the fire witness

the fire witness

lars kepler

translated from the swedish by laura a. wideburg

sarah crichton books
farrar, straus and giroux   new york

Sarah Crichton Books
Farrar, Straus and Giroux
18 West 18th Street, New York 10011

Library of Congress Cataloging-in-Publication Data
Kepler, Lars.
    [Eldvittnet. English]
    The fire witness / Lars Kepler ; translated from the Swedish by Laura A. Wideburg. —
First American edition.
        pages cm.
    "Sarah Crichton Books."
    "Originally published in 2011 by Albert Bonniers Förlag, Sweden, as Eldvittnet."
    ISBN 978-0-374-29866-1 (hardcover)
    I. Title.

PT9877.21.E65 E4413 2013
839.73'8—dc23
                                                                    2013011080

Designed by Abby Kagan

www.fsgbooks.com
www.twitter.com/fsgbooks · www.facebook.com/fsgbooks

10 9 8 7 6 5 4 3 2 1

All liars shall have their part in the lake which burneth with fire and brimstone . . . —REVELATION 21:8

A medium is someone who claims to have paranormal talent: the ability to interpret circumstances that lie beyond the limits of science.

Some mediums act as intermediaries to the dead at séances, while others offer guidance based on, for example, the reading of tarot cards.

Humans have tried to contact the dead through mediums since the beginning of history. One thousand years before the birth of Christ, King Saul of Israel sought advice from the spirit of the recently deceased prophet Samuel.

All over the world, the police accept the help of psychics and mediums when they are baffled by a case. This happens several times a year, even though there is not a single documented instance where a medium has actually solved a crime.

the fire witness

Elisabet Grim is fifty-three years old. Her hair is streaked with gray, but her eyes are bright and happy, and when she smiles, one of her front teeth juts out impishly.

She is a nurse at Birgittagården, a state-approved home for especially troubled girls north of Sundsvall. It's a small, privately owned residence. Rarely are there more than eight girls there at a time. They range from twelve to seventeen in age. Many are drug addicts when they arrive. Almost all have a history of self-injury—eating disorders, for instance. Some can be violent. For these girls, there is no alternative to Birgittagården, with its alarms and double-locked doors. The next step would be prison or forced confinement in a psychiatric unit. This home, by comparison, is a hopeful place, with the expectation that the girls can make it back someday to open care.

As Elisabet often says, "It's the nice girls who end up here."

Right now, Elisabet is savoring the last bite of a bittersweet bar of chocolate. She can feel her shoulders begin to relax.

The day started well but the evening was hard. There were classes in the morning, and in the afternoon, the girls spent time at the lake. After the evening meal, the housemother went home, leaving Elisabet in charge on her own. The night staff was recently let go when the company changed hands. Elisabet had sat in the nurse's office, catching up with reports, while the girls watched television, which they were allowed to do until ten.

And then she'd heard the yelling. It was loud, very loud. She'd hurried to the television room, where Miranda was beating up tiny Tuula. Miranda was screaming that Tuula was a slut and a whore. She'd yanked the little girl off the sofa and was kicking her in the back.

It was not unusual for Miranda to explode violently. Elisabet was used to her outbursts. She pulled her away from Tuula, and Miranda slapped Elisabet in the face. Elisabet was used to that, too. Without further discussion she led Miranda down the hall to the isolation room. Elisabet wished Miranda a good night, but Miranda didn't answer. She just sat on the bed and studied the floor with a secretive smile as the nurse shut and locked the door behind her.

Elisabet was scheduled to have a private talk with the new girl, Vicky Bennet, but after the conflict, she found she was exhausted and couldn't face it. When Vicky came by and timidly mentioned that it was her turn for a chat, Elisabet put her off. This made Vicky so unhappy, she broke a teacup and slashed her stomach and wrists with the sharpest piece.

When Elisabet checked on her a while later, Vicky was sitting in her room with her hands in front of her face and blood running down her arms.

The wounds were superficial. Elisabet washed the blood off, wrapped gauze around the girl's wrists, and put a Band-Aid on her stomach. And Elisabet comforted her, soothing her with sweet names, telling her not to worry, coaxing her until a tiny smile crossed the troubled girl's face. For the third night in a row, Elisabet gave the girl ten milligrams of Sonata so she could sleep.

All the girls are finally asleep and Birgittagården is quiet. Outside the office window, the September darkness has settled on the forest, but Himmelsjö Lake's smooth surface shines like mother-of-pearl. Elisabet sits in front of her computer entering the evening's events into the log.

It's almost midnight and she realizes she hasn't taken her sleeping pill yet. *My own little drug,* she calls it. Difficult days followed by nights on call are interfering with her sleep. She needs a few hours of rest; ten milligrams of Stilnoct by ten and she's asleep by eleven. She pulls her shawl tight and thinks that a glass of red wine would hit the spot right now. She longs for her own bed, where she can curl up with a book, or with her husband, Daniel. But not tonight; she's on call and has to stay here.

In the yard outside, Buster begins to bark. Insistently, stridently.

It's very late. She's usually asleep by now. She takes her pill, shuts down her computer. She grows aware of the sounds she's making: the hiss of her chair's hydraulic lift as she stands; the creak of the tiles beneath her feet as she moves to the window. She tries to look out, but all she can see is the reflection of her face. And of the door gliding open behind her.

Must be the draft, she thinks. *The tile stove in the dining room draws such a great deal of air.*

She shakes off the disquiet she feels and switches off the lamp before she turns around.

Now the door is wide open. She shudders faintly, and steps through it. The lights are on in the hallway between the dining room and the girls' bedrooms. *I should check the tile stove,* she thinks; *make sure the lids are shut.* But there is whispering coming from one of the bedrooms.

At first all Elisabet hears is a delicate hiss. The whisper is hardly perceptible. Then she hears words.

"It's your turn to close your eyes," someone murmurs.

Elisabet keeps still, staring so hard down the hall her eyes are frozen open. *It must be one of the girls talking in her sleep,* she thinks. Then there's a noise, like an overripe peach dropping on the floor. Then another, heavy and wet. A table leg scrapes the floor and there's the sound of two more peaches falling.

Out of the corner of her eye, Elisabet catches a movement, a shadow gliding past. She turns around and sees the door to the dining room slowly close.

"Wait!" she calls out, even while trying to convince herself it's nothing; it must be the draft.

She grabs the doorknob to the dining room, but something stops the door from opening and she has to yank it before it finally gives way. Stepping inside, she can see herself in the dull reflection from the scratched dining-room table, and again in the brass fire doors of the tile stove. She checks it: the lids are all shut. The stove suddenly knocks, and Elisabet takes a quick step back, tilting over a chair. It's nothing. Just the slipping of a log.

She heads to her room, pausing outside the girls' bedrooms. She detects a sour, slightly metallic aroma. She searches for movement in the hallway, but all is still. To the right are the bathrooms and the alcove leading to the isolation room. Miranda should be fast asleep in there. The peephole in the door glimmers weakly.

Now, again, there's that light voice, whispering.

"It's time to be quiet," Elisabet calls out.

A series of quick thuds. It's hard to locate the noise, but it sounds as if Miranda is lying in bed and kicking her bare feet against the wall. Elisabet decides to check on her through the peephole. It is then that she sees a shadowy figure in the alcove. With a gasp, she backs away. She knows how dangerous the situation is, but fear makes her slow; her body feels as if it's moving in the heavy water of a dream. But the creaking of the floor startles her awake, and she whirls around and starts to run.

A soft voice behind her urges her to stop, but she knows she mustn't.

Elisabet makes it to the front door. Throwing the lock, she races out into the cool air of the night. She slips on the front steps, smacking her hip and twisting a leg beneath her. Her ankle hurts so badly she cries out, and she crawls for a stretch, losing her slippers. Then she forces herself to her feet.

The dog is barking at her. He runs circles around her as she limps away across the gravel driveway. She knows there is no escape in the forest, and it's several hours' walk to the closest farm, so she drags herself behind the drying shed, toward the former brewery. Hands shaking, she opens the door, slips inside, and pulls the door tight.

"Oh God! Oh God!"

She searches her pockets for her cell, but her hands jerk so badly she drops the phone. The back bursts off and the battery flies out. She scrambles to pick up the pieces as she listens to the footsteps crunch the gravel.

She crawls to the low window and peers out. Buster, who has followed her, scratches frantically at the door. Elisabet creeps over to the masonry fireplace and crouches behind the woodpile, where with uncooperative hands she tries to shove the battery back into place.

The door flies open. There's nowhere to go.

She can see the boots, the twisted face, the raised hammer, its heft and shine. She listens to the voice, nods, and then covers her face with her hands.

The shadowy figure pauses a moment before knocking her flat on the ground, holding her down, and smashing her hard. Along the hairline, her forehead burns. Her sight is gone, and she's in agony, but the warm blood running over her ears and down the sides of her throat feels like a caress.

The next blow lands in the same spot. Her head is knocked askew and now the only thing she knows is how to breathe. She thinks how wonderfully sweet oxygen is.

She cannot feel her body jerk from the next round of blows. She cannot tell when the keys to the office and the isolation room are taken from her pocket. She cannot see her body lying on the floor or the dog sneaking in and tentatively lapping the blood leaking from her crushed head. She cannot sense her life ebb away.

5

Someone has left a large red apple on the table. It gleams and looks wonderfully tasty. Perhaps she'll just eat the whole thing and then pretend she knows nothing about it. She'll sit there looking glum, ignore the harangues, and refuse to answer their questions.

She reaches for the apple, but her fingers sink into cold, mushy flesh. It's completely rotten.

Nina Molander wakes up as she jerks her hand away. It's the middle of the night. She's lying in her bed. The only thing she hears is the dog barking in the yard. This new drug makes her wake at night. She has to get up and go to the bathroom. She needs to take the drug, even though it makes her feet and calves swell. Without it, dark thoughts consume her to the point where she no longer cares about anything and can't get out of bed. She knows she needs something to look forward to instead of thoughts about death.

Nina throws off her blanket and sets her feet on the warm wooden floor. She's fifteen years old, with straight blond hair, wide hips, and large breasts. Her white flannel nightgown is tight around her belly.

In the hallway, the only light on is the green emergency exit sign. She hears whispers behind one of the doors. Nina thinks the other girls are having a party and didn't invite her. *As if I'd ever want to go.*

She can smell cinders, an old fire that has gone out. The dog starts barking again. Nina doesn't worry about whether she's quiet or not. She feels like slamming the door over and over. She doesn't give a damn that Almira will get angry and throw things at her.

The floor is colder out in the hall. The old tiles creak. She heads toward the bathroom, but stops when she steps in a wet patch. A dark pool is spreading from beneath the door of the isolation room where Miranda is sleeping. Nina doesn't know what to do at first, but then she sees that the key to the room has been left in the lock.

That's weird.

She opens the door, walks inside, and flips on the light. There's blood everywhere; it runs down the walls. Miranda is lying on the bed.

Nina takes a few steps backward and sees bloody shoe prints on the floor. She thinks she's going to faint. She doesn't notice that she's peeing herself.

Back in the hall, she opens the door to the next room, and crouches down to shake Caroline's shoulder.

"Miranda's hurt," she whispers. "I think Miranda's hurt."

"What the hell are you doing in my room?" Caroline asks as she sits up. "What time is it, anyway?"

Nina stops whispering. "There's blood all over the floor!"

Nina can hardly breathe as she looks into Caroline's eyes. She needs to make her understand, and she's surprised when she realizes that she's screaming at the top of her lungs.

"Shut up!" Caroline hisses as she gets out of bed. "Calm down!"

Nina's screams have woken the other girls. Alarmed voices ring out from the other rooms.

"Come and see for yourself," Nina says, and she begins to scratch her arms. "Miranda looks weird. You've got to take a look at her! You've got to!"

"Can you please cool it? I'll look, but I'm sure—"

Another scream erupts in the hallway. Caroline scrambles out of her bedroom. Tuula is staring into the isolation room and her eyes are as wide as saucers.

Indie walks out of her room, too, scratching her armpit.

Caroline pulls Tuula away and catches sight of the blood on the walls and Miranda's pale body. She blocks Indie, thinking that no one should have to see another suicide.

"There's been an accident," she explains quickly. "Can you ask everyone to go to the dining room, Indie?"

"What's wrong with Miranda?" Indie asks.

"We have to wake up Elisabet."

Lu Chu and Almira come out of their double room. Lu Chu is wearing only pajama bottoms and Almira is wrapped in a blanket.

"Go to the dining room," Indie orders.

"Don't I have time to wash my face first?" Lu Chu pouts.

"Take Tuula with you."

"What the fuck is going on?" asks Almira.

"We don't know," Caroline says.

While Indie tries to gather everyone in the dining room, Caroline rushes to the staff room. She knows that Elisabet takes sleeping pills and never hears when the girls get up and wander around at night. Caroline bangs on the door as loud as she can.

"Elisabet, you have to wake up!" she yells.

Nothing happens.

Caroline hurries past the registration room and over to the nurse's office. The door is open and she runs to the telephone and calls Daniel.

There's static on the line.

Indie and Nina press in at the office door. Nina is shaking and her lips are white.

"Go wait in the dining room!" Caroline snaps.

"But the blood! Did you see all that blood?" Nina says and scratches her arm furiously.

"Daniel Grim," a sleepy voice says on the other end of the line.

"It's me, Caroline. There's been an accident and I can't wake Elisabet. I called you because I don't know what else to do."

"There's blood all over my feet!" screams Nina. "I have blood all over my feet!"

"Calm down!" Indie shouts at her as she tries to pull Nina out of the office.

"What's going on?" Daniel asks. His voice is sharper now and in control.

"Miranda's in the cell, but it's all full of blood," Caroline says. She swallows. "I don't know what we should—"

"Is she seriously hurt?" asks Daniel.

"Yes, I think so . . . or I—"

"Caroline," Daniel says. "I'm going to call for an ambulance. And then—"

"What should I do? What should I—"

"Go wake Elisabet."

The emergency center in Sundsvall is in a three-story redbrick building on Björneborgsgatan, next to Bäckgatan. Jasmin usually has no problem working nights, but at the moment she's having trouble staying awake. It's four in the morning and the witching hour has passed. She sits at her computer with her headset on, blowing on her coffee. Laughter pours out from the cafeteria. The evening newspaper reported that one of the center's police officers might have earned extra cash as a phone sex worker. The reality is likely more complicated than that, but at this hour, nothing could be funnier than the idea that two very different kinds of calls have been coming into the emergency center.

Jasmin stares out the window. There is no light in the sky yet. A truck thunders past.

She puts down her mug to answer an incoming call.

"SOS 112. What's going on?"

"My name is Daniel Grim and I'm a therapist at Birgittagården. One of the girls has just called me . . . You have to send someone to the home right away."

"Can you give me more details?" Jasmin searches for Birgittagården on her computer.

"I don't know anything. One of the girls called, but I didn't really understand what she was saying. She was crying . . . Everybody was screaming in the background . . . The girl said there was blood everywhere."

Jasmin signals to her colleague, Ingrid Sandén, that more operators are needed on this call.

"Are you at the scene now?" Ingrid asks as Jasmin tries to refine her search.

"I was home asleep when they called—"

"You are talking about Birgittagården north of Sunnås?" asks Jasmin.

"Hurry, please!" The man's voice is shaking.

"We're sending police and an ambulance to Birgittagården, north of Sunnås," Jasmin says clearly to give the man time to correct her if she's wrong.

She turns away for a moment to issue the alarm, and Ingrid picks up the questioning.

"Isn't Birgittagården a youth home?"

"Yes, for girls."

"Shouldn't there be staff on the premises?"

"Yes, my wife, Elisabet, is on duty tonight. I'm going to call her now . . . I don't know what's happening . . . I know nothing . . ."

Ingrid can see blue lights flash across the deserted street as the first car pulls out of the garage. "The police are on their way," she says in a calming voice.

The turnoff from Highway 86 leads directly into the dark forest and toward Lake Himmelsjö and Birgittagården. The car's headlights play between the tall trunks of the pine trees. "Have you been there before?" asks Rolf Wikner as he shifts into fourth gear.

"Yes, a few years ago when a girl tried to set fire to one of the buildings," Sonja Rask says.

"Why the hell can't anyone reach the person on duty?" Rolf mutters.

"They're probably too busy, no matter what's going on."

"I wish we knew more."

"So do I."

The officers fall silent so they can hear the voices coming over the police radio. An ambulance is on its way and another police car has been dispatched.

The gravel road runs completely straight. It's in need of grading, and their tires thunder across the potholes. Little missiles of gravel strike their fender as tree trunks flicker past and flashes of blue light stab far into the forest. As soon as they reach the yard between Birgittagården's dark red buildings, Sonja reports in.

A girl wearing nothing but a nightgown is standing on the front steps. Her eyes are wide open but her face is pale. Rolf and Sonja get out of the car and hurry toward her. The pulsing blue light swirls all around them. The girl doesn't appear to notice.

A dog is barking excitedly.

"Is someone hurt?" asks Rolf in a loud voice. "Is there someone who needs help?"

The girl waves vaguely toward the edge of the forest, sways, and then, when she tries to walk toward them, her legs give way.

Sonja has reached the girl. "Are you all right?" she asks.

The girl lies absolutely still on the steps, staring up at the sky, breathing shallowly. Sonja notices that she has fresh scratches all over her arms and neck.

"I'll go inside," Rolf says.

Sonja stays by the girl, who has gone into shock, while Rolf enters the main building. Bloody prints, marks from both shoes and bare feet, seem to fly in all directions. One set, going up and down the hall, belongs to someone with long strides. Rolf moves swiftly, while being careful not to mess the prints.

In a brightly lit room, four girls are huddled on a sofa.

"Is anyone hurt here?" he asks.

"Maybe. Miranda—a little," says a tiny girl with red hair.

"Where is she?"

"Miranda's in bed," says an older girl with straight black hair.

"This way?" He points down the hall.

The older girl nods and Rolf follows the bloody footprints past a dining room with a large wooden table and tile stove, and comes to the dark hall leading to the girls' private rooms. He shines his flashlight along the Bible quotes on the walls and then aims at the floor again. Blood has seeped out from under a door at the back of the alcove. The door is shut and the key is in the lock. He walks over, shifting the flashlight from one hand to the other. He presses down on the tip of the door handle. There's a click and the door swings open.

"Hello. Miranda? My name's Rolf and I'm a police officer," he says into the silence. "I'm coming inside now."

The only thing he can hear is his own breathing. He pulls the door all the way open, but the violence of the sight inside stops him short and he slumps against the doorjamb. Instinctively he looks away, but his eyes have already registered what he wishes he'd never seen.

A young woman is lying on the bed. A great part of her head seems to be missing. Blood has spattered the walls; it drips from a lampshade.

The door behind Rolf slams shut and he's so startled that he drops his flashlight. Now there's nothing but darkness. He turns around and fumbles for the door handle. He can hear the sound of hands on the outside of the door.

"Now she can see you!" shrieks a young voice. "Now she's looking right at you!"

He presses down on the door handle, but the door is blocked. There is only a glimmer of light through the peephole. He presses down again and throws his shoulder against the door. It flies open and Rolf stumbles into the hallway. The little red-haired girl is standing there, staring at him with her wide eyes.

Detective Inspector Joona Linna stands at the window of his hotel room in the town of Sveg, 440 kilometers north of Stockholm. The dawn light is cool and misty blue. The streetlights along Älvgatan have already switched off, but it will be many more hours before he knows whether he's found Rosa Bergman.

His shirt hangs loose and unbuttoned over black suit pants. His blond hair is, as usual, disheveled. His service pistol lies on the bed, still in its shoulder holster.

The last few months have been unsettled ones for Joona Linna. Last summer, he was accused of alerting an extremist left-wing group to a sweep by Säpo, the security police. The matter is now in the hands of the National Police's Internal Review Board. While it investigates, Joona has been removed from many duties though not formally barred from the force. But the head of the investigation has made it clear that he intends to forward Joona's file to the Swedish Prosecution Authority if he finds the slightest cause for an indictment.

It is a serious charge, but this is not the first time Joona has run up against the authorities. It seems to be his nature. He works as a lone wolf, and that can be irritating, especially to a team organization like the National Police. But what they can't ignore is that in the almost fifteen years Joona's been on the job, he's solved more challenging cases than any other Scandinavian police officer. And while he may be independent to a fault, he is also loyal. Despite repeated offers from other organizations, Joona's allegiance is to the force.

But right now Joona isn't worrying about the outcome of the investigation. His mind is not on the future, but on the recent past. It's on the old woman who followed him outside the Adolf Fredrik Church in Stockholm and delivered a message from Rosa Bergman.

Her thin hands had held up two tarot cards.

"This is you, isn't it?" she'd asked. "And here is the crown, the bridal crown."

"What do you want?"

"I don't want anything," the old woman had said. "But I have a message for you from Rosa Bergman."

Joona's heart had begun to pound, but he'd forced himself to shrug and say nonchalantly that there had to be some kind of mistake "because I don't know anyone by that name."

"She wants to know why you pretend your daughter is dead."

"I'm very sorry, but I have no idea what you're talking about." Joona had forced himself to smile as he answered. His voice had sounded odd in his own ears, foreign and cold, as if it came from underneath a large stone, and he'd been tempted to grab her skinny arms and demand to know what was going on. But he didn't. He managed to stay calm.

"I have to go," he had said, and was about to turn away when a migraine had shot through his brain like a knife stabbing his left eye. His vision disintegrated into a shimmering, pulsating halo.

When he was able to see again, a circle of people had gathered around him, a circle that broke only for the paramedics. And the old woman had disappeared.

He'd lied when he'd told her he didn't know Rosa Bergman.

Of course he knows who Rosa Bergman is. She's in his thoughts every day. Rosa Bergman is the only person who knows where his wife and daughter are. But she should not know about him. If she knows who he is, then something has gone terribly wrong.

Joona left the hospital a few hours after the migraine attack, and immediately began his search for Rosa Bergman. He requested and was granted a leave of absence. He soon learned that no such person was listed in any of Sweden's public registers, but there are at least two thousand people with the last name Bergman in Scandinavia.

He began to systematically work his way through register after register.

Two weeks ago, he began digging through archived church records. For hundreds of years, the Church of Sweden was responsible for keeping population registers, until 1991, when the responsibility was shifted to the Tax Office, where these records are now kept in digital form.

He started in the south of Sweden at the archives in Lund, where he pored through drawers of index cards, searching for any Rosa Bergman whose birth date might be right. He then traveled to Visby on the island of Gotland, and then to Vadstena, and after that to Gothenburg. Then he headed north to Uppsala and on to the massive archive in Härnösand. He searched through hundreds of thousands of files that recorded birth dates, places of birth, and parentages.

It was late in the afternoon yesterday, sitting in the Östersund archive, surrounded by the sweet scent of aged, stained paper and loose-leaf binders, that Joona found the record of a girl born eighty-four years ago. She was baptized Rosa Maja in the parish of Sveg, municipality of Härjedalen, Jämtland Province. Her parents were Kristina and Evert Bergman. He was unable to find any record of their marriage, but the mother had been born nineteen years earlier in the same parish. Her maiden name was Stefansson.

It took Joona three more hours to locate the name of Maja Stefansson, born the same year as Rosa Bergman, whose address was listed as a home for assisted living in Sveg. It was already seven in the evening by then, but Joona decided to drive there immediately. When he arrived, the residents were already in bed so he was denied entry.

Joona checked into the Lilla Hotellet. He went to bed early and woke at four. Since then, he's been standing at the window, waiting for dawn to break.

Sunlight slowly marches around the high walls of the room, dancing briefly in the glass panel of a grandfather clock. Joona's fairly sure he's found the right Rosa Bergman. She's changed her last name to her mother's maiden name and used her original middle name as her first name. Joona glances at his watch and decides it's time to go. Buttoning his jacket, he leaves the room, walks through the lobby, and heads out the door into the tiny town of Sveg.

The nursing home is called Blåvingen. It occupies a group of buildings, all of them faced in yellow stucco, surrounding a well-groomed lawn. There are paths and benches for resting.

Joona opens the door to the main entrance and steps inside. Now that he's this close to meeting her, he's suddenly apprehensive and has to force himself to walk down the hall, past the closed office doors, under the harsh fluorescent lights.

She was not supposed to find me, he thinks. *She wasn't even supposed to know of my existence. Something has gone very wrong.*

Joona never talks about what led him to be such a loner. Still, the reasons are with him every waking moment. His life had burned like magnesium, flaring and then out. From bright white to smoking ruin in an instant.

A thin, bent old man watches television in the activity room, staring intently as a chef heats up oil in a sauté pan while describing a new recipe for the traditional crayfish festival. He peers at Joona.

"Anders? Is that you?" he asks.

Gently, Joona replies, "My name is Joona," his soft Finnish accent coming through. "I'm looking for Maja Stefansson."

The old man stares at him, with eyes that are damp and red.

"Anders, my boy, please listen to me. You have to get me out of here. There are only old people in this place." The man slams his bony fist onto the armrest of the sofa but freezes the moment he sees a nurse enter the room.

"Good morning," Joona says to the nurse. "I'm here to visit Maja Stefansson."

"How nice," she replies. "But I must warn you Maja has started to suffer from dementia. She tries to run away at every opportunity."

"I understand."

"Last summer she managed to get all the way to Stockholm."

The nurse leads Joona through a freshly scrubbed but dimly lit hallway and opens a door.

"Maja?" she says. "There's someone here to see you."

An old woman is making her bed. She looks up and Joona recognizes her at once. It is the woman who approached him outside Adolf Fredrik Church and who showed him the tarot cards.

"Are you Rosa Bergman?" Joona asks.

"Yes," she says, shyly holding out her hand.

"You had a message for me," he says softly.

"Oh my goodness . . . I don't remember," she says, and sits down on her sofa.

Joona swallows hard and steps closer.

"You asked me why I'm pretending my daughter is dead."

"Well, you shouldn't do that," she reprimands him. "It's not a nice thing to do at all."

"What do you know about my daughter?" Joona asks gently, taking another step. "Have you heard anything at all?"

She smiles absently and Joona has to look away. He tries to think clearly. His hands are shaking. He goes to her tiny kitchenette to steady them and makes two cups of coffee.

"Rosa, this is very important," he says slowly as he sets the cups down on her coffee table. "It's extremely important to me."

Rosa blinks a few times. It is clear she's grown suddenly frightened. "Who are you? Has something happened to Mother?"

"Rosa, do you remember a little girl named Lumi? Her mother's name is Summa and you helped them to . . ."

Joona falls silent as he sees her wandering, lost gaze.

"Why did you come to Stockholm to find me?" he asks, although he knows his question won't be answered.

Rosa Bergman begins to cry. A nurse comes in and comforts her in a practiced manner.

She says quietly to Joona, "Come with me. I'll show you out."

They walk along the wide hall, designed for wheelchairs.

"How long has she been suffering from dementia?" Joona asks.

"Things went quickly for Maja. We started to see the first signs last summer, so, for about a year. In the old days, they used to call it a second childhood, which is not so far from the truth."

"If she . . . if she's able to think clearly at all . . ." Joona says seriously.

"It's unlikely," the nurse says, but you never know. "I can call you."

"My card," Joona says, and hands it to her.

She looks impressed. "Detective Inspector?" She tacks it to the bulletin board behind her desk.

Joona steps into the fresh air and takes a deep breath. *Perhaps Rosa Bergman did have something important to tell me,* he thinks. *Maybe someone
sent her, but she began to suffer from dementia before she could do anything about it.*

Perhaps he'll never know what the message was.

It has been twelve years since he lost Summa and Lumi, and the last
trace of them has disappeared with Rosa Bergman's memory.

Joona climbs into his car and wipes the tears from his cheeks. He
closes his eyes for a moment, then starts the drive back to Stockholm.
He's barely gone thirty kilometers along the E45 when he gets a call from
Carlos Eliasson, chief of the National Police.

"There's been a murder in Sundsvall. A girl," Carlos says. "The call
came in just after four this morning."

"I'm on leave," Joona says. His voice is barely audible. He's driving
through a forest that offers glimpses of a distant silvery lake between the
trees.

"Joona? What's going on?"

"Nothing."

In the background, someone yells for Carlos.

"There's a damned board meeting I've got to go to, but I would like . . .
You see, I just talked with Prosecutor Susanne Öst and she thinks that the
police in Västernorrland do not intend to request our help in the case."

"So why call me?"

"I told them we would send an observer anyway."

"Since when do we send observers?"

"As of now," says Carlos. He lowers his voice. "Things are kind of touchy around here these days. Remember the mess with the captain of the hockey league, Janne Svensson? The press had a field day with the police department's incompetence."

"Because they didn't find—"

"Let's not discuss it. That was Susanne Öst's first big prosecution. I don't want to say the press had it right, but the Västernorrland police could certainly have used you that time. They were just too slow and kept going by the book. Time ran out. Not unusual, perhaps, but it can lead to media unpleasantness."

"I can't talk anymore," Joona says, trying to cut short the conversation.

"You know I wouldn't trouble you if this was just an average murder case," Carlos says. Joona can hear him breathing deeply over the phone. "The press is going to be all over this one, Joona. It's extremely violent, extremely bloody. And there's one especially nasty thing: the girl's body has been arranged."

"Meaning what?"

"She's lying in bed with her hands over her face."

Joona says nothing. His left hand is on the wheel. The trees flash past as he drives, and Joona can hear a babble of voices in the background. Carlos waits patiently, and Joona turns off the E45 and onto the E14, leading east to Sundsvall, on the coast.

"Just go there, Joona," Carlos says. "Be nice and let them solve the case themselves, preferably before the press gets to town."

"So now I'm more than just an observer?"

"No, no. That's what you are, but stick around and keep an eye on the investigation. Make a few suggestions. Just keep in mind that you have no authority in the case."

"Because I'm under internal investigation?"

"It's important you keep a low profile."

North of Sundsvall, Joona leaves the coast and turns onto Highway 86, which heads inland toward Indalsälven. After two hours, he's close to where the home for troubled girls should be. He slows down and eventually turns onto a gravel road. Rays of sunshine stream past the dark trunks of the tall pines.

A *dead girl*, thinks Joona.

During the night while everyone slept, a girl was murdered and then set up, "arranged," in her bed. According to the local police, the crime was brutal. They have no suspect and now it's too late to close off the roads, but all officers in the area are on alert. Commissioner Olle Gunnarsson is leading the preliminary investigation but, Carlos tells Joona, the situation has been so chaotic, the girls have been so agitated, so uncontrollable, that the investigation has not yet begun.

It's ten by the time Joona reaches the home. He parks outside the line of police tape and gets out. The only sound he can hear is the buzz of insects in the ditch beside the road. Here the forest has opened into an enormous glade. Tree trunks, still damp with dew, shimmer in the sunshine. A hill slopes down to Lake Himmelsjö, and a metal sign beside the road reads BRIGITTAGÅRDEN, HVB: A HOME FOR YOUTH WITH SPECIAL NEEDS.

Joona heads toward the group of red buildings, which form a square around a gravel yard. An ambulance, three police cars, a white Mercedes, and three other cars are parked near the buildings.

A dog is barking. His leash is attached to a line running between two trees.

An older man with a walrus mustache and a beer belly, wearing a wrinkled linen suit, is standing by the main building. He's noticed Joona but does not acknowledge him. Instead, he taps a cigarette out of a full packet and starts to light it.

Joona swings his legs over a second ring of police tape while the man reconsiders and puts the cigarette behind his ear.

"Joona Linna from the National Police."

"Gunnarsson," the man replies. "Detective Gunnarsson."

"I'm supposed to observe your work."

"As long as you don't get in the way," Gunnarsson says coldly, looking Joona over.

Joona glances at the big house. The technicians are already busy. Floodlights are blazing in all the rooms, making the windows shine with an unnatural light.

A white-faced officer comes out of the house. He's holding his hand over his mouth and wobbles down the steps, then, leaning on the wall for support, he bends forward and throws up into the nettles by the rain barrel.

"You'll do the same once you've been inside," Gunnarsson says, grinning at Joona.

"What do we know so far?"

"We don't know a damn thing. The alarm came early this morning. The therapist in charge here called. His name's Daniel Grim. It was four o'clock. He was at home on Bruksgatan in Sundsvall. He'd just got a phone call from the place. He didn't know what was going on when he called us, but said the girls were screaming about a lot of blood."

"So it was the girls themselves who called him?" Joona asks.

"That's right."

"They didn't call emergency? They called the therapist in Sundsvall?"

"Exactly."

"Shouldn't there be staff on-site?"

"Apparently there's not."

"But some adult?"

"We don't know. It's impossible to talk to the girls," Gunnarsson says. He sounds weary.

"Which one of them made the call?"

"One of the older ones"—Gunnarsson glances at his notebook—"by the name of Caroline Forsman. From what I understand, she was not the one who found the body, but the crime scene's a mess, several of the girls have looked into the room. One of them got so hysterical they had to take her to the hospital. Let me tell you, it's a gruesome sight."

"Who were the first officers on the scene?" Joona asks.

"There were two, Rolf Wikner and Sonja Rask. And I got here around a quarter to six. I called the prosecutor. She must have shit her pants over it, since she called you guys in Stockholm. And now I have you hanging around my neck."

Gunnarsson smiles again at Joona. It's not a friendly smile.

"Any suspects yet?"

Gunnarsson sighs and then says, as if he's giving a lecture, "I've been at this sort of thing for a long time and my experience tells me to let the investigation take its course. Start from the beginning, find witnesses, secure evidence—"

"May I go inside and take a look?" Joona asks, glancing at the front door.

"I wouldn't recommend it. We'll soon have photos for you."

"I need to take a look at her body before it's moved," Joona says.

"It's blunt trauma," Gunnarsson says. "The perpetrator is tall. After she died, the victim was placed on her bed and no one noticed anything until one of the girls had to go to the bathroom and stepped into blood that had come out from under the door."

"Was it still warm?"

"You know, these aren't the easiest girls in the world to work with," Gunnarsson says. "They're frightened and angry all the time and they've been arguing about everything we say and not listening at all. They've been screaming at us. Earlier this morning they tried to cross the police tape to fetch things from their rooms, iPods and jackets and so on, and when we tried to move them out to the smaller building, two ran off into the woods."

"Ran off?"

"Oh, we caught up with them, and we're trying to get them to return on their own. Right now they're lying on the ground and demanding that Rolf give them a piggyback ride."

Joona puts on his protective gear and walks up the steps into the big house. Inside the entrance, he can hear floodlight fans humming, and the air is already too warm. Dust motes float through the air.

He walks across the protective mats that have been placed on the tiled floor. A picture has fallen from the wall and the broken glass glitters in the bright light. There are bloody footprints in all directions, to and from the front door.

The home has retained some details from when it was a wealthy farmhouse. The colors of stenciled patterns on the walls are a bit faded, but fanciful vegetables and vines, painted by itinerant painters from Dalarna two hundred years ago, still meander along the walls and around the chimneys.

A technician, who introduces himself as Jimi Sjöberg, is aiming a green light beam at a black chair he's sprayed with Hungarian Red.

"Any blood?" asks Joona.

"Not on this one," answers Jimi, continuing to look for traces of blood.

"Found anything unusual?"

"The Head of Crime Scene Investigation in Stockholm told us not to move even a single piece of fly shit until Joona Linna gives us permission," Jimi replies, smiling.

"And I'm very grateful."

"So, the thing is, we haven't really started yet," Jimi says. "We've put down these damned mats and we've taken photos and filmed every-thing, and I've taken the liberty of swabbing a blood sample from the hallway so we could send it to the lab."

"Good."

"And Siri lifted prints in the hallway before they could be ruined."

A second technician, Siri Karlsson, has just removed the brass han-dle from one of the doors. She puts it in a paper bag and comes over.

"This guy needs a look at the crime scene," Jimi says.

"Not a pretty sight," Siri says through the dust mask covering her mouth and nose. Her eyes look strained and tired.

"So I understand," Joona says.

"You can take a look at the photos instead if you'd like," Siri says.

"This is Joona Linna," Jimi says.

"Sorry, I didn't recognize you."

"I'm here only as an observer," Joona says.

Siri looks away and the mask can't hide her flushed cheeks when she looks back at him. "Sorry. Everyone's talking about what's happening to you. And I . . . that is . . . I don't care about the internal investigation. I think it'll be great to work together."

"I think so, too," Joona replies.

He stands for a moment longer, listening to the hum of the flood-lights. He's searching for that mental stillness that will allow him to ob-serve and not give in to the impulse to look away.

Joona goes down the hall to the door from which Siri removed the handle. The key is still in the lock. He closes his eyes a moment and then walks into the room. It's completely silent and fully lit, and the heated air is filled with the smell of blood and urine. Joona concentrates on breathing and in a moment he begins to distinguish other smells: damp wood, sweaty sheets, deodorant. The hot metal of the floodlights makes a pinging sound.

Joona does not move. He takes a long look at the body on the bed and lets each detail sink in, even though he'd much rather turn around and head for the fresh air of the forest.

Blood is all over the floor and splashed on the bolted-down furniture and the faded pictures of Bible scenes on the walls. It has spattered the ceiling and all the way to the toilet in the washroom, which has no door. A skinny girl, barely into puberty, is lying on the bed. She's on her back wearing only a pair of white cotton panties. Her hands are over her face. Her elbows protect her breasts, her legs are straight, and her feet are crossed at the ankles.

Joona can feel his heart beating and the pulse throbbing in his temples.

He forces himself to look, register, and think.

The girl's face is hidden as if she were afraid, as if she did not want to see her killer.

Before the girl was arranged on the bed, she had been hit repeatedly on her head and forehead by a blunt object. Her skull is smashed in.

Such a young girl; she must have been terrified. What chain of events had brought her to this home for troubled girls, to this room? Perhaps her parents or her foster parents couldn't cope anymore. Perhaps they'd needed help and brought her here to be safe.

Joona takes in every grisly detail until he can absorb no more. He closes his eyes and thinks about his daughter's face and the stone set over a grave that's not hers. Then he opens his eyes and continues his investigation.

Everything indicates the victim was sitting on the chair next to the small table when the suspect attacked her. Joona tries to figure out the sequence of events that caused the blood to spatter in this pattern. He knows that each drop of blood, flying through the air, forms a sphere with a diameter of about five millimeters. If the drop is smaller, it means that the blood was traveling at such high speed it split into smaller drops.

He stands on two protective mats in front of the table; most likely the spot where the killer stood just a few hours earlier. The girl would have been sitting on the chair on the other side of the table. Joona follows the spatter pattern with his eyes. He leans back to trace a high arc on the walls. The weapon must have been swung back to gain momentum, and each time, as its direction changed slightly for the next blow, blood was flung off in a backward trail.

Joona has already spent more time on this crime scene than most inspectors would, yet he knows he's not through yet. He steps over again to the girl on the bed. He notes her pierced navel, the lipstick stain on the glass by her bed, the scar, possibly from the removal of a birthmark, under her right breast. He sees the hair on her shins and a yellowed bruise on her thigh.

Joona leans over her and feels slight warmth still rising from her naked skin. He takes a closer look at her hands. There's nothing under her nails. She didn't scratch her assailant.

He steps to one side and examines her body once more: her white skin, her hands over her face, her crossed ankles. There is almost no blood on her body at all. Only her pillow is drenched. Her panties are white. Her skin is clean.

Joona looks around the room. Behind the door is a small shelf with two hooks. On the floor beneath the shelf is a pair of sports shoes with white socks balled inside. A faded pair of jeans, a black sweatshirt, and a denim jacket hang from one of the hooks. On the shelf, there's a small white bra.

Joona does not touch the clothes. They do not appear to be bloody. She had most likely undressed and hung up her clothes before she was killed.

But why is her body so clean? Something must have protected her. But what? There's nothing else in the room.

Joona walks back outside into the sunshine. He's puzzled. Such terrible violence was done to this young girl, but her body was left as pure as a sea-washed stone.

Gunnarsson had warned him that the level of violence was intense, and it was certainly forceful, extremely so, but not aggressive in the sense that her killer lost control. The blows were purposeful and were meant to kill, but in all other respects her body was treated with care.

Gunnarsson is sitting on the hood of his Mercedes, talking on his cell phone.

Unlike almost everything else, a murder investigation does not descend into chaos if left to itself. In most cases, a solution makes itself known eventually. But Joona has never expected a case to solve itself or trusted that order will eventually prevail.

He does know that the killer almost always knows the victim. Often the murderer will turn himself in to the police and confess a short time later. Joona never counts on this, either.

She's lying on the bed now, he thinks. *But the only clothes she was wearing when she died were her panties. None of this could have happened in complete silence. In a place like this there has to be a witness. One of the girls has heard or seen something. Someone must have guessed that something was about to happen, that there was a threat, or was aware of a conflict.*

Joona walks over to the smaller house. The dog is barking under a tree. It bites the leash attached to the running line and then starts to bark again.

There are two men talking outside the smaller house. One of them has muttonchops and is wearing a dark blue police sweater. He looks about fifty years old. Joona assumes that he is the crime scene coordinator. The other man does not look like a policeman. He's unshaven and his face looks compassionate and exhausted.

"I'm Joona Linna, here as an observer from the National Police," Joona says, extending his hand.

"I'm Åke," says the coordinator.

"My name's Daniel Grim," says the man with the tired eyes. "I'm the therapist in charge here. I got here as soon as I knew there was something wrong."

"Do you have a moment?" Joona asks. "I would like to meet the other girls and it would be best if you came along."

"Right now?"

"If you can spare the time."

Daniel blinks behind his glasses and says, "It's just that two of the girls have taken off into the forest."

"They've been found," Joona says.

"Yes, I know, but I have to talk seriously with them first." He smiles suddenly. "They're demanding piggyback rides from one of the officers before they'll come back."

"Gunnarsson will make sure they get their rides," Joona says, then continues on his way to the smaller house.

He knows he will have to watch carefully how the girls interact with each other to catch all the undercurrents swirling among them. If someone's seen something, the others will turn toward her like a compass needle. Joona knows he has no authority to question the girls, but he has to find out if anyone was a witness. He bends down to pass under the low doorframe.

The floorboard creaks under his weight as Joona steps into the cramped room. There are three girls there. The youngest is no more than twelve. She has pink skin and copper hair and sits on the floor, leaning against the wall, while she watches television. She is whispering to herself, then she suddenly bangs the back of her head against the wall. A second later, she's watching the show again.

The other two girls pay no attention to her. They're lounging together on a brown corduroy sofa and flipping through a fashion magazine.

A psychologist from the district hospital in Sundsvall enters the room behind Joona and sits down on the floor next to the little red-haired girl.

"My name is Lisa," she says. "What's your name?"

The girl does not take her eyes off the television. It's showing a rerun of an episode from *Blue Water High*. The volume is loud and the cool glow from the screen washes over their faces.

"Have you heard the fairy tale of Thumbelina?" asks Lisa. "I sometimes feel the way she does, as small as a thumb. How do you feel?"

"Like Jack the Ripper," the girl answers, her eyes on the show.

Joona sits down in an armchair in front of the television. One of the girls on the sofa looks at him with wide eyes, but returns to her magazine with a smile when he greets her. She's a big girl. She's bitten her nails to the quick. She wears jeans and a black sweater that has "Razors pain you less than life" written on it. She's wearing blue eye shadow and there's a glittering hair band around her neck. The other girl looks older and is wearing a cutoff T-shirt with a picture of a horse, a choker with white beads around her neck, and is using a rolled-up military jacket as a pillow. There are injection scars on the insides of her elbows.

The older one says, "Indie? Did you get a look before the cops got here?"

"I don't want nightmares," the hefty girl says lazily.

"Poor little Indie," the older one teases.

"And?"

"Afraid of nightmares!"

"So what?"

"You're such an egomaniac."

"Shut up, Caroline!" yells the little red-haired girl.

"Miranda's been murdered," Caroline says, "and all you care about is your nightmares."

"Oh, shit on Miranda. Thank God I don't have to deal with her anymore," Indie says.

"You're sick." Caroline smiles.

"She's the one who was sick, always burning me with her cigarette butts—"

"Stop your bitching," the red-haired girl says.

"—and hitting me with the jump rope," Indie says.

"You're the real bitch," says Caroline with a sigh.

"Okay, I'm the bitch, if that makes you feel better," Indie retorts. "Too bad the idiot is dead, but I for one—"

The little red-haired girl bangs her head against the wall again and then closes her eyes. The front door opens and Gunnarsson escorts the two runaways inside.

Joona leans back calmly in the chair. His dark jacket has fallen open. His muscular body is relaxed, but his eyes are as gray as ice as he watches the girls walk in.

Almira enters first, followed by Lu Chu, who sashays in with an exaggerated swing of her hips and makes the V sign with her fingers. The two girls on the sofa laugh and boo.

"You lesbian loser," Indie yells.

"Let's go take a shower together," says Lu Chu.

Daniel Grim comes in behind the girls, pleading with Gunnarsson to listen to him.

"I just want you to take it easy with these girls," he says. He lowers his voice. "Just your presence scares them."

"Don't worry," Gunnarsson says.

"But I *do* worry."

"What?"

"I am actually very worried about them," he says.

"Well," Gunnarsson says sighing, "then, sorry, but I can't help you out here. You're going to have to keep out of my hair and let me do my job."

"I *must* explain to you that . . . that for these girls police officers don't exactly mean safety and security."

Joona notices that Daniel's T-shirt is inside out.

"Yes, they do," Caroline jokes.

"Well, that's nice to hear." Daniel turns to her with a smile and then looks back at Gunnarsson. "But, seriously, for these girls, the police usually show up in their lives only when things are very bad."

Joona understands that Daniel knows he's being a pain but is determined to make his point. "I was just talking to the coordinator outside about finding—"

"One thing at a time," Gunnarsson brushes him off.

"It's really important because—"

"Cunt," Indie says to Lu Chu.

"Go piss yourself," Lu Chu says.

"—because it would be harmful for the girls to stay here tonight."

"Can we put them in a hotel?" asks Gunnarsson.

"You should have been the one that got killed!" Almira screams and throws a glass at Indie.

The glass breaks against the wall and shards scatter across the floor. Daniel rushes toward them. Almira ducks away, but not before Indie manages to land a few good blows on her back. Daniel separates them.

"Stop all this! Pull yourselves together, damn it!" he yells.

"Almira is a fucking cunt."

"Calm down, Indie," Daniel says. He grabs her hand, waits a second, and then in a soft voice says, "We've talked about this before, haven't we?"

"Yes," Indie says, slightly calmer.

"You're a good girl. You really are," Daniel says, smiling.

Indie nods and begins to pick up the glass pieces from the floor. Almira helps her.

"I'll get the vacuum cleaner," Daniel says and walks out, closing the door behind him. It swings open again and he bangs it shut so hard that a Carl Larsson picture on the wall rattles.

"Did Miranda have any enemies?" says Gunnarsson to no one in particular.

"No," Almira says and giggles.

Indie casts a sidelong look at Joona.

"Listen up!" Gunnarsson says loudly. "Just answer the questions without all this fuss and noise. That can't be too hard, can it?"

"Depends on the question," Caroline says.

"I'm going to scream no matter what," says Lu Chu.

"Truth or dare," Indie says and points at Joona.

"Truth," replies Joona. Gunnarsson swings toward him.

"I'm the one in charge of this investigation!" he protests.

Joona ignores him.

"Tell me what this means," Joona says to the girls, and he puts his hands over his face.

"That? I don't know," Indie says. "It's a game Miranda and Vicky played."

"I can't take this!" Caroline shrieks. "You're not the one who saw Miranda, Indie. She looked just like that and there was blood all over, there was so much blood all over the whole room!"

Caroline's voice breaks and she starts to cry. The hospital psychologist crouches beside her and in a low, calm voice tries to soothe the girl.

"Which one of you is Vicky?" asks Joona, getting up from the armchair.

"She's the newest one."

"But where the fuck *is* she?" demands Lu Chu.

"Which room is hers?" asks Joona.

"I bet she's snuck off to the guy she likes to fuck," Tuula says.

"We like to collect Stesolid and sleep like—"

"Who are you talking about now?" asks Gunnarsson loudly.

"Vicky Bennet," Caroline says. "I haven't seen her all—"

"Where the fuck is she?"

"Vicky's name has too many letters," Lu Chu says.

"Turn off that television!" Gunnarsson roars. "I want everyone to calm down!"

"Don't yell!" Tuula yells as she turns the volume up even higher.

Joona bends low and looks Caroline in the eyes. He is serious and calm.

"Which one is Vicky's room?"

"The one farthest down the hall."

Joona crosses the yard again, meeting Daniel going in the opposite direction, lugging the vacuum. He nods at the technicians and heads up the steps back into the main house. It's dark now. The floodlights have been switched off. The protective mats glisten like wet stones.

One girl is missing, Joona thinks. *Nobody's seen her. Maybe she ran away in all the chaos. But maybe the other girls are letting her hide.*

Joona shudders at the thought that the missing girl might have seen something. Perhaps she sought refuge in her room and is too frightened to come out.

He walks down the hall toward the girls' bedrooms. The crime scene investigation has just begun so the rooms have not yet been searched. The entire area will be gone over with a fine-tooth comb, but there hasn't yet been time for that with all the commotion. The girls are frightened and stressed. The Emergency Services for Victims of Violent Crime has still not arrived. The police need more officers, more technicians, more resources.

The timber walls creak, but otherwise the house is silent. In the alcove, the door that's missing its handle is slightly open. Inside, the dead girl is still lying on the bed, her hands over her eyes.

Joona remembers noting earlier three horizontal lines of blood on the corner of the alcove, the bloody marks of three fingers but no fingerprints. The first time he saw them, he had been concentrating on signs that led away from the crime scene. He hadn't realized that the streaks lead in the other direction, not toward the front door but farther down the hall. The person with blood on his or her hands was headed for one of the other bedrooms.

No more dead, Joona whispers to himself.

He pulls on latex gloves as he walks toward the last room in the hall. He hears a rustling sound as he opens the door. He stops and tries to see what's inside the dim room. The sound stops. Joona carefully feels for the light switch.

He hears rustling again as well as the clank of metal.

"Vicky?" he calls gently.

He flips the switch and light fills the small cell-like room with a yellow glow. There's another bang, and a moment later the window swings open toward the trees and Lake Himmelsjö. The rustling noises are coming from the corner. Joona sees a birdcage on its side on the floor. Inside, a yellow canary flaps its wings and climbs around.

There's a strong smell of blood in the room: iron and sweetness mixed together.

Joona fetches some protective mats for the floor before he enters.

There are flecks of blood next to the window fasteners. Bloody handprints mark how someone climbed on the windowsill, held onto the frame for a moment, and then jumped out, landing on the lawn below.

Joona walks over to the bed. He feels ice-cold as he pulls away the blanket. The sheets are smeared with dried blood, but the person who was sleeping here was not the one who bled. Whoever was in the bed was covered with someone else's blood.

Joona stands still and reads the traces of movement left by the bloodstains.

She was actually sleeping here, he thinks.

He tries to lift the pillow, but it feels stuck. Joona pulls it loose. Beneath the pillow is a hammer covered in blood. He can also see strands of brown hair. Most of the blood has been absorbed by the pillow and sheets, but the head of the hammer still gleams, shining wet.

20

Birgittagården is bathed in a beautiful soft light and Lake Himmelsjö is shimmering magically between the tall, ancient trees. Just a few hours ago, Nina Molander got up in the middle of the night to pee and found Miranda dead. The girls panicked. They could not find the night nurse. Frantic, they called the therapist, Daniel Grim. When the police arrived, Nina was in such severe shock that she was taken by ambulance to the provincial hospital in Sundsvall.

Gunnarsson stands in the middle of the yard with Daniel Grim and Sonja Rask. He's opened the hatchback of his white Mercedes and laid out the sketches, which the technicians have just finished, on the platform for baggage.

The dog, still fastened to the running line, has not yet stopped barking and pulling on its leash.

Joona Linna comes up to the back of the car.

"The girl's run away. She climbed out the window," he says.

"Run away?" asks Daniel Grim. "Vicky's run away? Why would—"

"There is blood on the windowsill, blood on the bed, and—"

"That doesn't mean—"

"—and a bloodstained hammer beneath her pillow," Joona finishes.

"Can't be right," Gunnarsson says. "Can't be right. This murder was committed with brutal force."

Joona turns to look at Daniel Grim. Grim's face is naked and fragile in the sunlight.

"What do you think?" Joona asks.

"About what? That Vicky would . . . That's just sick," Daniel says.

"How so?"

"Just a minute ago you policemen were saying that this had to be a grown man," he says. "Vicky is a small girl who weighs not much more than a hundred pounds and her wrists are as thin as—"

"Is she violent?" asks Joona.

"Vicky did not do this," Daniel says calmly. "I've been working with her for two months and I can tell you for a fact that she didn't do this."

"Was she violent when she arrived here?"

"I'm sorry, I can't tell you. Patient confidentiality."

"Your damned patient confidentiality is a waste of our time," Gunnarsson says.

"All I can tell you is that I work with certain students to help them find alternatives to their aggressive reactions, for instance, disappointment or fear," Daniel said, keeping his composure.

"Vicky wasn't one of them," Joona says.

"She was not."

"So why was she here?" asks Sonja Rask.

"I am sorry, I cannot comment on specific students."

"But you believe she is not violent?" Sonja insists.

"She's nice," he says simply.

"What do you think happened? Why is there a bloody hammer under her pillow?"

"I have no idea. It doesn't add up. Maybe she helped someone. Wanted to hide it for someone else."

"Which students here are violent?" snaps Gunnarsson.

"I can't single out any one student. You must understand."

"We understand," Joona says.

Daniel turns toward Joona gratefully.

"You can try to talk to them yourself," Daniel says to Joona. "You can tell which ones I indicated earlier fairly quickly."

"Thanks." Joona starts to leave.

"Keep in mind that they've just lost a friend," Daniel calls after him.

Joona stops and turns to look at him. "Are you aware which room Miranda was found in?"

Daniel shakes his head. "No, but I assumed . . ."

"I find it hard to believe that the room she was found in was her own room," Joona continues. "It is almost empty. On the right side of the hall, next to the bathrooms."

"The isolation room," Daniel says.

"Why are the girls put in that room?"

"Because . . ." Daniel falls silent and appears to think of something.

Joona asks, "What is on your mind?"

"The door should have been locked."

"There is a key in the lock."

"Which key?" Daniel asks. "Only Elisabet has the key to the isolation room."

"Who is Elisabet?" asks Gunnarsson.

"My wife," Daniel replies. "She was the one on call last night."

"Where is she now?" asks Sonja.

"What do you mean?" Daniel asks.

"Your wife—is she at home?" Sonja asks.

Daniel appears surprised and unsure of himself.

"I assumed that Elisabet went with Nina in the ambulance," he says slowly.

"No, Nina Molander was alone," Sonja says.

"Of course Elisabet went with Nina! She would never let a student—"

"I was the first person on the scene," Sonja says abruptly. Her exhaustion has made her voice hoarse and brusque. "There was no staff here. Just a group of terrified girls."

"But my wife—"

"Call her now," Sonja says.

"I've tried repeatedly. Her phone is off," Daniel says softly. "I thought . . . I assumed—"

"This is a real goddamn mess," Gunnarsson says.

"My wife, Elisabet . . . She has heart trouble," Daniel Grim continued. His voice becomes even shakier. "Maybe she . . . she could have . . ."

"Try to speak calmly," Joona says.

"My wife has an enlarged heart and she . . . she worked here last night . . . She should be here . . . Her phone is off . . ."

21

Daniel looks at the two officers in despair. He pulls at the zipper on his jacket and keeps repeating that his wife has heart trouble. The dog barks and pulls on its leash hard enough that it almost strangles. It wheezes and then starts barking again.

Joona walks up to the dog, murmuring in a soothing tone, and lets him off the leash. The second it's released, the dog dashes across the yard. Joona sprints after it. The dog starts scratching at the door to an outbuilding, whining and panting.

Daniel stares at Joona and the dog for a moment and then starts to walk toward them. Gunnarsson yells at him to stay put, but he keeps walking. His body is stiff and his face contorts with fear. The gravel crunches beneath his feet.

Joona tries to calm the dog down. He grabs it by the collar and drags it away from the door, while Gunnarsson runs across the yard and grasps Daniel's coat, but Daniel tugs loose. As he yanks free, he slips on the gravel and scrapes his hand. He gets back up. The dog keeps howling, straining at its collar, its body quivering. A uniformed police officer moves to block the door, but Daniel tries to push past him.

"Elisabet! Elisabet! I have to—"

The police officer grips Daniel by the shoulder and steers him away, while Gunnarsson reaches Joona and helps him get the dog under control.

"It could be my wife in there!" screams Daniel. "My wife—"

Joona feels a pang of pain behind his eyes as he pulls on a pair of latex gloves.

There's a wooden sign hanging below the low roof. It says BREWERY.

Joona opens the door slowly and peers into the dark. A tiny window is cracked and hundreds of flies are buzzing in the air. There are bloody paw prints all over the glazed tile floor. Joona makes sure not to step on them as he moves to the side to look beyond the stone fireplace.

He sees the back panel of a cell phone next to a trail of smeared blood. The flies grow louder. A woman is lying on the ground with her head in a pool of blood. She looks about fifty years old. Her mouth is open. She is wearing jeans, rose-colored socks, and a gray cardigan. From her posture, it looks as if the woman had tried to slither away, but then her head and face were smashed in.

22

Pia Abrahamsson knows she's driving over the speed limit. She'd hoped to get on the road a bit earlier, but the meeting in Östersund for pastors of the Church of Sweden dragged on later than usual. She glances at her son, Dante, in the rearview mirror. His head is leaning on the side of the child seat and his eyes are closed beneath his glasses. His little face is calm, and the car seems softly cloaked by the morning fog.

She reduces her speed to eighty kilometers an hour, even though the road heads straight through the spruce forest. The highway is hauntingly empty. Twenty minutes ago she passed a lumber truck filled with logs, but since then she hasn't seen a single vehicle.

She screws up her eyes to see the road properly. Tall fences flash past her on either side. They are meant to keep wildlife off the road. They're not meant to protect wildlife but to protect people. People are the most frightened animals on the planet, she thinks.

She glances again at Dante in the child seat.

She was already a pastor in the parish of Hässelby when she found out she was pregnant. The father was the editor of the newspaper *Church Times*. She found herself standing and staring at the results of the pregnancy test, realizing that she was thirty-six years old. She decided to keep the baby but not the father. Her son was the best thing that had ever happened to her.

The sleeping boy's head has fallen to his chest and his security blanket has slipped to the floor. Before falling asleep, he was so tired that he cried at the slightest frustration. He cried because he didn't like the way the car smelled like Mamma's perfume; he cried because Super Mario had been eaten up.

Pia Abrahamsson realized she had to pee urgently. She'd had too much coffee at the meeting. It's at least twenty kilometers to Sundsvall and more than four hundred to Stockholm. There has to be an open gas station soon.

She tells herself that she shouldn't stop the car in the middle of the forest. She shouldn't and yet she finds she is stopping anyway.

Pia Abrahamsson, who often preaches that there is a reason for everything that happens, is about to be the victim of chance.

She turns onto a logging road and stops at the boom that prevents traffic from entering. Behind the boom, a gravel road stretches through the forest to a storehouse for lumber. She thinks she'll walk just beyond the view of the road and she'll leave the car door open in case Dante wakes up. Which he does.

"Mamma, don't go."

"Sweetie," Pia says. "Mamma has to pee. I'll leave the door open so I can see you the whole time."

He looks at her with sleepy eyes.

"Don't leave me alone," he whispers.

She smiles and pats his sweaty cheek. She knows that she's overprotective, but she can't help it.

"Just an itty-bitty minute," she says.

Dante grabs for her hand, but she pulls away. She ducks under the boom and walks along the gravel road. She turns and winks at Dante.

What if someone sees her with her bare backside and films her with a cell phone? Pia envisions the clip circulating on YouTube, Facebook, and Twitter: "The Pissing Pastor."

She shudders at the thought, then steps off the road and into the trees. Heavy forestry machinery, harvesters, and bulldozers have torn up the earth.

As soon as she's sure that no one can see her from the main road, she lifts her skirt, moves her underwear to one side, and squats. She's tired, and she steadies herself with one hand in the soft moss that grows at the base of the trees.

Relief fills her as she shuts her eyes. When she looks up again, she sees something incomprehensible. An animal has come out of the forest on two legs. It's walking on the logging road, bent over and stumbling. A tiny figure covered in dirt, blood, and clay.

Pia holds her breath. It isn't an animal after all. It's almost as if a part of the forest has freed itself and come alive. As if it's a little girl made from twigs.

She gets up and follows it. She tries to say something but can't find her voice. A branch breaks beneath her foot. Rain has started to fall.

She moves as if she's in a nightmare. She can't make her legs run.

She sees between the trees that the creature has reached the car. There are dirty cloth bands hanging from the strange girl's hands.

Pia stumbles up the gravel road and watches the girl sweep her purse off the driver's seat onto the ground. She gets in and shuts the door.

"Dante!" Pia struggles to say.

The car starts up and drives over her cell phone. It scrapes the guard-rail as it turns around and onto the road. Then it straightens out and roars away.

Pia is crying as she reaches the boom. Her whole body is shaking. How could this have happened? The twig girl appeared from nowhere, and now the car and her son are gone.

She bends down under the boom then walks onto the long, empty road. She is not screaming. She can't scream. The only sound she hears is her own breathing.

23

The rain is beginning to beat against his windshield. Mads Jensen, a Danish long-haul trucker, sees a woman standing in the middle of the road barely two hundred yards in front of him. He swears and blows the horn. The woman seems to come alive at the sound of the horn, but instead of moving, she stays in the middle of the road. The trucker honks the horn again and the woman takes a step toward him, lifting her chin to look right at him.

Mads has already put on the brakes and feels the weight of the semi-trailer press against the old Fliegel cab. He has to brake harder while gearing down. The transmission is bad and there's knocking in the steering axle. A shudder goes through the trailer before he manages to bring the vehicle to a full stop.

The woman is just standing there, barely three yards from the headlights. Now Jensen can see that she's wearing the dress of a Lutheran pastor beneath her jean jacket. The little white rectangle at her collar shines against the black backdrop of her shirt. The woman's face is devoid of color. When their eyes meet through the windshield, tears begin to stream down her face.

Mads turns on his warning lights and leaves the cab. Heat and the smell of diesel stream from the motor. As he walks around the cab, he sees that the woman is now leaning on a headlight and is having trouble breathing.

"What is all this?" asks Mads.

She turns to look at him. Her eyes are wide open.

"Do you need help?"

She nods and he leads her to the side of the cab. The rain is getting heavier and the skies are darkening.

"Has someone done something bad to you?"

At first she hesitates, but then she climbs into the passenger seat. He closes the door behind her, hurries around the cab, and gets into the driver's seat.

"I can't keep blocking the road," he says. "Do you mind if I get going again?"

She doesn't answer, so he starts the motor and the tractor-trailer moves forward. He turns on the windshield wipers.

"Are you hurt?" he asks.

She shakes her head and holds her hand in front of her mouth.

"My son," she whispers. "My son . . ."

"What did you say? What happened?"

"She took my child . . ."

"Would you like me to call the police?" he asks. "Let me call the police."

"Oh God!" the woman moans.

24

The wipers sweep the rain away as fast as they can. The road ahead appears to be boiling under the downpour.

Pia is shivering and she can't calm down. She realizes she can't speak coherently, but she's able to listen as the truck driver talks with the emergency center. He's being advised to continue along Highway 86 and then take Highway 330 to Timrå, where an ambulance can take Pia to Sundsvall Hospital.

"What are you talking about?" asks Pia, suddenly finding her voice. "I don't need an ambulance! You have to stop the car! That's all that matters!"

The truck driver gives her a look and Pia realizes that she has to pull herself together and make herself clear. Even though she feels as if she's falling through space, she must sound rational.

"My son has been kidnapped," she says.

"She is saying that her son has been kidnapped," reports the truck driver.

"The police must stop the car. It's a Toyota . . . a red Toyota Auris. I can't remember the license plate number."

The truck driver asks the operator to hold on for a minute.

"It should be ahead of us on the road. You have to stop it. My son is only four years old. He was still in his car seat when I had to . . ."

The truck driver repeats her words and then explains that he is on Highway 86 just thirty-eight kilometers from Timrå.

"We have to hurry!"

The truck driver slows down as they approach a broken traffic light before a roundabout. The truck thunders as it rolls over the speed bumps. They pass a white brick building as they pick up speed and keep heading down Highway 86.

The emergency center has connected the truck driver to the police. A female officer in a roaming squad car picks it up. She explains that her name is Mirja Zlatnek and she is only twenty-nine kilometers away from them on Highway 330 in Djupängen.

Pia Abrahamsson takes over the telephone. She swallows hard to force away her nausea. Her voice is calm even though it is shaking.

"Listen to me," she says. "My son has been kidnapped. The car is on—" She turns to the truck driver. "What highway is this?"

"Highway 86," he says.

"How far ahead are they?" asks the policewoman.

"Perhaps five minutes ahead of us," Pia says.

"Have you already driven past Indal?"

"Indal," Pia says loudly.

"Nineteen kilometers ahead of us," the truck driver says.

"Then we'll get them," the policewoman says. "We'll catch them."

As Pia Abrahamsson hears those words, tears begin to flow. She wipes them from her cheeks and listens to the policewoman talk to a colleague. They're going to erect a blockade on Highway 330 where there is a bridge over the river. The officer says that he's just five minutes away and will be able to get there in time.

"Good," the policewoman says quickly.

The truck driver keeps driving along the highway, which follows the river through the empty spaces of Medelpad Province. They know that the car with Pia's son has to be ahead of them, although they can't see it. There are no alternatives. The highway runs past small collections of houses, but there are no other roads and no turnoffs except for lumber roads leading to the occasional clearing.

"I can't take this," Pia says to herself.

The road forks a few kilometers ahead, past the village of Indal. One branch leads south to a bridge over the river, and the other continues east along the river toward the coast.

Pia is sitting with her hands clasped as she prays.

The police are setting up blockades on both forks of the road. One is on the other side of the bridge and the other is eight kilometers to the east.

The tractor-trailer with its driver from Denmark and the Lutheran pastor Pia Abrahamsson is now passing through Indal. Through the downpour, they can see the empty bridge over the river and the blue light of a squad car rotating on the other side.

25

Police officer Mirja Zlatnek has parked her squad car diagonally across the road and pulled up the emergency brake. To get past her, a car would have to leave the road and then at least two wheels would go into the ditch.

There's a long stretch of road before her, and the rain beats against the roof of her car. Mirja peers through the windshield, but it's hard to see in the increasingly heavy rain.

She'd thought she'd have a quiet day, since all the other police officers in the region were sent to Birgittagården after the dead girl was found there. She started at her desk, reading recipes on a food website. Baked fillet of moose, potato wedges, and Karl Johan mushroom sauce. Full-bodied puree of Jerusalem artichoke. Then she had to get in the squad car and check out a stolen trailer in Djupängen, which was where she was when the call came in about the kidnapped boy.

Although she's never been involved in a case involving violence, Mirja has started to fear the operative side of police work. She can trace this back many years to when she tried to mediate a family conflict, which ended badly. Over the years since, her fear has crept up on her to the point that she prefers administrative work and preventive tactics. But she tells herself that she can handle the situation. There's no other place where the car with the four-year-old boy could go. This road is like a single long tunnel—a fish trap. Either the car will drive over the bridge after Indal, where her colleague Lasse Bengtsson is waiting for it, or it will come here—and here's where I'm waiting, Mirja thinks.

The tractor-trailer should be about ten or eleven kilometers behind the car. Much depends on how fast the car is going. In twenty minutes, no less, it will be here. Mirja tells herself that this is probably not a random kidnapping. It could be a custody battle. The woman on the phone was too upset to give much concrete information, but her car should be somewhere on this highway, this side of Nilsböle.

It'll soon be over, she thinks. In a little while, she'll be able to return to the office, have a cup of coffee, eat her ham sandwich.

But there is something that bothers her. The woman kept talking about a girl with twigs for arms. Mirja didn't ask the woman for her name. There wasn't time. She assumed that the emergency center had taken it down. The woman's agitation was frightening. She had described what happened as if it were some incomprehensible or supernatural event.

The rain keeps beating down. Mirja picks up the radio and calls her colleague Lasse Bengtsson.

"What's going on?" she asks.

"Raining like hell, but otherwise not much. Not a single car," he says. "Wait, now I see a truck, a huge tractor-trailer. On Highway 330."

"He's the driver who placed the call," she says.

"Then where the hell is the Toyota?" asks Lasse. "I've been here for fifteen minutes and I haven't seen it. Unless the car is a UFO, it should reach you in less than five minutes."

"Just a minute," Mirja says quickly, and cuts off communication. She can see headlights in the distance.

26

Mirja Zlatnek leaves the squad car and peers through the curtain of rain at the approaching car. She places one hand on her holstered gun as she walks toward it and motions for it to stop. Water runs over the road and puddles in the grass at the bottom of the ditch. Her own shadow cast by the rotating blue light behind her leaps around on the asphalt.

Mirja sees that the car is slowing down just as she hears a call come through on her radio. She stays on the road. It sounds as if the voices on the radio are coming from inside a can. There's hiss and crackle, but she can tell what's being said.

"There's blood everywhere," a voice says. Another body has been found at Birgittagården. A woman in her fifties.

The vehicle swings to the shoulder as it comes to a stop. Mirja Zlatnek walks over to the driver's side. The vehicle is a Mazda pickup truck. The driver's door opens and a huge man in a green hunting vest gets out. He has shoulder-length hair, a powerful nose, and narrow eyes. He's smiling broadly.

"Are you the only person in the vehicle?" asks Mirja, wiping water from her face.

He nods and looks away toward the forest.

"Move aside," she says as she reaches the vehicle.

The man takes a small step back and Mirja leans forward to look inside the truck's cab. Her hair is soaked and water runs down her back.

It's hard to see anything through the windshield. A newspaper is spread out on the driver's seat. She can tell he was sitting on it. She walks around and peers into the tiny backseat compartment. Nothing but a thermos and an old blanket.

There's another call on her radio, but she can't make out the words.

The huge man's hunting vest is already turning dark green from the rain. She hears a scratching sound, something scraping against the metal. She turns to look at the man. He's come closer, or perhaps she's just imagining it, she's no longer sure. He's taking a good look at her, neck to knee, and his fleshy forehead wrinkles.

"Do you live around here?" she asks.

She rubs the mud off the license plate with her foot and writes down the number. Then she walks around the front of the vehicle.

"No," he says slowly.

There's a pink sports bag on the passenger seat. Mirja keeps going around the truck. There's a tarp held down by bungee cords over the flatbed and something's underneath it.

"Where are you headed?" asks Mirja.

The man doesn't move but he follows her with his eyes. Suddenly she spots a trickle of blood running out from beneath the tarp in one of the grooves otherwise filled with mud and pine needles.

"What's this?" she asks.

When he doesn't answer, Mirja reaches over the side of the flatbed. It's not easy to reach—she has to press against the wet truck. The man moves to the side. She can just reach the tarp with her fingertips, but she doesn't take her eyes off the man. He's licking his lips as she begins to pull the tarp away. She unsnaps the holster of her gun and then turns quickly to look at the flatbed, where she sees the slender hoof of a young deer, a fawn.

The man stops moving, but Mirja still puts her hand on her gun as she walks away from the pickup truck.

"Where'd you shoot the deer?"

"It was roadkill."

"Did you mark the spot?"

He spits on the ground between his own feet.

"Please show me your driver's license," she says.

He doesn't reply and shows no indication that he is going to comply.

"Your driver's license," she says again, and she can hear the insecurity in her voice.

"I'm through with you," the man says and gets into his truck.

"It's the law to report any animals which have been hit—"

The man is in the driver's seat and slams the door. He starts the truck and drives around the squad car, even though two wheels dip into the ditch. As he swings back up onto the road, Mirja thinks that she should have inspected the vehicle more carefully. She should have removed the entire tarp and checked to see if anything else was underneath it.

She can hear a crow cawing from a perch in the treetops. Then she hears the noise of a vehicle coming up behind her. She whirls around with her pistol out, but she can't see anything in the downpour.

27

Mads Jensen is on his radio, being told off by his manager. He's doing his best to explain the situation while his boss is yelling about missed times and ruined logistics.

"But—" Mads keeps trying to break in. "Don't you have to help other peo—"

"The only help you'll get from me is a cut in your pay!"

"Well, thank you very much, then," Mads says, and breaks off communication.

The rain thunders on the roof of the cab. Pia is staring into the sideview mirror, looking at the trailer and watching the trees fade into the distance. Mads takes out a piece of nicotine gum. He's staring straight ahead at the road. The rumbling from the motor and the hiss of heavy tires on wet asphalt fills the cab.

Pia glances at the calendar, which is swinging with the movement of the truck. A curvy woman in a swimming pool holding a plastic swan. Beneath the picture is the date, August 1968. The road is sloping downhill and the weight of the load of bar iron is making the tractor-trailer speed up.

In the distance, a blue light flickers through the gray sheet of rain. A squad car is blocking the road.

Pia's heart begins to pound. She stares at the police car and the woman in her dark blue sweater waving for them to pull over. Even before the tractor-trailer has come to a complete stop, Pia is opening the door. The sound of the engine is overwhelming.

She feels dizzy as she climbs down and runs over to the waiting policewoman.

"Where's the car?" asks the policewoman.

"What are you saying?"

Pia reads the woman's wet face and is frightened by the look. She feels as if her legs are about to give way beneath her.

"Did you see the car as you passed it?" the policewoman asks.

"Passed it?" says Pia in confusion.

Mads joins them.

"We haven't seen anything on the road," he says. "You must have put up the roadblock too late."

"Too late? I drove up here on this road from the other direction!"

"So where the hell is the car, then?" asks the trucker.

Mirja Zlatnek runs back to the patrol car and radios her colleague.

"Lasse?" she asks, out of breath.

"I've been trying to get you," said Lasse. "You weren't answering—"

"I was—"

"Did you get him?"

"Where the hell is the car?" She is practically screaming. "The truck is here, but no car has come past!"

"There aren't any other roads," he says.

"We have to put out a bulletin and close Highway 86 in the other direction."

"I'm on it," he says and breaks off.

Pia leans into the squad car. The rain has soaked through her clothes. Mirja Zlatnek is sitting in the driver's seat with the door open.

"You told me you'd get him," Pia says.

"Yes, I—"

"I believed you."

"I know. I don't understand it, either. It's impossible to drive at high speed on this road, and there's no chance the car could have reached the bridge before Lasse did."

"But it has to be somewhere," Pia says. She pulls off her pastor's collar.

"Wait a minute," Mirja says.

She contacts the central station.

"This is car 321. We need a roadblock immediately, before Aspen.

There's a small road there. If you know where the road is you can drive from Kävsta up to Myckelsjö. That's right. Who's going there? Good, I imagine it'll take him eight to ten minutes."

Mirja gets back out of the car and stares down the road as if she still expects the Toyota to appear.

"Where's my boy?" Pia asks her.

"There's no other place for them to go," Mirja says, trying to be patient. "I understand your worry, but we will get them. They must have turned off the road somewhere, but there's nowhere for them to go."

She wipes the rain from her eyes. "We're closing the last road and then we'll get the helicopter from the rescue station."

Pia unbuttons the top button of her shirt and then leans on the front of the squad car. She's breathing much too heavily and it feels as if her chest has burst open. She thinks she should be making demands, but she can't think clearly. She is desperate and afraid.

28

A large white command bus is parked in the middle of the yard between the buildings at Birgittagården. Command Central is inside. A group of men and women sit around a table covered in maps and laptops, analyzing the investigation, until a bulletin comes in about a kidnapped boy and they stop.

Roadblocks have been thrown up on Highway 330 and Highway 86 going north, as well as at the bridge south of Indal. It should be doable, their colleagues say, to stop the kidnapper—but they hear nothing more for the next ten minutes at least. Then the radio breaks in again.

"It's gone!" a policewoman reports breathlessly. "The car should have been here, but it hasn't shown up. We've closed each and every damned road. It's just gone. I don't know what to do." Mirja sounds exhausted. "The mother is sitting in my car. I'm going to try to talk to her."

The police in the bus listen silently; then they all turn to the map spread out on the table. Bosse Norling traces the route of Highway 86 with his finger.

"If they've blocked here and here, then the car can't just disappear," he says. "Obviously, the kidnapper could have driven it into a garage in Bäck or Bjällsta, or onto a logging road, but that would be a damned strange thing to do."

"And there's nowhere to go," Sonja Rask says.

"Am I the only one who's thinking that Vicky Bennet could have taken this car?" asks Bosse.

The rain is starting to ease up, but water is still washing down the bus's windows.

Sonja turns back to her computer and starts to go through lists of pedophiles and custody disputes via the police intranet.

"Nine times out of ten," Gunnarsson begins as he leans back and starts peeling a banana, "these kinds of events solve themselves. I think she had a guy with her in the car. They fought and he took off, leaving her at the side of the road."

"She's not married," says Sonja.

"According to our statistics," Gunnarsson says, keeping his pedagogic tone of voice, "most of the children born in Sweden are born outside marriage and—"

"Here we go," said Sonja. "Pia Abrahamsson requested sole custody of her son, Dante, and the father tried to contest it."

"So we're going to drop the possible connection to Vicky Bennet?" asks Bosse.

"Look for the father first," says Joona.

"On it," says Sonja. She heads to the back of the bus.

"What did you find beneath Vicky Bennet's window?" Joona asks one of the technicians.

"There wasn't anything on the ground. We found prints and some coagulation traces on the windowsill."

"And what did you find near the edge of the forest?"

"Nothing, and then it started to rain."

"But apparently Vicky Bennet headed directly into the forest," Joona says thoughtfully. He watches Bosse Norling, who is leaning over the map, place a pin on Birgittagården and then draw a circle around it with a compass.

"Vicky didn't take the car," says Gunnarsson. "It doesn't take three whole damn hours to get from the forest to Highway 86 and then go—"

"On the other hand, she was running at night. It's not easy to find your way in the dark. She could have walked all the way there," Bosse says. He jabs the map to the east of a forested area and then traces a line going north.

"The timing would work," Joona says.

"Dante's father is in the Canary Islands right now," Sonja calls from the back of the bus.

Olle Gunnarsson swears, then picks up the radio to call Mirja Zlatnek.

"Gunnarsson here," he says. "Has the mother given us her statement?"

"Yes, and I—"

"Can she describe the suspect?"

"It wasn't easy. The mother is emotional and the picture of the suspect is somewhat unclear," Mirja says. "The mother is obviously in shock. She's talking about a skeleton with rags hanging down coming out of the forest. A girl with a bloody face and twigs instead of arms."

"But she says it's a girl?"

"I've recorded her testimony, but it's really odd. She keeps saying the strangest things. She'll have to calm down before we can get a decent—"

"But she says it's a girl?"

"Yes. Over and over."

29

Joona stops his car at the roadblock on Highway 330. He greets one of the policemen on duty, shows his ID, and then keeps driving along the road, paralleling the Indal River. He's been told that the students from Birgittagården are being housed at the Hotel Ibis in Sundsvall; Daniel Grim has been checked into the psychiatric ward of the provincial hospital; the housemother, Margot Lundin, is now at her home in Timrå; and Faduumo Axmed, who works part-time as an assistant, is with his parents in Vänersborg.

When they heard Mirja Zlatnek tell them that Pia Abrahamsson insisted she'd seen a small girl with rags on her hands, everyone understood that Vicky Bennet had taken the car with the little boy in the backseat.

"It's a mystery how she didn't get caught in the roadblocks," Bosse Norling said.

They'd put a helicopter up, but the pilot could not see the car anywhere. Not in Indal and not on any of the logging roads.

It's not much of a mystery, Joona thought. *The logical explanation is that she managed to find a hiding place before she reached any of the roadblocks. But where? She must know someone who lives in the village, someone who owns a garage.*

Joona asked to speak with the girls at the hotel and agreed that there should be a child psychologist and a support person from the Office of Victim Services in the room with him.

He's been thinking over the girls' behavior when they were in the small house. Gunnarsson had returned with the two who'd run into the forest. The little red-haired girl had been watching television while banging the back of her head against the wall. The girl named Indie had said putting hands over her face was a game Vicky played. Then everyone realized Vicky had disappeared and had started screaming and carrying on. A couple of the girls had been sure she was still sleeping off a heavy dose of Stesolid. The girl called Almira had spat on the floor and Indie had rubbed her eyes so hard that she'd smeared blue eye shadow over her hands.

Joona thinks that the red-haired girl, Tuula, was onto something. Tuula was so pale even her eyelashes were white. She wore shiny pink sport shorts. She'd said something while the others were all jabbering away.

She'd said that Vicky must have run off to meet the guy she likes to fuck.

30

The two-star Hotel Ibis is on Trädgårdsgatan not far from the police station in Sundsvall. When Joona pulls the front door open, he is greeted by the smell of vacuum cleaners, musty carpets, and cigarette smoke. There's a dish at the reception desk filled with stale candies. The police have assigned the students from Birgittagården to five adjacent rooms and placed two uniformed officers in the hallway. Joona strides over the worn wooden flooring.

The psychologist, Lisa Jern, is waiting for Joona outside one of the bedrooms. Her dark hair is streaked with gray. Her mouth is narrow and nervous.

"Is Tuula here already?" asks Joona.

"Yes, but wait," she says as Joona lays his hand on the door handle. "From what I understand, you are an observer from the National Police—"

"A little boy's in danger," Joona says.

"Tuula is hardly speaking, and my recommendation as a child psychologist is that you wait until she starts speaking about it on her own initiative."

"No time for that." Joona pushes down the handle.

"Wait. It's really important that you keep yourself on the same level as the children. They must not feel as if they're sick or—"

Joona is already in the room. All the furniture has beech-wood veneer and the floor is covered in green wall-to-wall carpet. Tuula Lehti is sitting with her back to a row of windows. She's a tiny girl, just twelve years old, and she's still dressed in her pink shorts and tennis shoes.

Between the slats of the venetian blinds, Joona can see the parked cars in the street. Standing in the farthest corner of the room, there's a man wearing a blue flannel shirt, with his hair combed back. He's tapping the screen on his cell phone. Joona assumes he is the support person for the students.

Joona sits directly across from Tuula and studies her. She has light blond eyebrows and her red hair is straight and needs washing.

"We met briefly this morning," Joona says.

Tuula crosses her freckled arms over her chest. Her lips are narrow and almost colorless.

"Pop a cop," she says.

Lisa Jern has followed Joona into the room and now sits down next to the tiny girl.

"Tuula," she says in a mild voice. "Remember how I told you that I sometimes feel like Thumbelina? It's not strange to feel little, just like Thumbelina, even when you're grown up."

"Why do people always talk like idiots?" Tuula asks, looking Joona directly in the eye. "Is it because you grown-ups are idiots, or because you think we're idiots?"

"We grown-ups probably think you're a bit idiotic," Joona says.

Tuula smiles, surprised. She is about to say something when Lisa Jern breaks in and tries to reassure her that Joona wasn't telling the truth. The officer was just making a joke.

Tuula hugs her arms closer to her chest, stares at the table, and puffs out her cheeks.

"You're not an idiot at all," Lisa Jern keeps repeating.

"Yes, I am," Tuula whispers.

She spits, and a long string of saliva hits the table. She says nothing but begins to draw with the saliva on the table. She draws a star.

"Do you want to talk?" Lisa says quietly.

"Only with the Finn," Tuula replies, her voice so low as to be almost inaudible.

"What did you say?" asks Lisa Jern with a smile.

"I only want to talk to the Finn!" Tuula lifts her chin, pointing at Joona Linna.

"How nice," the psychologist says stiffly.

Joona turns on the recorder and quietly states the formalities: time, place, people present, and the reason for the conversation.

"Why are you at Birgittagården?" he asks.

"I was at Lövsta, and some things happened that weren't so good," Tuula says. "So they put me with the girls who are locked in, even though I'm too young. I kept my nose clean, just watched TV, and one year and four months later they moved me to Birgittagården."

"What's the difference between Lövsta and Birgittagården?"

"Well, Birgittagården is more like a real home, at least as far as I'm concerned. They have rugs on the floors, and they haven't bolted down the furniture, except in the isolation room, and they don't have alarms connected to everything, and you can sleep in peace and quiet, and they give you homemade food."

Joona nods and notices that the support person is still flipping through pages on his cell phone. The psychologist Lisa Jern is breathing heavily as she listens to them.

"What food did they make for you yesterday?" Joona asks.

"Tacos."

"Was everyone at dinner?"

Tuula shrugs. "I guess so."

"Miranda, too? Did she eat tacos with you?"

"Cut open her stomach and you'll find out. Haven't you done that yet?"

"No, we haven't."

"Why not?"

"We haven't had time yet."

Tuula semi-smiles and starts pulling at a loose thread on her shorts. Her nails have been bitten to the quick and the cuticles are raw.

"I looked into the isolation room," Tuula says, and she starts to rock. "It was pretty cool."

"Did you see how Miranda was lying there?" asks Joona.

"Yeah, like this," Tuula says and puts her hands over her face.

"Why do you think she was doing that?"

Tuula starts kicking at the carpet. "Maybe she was scared."

"Did you ever see anyone else do that?"

"No," Tuula says, scratching her neck.

"So you're not locked into your rooms," Joona says.

"No, it's almost like open wards," Tuula says and smiles.

"Do you often sneak out at night?"

"Not me." Tuula's mouth becomes tight and hard as she pretends to shoot the psychologist with her index finger.

"Why not?" asks Joona.

She looks back at Joona and says in a small voice, "I'm afraid of the dark."

"What about the others?"

Lisa Jern stands up and frowns as she continues to listen.

"Yes," Tuula whispers.

"What do they do when they sneak out?" asks Joona.

The girl looks down and smiles to herself.

"Of course, those girls are older than you are," Joona says.

"Right," Tuula says. She is blushing.

"Do they meet boys?"

She nods.

"Does Vicky meet boys, too?"

"Yes, she sneaks out at night," Tuula says. She leans on the table in Joona's direction.

"Do you know who she goes to see?"

"Dennis."

"Who is Dennis?"

"I don't know," she whispers. She wets her lips with her tongue.

"But his name is Dennis? Do you know his last name?"

"No."

"How long is she gone?"

Tuula shrugs and pulls at a bit of tape stuck to the underside of the chair cushion.

31

The prosecutor Susanne Öst is waiting outside the Hotel Ibis. She's leaning against a Ford Fairlane. There's not a trace of makeup on her round face, and her blond hair is gathered up in a messy ponytail. Her shirt collar sticks straight up out of her gray suit jacket.

"Do you mind if I play police officer with you?" she asks, blushing.

"Not at all," Joona says, shaking hands with her.

"We're supposed to go knocking on all the doors, looking into each and every garage, shed, and parking lot, et cetera, et cetera," she says. "We'll close the net. There aren't many places where you can hide a car."

"Right," says Joona.

"It'll go faster now that we have a name," she says, smiling, as she opens the door to the Ford Fairlane. "There are only four people with the first name of Dennis in the area."

"I'll follow you," Joona says, and walks over to his Volvo.

The American car sways as it turns onto the road and starts toward Indal. Joona follows it and thinks about what he knows so far about Vicky Bennet.

Her mother, Susie Bennet, was a drug addict and homeless at the time of her death last winter. Vicky had lived with various foster parents and institutions from the age of six and had probably learned to create and let go of relationships quickly.

If Vicky goes out at night to meet a boy, she must meet him close-by. Perhaps he waits for her in the forest or on the gravel road. Perhaps she walks along Highway 86 until she reaches his house in Baggböle or Västloning.

The asphalt is starting to dry. The rainwater is pooling in the ditches. The skies are brightening although raindrops still drip from the trees.

The prosecutor calls Joona and he can see her glancing at him in her rearview mirror as she talks.

"We've only found one Dennis in Indal," she says. "He's seven years old. The second Dennis lives in Stige, but he's working in Leeds in England right now."

"So that leaves only two," Joona says.

"Right. Dennis and Lovisa Karmstedt live in a house on the outskirts of Tomming. We haven't got to them yet. And then there's Dennis Rolando. He lives with his parents just south of Indal. We've just visited the house and there's no one there at the moment. This Dennis owns a large industrial building in Sundsvall, on Kvarnvägen, which we haven't entered yet. There's probably nothing there. At the moment, this Dennis is in his car on the road to Sollefteå."

"Break down the door," says Joona.

"Okay," she says and ends the call.

The landscape opens up and fields line both sides of the highway. Red farm buildings press against the edge of the forest and, behind them, the forest stretches endlessly. Everything is shimmering after the rain.

As Joona passes through the sleepy village of Östanskär, two uniformed police officers in Sundsvall are sawing through the massive iron rail across the steel door of the industrial building with an angle grinder. A cascade of sparks flashes around the walls. Then the bar separates and the officers lever the door with a hefty crowbar. The door bends open and they walk inside. In the beams of their flashlights they can see dark heaps on the floor. They find about fifty ancient video games—Space Invaders, Asteroids, and Street Fighter—beneath dusty plastic sheets.

Meanwhile, Joona observes Susanne Öst speak on the cell phone and then cast him a glance via her rearview mirror. A second later, his cell phone rings. Susanne tells him they now only have one address left to check. It's not far from where they are, and it should take ten minutes to get there.

Finally she slows down and Joona follows her as she turns onto a road between two waterlogged fields and drives up to a yellow wooden house. Its blinds are drawn. Apple trees are growing in a well-tended yard and a blue-and-white-striped hammock hangs between two of them. They park their cars and walk toward two police offers standing by a squad car.

Joona greets the officers and then studies the house. He says, "We don't know if Vicky took the car in order to steal the child, or if she just wanted a car and the child happened to be in the backseat. At the moment, we must think of the child as a hostage."

"A hostage," the prosecutor repeats in a low voice.

She walks up to the door and rings the bell. No response. She shouts a warning that the police will break down the door if they are not let inside. There's someone inside. A piece of heavy furniture is being moved. She can hear the floor groan as the piece is turned over.

"I'll go in," Joona says.

One of the policemen stays to watch the front of the house and the garage. The other follows Joona around the rear. The back of the house has a small set of concrete steps up to a back door with a window of frosted glass. Joona kicks the door, the window breaks and shards of glass fall onto a blue doormat.

"Stay here," he tells the policeman, and he slips inside.

32

The slivers of glass crunch under Joona's shoes as he enters a neat laundry room complete with a hand-crank mangle fastened to a sink.

Miranda was sitting in a chair when she was killed, Joona thinks. *Elisabet, wearing only socks on her feet, was hunted across the yard and into the brewery. She tried to crawl away but was beaten to death.*

Joona can feel the weight of his new pistol in its holster underneath his arm. It's a semiautomatic Smith & Wesson .45 caliber ACP. It weighs slightly more than his previous one and carries fewer bullets, but its first shot is quicker.

Joona slowly opens a creaky door and finds himself looking into a traditional Swedish country kitchen. A large ceramic bowl with apples is on the round wooden table and there's the scent of a fire burning in the beautiful old wood-fired stove. He sees frozen cinnamon buns thawing on a tray and a drawer with sharp knives has been left open. He catches a glimpse of the yard between the drawn curtains.

He shuts the door and walks down the hall. He stops when he hears the sound of tinkling from the ceiling lamp. Its glass prisms are swaying and colliding. Someone is upstairs.

Hugging the wall, he climbs the stairs. Between the open treads he can see clothes hanging in neat rows beneath the staircase. When he reaches the landing, he creeps silently to the closest bedroom. There's a double bed covered by a crazy quilt and a wardrobe, its sliding door partially open. The curtains are closed and the ceiling light is off. Joona steps into the room, his line of fire clear, and moves to the side. The front sight of a rifle is lying on the bed.

He hears someone breathing close-by. Joona aims his gun at the corner of the room as he steps farther inside. Beside the wardrobe, there's a man with stooped shoulders and light brown hair. He's staring at Joona. He's barefoot and wearing dark blue jeans and a white T-shirt with the words "Stora Enso." He's hiding something behind his back and is slowly moving toward the center of the room and closer to the bed.

"I'm from the National Police," Joona says. He lowers his gun slightly.

"This is my house," the man says.

"You should have opened the door."

Joona sees that sweat is running down the man's face.

"Did you bust my back door?"

"I'm afraid so."

"Can it be fixed?"

"I'm afraid not."

Something glints in the smoke-tinted mirror on the wardrobe door. Joona sees in the reflection that the man is holding a large kitchen knife behind his back.

He says calmly, "I need to see what's in your garage."

"The only thing there is my car."

"Put the knife on the bed and take me to your garage."

The man moves the knife and looks at it. It has a stained wooden shaft, and the blade has been worn down by sharpening.

"I don't have time to wait," Joona says.

"You shouldn't have broken my—"

Joona hears bare feet moving in his direction. He moves slightly to the side while keeping his eyes on the knife. A shadow is heading for his back. Joona turns his body and puts his energy into lifting his elbow to meet the rushing shadow.

Joona's gun is still aimed at the man with the knife as his elbow hits a boy in the middle of his chest, knocking the wind out of him. The boy tries to stay upright, but he falls to the floor, gasping for breath. He pulls himself into a fetal position on his side, the rag rug rucked up beneath him.

"They're from Afghanistan," the man says. "They needed help."

"I am going to shoot you in the leg if you don't throw the knife on the bed right now," Joona says.

The man glances down at the knife in his hand, then throws it on the bed.

Two small children appear at the door. Transfixed, they stare at Joona.

"You're hiding refugees?" Joona asks. "How much do they pay you?"

"You think I can change them?" the man says indignantly.

"Do you?"

"No, I don't."

Joona looks at the dark-eyed boy. He asks in English, "Do you pay him?"

The boy shakes his head.

"No human being is illegal," the man says in Swedish.

"You don't have to be afraid," Joona says to the boy, still in English. "I promise I will help you. Are you being abused?"

"Dennis is a good man," the boy whispers.

"I'm happy to hear that," Joona says. He looks the man in the eye then leaves the room.

He walks down the stairs and out the back door. He heads to the garage. He stands there looking through the window at a dusty old Saab inside. He's thinking that Vicky and the boy, Dante, are still missing and there are not many more places to look.

33

Flora Hansen is mopping the floor in the hall of Ewa and Hans-Gunnar's second-floor apartment. Her left cheek is still burning from the blow and her ear is ringing. The shine was rubbed off the vinyl long ago, but the water makes it glisten again for a short time.

Flora has beaten all the rugs and mopped the living room, the narrow kitchen, and Hans-Gunnar's room, but she's waiting to do Ewa's until *Solsidan* starts. Both Ewa and Hans-Gunnar are fans of the show and never miss an episode.

Flora shoves the mop into every crevice and corner. Walking backward, she bumps against a picture she made at nursery school more than thirty years ago. All the children glued pasta to a wooden board and then sprayed their pictures with gold paint. She hears the theme music of the TV show start. Now is her chance.

Her back twinges as she lifts the bucket and carries it into Ewa's room. She closes the door behind her and blocks it with the bucket so that no one can fling the door open. Her heart starts to pound as she dips the mop into the bucket, presses out the excess water, and glances at the wedding photo on the nightstand. Ewa has hooked the key to her desk on the back of the photograph.

Flora does all the housework in exchange for a place to stay. She'd had no choice but to return to Ewa and Hans-Gunnar after she lost her job as an assistant nurse at Saint Göran's Hospital and her unemployment ran out. She lives in the maid's room.

As a child, Flora used to dream that her birth parents would find her and take her away, but apparently they were drug addicts, and Hans-Gunnar and Ewa say they know nothing about them. Flora came to their house when she was five and doesn't remember anything about her earlier life. Hans-Gunnar always treated Flora like a burden, and ever since she was a young teenager, Flora has longed to escape. When she was nineteen, she'd gotten the job as an assistant nurse and moved to her own apartment in Kallhäll that same month.

The mop drips as she carries it over to the window. Beneath the radiator, the vinyl is black from old leaks. The venetian blind hangs crookedly in the window. There's a Dala horse from Rättvik between the geraniums on the windowsill.

Flora moves slowly toward the nightstand. She stops and listens. She can hear the television.

Hans-Gunnar and Ewa are young in their wedding photo. She's wearing a white dress and he's in a tuxedo with a silver tie. The sky behind them is white. On a hill beside the church, there's a black bell tower with an onion dome. The tower sticks up behind Hans-Gunnar's head like a strange hat. Flora doesn't know why, but she finds the picture unpleasant.

She tries to breathe evenly.

Silently, she leans the shaft of the mop against the wall. She waits until she hears her foster mother's laughter before she picks up the photo and unhooks the ornate bronze key hanging behind it. Her hands shake so much she drops the key, which hits the floor and bounces beneath the bed. Flora has to support herself on the nightstand as she bends down to retrieve it. The blood beats in her temples and the floor outside creaks, but then goes silent again.

The key has landed by the dust-covered electrical cords that run along the wall. Flora can just reach it. She stands back up and waits a moment before she goes to the secretary desk and unlocks it. She lowers the heavy lid and slides open one of the tiny drawers inside. Beneath two postcards from Majorca and Paris, there's an envelope where Ewa keeps cash for immediate expenses. Flora opens the envelope for next month's bills and takes half. She stuffs the bills into one of her pockets and puts the envelope back. She tries to shut the tiny drawer, but it sticks.

"Flora!" Ewa calls.

Flora opens the drawer and doesn't see anything strange about it, so she tries to shut it again, but she's shaking so hard that she can't. She can hear footsteps head down the hall. She shoves the drawer, and it jerks in, although it is crooked now. She lifts the desk lid back into place, but doesn't have time to lock it.

The door is pushed open and water from the bucket sloshes out.

"Flora?"

Flora grabs the mop and moves the bucket as she starts cleaning up the spilled water.

"I can't find my hand cream," Ewa says.

Ewa's eyes are tense, her lips pursed. She's barefoot in sagging yellow sweatpants, and her white T-shirt strains over her stomach and voluminous breasts.

"It's next to the shampoo in the bathroom cabinet," Flora says as she twists the mop.

There's a commercial break—the sound is louder and a shrill voice is talking about foot fungus. Ewa keeps standing inside the doorway, looking at Flora.

"Hans-Gunnar did not like his coffee," she says.

"I'm sorry."

Flora squeezes out the excess water.

"He says that you're putting cheaper coffee into the expensive packet."

"Why would I—"

"Don't lie to me!"

"Well, I don't," mutters Flora.

"Go get his cup now, right now, and brew him a new one, a decent one."

Flora leans the mop against the wall. She asks forgiveness as she walks out and heads for the living room. She can feel the key and the bills in her pocket. Hans-Gunnar does not even look at her as she takes his coffee cup from the tray.

"Ewa, get the hell back here!" he yells. "The show's starting again!"

Flora jumps at his voice and hurries away. She meets Ewa in the hallway and catches her eye.

"Do you remember that I'll be gone this evening for a job-search class?"

"Like you would ever find a job."

"But I have to go, those are the rules. I'm making new coffee now and then I'll finish the floors. Maybe I can do the curtains tomorrow instead."

34

Flora hands over the cash to a man in a gray coat. His umbrella drips water on her face as he gives her the key and tells her that, as usual, she should drop it in the antique dealer's mail slot when she's finished. Flora thanks him and hurries down the sidewalk. The seams in her old coat are beginning to rip open. She is forty, but her face is childlike. It radiates loneliness.

The first block on Upplandsgatan after Odenplan in Stockholm is filled with antique and curiosity shops. Crystal chandeliers and display cases, old toys made of painted tin, porcelain dolls, medals, and mantel clocks clutter the shop windows.

Next to the barred windows of Carlén Antiques there's a narrow door. Flora tapes a piece of white cardboard onto the door's thick glass window. On it she's written "Spiritualist Evening."

A steep staircase leads to the basement. There are two rooms here: a small pantry and a larger meeting room. The pipes in the walls roar whenever anyone in the upper floors flushes the toilet or turns on the faucets. Flora has hired the larger room for seven séances. Four to six people usually attend, which barely covers the rent. She's written letters to a number of newspapers to inform them of her ability to contact the dead, but nobody has replied. She's put an advertisement in the New Age magazine *Fenomen* for this evening's séance.

She only has a few minutes before the participants will arrive, but she knows what to do. She quickly pushes the excess furniture to one side and takes twelve chairs and puts them in a circle around a table. In the center of the table she places the porcelain figurines of a man and a woman wearing clothes from the nineteenth century. She believes that they will help evoke a feeling of the past. As soon as the séance is over, she'll return them to their place in an oak cabinet because she's not fond of them. She arranges twelve tea lights around the figurines after pressing a little strontium salt into one of the candles with the end of a match and covering the hole.

Then she goes to the cabinet and sets an ancient alarm clock to ring. She first tried this trick four weeks ago. The bell is gone, so the only thing that can be heard is a chattering sound inside the cabinet. Before she can wind up the clock, however, she hears the door upstairs open. The first guests have arrived. She hears people shake their umbrellas and start walking down the stairs.

Flora catches a glimpse of herself in the square mirror. She stops, takes a deep breath, and presses her hand along the front of the gray dress she bought at the Salvation Army store. She smiles at her reflection. She appears calm. She lights some incense and smiles kindly as Dina and Asker Sibelius enter the room. They hang up their coats, talking quietly to each other.

The outer door opens again, and more people come down the stairs. This time, it's an elderly couple that she hasn't met before. The participants of Flora's séances tend to be old people near the end of their lives. They can't accept the fact that many of their loved ones are gone and that death is final.

Flora greets the new couple in her usual, quiet manner and starts to turn away. Then she stops and studies the man as if she's seen something particular about him, and she makes as if to shake off that feeling as she motions for them to take a seat. The door opens again. A few more guests have arrived.

At ten past seven, Flora realizes that no one else is coming. There are nine people seated around the table. It's the highest number yet, but not enough to pay back the money she's taken from Ewa. Her legs are shaking as she pulls out a chair and sits down. The conversation stops and everyone looks at her.

35

Flora lights the candles on the tray and then lets her gaze wander over the participants. She's met five of them before. The others are new. Directly across from her, there's a man who looks barely thirty. His face is open and handsome in a boyish way.

"Welcome," she begins. "Welcome to our séance. I believe we should get started right away."

"Yes, indeed," old Asker says.

"Take each other's hands and close the circle," Flora commands in a warm, friendly way.

The young man is looking directly at her. He's smiling and obviously curious. A feeling of excitement and expectation begins to flutter in Flora's stomach. For several minutes, there is only silence. It feels powerful and dark. Ten people have made a circle and they can sense the dead arriving behind their backs.

"Don't break the circle," Flora cautions the group. "No matter what happens, don't break the circle. Our visitors might not find their way back to the other side."

Her guests are so old that most of their relatives and friends have already died. Death is a country with many well-known faces.

"Never ask the date of your own death," Flora continues. "And never ask about the Devil."

"Why not?" asks the young man, smiling.

"Not every spirit is good, and the circle is just a gateway to the other side."

The young man's black eyes shine.

"Demons?" he asks.

"I don't believe in demons," Dina Sibelius says. She sounds nervous.

"I keep watch on the gate as best as I can," Flora says. "But all the spirits feel our warmth, see our lights."

Everyone is silent again. There's a noise in the pipes—an odd, busy buzzing as if a fly is caught in a spiderweb.

"Are you ready?" Flora asks gently.

The participants all nod, and Flora is pleased by how serious they seem. She thinks she can hear their hearts beating and their blood pulsing through the circle.

"Now I'm going into a trance."

Flora holds her breath and presses Asker Sibelius's hand as well as the hand of one of the new women. She keeps her eyes closed and waits as long as she can, fighting the impulse to breathe until she starts to shake. Then she takes a deep breath and fills her lungs.

"We have many visitors from the other side tonight," Flora says after a few moments.

The participants who have been here before hum in agreement.

Flora senses the young man is looking at her. She feels his watchful, interested gaze on her cheeks, her hair, her neck.

She lowers her face and thinks she should begin with Violet so that the young man will be convinced. Flora knows Violet's history but up to now has let her wait. Violet Larsen is a terribly lonely person. She lost her only son fifty years ago when he became ill with meningitis and no hospital would admit him for fear of infection. Violet's husband had driven the boy from hospital to hospital the entire night. When dawn came, the boy died in his arms. Violet's husband broke down in grief and died a few years later. One terrible night had eliminated the woman's happiness for the rest of her life.

Flora opens her eyes.

"Violet," she whispers.

The old woman turns hungrily toward Flora.

"Yes?"

"I have a child here, a child who is holding the hand of a grown man."

"What are their names?" Violet asks. Her voice trembles.

"Their names are . . . The boy says you used to call him Jusse."

Violet gasps. "It's my little Jusse," she whispers.

"The man, he says that you know who he is. You are his beautiful flower."

Violet nods and smiles. "That's my Albert."

"They have a message for you, Violet," Flora continues. "They say that they follow you day and night so that you are never alone."

A large tear runs down Violet's cheek.

"The boy asks you not to be sad. Mamma, he is saying, Mamma, I am fine. Pappa is with me all the time."

"I miss you so much," Violet says.

"I can see the boy," Flora whispers. "He is standing next to you. He is touching your cheek."

Violet is crying quietly and the room is silent. Flora is waiting for the tea light to ignite the strontium salts, but it's taking its time.

She mumbles to herself and wonders which person she should choose next. She closes her eyes and sways her upper body.

"So many here. So many here," she mutters. "They're crowding at the small gate. I feel their presence. They are longing to talk to you."

She falls silent as the candle begins to sparkle.

"Don't crowd at the gate," she says.

The candle suddenly flashes a red flame and someone in the room screams.

"You are not invited," Flora says sternly. She waits until the flame dies down. "Now I would like to speak with the man wearing glasses. Yes, please come closer. What is your name?"

She appears to listen inwardly. "You are telling me that you want things to be as they were." Flora looks at her guests. "He says he wants things as they always were. Skinless sausage and boiled potatoes."

"It's my Stig!" says the woman holding Flora's hand.

"It's hard to hear what he is saying," Flora continues. "There are so many people here. They keep interrupting him."

"Stig," the woman whispers.

"He says forgive me. He wants you to forgive him."

Flora feels the woman shaking.

"I have already forgiven you," she whispers.

36

After the séance, Flora sends her guests off with a brief farewell. She knows that people like to be alone with their fantasies and memories.

She walks around the room slowly, blowing out the candles and returning the chairs to their original positions. She is pleased that everything has gone so well. Then she goes to the entryway, where she's placed a box for contributions, and counts the money inside. Next week is her final spiritual evening and her last chance to recover the money she's taken from Ewa. Too few people came in spite of her ad in *Fenomen*. She's started to lie awake at night and stare into the darkness dry-eyed, wondering what she's going to do. When Ewa pays her bills at the end of the month, she's going to realize that the money is missing.

The rain has stopped by the time she gets outside. The sky is black, and the reflections of streetlights and neon signs glitter on the wet pavement. Flora locks the door and slips the key into the mailbox for Carlén Antiques. She takes down her cardboard sign and stuffs it into her bag, then notices that someone is standing in the doorway one building down. It's the young man who attended the séance. He takes a step toward her and smiles apologetically.

"Hi, I was wondering . . . Could I ask you out for a glass of wine or something?"

"Not possible," she says, feeling her usual shyness.

"You were really great," he says.

Flora has no idea what she should say. Her face colors more and more the longer he looks at her.

"It's just that I'm going to Paris," she lies.

"Would I be able to ask you a few questions?"

She realizes that he must be a journalist from one of the newspapers she's tried to contact.

"I'm leaving really early tomorrow," she says.

"Just half an hour, no more," he says.

As they cross the street to the nearest bistro, he tells her that his name is Julian Borg and he writes for the magazine *Nära*.

A few minutes later, Flora is sitting across from him at a table with a white paper cover. A waiter delivers red wine and she cautiously takes a sip. It tastes both sweet and bitter and soon she feels warmth spreading through her body. Julian Borg is eating a Caesar salad and he's looking at her with curiosity.

"So how did this start?" he asks. "Were you always able to see spirits?"

"When I was little, I thought everyone could see them. I didn't find it strange," she said, and blushed again because the lie came so easily.

"What did you see?"

"People I didn't know were in our house. I only thought they were lonely. Once in a while a child came into my room and I'd try and play."

"Did you tell this to your parents?"

"I learned quickly not to say anything," Flora says, and takes another sip of wine. "It's only recently I realized that many people need the spirits, even if they can't see them, and the spirits need people. I've finally found my calling. I'm between them and help them meet each other."

She finds herself resting in Julian Borg's warm gaze.

In reality, the whole thing started when she lost her job as an assistant nurse. She saw less and less of her former colleagues, and within a year, she had no friends left. The unemployment office paid for a course in nail aesthetics, and she got to know another person in the class, Jadranka from Slovakia. Jadranka had periods of depression, but during the months she felt well, she earned a bit of extra money by handling calls for a website called Tarot Help.

Flora and Jadranka started to hang out together. Jadranka took Flora to a séance held by the Sanningsökarna. Afterward they chatted about how much better they could do it themselves. A few months later, they found the basement space on Upplandsgatan. Two séances later, Jadranka's depression worsened and she was admitted to a clinic south of Stockholm. Flora decided to continue the séances on her own.

She took out books from the library on healing, previous lives, angels, auras, and astral bodies. She read about the Fox sisters, the mirrored cabinet, and Uri Geller, but she learned the most from the skeptic James Randi's efforts to expose the bluffs and tricks mediums use.

Flora has never seen ghosts or spirits, but she realized she was good at saying the things that people longed to hear.

"You use the word 'spirits' and not ghosts," Julian says.

"They're the same thing really. But 'ghosts' is such a negative word."

Julian smiles and his eyes are sympathetically honest as he says, "I have to confess . . . I have difficulty believing in spirits."

"You have to have an open mind," Flora explains. "Arthur Conan Doyle was a spiritualist, for example—you know, the man who wrote the Sherlock Holmes stories."

"Have you ever been called in to help the police?"

"No, no."

Flora turns beet red and doesn't know what to say. She looks at her watch.

"I'm sorry, I know you have to get going," Julian says, and he takes her hands. "I just want to say that I know you really do want to help people and I think that's wonderful."

Flora's heart pounds from his touch. She doesn't dare meet his eyes as they say goodbye and go their own ways.

37

The red buildings of Birgittagården look idyllic in the light of day. Joona is standing by a birch tree, talking with Susanne Öst. Raindrops loosen from the branches and fall sparkling through the air.

"The police are still knocking on doors in Indal," the prosecutor is saying. "Someone crashed into a traffic light and there's a bunch of glass on the road. After that, nothing."

"I'll have to talk to the students again," Joona says.

"I really hoped this lead on Dennis would give us something," Susanne says.

Joona is picturing the scene he observed in the isolation room. His intuition is on alert. He tries to imagine the sequence of violence, but he only sees shadows moving between the furniture. The human beings are fuzzy, as if he were seeing them through frosted glass, shimmering and impossible to differentiate.

He takes a deep breath and his picture of the room where Miranda is lying with her hands over her face shifts into focus. He sees the velocity shown by the blood spatter and the heavy blows. He can follow each and every blow and see how the angle changes after the third one. The lamp starts swaying. Miranda's body is covered in blood.

"But there was no blood on her body," he mutters.

"What did you just say?" asks the prosecutor.

"There's something I have to check," Joona says, just as the door to the main building opens and a small man in a tight, protective jumpsuit comes out.

This is Holger Jalmert, a professor of criminology at Umeå University. He takes off his mask and wipes the sweat from his face.

"I'll arrange for you to question the girls at the hotel in one hour from now," Susanne says.

"Great, thanks," Joona says and he starts across the yard.

The professor is by his van, taking off his jumpsuit and putting it in a garbage bag. He closes the bag tightly.

"The blanket is missing," Joona says.

"Finally I get to meet the famous Joona Linna in person," the professor says with a smile. He's opening a new package of disposable clothing.

"Were you just in Miranda's room?" asks Joona.

"Yes, I was. I'm done there now."

"There's no blanket in it."

Holger stops what he's doing and wrinkles his brow. "You're right."

"Vicky must have hidden Miranda's blanket in the wardrobe or under the bed in her own room," Joona says.

"I'm going there now," Holger says, but Joona is already on his way.

The professor looks after him and remembers hearing that Joona Linna is so stubborn he'll stare at a crime scene until it opens before him like a book. He tucks the new jumpsuit under his arm and follows.

Before opening the door to Vicky's room, they both pause to put on their protective clothes and their shoe covers and latex gloves.

"It looks like there's something under the bed," Joona says.

"One thing at a time," says Holger. He puts on a mask.

Joona waits at the door while Holger photographs and measures the room with a laser. They will mark all their discoveries in a three-dimensional coordinating system.

A poster of Robert Pattinson, with his pale face and dark eyebrows, covers a painted Bible scene. On a shelf, there's a bowl of security tags from H&M.

Joona follows Holger as he covers the floor bit by bit with black plastic film, presses it down with a rubber roller, lifts it carefully, photographs it, and packs it. Holger works methodically from the door to the bed and then over to the window. This time when he lifts the film from the floor, a weak print of a running shoe shows on the yellow gelatin layer.

"I have to get going soon," Joona says.

"You want me to look underneath the bed first?"

Holger shakes his head at Joona's impatience but then spreads protective plastic on the floor by the side of the bed. He gets on his knees, reaches in, and catches the corner of some fabric shoved up against the wall.

"It probably is a blanket," Holger says, stretching his arm farther.

Holger carefully drags the heavy blanket onto the plastic sheet. It's twisted and soaked in blood.

"I think Miranda had the blanket around her shoulders when she was killed," Joona says in a low voice.

Holger folds the plastic sheet over the blanket and then pulls a large sack over the bundle. Joona glances at the clock. He can stay for just ten more minutes. Holger is doing a new test. He's using damp cotton swabs on the smears of dried blood on the bed sheet, letting them dry a second before he packs them.

"If you find anything that indicates a place or a person, call me immediately," Joona says.

"Sure, sure."

Around the hammer beneath the pillow, Holger uses one hundred and twenty swabs, which he packs individually and marks. He tapes hairs and fibers onto clear plastic film and carefully folds white paper around tufts of hair. He has tubes for tissue scraps and skull fragments. These will be chilled to prevent bacteria growth.

38

At the hotel where the girls are staying, the conference room is occupied, so Joona has to wait in the breakfast room. Susanne Öst is talking to the nervous hotel manager about another room they can use for questioning. Joona rings Anja Larsson back in Stockholm and is connected to her voice mail. He leaves a message requesting information on a good forensic doctor in Sundsvall. Anja may be eccentric, but she is good at her job. Even though she knows her love for Joona is hopeless and she can't quite let go.

A television is suspended from the ceiling on metal wires. The lead story on the news tonight is about the murders at Birgittagården. They're giving up-to-the-minute dramatic reports. There are pictures of the police tape, the red buildings, and the sign at the end of the driveway: BIRGITTAGÅRDEN, HVB: A HOME FOR YOUTH WITH SPECIAL NEEDS. The probable route of the killer's flight is marked on a map, and a reporter is standing in the middle of Highway 86 talking about the kidnapping and the failed roadblocks.

Joona stands up and walks closer to the television when the news anchor says that the mother of the kidnapped child has asked to plead with the kidnapper on live television.

The screen now shows Pia Abrahamsson sitting at a kitchen table and holding a sheet of paper. Her face looks tortured.

"If you can hear this," she starts, "please listen to me. I understand

that you're the victim of injustice. But, please, Dante doesn't have anything to do with it."

Pia looks directly into the camera. "Please bring him back," she whispers, her voice shaking. "You are probably a kind person at heart. Dante
is only four years old, and I know how frightened he must be. He is so . . ."

She looks down at the sheet of paper and tears start running down
her cheeks.

"Please don't hurt him. Please don't hit him or . . ." She starts to sob
and turns her face away from the camera.

The news returns to the studio in Stockholm. A forensic psychologist
from Säter Hospital explains to the news anchor how dangerous the situation is.

"I have not seen the girl's medical records and I do not want to
speculate on whether or not she is guilty of these two murders, but just
considering where she has been placed, she is most likely psychologically unstable. Even if—"

"What kind of threat does she pose to the child?" asks the anchor.

"It could be that she's not concerned about the boy at all. She might
have forgotten about him entirely. He's just four years old, though, and if
he starts crying or calling for his mother, she could become angry and
dangerous."

Susanne smiles as she arrives to get Joona. He follows her to the
elevator and they ride to the top floor and enter a gloomy bridal suite.
The minibar is padlocked and there's a Jacuzzi with golden feet in the
bedroom.

Tuula Lehti is lying on a king-size bed covered with bolsters. She's
watching the Disney Channel. The person from the Office of Victim
Services nods as they enter. Susanne closes the door and Joona pulls out
a chair with red plush cushions and sits down.

"Why did you tell me that Vicky was meeting a man named Dennis?" Joona asks.

Tuula sits up and clutches a heart-shaped pillow to her chest.

"I thought she was," she replies.

"Why did you think that?"

Tuula shrugs and looks back at the television.

"Did she tell you about a man named Dennis?"

"No." Tuula smiles.

"Tuula, I really need to find Vicky."

Tuula kicks the bedcover off the bed and turns her gaze back to the television.

"Do I have to be stuck here all day?" she asks.

"No, you can return to your room whenever you want," the support person says.

"*Sinä olet vain pieni lapsi*," Joona says in Finnish. "You're just a small child."

"*Ei*," she replies and looks him in the eye.

"You shouldn't have to live in institutions."

"I'm fine here," she says flatly.

"Don't bad things happen to you?"

She turns red and her white eyelashes flutter.

"No," she snaps.

"Miranda hit you yesterday."

"That's right." Tuula holds the pillow even tighter.

"Why was she angry?"

"She thought I went to her room and was messing around."

"Did you?"

Tuula licks the pillow. "Yeah, but I didn't take anything."

"Why were you messing around in her room?"

"I mess around in everyone's room."

"Why?"

"For fun."

"But Miranda thought you'd taken something from her room."

"Yeah, she got mad."

"Why did she think you'd taken something?"

"She didn't say," Tuula says, and smiles.

"What do you think?"

"I don't know. Usually people think I take their pills. Lu Chu pushed me down the stairs when she thought I'd taken her freaking uppers."

"If it wasn't pills, what did Miranda think you'd taken?"

"Who cares? Makeup, earrings."

Tuula moves until her legs are dangling off the edge of the bed and then flops backward. She whispers something and Joona catches the words "rhinestone necklace."

"What about Vicky?" asks Joona. "Did Vicky like to hit people?"

"No." Tuula smiles again and sits up.

"What does she do?"

"I can't say because I don't know her. She hasn't said a single word to me. But . . ." The girl shrugs and stops talking.

"Why didn't she talk to you?"

"Don't know."

"You must have seen her angry at some point?"

"She cuts herself . . . You can . . ." Tuula shakes her head.

"What were you going to say?"

"You can forget about her. She'll kill herself soon enough, then you'll have one less problem."

Tuula looks at her fingers, says something inaudible, then gets up abruptly and leaves the room.

39

Caroline, who looks somewhat older than the others, enters the room with the support person. She's wearing a long, baggy T-shirt with a picture of a kitten on it. There's a tattoo of runes along one of her arms and there are old injection scars on the insides of her elbows.

As she greets Joona, she smiles shyly. Then she sits down in the armchair next to the brown desk.

"Tuula says that Vicky usually sneaks out at night to meet a guy," Joona begins.

Caroline laughs. "No, she doesn't."

"Why do you say that?"

"I know she doesn't." Caroline is smiling.

"You're absolutely sure?"

"Tuula believes that we're all sluts."

"So Vicky doesn't sneak out?"

"No, she does." Caroline looks serious.

"What does she do when she sneaks out?"

Caroline looks him briefly in the eye and then looks out the window.

"She goes behind the brewery and calls her mother."

Joona knows that Vicky's mother died before Vicky arrived at Birgittagården. He decides not to confront Caroline with this information. Instead, he calmly asks, "What did they usually talk about?"

"Well, the thing is, she just leaves messages on her mother's voice mail. I don't think her mother ever calls her back."

Joona nods and thinks that perhaps no one has told Vicky that her mother is dead.

"Has she ever mentioned someone named Dennis?" he asks.

"No."

"Think back."

She looks at Joona, and jumps when Susanne Öst's cell phone rings. Susanne checks it for a message.

"Who would Vicky run to for help?" asks Joona, although he realizes the energy has gone out of the interview.

"I think the only person she'd run to is her mother."

"No friends or boys?"

"No," Caroline says. "But I really don't know her. We're both ADL and so we meet often, but she never talks about herself."

"What is ADL?"

"It sounds like a diagnosis but it means All Day Lifestyle. It's for those who behave. They let you go with them to Sundsvall to go shopping for groceries and stuff. Exciting, isn't it?"

"But you'd have the chance to talk?"

"Yes, but we didn't say much."

"So whom did she talk to?"

"Nobody," Caroline says. "Except Daniel, of course."

40

Joona and Susanne walk back to the elevator in silence, but she laughs when they both hit the button simultaneously.

"When can we question Daniel Grim?" asks Joona as they ride down.

"The doctor thought it was too early yesterday, which is understandable," Susanne says, giving him a brief glance. "This is not an easy case, this one. I'll give them a reminder call and let's see what they say."

Gunnarsson is waiting for them on the ground floor.

"Oh, right, I got a text message while you were talking to Caroline. The autopsy is under way," Susanne says to Joona.

"Good. When will we have the first report?" asks Joona.

"Go home," says Gunnarsson angrily. "You are not supposed to be here. You are not supposed to read any reports, you are not to—"

"Calm down," says Susanne, surprised.

"We're so damned slow on the uptake that we've let a damned observer come and take over the entire investigation just because he's from Stockholm!"

"I'm only trying to help," says Joona. "Since there's—"

"Shut up!"

"This is my preliminary investigation," Susanne says, glaring at Gunnarsson.

"Then I have to inform you that Joona Linna has the Internal Review Board after his ass—"

"Is it true? Have you been reported to the Internal Review Board?" Susanne asks.

"Yes, but my case hasn't gone to any prosecutor—"

"And I let you into the investigation?" She purses her lips. "This is about trust. You lied to me."

"I'm still formally on duty, and I don't have time for this," says Joona. "I have to question Daniel Grim."

"That's my job," Gunnarsson says.

"You have to understand how important it is," Joona says. "Daniel Grim may be the only person who—"

"I am not going to work with you," Susanne interrupts.

"We're cutting you off from the investigation," says Gunnarsson.

"I've lost all trust in you," Susanne says, and turns on her heels and heads for the exit.

Gunnarsson takes off after her.

"If you talk to Daniel, you have to ask him about Dennis!" Joona calls after them. "Ask Daniel if he knows who Dennis is, and ask if he knows where Vicky would go. We need a name or a place. Daniel is the only person Vicky talked to and he—"

"Go home!" Gunnarsson waves without turning back.

41

Commissioner Gunnarsson has a fresh cigarette in his mouth as he leaves the elevator. He's headed for Ward 52A in the psychiatric unit at Västernorrland provincial hospital.

A young man in a buttoned-up lab coat walks over to greet him. They shake hands and Gunnarsson follows him down a hall painted light gray.

"As I said on the phone, I don't believe that questioning him will be useful at this time, so soon after —"

"You're right, but I want to have a little chat with him anyway."

The doctor stops and turns to look at Gunnarsson. "Daniel Grim is in a traumatic state of stress that we call arousal. It is activated by the hypothalamus and the limbic system—"

"I don't give a shit," said Gunnarsson. "Just tell me if he's been stuffed with so many drugs he's on Mars."

"He's able to talk, but I won't let you near him if you—"

"We're dealing with a double murder—"

"You know very well who has the last word in this building," the doctor says calmly. "If I believe that the patient's recovery will be hindered by a talk with the police, I will forbid it."

"I understand." Gunnarsson sighs.

"However, the patient himself has said that he would like to help the police, so I will allow you to ask a few questions in my presence."

"Thank you." They start along the hall again, turn a corner, and pass a row of dormer windows that overlook a courtyard. A few moments later, the doctor opens a door to a single-patient room. There's a sheet and a blanket on the small sofa, but Daniel Grim is sitting on the floor with his back to the radiator. He looks serene and he doesn't even glance at them when they come in.

Gunnarsson moves a chair near Daniel and sits down. Then he swears, gets off the chair, and squats in front of him.

"I have to talk to you," Gunnarsson starts. "We are searching for Vicky Bennet. She's a suspect in the murders at Birgittagården, and I—"

"But I . . ." Daniel murmurs.

Gunnarsson stops talking as Daniel keeps whispering. Finally he says, "Sorry, I can't hear you."

The doctor stands by the door listening to them.

"I don't believe she did it," says Daniel. "She's much too nice."

He wipes the tears from his cheeks and from beneath his eyeglasses.

"I know that you are bound by patient confidentiality," Gunnarsson says. "But is there any way you can help us find Vicky Bennet?"

"I'll try," Daniel says, but then presses his lips firmly together.

"Does she know anyone who lives near Birgittagården?"

"Maybe. I'm having trouble collecting my thoughts right now."

Gunnarsson groans and decides to change tactics. "You were Vicky's counselor," he says. "Where do you think she went? We don't give a shit whether she's guilty. We don't know anything yet. But there's one thing we do know—she's kidnapped a child."

"No," Daniel whispers.

"Who is she trying to find? Where is she going?"

"She's afraid," Daniel says. His voice is shaking. "She crawls beneath a bush and tries to hide . . . it . . . it . . . What did you ask, again?"

"Is there a hiding place you know about?"

Daniel starts mumbling about Elisabet's heart and how he thought she'd died from her heart problems.

"Daniel," the doctor says, "you don't have to do this unless you want to. I can ask the police to come back later after you've had a chance to rest."

Daniel shakes his head and tries to breathe calmly.

"Just give me a place," Gunnarsson says.

"Stockholm."

"Where in Stockholm?"

"I . . . I don't know anything."

"What the hell!" barks Gunnarsson.

"I'm sorry, I'm sorry." Daniel's chin is quivering. He turns his face away and starts sobbing.

"She killed your wife with a hammer and—"

Daniel throws his head back against the radiator so hard his glasses fall off into his lap.

"It's time for you to go," says the doctor. "Not another word. Bringing you here was a mistake, and I will not allow any further questioning."

42

The parking lot outside the provincial hospital in Sundsvall is almost empty. The long, low building looks depressing, especially under these gray skies. Its brown brickwork is broken by windows that seem to have closed their eyes to the world. Joona strides up a path lined by bushes and through the front door.

There's no one at the reception desk but in a moment a janitor comes by.

"Where's your forensics department?" asks Joona.

"Two hundred and forty kilometers north of here," the janitor says with a smile. "But if you want pathology, I can show you the way."

He takes Joona down to the basement and through a pair of heavy metal doors. Down the hall Joona sees a sign over another door: DEPARTMENT OF CLINICAL PATHOLOGY AND CYTOLOGY.

"Good luck," the janitor says as he points to the door.

Joona thanks him and walks down the empty hall. It's cold and the tiled floor is cracked in places and scuffed with wheel marks from gurneys and carts. He passes a laboratory and opens the door to the autopsy room. No one is there and the stainless-steel autopsy table is empty. The overhead fluorescent fixtures bounce a cold, hard light off the white tiled walls. Joona waits and after a few minutes the door squeaks open, and two people wheel in a gurney from the morgue.

"Excuse me," says Joona.

A thin man in a lab coat turns around and his aviator glasses glare in the light. He's one of Joona's old friends, Dr. Nils Åhlén, the head doctor at the National Forensic Laboratory, in Stockholm. His colleagues and friends call him "The Needle." With him is his assistant, a young doctor Joona knows only as Frippe. Frippe's dyed black hair hangs in wisps down to his shoulders.

"What are you doing here?" Joona asks.

"A woman from the National Police threatened me," The Needle says.

"Anja."

"She terrified me. She was yelling that you're not allowed to go all the way up to Umeå to talk to anyone in forensics."

"But we're going to Nordfest as long as we're here," Frippe says. Joona notices black leather pants under his lab coat and cowboy boots swathed in blue protectors.

"The Haunted are playing at Club Deströyer." The Needle smiles.

"That explains it," says Joona.

Frippe laughs.

"We've just finished the woman, Elisabet Grim," The Needle says. "The only unusual thing about her were the injuries on her hands."

"Defensive wounds?" asks Joona.

"Except they're on the wrong side," says Frippe.

"Perhaps she held her hands in front of her face," Joona says quietly.

"We'll get back to her in a moment," says The Needle. "First, let's take a look at Miranda Eriksdotter."

"When did they die? Can you determine that?" asks Joona.

"As you know, body temperature sinks."

"Algor mortis," Joona says.

"Right, and this cooling follows a billowing graph, which evens out to room temperature."

"He knows all that," Frippe says.

"So, with that and the rigor mortis as well as the lividity, we've determined that the girl and the woman died at approximately the same time late Friday night."

Joona watches them roll the gurney over, count to three, then effortlessly lift the body bag onto the autopsy table. Frippe opens the bag and the smell of moldy bread and dried blood escapes. Miranda is in the same position in which she was found: her hands over her face and her ankles crossed.

Joona knows that the rigor mortis won't have passed yet and that it is going to take some effort to move her hands away from her face. For a moment he wonders if perhaps it isn't Miranda behind those hands. Perhaps her face is gone or her eyes were poked out. Perhaps she didn't want her face to be seen.

"We didn't receive an examination request," The Needle says. "Why is she covering her face like that?"

"I don't know," Joona says.

Frippe is photographing the body carefully.

"I take it this is a forensic autopsy and that you will need a certified autopsy report?" The Needle says.

Joona nods.

"I could use a secretary," mutters The Needle as he walks around the body.

"Now you're just complaining again," Frippe says, and smiles.

"So I was," The Needle says. He pauses behind Miranda's head and then completes his circuit.

Joona is reminded of Rainer Maria Rilke's idea that only the living insist on distinguishing between the living and the dead. Rilke thought that other beings, such as angels, didn't notice any difference.

"The lividity indicates that the victim has not been moved," The Needle starts.

"The way I read the blood spatter, I'm sure that she was moved immediately after she was killed," Joona says. "Her body would still have been limp when it was placed on the bed."

Frippe nods. "If she was moved right away, she won't show any lividity elsewhere."

Joona watches quietly as the doctors examine the body. He's thinking that his own daughter is not much younger than this girl whose life has been stolen.

The yellow network of veins has started to show beneath her white skin, and her flat stomach has started to bloat and has darkened.

Joona observes everything the doctors are doing and listens as they describe what they're seeing, but he's thinking of what he saw at the scene of the crime.

The Needle determines that there are no defensive injuries, no soft-tissue injuries, no indications of a fight or domestic abuse. Perhaps she didn't see the blow coming, Joona thinks. Perhaps she just sat there and waited for it.

The doctors pull some hair out by the roots for comparison tests and fill in EDTA tubes with blood, then The Needle scrapes beneath her fingernails and turns to Joona.

"No traces of skin. She did not defend herself."

"I know," Joona says.

They start examining the skull injuries, and Joona comes closer to watch.

"Strong, blunt trauma to the head. Most likely cause of death," The Needle says, noticing Joona's close attention.

"From the front?" Joona asks.

"From the front, though slightly to the side." The Needle points at the bloody hair. "Depression fracture on the temporal bone. We'll do a CT scan, but I imagine the major blood vessels behind the skull were ruptured and bone fragments impaled the brain."

"As with Elisabet Grim, we're going to find trauma to the frontal lobe," Frippe says.

"Brain tissue in the hair," The Needle says.

"There were broken blood vessels, and blood and cerebral spinal fluid had run through her nostrils," Frippe says.

"And in your opinion, they died at about the same time," Joona says. Frippe nods.

"They've both been hit from the front. The same cause of death for both of them," Joona says. "The same murder weapon—"

"No," The Needle says. "The murder weapon was not the same."

"But the hammer," Joona murmurs.

"Elisabet's skull was crushed by a hammer," The Needle says. "But Miranda was killed by a rock."

Joona stares at him. "She was killed by a rock?"

Joona stayed in the autopsy room until he saw Miranda's face. He felt uneasy as the doctors forced her hands away. His earlier thought that she didn't want her face to be seen rang in his brain.

Now he's sitting at Gunnarsson's desk in the Sundsvall police station. He's reading through the early technical reports. A woman is sitting a few feet away in front of a computer. Her telephone rings and she mumbles something as she checks the number display.

One wall is covered with maps and pictures of the little boy, Dante Abrahamsson. There are binders and heaps of paper in the bookshelves lining the other walls. A copier rumbles ceaselessly. A radio is playing in the lunch room and when the pop music stops, Joona is able to hear the police alert for the third time.

"We have a missing person alert," the radio host says. "The police are searching for a fifteen-year-old girl and a four-year-old boy, probably together. The girl has long blond hair and the boy is wearing a dark blue sweater and corduroy pants. They were last seen in a red Toyota Auris on Highway 86 heading toward Sundsvall. Please contact the police at 114 14 if you have any information regarding these missing children."

Joona gets up, goes to the empty lunch room, and changes the channel to P2. He pours himself a cup of coffee. The radio plays a scratched recording of an unusually clear soprano voice. It is Birgit Nilsson singing the role of Brünnhilde in Wagner's *Ring of the Nibelung*.

Joona sits back down at the desk and it occurs to him that the girl who took the little boy is probably psychotic. He pictures them hiding in a garage. Perhaps the boy has been forced to lie beneath a blanket with tape over his mouth. Perhaps he's tied up.

If he is still alive, he must be terribly frightened.

Joona continues to read the technical report. It confirms that it was Elisabet's key in the lock to the isolation room at Birgittagården and that the boots that had left bloody footprints in the main house were the same ones found in Vicky Bennet's closet.

We have two murders, Joona thinks. *One is primary and the other is secondary. Miranda is the primary victim, but to get to her, the suspect had to take Elisabet's key.*

The technicians' reconstructed chain of events suggest that an argument could have been the triggering factor, even if there had been rivalry for some time. According to the report Vicky Bennet had gotten the hammer and the boots before lights-out and waited in her room. Once the other girls had gone to sleep, she'd approached Elisabet and demanded the key. Elisabet refused and fled through the hallway, out the door, and into the brewery. Vicky had followed her, killed her with the hammer, and taken the key. She'd returned to the main building, unlocked the isolation room, and killed Miranda. For some reason, she'd lifted Miranda onto the bed and placed Miranda's hands over her face and crossed her legs at the ankles. She then returned to her room, hid the hammer, the blanket, and the boots, climbed out the window, and fled into the forest.

Joona puts the report down on the desk. He knows that it will be several weeks before the lab has the test results. Without that information, the crime scene investigators have assumed that both Elisabet and Miranda were killed with the hammer.

But Miranda was killed by a rock.

Why was she killed by a rock when Vicky had a hammer?

Joona looks carefully at every photograph sent with the report. There is Miranda, lying on the bed, her skin as pale as porcelain, her ankles crossed, a small bruise on her leg, a tiny jewel in her belly button, her hands over her face.

He puts himself in the mind of the killer, as he usually does, and forces himself to see each action, each frightening choice, as absolutely necessary: the simplest or the best solution right that minute.

It's unlikely that the killer thought this murder bestial or appalling. It could have been rational or even enticing.

Sometimes the killer can't see beyond one blow at a time. He needs to strike just this one blow—he justifies just this one blow—and there is no thought of the next until the need for it comes over him like a wave. Time is warped, and the murder can seem epic, starting with the first blow and ending years later with the last, although in reality it might take no more than thirty seconds.

The evidence points to Vicky Bennet. Everyone believes she killed both Elisabet and Miranda, and yet no one believes that she is capable, physically or mentally, of murder.

Every human being is capable of murder, Joona thinks. He puts the report back in Gunnarsson's folder. *We see this in our dreams and our fantasies. Everyone is violent inside, but most people have tamed and caged their inner beast.*

Joona gets up from the desk just seconds before Gunnarsson arrives. He hangs up his wrinkled coat and goes into the cafeteria. When he comes out with a cup of coffee in his hand and sees Joona, he breaks into a grin.

"Aren't they missing you in Stockholm yet?"

"Not yet," Joona says.

Gunnarsson searches his jacket for his cigarettes and turns to the woman at the computer.

"All reports go directly to me."

"Yes," she says, but she doesn't look up.

Gunnarsson mumbles to himself and fishes out a cigarette and lighter.

"How did the interview with Daniel Grim go?" asks Joona.

"Fine, not that it's any of your business. But I had to be damned careful."

"What did he know about Vicky?"

"Nothing the police can use."

"Did you ask about Dennis?"

"That doctor was on my ass like the man's mother and cut off questioning."

Gunnarsson pats his pockets, not noticing he's holding a cigarette.

"I want the report from Holger Jalmert as soon as it comes in," Joona says. "I also want the forensic examination results and—"

"Get the fuck out of my sandbox," says Gunnarsson. He smiles widely at the woman, but falters when he sees Joona's serious, steely gaze.

"You have no idea how to find Vicky Bennet and the boy," Joona says. "And you have no idea how to proceed with the investigation."

"I'm waiting for tips from the public," Gunnarsson says. "There's always someone who's seen something."

44

That morning, Flora woke up before her alarm clock went off. Hans-Gunnar needed breakfast in bed at eight fifteen sharp. Once he got up, Flora aired out his room and made his bed, while Ewa sat in a chair, dressed in yellow sweatpants and a skin-colored bra, keeping an eye on Flora. She got up to check that the sheet was completely smooth and that the corners were tucked in precisely. The crocheted bedcover needed to hang evenly on each side of the bed. Flora had to remake the bed before it passed Ewa's inspection.

Now it's lunchtime. Flora returns home with groceries as well as cigarettes for Hans-Gunnar. She hands him the change and waits while he examines the receipt.

"Goddamn, that cheese was expensive," he says.

"You told me to be sure to buy cheddar," Flora says.

"Not if it's this damned expensive. You should realize you need to buy a different kind if this one is too expensive."

"I'm sorry. I thought—"

Flora is stopped by a powerful blow to the side of her head. She's knocked to her knees and her ear begins to ring. Her cheek is burning. Hans-Gunner stands over her, staring, until she gets up.

"You said cheddar," Ewa says from the sofa. "You said cheddar or nothing, so it's not her fault."

Hans-Gunner mutters that they're both idiots and goes out onto the balcony to smoke. Flora puts away the groceries, then goes into the maid's room and sits on the bed. She touches her cheek and thinks that she's tired of Hans-Gunnar's punches. There are days when he hits her more than once. She can tell when he's working up a head of steam because he keeps looking at her, and normally he ignores her. The worst thing is not the blows but the way he looks at her and breathes afterward.

He never hit her when she was a child. In those days, he worked and was almost never home. She remembers once his showing her different countries on the globe he kept in his bedroom.

She can hear Ewa and Hans-Gunnar leave the apartment. Flora looks over at the glass horse-and-carriage on her dresser. It was a gift from one of her teachers. In one of the dresser drawers there's an old toy from her childhood, a bright blue Smurf with blond hair and high-heeled shoes. In the middle drawer is a pile of pressed handkerchiefs. Flora gets up and opens the drawer, shifts the handkerchiefs, and takes out an elegant green dress, which she bought at the beginning of the summer at the Salvation Army store. She never wears it except in her room, but she likes to try it on whenever Ewa and Hans-Gunnar are out.

She's buttoning it up when she hears voices coming from the kitchen. The radio is on. She walks out to turn it off and notices that Ewa and Hans-Gunnar snacked on cake before they left. There are crumbs on the floor by the pantry. They've left a glass of strawberry juice on the counter by the sink. It's half full. The bottle is still out as well.

Flora gets a dishrag, washes the glass, then wipes up the crumbs from the floor.

There's a news report on the radio about a murder in northern Sweden. A young girl has been found dead in a youth home for girls.

Flora rinses out the dishrag and hangs it on the faucet.

The police are refusing to comment, but a reporter has tracked down a few of the girls who'd been living at the home and the girls are being interviewed live.

"I wanted to see what was going on, so I pushed ahead of the other girls," says one girl. "I couldn't see much because the others pulled me away from the door. I screamed for a bit, but then I realized it didn't matter much."

Flora picks up the bottle of strawberry juice and heads to the refrigerator.

"Can you tell us what you saw?"

"Yes, I saw Miranda and she was lying on the bed, like this, just like this, see?"

Flora stops to listen.

"Her eyes were closed?" asks the reporter.

"No, no, like this, with her hands in front of her face—"

"You're such a fucking liar," another girl's voice breaks in.

Flora hears a crash. She glances down and sees she's dropped the bottle. Her feet are wet. Her stomach suddenly flips and she barely makes it to the toilet before she throws up.

45

A woman with a German accent is discussing fall recipes when Flora gets back to the kitchen. She cleans up the mess of glass and juice and stands for a while, staring at her cold white hands. Then she walks into the hallway to call the police.

Flora listens to the crackle on the line before the first signal.

"Police," says a woman with a tired voice.

"Yes, hi, my name is Flora Hansen and I—"

"Just a second, I didn't catch that."

"All right." Flora starts over. "My name is Flora Hansen. I want to leave a tip about the murdered girl in Sundsvall."

There's a moment of silence and then the same tired voice says, "What do you want to tell us?"

"Do you pay for tips?" asks Flora.

"No, sorry."

"But I . . . I saw the dead girl."

"Are you saying that you were present when the girl was killed?"

"I'm a psychic," says Flora in her most mysterious voice. "I can contact the dead. I saw everything, but I need to get paid to remember things better."

"You can contact the dead. Is that it?"

"The girl held her hands in front of her face."

"The headlines say that already." The policewoman sounds impatient.

Flora feels her heart shrink from shame. She feels sick. She hadn't planned what to say, but she realizes she should have said something else. It was already front-page news in the tabloids stacked at the grocery store when she was buying food and cigarettes for Hans-Gunnar.

"I didn't know," she whispers. "I can only tell you what I see. I've seen other things that you might want to pay for."

"As I said, we don't pay."

"I saw the murder weapon," she says. "Maybe you think you've found the murder weapon, but you haven't. It's not the right one. I saw—"

"Do you know that it is against the law to call the police without cause?" the policewoman interrupts. "It's actually a criminal offense. I don't mean to sound angry, but you've been taking up my time when someone with real information could be trying to get through."

Flora is about to tell the policewoman about the murder weapon when she hears a click. She looks at the phone for a moment; then she dials the number again.

46

The Church of Sweden has loaned Pia Abrahamsson a temporary apartment in Sundsvall in a large wooden house filled with furniture designed by Carl Malmsten and Bruno Mathsson. The deacons, who come by with groceries for her, keep urging her to talk to one of the other Lutheran pastors, but Pia can't bring herself to do it.

She's been driving her rented car up and down Highway 86 the entire day, going through all the small villages and along all the timber roads. Several times she's run into police officers, who keep telling her to go home.

It's night now and she's lying on the bed in this strange house, fully dressed, and staring at the ceiling. She has barely slept since Dante disappeared. She keeps hearing him cry. He's frightened and keeps begging to go home.

Her cell phone rings. She reaches for it and looks at the number before turning off the ringer. It was her parents. They call all the time.

Pia gets up, puts on her jacket, and leaves. There's a taste of blood in her mouth. She gets into the rental car and begins to drive. She has to find Dante. *What if he's in a ditch at the side of the road? What if the girl just left him in the woods?*

The road is dark and empty. It appears that everyone is asleep. She tries to peer through the mist beyond her headlights.

She drives to the logging road where her car was stolen. She sits there for a while, clutching the steering wheel to stop herself from shaking. Then she turns around and drives back to Indal. She drives slowly past a preschool and turns at the next street, Solgårdsvägen. The houses she passes are all quiet, their windows dark. She sees something move under a trampoline and stops. She gets out and pushes through a row of roses to get to the front yard, the thorns tearing at her legs. She reaches the trampoline and a cat darts out from underneath.

She turns toward the house, her heart racing.

"Dante?" she cries. "Dante! Where are you? Mamma's here!"

Lights go on inside the house. Pia runs across the lawn to the next house and rings the bell.

"Dante!" she screams as loud as she can. She hammers on the door then abruptly heads to the shed.

She runs from house to house, calling for her son, pounding on closed garage doors, opening the doors to playhouses, pushing her way through hedges, and finally through a ditch until she finds herself back on Indalsvägen.

A car races up behind her and screeches to a stop. Pia starts running but trips, landing on all fours. She rolls onto her back, blinking back tears. A policewoman hurries up to her.

"Are you all right?"

The policewoman helps Pia to her feet.

"Have you found him?" asks Pia.

A second police officer comes up and says that they'll drive her home.

"Dante is afraid of the dark," Pia says. Her voice is hoarse. "I'm his mother, but I haven't been patient enough with him. He comes into my bedroom at night, and I make him go back to bed. He just stands there in his pajamas, scared, and I just—"

"Where did you park your car?" asks the policewoman as she takes Pia's arm.

"Leave me alone!" Pia screeches. "I have to find him!" She jerks free and slaps the woman's face. The two officers grab her and force her, screaming, facedown onto the asphalt. She thrashes against their hold, scraping her chin, but they've pulled her arms behind her. She starts to weep as helplessly as a child.

47

Joona Linna is driving along a beautiful stretch of road between lush meadows and glittering lakes, wondering why there are no witnesses. No one seems to know anything about Vicky Bennet, and no one saw a thing. There are no witnesses. He puzzles over this until he arrives at a white stone house. There's a lemon tree in a huge pot on the veranda. He rings the doorbell, waits a moment, and then walks around to the back.

Nathan Pollock is sitting at a table beneath an apple tree. He has a cast on one leg.

"Nathan?"

The thin man twists around, shading his eyes with a hand, and smiles in surprise.

"Joona Linna, as I live and breathe!"

Nathan's a member of the National Criminal Investigation Department, a group of six experts who help both the national and the county police with difficult homicide cases. He has long silver hair that is tied in a thin ponytail and hangs over one shoulder, and he's dressed in black pants and a loosely knitted sweater.

"Joona, I'm really sorry about the internal investigation. I shouldn't have tried to stop you from seeing the Brigade."

"It was my decision to handle it the way I did," Joona says. He sits down.

Nathan shakes his head slowly. "I had a real fight with Carlos over it. They were clearly making an example of you, and I said so."

"Is that how you broke your leg?"

"No, this came from an angry mamma bear that rushed into our yard." Nathan grins so that his gold tooth shows.

"Or perhaps the truth of the matter is that he fell off the ladder when he was picking apples," a bright voice says behind them.

"Hello, Mathilda," Joona says.

He gets up from his chair to give the freckled woman with thick reddish-brown hair a big hug.

"Hello, Detective Inspector," Mathilda says as she sits down beside Nathan. "I hope that you have some work for my beloved husband to do for you. Otherwise he's going to have to learn how to do sudoku."

"Yes, I might have something," Joona says. "The murders at Birgittagården."

"Really?" Nathan looks up from scratching beneath his cast.

"I've gone to the crime scenes and I've examined the bodies, but they won't let me look at the reports or the results from the tests."

"Because of this internal investigation business?"

"It's not my preliminary investigation," Joona says. "But I would like to hear your thoughts."

"You've made my Nathan a happy man," says Mathilda as she leans over to pat her husband on the cheek.

"Nice that you're thinking of little old me," Pollock says.

"You're the best investigator I know," Joona says.

Nathan is particularly good at psychological profiling—extrapolating from the evidence what kind of person most likely committed the crime. So far, he's been right every time.

Joona sits back down and begins to report everything he knows about the case. After a while, Mathilda heads indoors, but Pollock listens intently, occasionally interrupting with a question. A gray tabby cat winds itself around Nathan's legs, and warblers sing in the apple tree while Joona describes the position of the bodies, the pattern of the blood spatter, where the blood pooled, where it dripped, where it was smeared, the tracks of bloody footprints, where there were traces of liquid and crusted blood. Nathan closes his eyes and listens as Joona tells him about the hammer beneath the pillow, the blood-soaked blanket, and the open window.

"Let's see," Nathan starts. "The killer was extremely violent, but there are no bites, no hacking or dismembering . . ."

Joona says nothing and watches Nathan's lips move as he thinks things through. At times, he whispers something to himself or he pulls his ponytail absentmindedly. After a few minutes, he starts to talk.

"All right, I can see the bodies in my mind and I see how the blood spattered as it did. You already know this, of course, but most murders are committed in a moment of frenzy. Then the killer is panicked by all the blood and chaos. That's when they'll grab a sander and a garbage bag or skid around in the blood with a scrub brush and leave evidence everywhere."

"Not here."

"This killer did not attempt to hide a thing."

"I agree."

"The violence was severe and methodical. It's not punishment that's gone too far. In both cases, the intent was to kill and nothing more. Both victims were in small rooms. They couldn't escape. The violence is not passionate. It's more like an execution or a slaughter."

"We think the murderer is a girl," Joona says.

"A girl?"

Joona meets Nathan's surprised look and hands him a photograph of Vicky Bennet.

Nathan laughs. "Sorry, but, really, I don't buy it."

Mathilda reappears with a tea service and jam cookies on a tray. She sits down at the table and Nathan pours the tea into three cups.

"So you don't believe a girl is capable of this?" Joona asks.

"Never had a case like that," Nathan says.

"Not all girls are nice girls," Mathilda points out.

Nathan jabs a finger at the photograph. "Is she known to be violent?"

"No, the opposite."

"Then you're looking for the wrong person."

"We're certain she kidnapped a child yesterday."

"But she hasn't beaten the child to death?"

"Not as far as we know," Joona says as he helps himself to a cookie.

Nathan leans back in his chair.

"If the girl is not known for violence, if she hasn't been punished for being violent, if she hasn't ever been suspected of a similar kind of violence, she's not the one you're looking for," Nathan says, and looks at Joona sharply.

"What if it is her in spite of that?" Joona asks.

Nathan shakes his head and blows on his tea.

"Can't be," he says. "I've just been reading a paper by David Canter. He says what I've always thought, that during the commission of the crime, the suspect assigns the victim the role of an opposing player in an interior drama."

"Yes, that makes sense," Joona says.

"According to his hypothesis, a covered face means that the killer wants to remove the victim's face and make her into nothing more than an object. Men in this category often use exaggerated violence."

"What if they were just playing hide-and-seek?" Joona asks.

"Where are you going with that?"

"The victim covers her eyes and counts to one hundred while the killer hides."

Nathan lets this thought sink in.

"Then I believe the killer intends for *you* to do the seeking."

"But where?"

"All I can tell you is to go back and seek the answer in the old places," Pollock says. "The past always reveals the future."

Carlos Eliasson, the National Police chief, is standing by his office window on the eighth floor. He's looking out at the steep hillsides of Kronoberg Park. He has no idea that Joona Linna is walking through the park after a brief visit to the old Jewish cemetery.

Carlos goes back to sit at his desk and doesn't see the detective with the disheveled hair cross Polhemsgatan and head for the main entrance of the police station.

Joona walks past a banner proclaiming the role of modern police in a changing world. He passes Benny Rubin, who is sitting hunched in front of his computer, and Magdalena Ronander's office, where she's on the phone, saying something about cooperation with Europol.

Joona is back in Stockholm because he's been summoned to a meeting with both of the internal investigators later this afternoon. He takes his mail from his box, goes to sit at his desk, and then flips through the messages and envelopes while thinking about what Nathan said. He agrees with Nathan. Vicky Bennet's profile doesn't fit these two murders.

In the admittedly incomplete psychological documentation the police have on Vicky Bennet, there's nothing to indicate that she could be dangerous. She is not on the police register. The people who have met her find her shy and withdrawn but nice.

But all the technical evidence points to her. Everything indicates that she took the little boy. Maybe the boy is already lying in a ditch with a broken skull. If the boy is still alive, they must find him quickly. Maybe he's with Vicky in some dark garage. Maybe she's in a rage at him right now.

Go seek the past. Nathan Pollock's usual advice.

It's as simple as it is clear. The past always indicates the future.

In her short life, Vicky has moved many times. She'd moved around with her homeless mother, then from foster home to foster home, into an urgent-care facility, then a youth home, and finally to Birgittagården. But where is she now?

Maybe the answer is hidden in one of her conversations with her counselors, social workers, or temporary foster parents. There must be someone whom she trusted and confided in.

Joona is about to look for Anja to ask if she's found any new names or addresses, when he sees her standing in the doorway. Her hefty body is squeezed into a tight black skirt and one of several angora sweaters she owns. Her blond hair is artfully pinned up and her lipstick is bright red.

"Before I tell you what I've found, let me just say that fifteen thousand children are placed in foster homes every year," Anja starts. "And let me remind you that it was called health reform when politicians opened the door of health care to the private sector. Now venture capitalists own the youth homes. It's like the olden days when they used to auction off orphans. They save money on staff, on education, on therapy, and even on dentists, all to stoke their coffers."

"I know," Joona says. "Just tell me about Vicky Bennet—"

"I thought I would start by finding out who was responsible for her last placement."

"And?" asks Joona.

She smiles and leans her head to the side. "Mission accomplished, Joona Linna."

"Fantastic."

"I do whatever I can for you."

"I don't deserve it," Joona says.

"I know," she says, and leaves the room.

He waits in his chair for a few minutes, then he goes to Anja's office and knocks on the door.

As he enters, she says, "The addresses are there," and nods at the printer.

"Thanks."

"When the last person responsible for Vicky's placement heard my name, he said that Sweden once had a famous butterfly swimmer by the same name," she says, and blushes.

"So you told him you were that famous swimmer?"

"No, I didn't. But he told me that Vicky Bennet doesn't appear in any records before the age of six. Her mother, Susie, was homeless and appears to have given birth alone and kept Vicky out of the health system. When Susie was committed to a mental hospital, Vicky was placed with foster parents here in Stockholm."

Joona is holding the list in his hand. It's still warm from the printer. He glances down the list of dates and placements. He sees that Vicky's first foster parents were Jack and Elin Frank, who lived at Strandvägen 47. Among numerous other placements, there are two youth homes on the list: Ljungbacken in Uddevalla and Birgittagården in Sundsvall township. Against several names on the list there's a note saying that the child asked to be returned to her first foster family. Each one says the same thing: "The child requests to be returned to the Frank family, but the family declines." The sentence is dry and clinical.

The two youth homes are at the end of the list after other foster families, emergency placements, and treatment homes.

Joona thinks about the bloody hammer underneath the pillow and the blood on the windowsill. He thinks about the glum, thin face in the photograph. Her hair in tangled curls.

"Can you find out if Jack and Elin Frank are still living at this address?" Joona asks.

Anja's plump face shows her amusement. "You should read *See & Hear*. You'd learn a thing or two."

"What are you saying?"

"Elin and Jack are divorced, but she kept the apartment because, well, it's all her money."

"So they're celebrities?"

"You know Albert Frank, don't you?"

"Sure."

"Elin inherited the entire mining operation when she was just eighteen years old. These days she's often in the media for her charitable works. She and her former husband have given quite a bit of money to orphanages and foundations."

"There was a time when Vicky lived with them?"

"It probably didn't work out so well," Anja replies.

Joona heads to the door, holding the printout. He turns to look at Anja.

"What can I do to thank you?"

"I've registered us both in a class," she said. "Promise you'll go with me."

"What kind of class?"

"Relaxation. Kama Sutra something."

49

Strandvägen 47 is right across the street from Djurgård Bridge. It is a luxury five-story limestone apartment building with an elegant entrance and a dark, attractive stairwell. The name "Frank" is engraved on a shiny black plaque beside a door on the second floor, which opens almost as soon as Joona rings the bell. A man with gelled short hair and an even tan looks at him questioningly.

"I'm looking for Elin Frank."

"I'm Robert Bianchi, Elin's personal assistant," the man says as he holds out his hand.

"Joona Linna, the National Police."

A slight smile passes over the man's lips. "Sounds exciting, but—"

"I need to speak with her."

"May I ask what it concerns? She is not to be disturbed unnecessarily . . ." The man stops speaking as Joona's gaze turns cold.

"Please wait in the foyer while I ask her if she is able to receive visitors," Bianchi says, and disappears behind a door.

The foyer is white and empty. There is no furniture, no coats, no shoes. Just smooth white walls and a single enormous mirror in a white frame.

Joona tries to imagine Vicky Bennet in this environment. A nervous, chaotic girl who did not appear in the Swedish register until she was six years old. A child who had lived only in garages or tunnels or stairwells, and probably a different one each night.

Bianchi returns, smiling calmly, and asks Joona to follow him. They walk past a large lounge with several sofa arrangements and a tile stove, elegantly decorated. Thick rugs muffle the sound of their footsteps as they walk past the various rooms until they reach a closed door.

"You can knock," Robert says to Joona. His smile has become uncertain.

Joona knocks and hears someone in high-heeled shoes walk across a wooden floor. A thin middle-aged woman opens the door. She has dark blond hair and large blue eyes. She's wearing a close-fitting red dress and three strands of snow-white pearls. Her makeup is sparse. She looks beautiful.

"Come in, Joona Linna," she says. Her voice is low and well modulated.

The light-filled room has a desk, a group of sofas in white leather, and built-in bookcases painted white.

"I was just about to have some chai. Is it too early for you?" she asks.

"No, that sounds fine," Joona says.

Robert leaves the room and Elin gestures toward the sofas.

"Let's sit down."

She sits across from him and crosses her legs.

"Now, what do you want to ask me about?" she says.

"A number of years ago, you and your former husband, Jack, were the foster parents of a young girl—"

"We've helped many children over the years—"

"Her name is Vicky Bennet," Joona interrupts her quietly.

For just an instant she frowns slightly, but her voice remains calm.

"I remember Vicky very well," she says with a brief smile.

"What do you remember about her?" asks Joona.

"She was a sweet little thing and she . . ." Elin Frank falls silent and stares into space. Her hands lie completely still in her lap.

"We believe that she might be involved in the murder of two people at a youth home in Sundsvall," Joona says.

The woman turns her face quickly away from Joona, but not before he sees the frown return. She smoothes her skirt with her hands, which seem to be trembling slightly.

"How does this concern me?" she asks.

Robert knocks on the door and then pushes in a tea cart. Elin Frank thanks him and asks him to leave.

"Vicky Bennet has been missing since Friday," Joona says. "It is possible that she might come looking for you."

Elin bows her head slightly and swallows hard.

"No, she won't," Elin finally says in a chilly voice.

"Why not?" asks Joona.

"She will never attempt to contact me," Elin replies. She stands up. "It was a mistake to let you in my house without finding out your business first."

Joona stays seated and looks up at her.

"Who will Vicky try to contact, then? Will she try to contact Jack?"

"If you have any more questions, contact my lawyer," Elin says and leaves the room.

A moment later, Robert enters. "I will show you the door," he says shortly.

"Thank you very much," Joona says. He reaches for the cart and pours tea into a cup. He picks it up, blows on it, takes a careful sip, and helps himself to a lemon cookie. He eats the cookie and sips his tea unhurriedly. Finally he lifts the napkin from his knee and wipes his mouth, folds the napkin carefully, and places it on the table. Then he stands up.

Robert follows him as he walks past the enormous rooms and the lounge with the decorated tile stove. He walks through the white foyer and opens the door to the stairwell.

Robert finally speaks. "I must tell you. It is important that Elin not be associated with any negative—"

"I hear what you're saying," Joona interrupts. "But this is not about Elin Frank, but—"

"For me it is about Elin Frank. For her it's about Elin Frank," Robert says.

"I understand. However, the past is never concerned about anyone's reputation. When the past catches up to you, it has no regard for anyone at all," Joona says, and he heads down the stairs.

50

Elin usually runs eleven kilometers a day in the workout wing of her apartment. Some days she watches the television suspended from the ceiling; other days she listens to music. But today she just runs and looks out over the rooftaps, toward St. Olaf's steeple. All she can hear is the thump of her shoes, the humming motor of the treadmill, and her own breathing. After an hour her running shorts and sports bra are soaked in sweat.

She remembers when Vicky Bennet came to her house. Nine years ago. A little girl with messy blond hair.

As a teenager, during a trip to France to learn the language, Elin had contracted chlamydia. She didn't take it seriously, and by the time she saw a doctor, the bacteria had made her sterile. She didn't worry about it much back then; she didn't think she'd ever want to have children. And for years, she thought it was great that she never had to worry about birth control.

But she and Jack had been married barely two years when he started to talk about adoption. Every time he brought up the subject, she said that she didn't want kids. They were too much of a responsibility.

Jack was in love with her in those days, and he pushed. So Elin said they'd volunteer to help children temporarily, children who were having difficulty at home and needed to get away for a while.

Elin had called Stockholm's social services in the Norrmalm district, and less than six weeks later, after two lengthy interviews, a social worker rang to say that she had a child who needed a great deal of security and peace for a while.

"She's only six years old. I think it might work out. Well, you'll have to try it out. As soon as she is settled with you, we can arrange psycho-therapy for her," the woman said.

"What has happened to her?"

"Her mother is homeless and mentally ill. The authorities stepped in when they found the girl asleep on a subway car."

"How is the girl? Is she well?"

"She was dehydrated but otherwise fine. The doctor said she's healthy. I've tried to talk to the girl myself, but she's extremely with-drawn. She appears nice, though."

"What's her name? Do you know?"

"Yes, Vicky. Vicky Bennet."

Elin Frank quickens her pace. The treadmill hums, her breathing grows more labored.

Afterward, she stretches at the ballet barre in front of the large mir-ror. She avoids looking at her own eyes. Her legs feel heavy. Finally she kicks off her shoes and heads for the shower. She lets the stream of warm water pummel her back until her muscles begin to relax, but then her anxiety returns. It's as if hysteria has crept beneath her skin. She wants to scream or sob and never stop. Instead she turns the water to cold and forces herself to stand beneath the flow until her temples throb from the chill. Then she turns off the water.

51

Elin emerges from her walk-in closet wearing a mid-length velvet skirt and a nylon bodysuit studded with small glittering stones. The cloth is so delicate she has to use silk gloves to put it on.

Robert is in the reading room, sitting in a lambskin armchair and shuffling through some papers, which he is sorting into various folders.

"What was that all about? Why are the police interested in this girl?"

"She's not important," Elin answers.

"Do we have to worry about this?"

"No, we don't."

Robert Bianchi has been her assistant and adviser for the past six years. Robert's gay. Jack thought it would be best if she had a homosexual assistant, since he wouldn't get jealous.

Elin settles into the chair opposite him, stretches out her legs, and shows off her new patent leather heels.

"They're magnificent," he says, smiling. "You have to be at the reception at the Clarion Hotel in one hour."

She doesn't move. Elin can feel Robert's eyes on her, but she doesn't meet them. She plays with the tiny diamond-studded cross she's wearing. She swallows hard.

"Once, Jack and I took care of a little girl by the name of Vicky. It was a long time ago."

"Took care of? You mean, like, adopted?"

"No, her mother was alive. We fostered her, but I . . ."

She falls silent and pulls at her cross.

"When was this?"

"A few years before you started here," she says. "I wasn't on the board then, and Jack had just started working for Zentropa." She falls back into silence.

Robert studies her closely. "You don't have to tell me if you don't want."

"I thought we were ready, as ready as anyone could be. We knew that it wasn't going to be easy, but . . . Do you have any idea of how the system works? There were unbelievable hoops to jump through. We had to meet with social workers and counselors. Everything had to be examined, from our finances to our sex lives, but as soon as we were approved, it only took them three days to hand over a child to us. It was really strange. They didn't tell us anything about her, and they gave us no help at all."

"Sounds typical."

"We really wanted to do some good. Vicky lived with us for nine months, off and on. They kept trying to send her home to her mother, but Vicky would always end up being found alone in some old cardboard box in a garage."

"Sad."

"Finally Jack couldn't take it anymore. All those times we were woken in the middle of the night to pick her up and take her to Emergency, or just put her in the bathtub or give her some food. One night Jack said I had to choose." She offers Robert a wan smile. "I still don't understand why."

"He only thinks about himself," said Robert.

"But we were supposed to be her parents until her mother could care for her properly. There was no way I could choose between him and a child who was only supposed to live with us for a few months. It was crazy. And he knew I was completely dependent on him at the time."

"Well . . ." Robert prompts.

"Yes, I was, it's true," Elin says. "So when Vicky's mother got a place to live, I agreed he should call social services. I mean, it looked like things were finally starting to go well for her mother this time." Her voice breaks and she's surprised to feel tears running down her face.

"Why didn't you tell me this before?"

Elin dries her tears. "It wasn't a big deal. I don't think about it all that much." She doesn't know why she's lying.

"You have to move on," Robert says, excusing her.

"That's right," she says, and then covers her face with her hands.

"What's wrong?"

"Robert," she says with a sigh, and then looks at him. "I have nothing to do with this whatsoever, but the policeman who was just here told me that Vicky has killed two people."

"You mean those murders up in Västernorrland?"

"I don't know."

"Do you have any contact with her now?"

"None at all."

"You must not be dragged into this."

"I know. Of course, I would do whatever I could to help her, but—"

"Keep out of it."

"Maybe I should give Jack a call."

"No, don't do that."

"He should know."

"He doesn't need to hear it from you, and it will only make you unhappy, you know that. Every time you talk to him . . ."

She tries to smile in agreement and leans over to place her hand on Robert's warm fingers.

"Come here at eight tomorrow morning and let's go through the week's schedule."

"Good," Robert says. He knows he's being dismissed, and he gets up and leaves the room.

Elin picks up the phone but waits until she hears Robert close the front door. Then she calls Jack. He sounds hoarse and sleepy.

"Elin, do you know what time it is? You can't keep calling me."

"Were you asleep?"

"Yes."

"Alone?"

"No."

"Are you being honest to hurt me?"

"We are divorced, Elin," he says.

Elin walks into her bedroom and looks at her huge empty bed.

"Tell me you miss me," she says.

"Good night, Elin," he says.

"I'll give you the apartment on Broome Street if you want it."

"I don't want it. You're the one who loves New York."

"The police were here. They seem to think that Vicky has murdered two people."

"Our Vicky?"

Elin's mouth trembles and tears leap to her eyes.

"Yes. They came here to ask about her."

"How sad," he says in a low voice.

"Can you just come here? I need you. Bring Norah if you want. I won't be jealous."

"Elin, you know I'm not going to come to Stockholm."

"Sorry I disturbed you," Elin says, and ends the call.

52

The Swedish Prosecution Authority for cases concerning police officers and the Internal Review Board of the National Police both have their offices at Kungsbro 21. Joona is sitting in a small room there with Mikael Båge, who is the head of internal investigations, and his secretary, Helene Fiorine.

"At this time, the security police cracked down on an extremist left-wing group called the Brigade," Båge is saying. "The report states that Detective Inspector Linna from the National Police was at the address at the same time or right before."

"It's true," says Joona. He's looking out of the window at the railroad tracks and the Bay of Barnhusvik.

Helene Fiorine puts her pen and notebook down. "Joona, I must ask that you take this inquiry seriously," she says.

"I am," he says, though his voice makes it clear his thoughts are elsewhere.

Helene waits until Joona looks at her before she nods and picks up her pen.

"Before we conclude," Mikael Båge says, "there is the matter of the main charge against you."

"Perhaps it's just a misunderstanding," Helene says quickly. "Two investigations happened to cross paths at the same time."

"In the report, the charge against you is that the crackdown on the Brigade by Säpo failed because you'd warned the inner circle."

"Yes, I did," Joona says.

Helene gets up from her chair but does not know what to say. She stares at Joona with sad eyes.

Båge smiles. "You warned the group about the crackdown?"

"They were just kids," Joona says. "They weren't dangerous."

"Säpo thought otherwise," Båge says.

"I know," Joona says quietly.

"This is the end of the preliminary investigation," Helene says, and collects her papers.

53

It's already four thirty in the afternoon by the time Joona drives past Tumba. He once investigated a brutal triple homicide in a town house there. On the seat next to him is a list of all Vicky Bennet's known residences through the years. The last one is Birgittagården and the first is Strandvägen 47.

He's sure Vicky must have talked to someone she stayed with. She must have confided in someone or have a friend somewhere. Elin Frank said that Vicky was sweet. That's all she'd said.

Sweet, Joona thinks.

For the wealthy Franks, Vicky was a child in trouble, a girl who needed help, someone who had to be shown mercy. It was a question of charity. But for Vicky, Elin was the first sane mother she'd had.

Life for her at Strandvägen must have been like a fairy tale. She was kept warm and ate regular meals. She slept in a bed and wore lovely clothes. She would have had toys to play with. The time she spent with Elin and Jack must shine bright in her memory.

Joona turns on the signal before he moves into the left lane.

He has studied the list. Before she was sent to Birgittagården, Vicky was at the Ljungbacken orphanage. Before that, she spent two weeks with a family named Arnander-Johansson in Katrineholm.

In his mind's eye, he sees The Needle and Frippe forcing Miranda's hands away from her face. They'd fought her stiff arms, as if the dead girl was resisting. As if she was ashamed to be seen. But her face was calm and as white as a pearl.

She'd been sitting with the blanket around her body when, according to The Needle, a large rock hit her. She'd been hit six or seven times. Then she was lifted onto the bed and her hands were placed in front of her face.

The last thing she saw in life was her killer.

Joona slows down as he reaches an older residential area. He parks by the side of the street, next to a hedge of flowering Öland cinquefoil. He gets out of the car. A woman is walking around the house carrying a bucket of apples. It's apparent she has trouble moving her hips and her mouth is tense with pain. She's hefty, with large breasts and thick upper arms.

"You just missed him," she says.

"Typical," Joona says.

"He had to go to the warehouse. Something about the invoices."

"Who are we talking about?" asks Joona. He's smiling.

She puts down the bucket.

"I thought you were here about the treadmill."

"How much does it cost?"

"One thousand. It's brand-new." She rubs her hand along the crease of her pants as she looks at him.

"I'm not here about the treadmill. I'm here from the National Police," Joona says. "I need to ask you a few questions."

"What's this about?"

"Vicky Bennet. She lived with you about a year ago."

The woman's face turns sad. She nods and points to the door. Joona follows her into a kitchen with a table covered by a crocheted cloth beside a window with floral curtains, which faces onto the backyard. Outside, the lawn is freshly mown. Plum trees and gooseberry bushes form a hedge along the property line, and a small swimming pool is tucked behind a wooden lattice fence.

"Vicky has run away," Joona says directly.

"I read about it in the newspapers," she says as she puts the bucket in the sink.

"Do you know where she might be hiding?"

"No idea."

"Did she ever mention friends or boys?"

"Vicky didn't really live here long," the woman says.

"Why is that?"

"It didn't work out." She fills a carafe with water and pours it into the coffee machine. Then she stops.

"I guess offering coffee is part of what you do when the police stop by," she says without any strength in her voice.

Joona is looking out the window at two blond boys playing karate in the backyard. They're thin and tanned and wearing swimming shorts that are too large. The play is rough and wild, but the boys are laughing.

"So you foster children?"

"Our daughter is nineteen now, so, well, we've done this for a few years."

"How long do the children usually stay with you?"

"It varies. They can go back and forth for a while," she replies. She turns to Joona. "Some of these kids come from really broken homes."

"Is it difficult?"

"No, not really. Of course, there are always conflicts, but you just have to be clear about the limits."

One of the boys jumps into the swimming pool and is followed by the second, who somersaults in.

"Vicky stayed only two weeks," Joona says looking at the woman. She avoids his gaze.

"We have the two boys," she says. "We've had them for two years now. They're brothers. We hoped it would work with Vicky, but we had to stop."

"What happened?"

"Nothing, I mean, nothing really. It wasn't her fault. It wasn't anyone's fault. We just weren't up to it."

"Did Vicky cause trouble? Was she hard to manage?"

"No, no," she says. "It was . . ." She stops speaking.

"What were you going to say? What happened?"

"Nothing at all."

"You were both experienced foster parents. Why did you decide to give up after only two weeks?"

"It is what it is."

"Something must have happened."

"No, really, it was just too much for us."

"Something must have happened," Joona repeats in the same soft tone of voice. "Tell me, please."

She reddens and the blush travels all the way down her neck to between her breasts.

"Someone visited us," she whispers.

"Who?"

She shakes her head. Joona hands her his notebook and a pen. Tears start to run down her cheeks. She looks at him, and then she takes the pen and notebook. She begins to write.

54

It takes Joona three hours to drive west to Bengtsfors. By the time he gets there, the tears on his notebook where the woman wrote the address have long since dried. He had to pry it gently from her hand, and when he tried to get her to say something, she just shook her head. Then she hurried from the kitchen and locked herself in the bathroom.

Joona drives slowly along Skrakegatan. Number 35 is the last house on the street. The front yard is overgrown and white plastic furniture is lying in the tall grass. The mailbox by the gate is stuffed with flyers, and black garbage bags have been taped to the inside of the front window.

Climbing out of his car, Joona walks through the weeds to the front door. A doormat has been printed with the reminder: keys, wallet, cell phone. When he rings the doorbell, a dog barks and after a while, an eye looks through the peephole. He can hear two locks being unlatched and then the door is opened as far as the security chain allows. He can't see the person in the dark hallway, but he can smell red wine.

"May I come in?" Joona asks.

"She doesn't want to see you." It's a boy's voice, husky and hoarse.

The dog is panting and Joona can hear the links of a choke collar click.

"I need to talk to her."

"We're not buying anything!" a woman shouts.

"I'm from the police," Joona says.

Joona hears steps inside the house.

"Is he by himself?" asks the woman.

"Yes, I think so."

"Hold on to Zombie."

"Mamma? Are you really going to open the door?"

Joona hears the woman approach.

"What do you want?" she says.

"Do you know anything about a girl named Vicky Bennet?"

Joona hears the dog's nails scratch against the floor. The woman yells at the boy then closes the door and takes off the security chain. The door opens a crack. Joona pushes it wider and steps inside. The woman is standing with her back to him. She's wearing flesh-colored leggings and a white T-shirt. Her blond hair hangs over her shoulders. As Joona shuts the door behind him, it's so dark he has to stop.

By the time his eyes adjust, the woman is at the far end of the hall. He walks past the kitchen, where a vague gray light shows a box of wine on the table and a pool of wine on the brown linoleum underneath. He goes into the television room, where the woman is already sitting on a denim sofa. Dark purple curtains reach the floor on either side of a window covered in more garbage bags. The door to the veranda lets in a ray of light, which lands on the woman's hand. Her nails are well cared for and painted red.

"Go ahead and sit down," she says.

"Thank you."

Joona sits across from her on a footstool and immediately notices that there's something wrong with the woman's face.

"What do you want to know?" she says.

"You visited the Arnander-Johansson family," Joona says.

"That's right."

"Why did you need to go see them?"

"I had to warn them."

"What did you need to warn them about?"

"Tompa!" the woman yells. "Tompa!"

A door opens and slow footsteps head toward them. A shadow comes in.

"Turn on the light."

"But, Mamma—"

"Do as you're told!"

The boy hits the light switch and a large globe of rice paper lights up the entire room. The tall, thin boy is standing with his head bowed. His face looks like it had been savaged by a dog and never healed properly. His lower lip is missing so that his teeth are showing. His chin and his right cheek are bright red like fresh beef and a deep red gash goes diagonally from his hairline through one eyebrow.

When Joona turns toward the woman, he sees that her face is even more ruined. Still, she's smiling at him. She's missing her right eye and there are several deep gashes in her face and neck—at least ten. Her eyebrow droops over her remaining eye and her lips have been slashed into sections.

"Vicky got angry at us," the woman says. Her smile disappears.

"What happened?"

"She cut us with a broken bottle. I never thought a human being could get so angry. I passed out and when I woke up, I could feel the gashes from the broken glass, all the wounds, and the bits of broken glass inside my body. I realized I had no face left."

55

The agreement that Sundsvall township has made with the company that owns Birgittagården is costing it a lot of money, but at least it deals with the difficult situation. To cut back on expenses, the girls have been moved from the Hotel Ibis to the small fishing village of Hårte on the Jungfru coast.

The school in Hårte closed more than a hundred years ago when a nearby iron mine was abandoned, and the grocery store closed a few decades later when its owners got too old to run it. But the village hangs on and, during the summer, comes alive with visitors to its white sand beaches.

The six girls are staying in a large old country house with a huge glass-enclosed veranda. It stands at the point where the small road in the village forks like a snake's tongue. They've finished dinner and a few are hanging out in the dining room next to the small kitchen. A guard is sitting where he can watch both the room and the front door as well as see out through the windows to the lawn facing the road.

Lu Chu and Nina are looking for potato chips in the pantry, but they can only find Frosted Flakes.

"So what are you going to do when the killer gets here?" asks Lu Chu.

The guard's tattooed hand jerks and he smiles stiffly at her.

"You're safe here," he says.

He's fifty years old, his head is shaved, and he has a stiff goatee. His large muscles bulge the arms of his dark blue security-company sweater. Lu Chu stares at him while she snacks on the breakfast cereal. Nina finds a packet of smoked ham and a jar of mustard in the fridge. At the other end of the house, sitting around a table on the veranda, Caroline, Indie, Tuula, and Almira are playing cards.

"I want all your jacks," Indie says.

"Go fish." Almira giggles.

Indie draws a card and looks at it happily.

"Ted Bundy was just a butcher," Tuula says in a low voice.

"God, how you talk!" Caroline sighs.

"He went from room to room and clubbed the girls like they were seal pups. Lisa and Margaret and—"

"Shut up," Almira says, laughing.

Tuula smiles too, but Caroline can't help shivering.

"What the fuck is that old lady doing here?" Indie says as loud as she can.

The woman sitting in front of the fireplace looks up and then goes back to her knitting.

"Come on, aren't we playing cards?" asks Tuula impatiently.

"Whose turn is it?"

"My turn," says Indie.

"Cheater!" says Caroline, but she's smiling.

"My phone is dead," Almira says. "I was charging it in my room and now—"

"Let me look at it," says Indie.

Indie opens the back, takes the battery out, and puts it back in again. Nothing happens.

"Weird," she mutters.

"Fuck that," says Almira.

Indie takes the battery out again and exclaims, "The fucking SIM card is missing!"

"Tuula!" Almira says severely. "Did you take my SIM card?"

"Don't know," Tuula says sullenly.

"I need that SIM card!"

The woman puts down her knitting. "What's going on?"

"We can take care of ourselves," Caroline replies calmly.

Tuula whines, "I haven't taken anything!"

"My SIM card is missing!" Almira's voice is loud.

"It doesn't mean that Tuula has taken it," says the woman.

"Almira says she's going to hit me!" says Tuula.

"We don't tolerate violence of any kind here," the woman says. Then she picks up her knitting.

"Tuula," Almira says in a low voice. "I really need to make phone calls."

"Well, too bad for you!" says Tuula, smiling.

The forest across the bay and the sky above it are dark, but the water is still shimmering like molten lead in the last rays of the sun.

"The police think that Vicky beat Miranda to death," Caroline says.

"They're so fucking stupid," Almira mutters.

"I don't know Vicky. No one knows Vicky," Indie says.

"Well, watch out, then!"

"What if she's on the way over here to kill us all?"

"Shh!" Tuula says. She gets up and looks out into the darkness. She's tense.

"Did you hear that?" She turns and looks at Caroline and Almira.

"No, I don't hear a thing." Indie sighs.

"We're soon going to be dead, all of us!" whispers Tuula.

"You're a sick little bitch, aren't you?" Caroline says, but she can't hide a smile. She catches Tuula's hand and pulls her onto her lap and strokes her hair.

"Don't be afraid. Nothing's going to happen," she says.

56

Caroline wakes up on the sofa. She sits up and looks around the empty room. A few embers are glowing in the fireplace. She realizes that everyone else has gone to bed and just left her sleeping.

She gets up and looks out the window. She can see the water beyond the fishing huts. Everything is silent and still and the moon, behind a few wisps of clouds, shines over the ocean.

She opens the door and feels the cool air of the hallway on her face. The shadows are deep and she can barely make out the doors to the girls' bedrooms. She can hear a bed creak. Caroline walks into the darkness, the floor icy cold beneath her bare feet. She stops when she hears someone softly moaning. The sound is coming from the bathroom. She tiptoes there, her heart pounding. The door is slightly ajar. Someone is inside and Caroline can hear the moan again.

She peeks through the gap.

Nina is sitting on the toilet seat with her legs wide apart and her face expressionless. There's a man kneeling on the floor with his face burrowed between her thighs. She's opened her pajama top and he's squeezing her breast as he licks her.

"You should be done by now," Nina whispers.

"Okay," he says, and gets up quickly.

As he pulls some toilet paper off the roll and wipes his mouth, Caroline can see that the man is the security guard.

"So where's my money?" Nina holds out her hand.

The guard starts digging around in his pocket.

"Damn it, I just have eighty," he says.

"You told me you had five hundred."

"What am I supposed to do? I only have eighty."

Nina sighs and takes the money.

Caroline hurries away and slides into her own cold little bedroom. She closes the door and turns on the light. She can see herself reflected in the black window and realizes that she's visible to anyone outside. She stands to one side as she pulls the blind down, so she can't be seen. For the first time in a long while, she feels afraid of the dark. She leans against the wall, suddenly remembering Tuula's light blue eyes as she talked about various serial killers. She knows Tuula was frightened and only wanted the others to be scared too when she said that Vicky had followed them to the fishing village.

Caroline decides to forget about brushing her teeth. Nothing can induce her to go back out into that cold hallway.

She moves the chair to the door and tries to wedge its back under the handle, but it's too short. She gets a stack of old magazines from the bookshelf and puts them underneath the rear legs until the back reaches the handle at an angle.

She thinks she hears someone outside in the hallway and a shiver runs up and down her spine.

There's a sudden bang behind her. The window blind has snapped up and is now spinning.

"Oh God." She sighs and pulls it back down.

She stands still in the room and listens. Then she turns off the ceiling light and hurries into bed, pulling the quilt tightly around her. As she waits for the sheets to warm up she stares fixedly at the door.

She thinks about Vicky Bennet. Vicky, who seemed so shy and withdrawn. Caroline doesn't think that she really did that awful thing; she just can't wrap her mind around that. Before she can force her thoughts in another direction, she remembers the sight of Miranda's crushed skull and the blood dripping from the lamp shade.

There are footsteps in the hallway. They fall silent for a moment, then start again. Whoever it is stops outside her door. Caroline can hear the faint scrape of the door handle being pushed down. Then it stops. She shuts her eyes and prays to God, who loves little children.

57

In the middle of the night, a child's car seat bumps against the dam by the hydroelectric plant at Bergeforsen, its gray plastic back barely breaking the glassy surface of the water. The car seat has floated here in the current of the Indal River.

The river has been high since the snow melted in the Jämtland mountains. The power company has been partially opening the sluice gates as needed to prevent water from spilling over the dam. The heavy rainfall of the past few days has aggravated the threat, and the sluice gates are now wide open. For months, the Indal River resembled a lake, but now its current is strong and evident. The car seat hits the dam, whirls back a short way, and then bumps against it again.

Joona is running along the lane at the edge of the dam. On the far side, a slick concrete wall falls straight down a hundred feet. It's dizzyingly tall. Water is gushing out of the dam's gates with chaotic violence and churning over black rocks far below. But on this side of the dam, the shining river is almost at the brim. Two uniformed policemen and a guard from the power plant are standing farther along the lane. One of the policemen is pointing at the water below and the other has a boat hook.

A great deal of garbage has collected around the car seat. The river has brought empty plastic bottles, branches, spruce logs, and half-dissolved cardboard boxes to the dam. Joona joins the three men and looks at where the officer is pointing. The current is swirling the car seat around and it repeatedly bumps into the wall. Only its gray plastic back is visible. It's impossible to tell whether a child is still strapped into the front.

"Turn it over," Joona says.

The other policeman nods and leans as far as he can over the rail. He lets the boat hook break the surface of the water and he pulls a spruce log to the side. Then he moves the hook over to the car seat and lets it sink. He lifts it again carefully so that the hook will catch. He draws it up and there's a splash when the car seat flips over. It's empty. The unbuckled seat belts trail in the water.

Studying the car seat, Joona thinks that the child's body could have slipped through the belts and sunk to the bottom.

"As I said on the phone," the policeman says, "it appears to be the right car seat. It's not noticeably beaten up, but it's hard to see the details from here."

"Tell the technicians to put it in a watertight plastic bag when they get it out of the water."

The policeman lets the car seat go and it begins to tumble in the current again.

"Meet me at the bridge near Indal," Joona says. He starts walking back to his car. "There's a beach there for swimming, right?"

"What are we going to do?"

"We're going swimming," Joona says, without a trace of a smile. He keeps walking to his car.

58

Joona stands at the point where the bridge meets the ground on the river's north bank. He's looking down the grassy slope, and at the floating swimming dock that stretches from the sandy edge of the beach out into the river's current.

The wind blows open his jacket.

He walks away from the bridge along the edge of the road and feels the humidity rising from the grass; he can smell the scent of sweet fireweed. He stops, bends down, and picks up a small cube of glass hidden among the plants. He lets it sit in his palm and then looks at the water again.

"Here's where they drove off the road," he says. He points out the direction.

One policeman walks to the sandy beach and shakes his head.

"There's no sign of anything here. Nothing at all," he calls back.

"I'm sure I'm right," Joona says.

"Well, we'll never know. There's been too much rain," the other policeman says.

"It didn't rain underneath the water," Joona says.

He strides past the two police officers to the water's edge. Walking upstream, he catches sight of tire tracks in the shallows. Parallel tracks in the sand head straight out to the deep water.

"Do you see anything?" yells one of the officers.

"Yes, I do," Joona shouts back, and then he walks into the river.

The cool water swirls around his legs and tugs him gently to one side. It's hard to see beneath the shimmering surface, but he can make out reeds dancing in the current. One of the policemen follows him into the river, swearing audibly. Now up to his thighs in the river, Joona makes out a dark form about thirty feet farther out.

"Let me call for a diver," says the policeman.

Joona takes off his jacket and hands it to the officer as he keeps going.

"What are you doing?"

"I need to know if they're dead," Joona says. He hands his pistol to the officer, who is also thigh deep in the river, and wades farther out. The water is cold here and the current pulls at his pants.

"Hey! There are logs floating in the river! You can't go swimming around in there!" yells the other policeman from the shore.

Joona keeps going. The riverbed is falling away beneath his feet and the water is up to his stomach. He dives in. His ears thud as water fills them. He opens his eyes. Rays of sunlight cut through the water. Mud whirls in the current. He kicks and glides deeper beneath the surface. Suddenly he can see the car. It's slightly to the side of the wheel tracks. The current has already shifted it toward midstream.

The red body panels glimmer. The windshield and the two side windows on the right are missing. Water glides through the interior.

Joona swims closer, trying not to think about what he might find. Still, his brain flashes images of the girl in the driver's seat, the seat belt diagonally across her body—her arms floating, her mouth open, her hair swirling.

His heart is beating hard now. This deep below the surface everything is dim and silent. He reaches the rear door on the right side and grabs the empty window frame. The power of the river is drawing him away. There's a groan of metal and the car shifts. Mud whirls up and he can't see. He swims a few strokes. The cloud of mud clears and he can see again.

About three meters above his head is the other world, drenched in sunlight. A waterlogged log is gliding just below the surface—a heavy projectile.

Joona's lungs are starting to spasm. The water current is strong down here.

Joona grabs the empty window opening and sees that blood is flowing from his hand. He forces his body down and tries to look inside the Toyota.

The car is empty. There is nobody there—no girl, no child. The windshield is gone. The bodies could have been washed out through the gap and drifted along the bottom of the river. He quickly registers the area around the car. There's nothing to catch a child's body. The stones are rounded and the plants are sparse.

His lungs are screaming for oxygen, but he knows he has just a bit more time. His body has learned to wait. When he was in the navy, he often had to swim twelve kilometers carrying the signal flag. He's left a submarine with an emergency balloon. He's swum beneath the ice of the Gulf of Finland. He can go without oxygen for a few more seconds.

He swims around the car and searches the smooth riverbed. The water pulls him like a strong wind. Shadows from the logs above pass swiftly over the bottom.

Vicky drove off the road, down the beach, and into the water. The windows were already broken from crashing into the traffic light in Indal. The car would have filled with water immediately but kept going for a few seconds before it settled on the riverbed.

But where are the bodies?

He sees something shining among the stones. It's a pair of glasses that have tumbled away from the car. Joona swims over and grabs them as they are about to whirl farther downstream. Bright spots flash before his eyes. He's out of time. He kicks, swimming up blindly. He breaks the surface and draws air into his lungs. He doesn't see the log until just before it hits his shoulder. It hurts so much he howls. His shoulder has been dislocated by the force of the blow. Joona finds himself underwater again. The ringing in his ears sounds like church bells calling him to service. Above him, the sun flares in broken rays.

59

The police on shore watch as the log slams into Joona, and within moments they are in the river, swimming out to grab him. They drag him up onto the beach.

"I'm sorry," Joona manages to pant. "I just needed to know . . ."

"Where did the log hit you?"

"There aren't any bodies in the car," Joona says. The pain in his shoulder is excruciating.

"Let's take a look at your arm," says an officer.

"Shit," another whispers.

Blood has spread through Joona's soaked shirt and his arm hangs at a weird angle. It's dangling loosely from its tendons.

They take the glasses from his good hand and put them in a plastic bag.

One of the police officers drives him at top speed the twenty-nine kilometers to Sundsvall hospital. Joona sits quietly, his eyes shut, and holds his arm close to his chest. In spite of the pain, he tells the other officer how the current had shifted the car over the riverbed and the direction of the water flowing through the broken windows.

"The children weren't there," he says, barely audible.

"Bodies can float pretty far in the current," the officer replies. "There's no reason to start a diving search just yet. Either they will be snagged by something and never surface, or they'll end up at the dam just like the car seat did."

At the hospital, two cheerful, chatty nurses who could be mother and daughter get him out of his wet clothes, but when they see his arm, they fall silent. They clean him up and take him to the X-ray unit.

Twenty minutes later, a doctor comes in to report that nothing is broken, the clavicle is intact, but Joona's shoulder is dislocated. Joona lies on his stomach, his arm hanging straight down, and the doctor injects twenty milligrams of lidocaine directly into the joint. Then the doctor sinks to the floor. He pulls the arm down while the two nurses press it back into position. Joona bites hard on a towel. Then he hears a crack, and he finds to his relief he can release his breath. And think. The car with Vicky Bennet and Dante had disappeared on a stretch of the road without intersections. And with the press hounding them, the police had searched every possible place a vehicle could be hidden. But what Joona realized when he saw the car seat at the dam was this: If the car had gone off the road and into the river, there was only one spot where it could have happened without being spotted. After Indal, Highway 86 swings to the right and over the bridge. There, Vicky must have missed the turn and headed the car straight down the riverbank and into the water.

The hard rain would have washed away the tracks on the sandy beach. And given its broken windows, the river would have rushed in to fill the car. In just a few moments, it would have disappeared from sight.

60

The air is cool inside the police garage, and Joona is thankful for it as he walks down the stairs, his arm in a dark blue sling.

A large plastic tent covers the car Vicky Bennet stole. Police used a four-point suspension crane to salvage it from the Indal River, then wrapped it in plastic and transported it here. All the seats have been removed and set aside. Plastic bags containing everything found inside the car have been marked and placed on a long bench. Joona takes a look at the secured evidence. There are fingerprints from Pia, Vicky, and Dante. There are bags of glass splinters, hairs, and fibers, an empty water bottle, a tennis shoe, which most likely belonged to Vicky, and the boy's tiny pair of glasses.

The door to the garage office opens and Holger Jalmert comes out holding a folder.

"You wanted to point out something to me," Joona says.

"Yes, it's just as well," Holger says and sighs. He gestures toward the car. "The entire windshield is gone. You saw that yourself when you dove down into the water. It was knocked out when the car collided with the traffic light. Unfortunately, I've found a few strands of hair from the boy in the windshield frame."

"That's sad to hear," Joona says. A wave of loneliness washes over him.

"Well, it's what everyone suspected."

Joona takes a look at the photograph of the strands of hair on the right side of the jagged windshield frame and at an enlargement showing that the hairs were pulled out by their roots. The only way hair could have been ripped from Dante's head was if he'd been thrown from the child seat, over the front seat, through the windshield frame, and into the river. Joona imagines the child hurtling through the car and being carried off by the strong current.

Vicky Bennet hadn't killed the boy, he realizes. She'd kept him with her in the car.

"Is it your opinion that the boy was alive when the car hit the water?" he asks.

"Yes. Probably he was knocked out and drowned, but we'll have to wait until the bodies appear at the dam to know for sure."

Holger shows Joona a plastic bag containing a red water pistol. "I have a little boy, too . . ." He stops speaking and sits down in an office chair.

Joona rests his good hand on Holger's shoulder.

"We'll have to tell the mother that we're going to stop the search and wait and see," Holger says, and he turns away.

It's unusually quiet at the small police station. A few men in uniform are standing around talking near the coffee machine. A woman is typing on her computer. The twilight outside is heavy and gray, like an endless dreary day at school.

When the front door opens and Pia Abrahamsson enters, the men stop talking. She is wearing jeans and a tight denim jacket. Her nut-brown hair hanging from beneath her black beret is unwashed. She's not wearing makeup and her eyes look exhausted, terrified.

Mirja Zlatnek gets up quickly and pulls up a chair.

"I don't want to sit down," Pia says weakly.

"We asked you to come here because we fear that . . ."

Pia steadies herself with a hand on the back of the chair but stays standing.

"What I'm trying to say," Mirja says, "what I'm trying to say is that . . ."

"Yes?"

"No one believes that they can still be alive."

Pia doesn't react. She doesn't break into sobs. She just nods slightly and licks her lips.

"Why do you believe that?" she asks, softly and strangely.

"We have found your car," Mirja says. "She drove it off the road and it landed in the river. The car was at a depth of twelve feet. It was heavily damaged and . . ."

Mirja's voice fades away.

"I want to see my son," Pia says with the same disturbing calm. "Where is his body?"

"It is . . . We haven't found it yet, but—this is difficult—the decision was made to stop the search. The divers haven't found anything."

"But . . ."

Pia Abrahamsson's hand reaches for the silver cross she's wearing underneath her shirt, but stops over her heart.

"Dante is just four years old," she says. "He can't swim."

"I understand," Mirja says, looking stricken.

"But he . . . he does like playing in the water," Pia whispers.

Her chin begins to tremble. She moves slowly, like an old and broken woman, as she finally sits down.

61

Elin Frank gets out of the gym shower and crosses the polished stone floor to the large mirror over the double washbasins. She dries off with a warm towel. Before the shower, she spent some time in the sauna and her skin is still hot and damp as she pulls on the black kimono Jack gave her the year they separated.

She leaves the bathroom and walks over the white parquet floor past all the pale rooms to her bedroom, where she's already laid out a copper-colored dress from Karen Millen and golden panties from Dolce & Gabbana. She hangs up the kimono, perfumes herself with La Perla, and waits a moment before putting on her clothes.

When she reaches the large salon, she sees Robert quickly hide the telephone behind his back. Worry sweeps through her, landing like a black stone in her gut.

"What's going on?"

Robert's boyish, striped T-shirt has pulled free from his white jeans. His round stomach is visible. He shouldn't have a little stomach.

"The photographer from French *Vogue* is ten minutes late," he says, but he avoids her gaze.

"I haven't had a chance to look at the newspapers," Elin says, trying to keep her voice light. "Do you know if the police have found Vicky yet?" For the past two days, she hasn't dared listen to the news or read the paper. Both nights she's taken a sleeping pill at ten p.m. and another at three just to get some rest. "Have you heard anything?"

Robert scratches his head.

"Elin, I really don't want to upset you."

"I'm not upset, but—"

"No one can connect you to any of this."

"There's nothing wrong with keeping an eye on the situation," Elin says, trying to appear nonchalant.

"You're not a part of any of this," he says stubbornly.

Elin smiles at him coolly. "Do I have to get angry with you?"

Robert shakes his head and tucks his T-shirt in.

"I caught the end of the news as I was driving over," he says. "Apparently they've found the car in the river. I think they were searching with divers."

Elin quickly turns her face away. Her lips are trembling and her heart is beating so hard she feels it will break.

"It doesn't sound good," she says in an empty voice.

"Would you like me to turn on the television?"

"No, that's not necessary," she whispers.

"It'll be sad, of course, if they've drowned."

"Don't be so blasé," Elin says.

She has to swallow but her throat hurts.

62

Elin has a vivid memory of the day Vicky arrived. The girl was standing inside the hallway, with a closed face and yellowing bruises on her arms. She'd never even fantasized about having children, but the minute she saw Vicky she realized how much she longed for one. Vicky was the daughter she'd always wanted.

Vicky was her unique self, just as a child should be.

In the beginning, she would run into Elin's bedroom at night and stare at her before turning away. Perhaps she hoped to find her real mother there; perhaps she regretted that she'd come in at all or couldn't risk being turned away. Elin still remembers the patter of her small feet running over the parquet floor as she disappeared back to her room.

Sometimes Vicky would sit in Jack's lap while watching TV, but she never wanted to sit in Elin's lap. Vicky didn't trust her, didn't dare trust her, but Elin noticed that she often glanced at her furtively.

Little Vicky, the silent girl who would play only if she was sure no one was watching her. Little Vicky, who didn't dare open her Christmas presents because she thought that such beautiful packages couldn't be hers. Little Vicky, who shrank from every hug.

Elin bought her a little white hamster and a large cage with ladders and tunnels of red plastic. Vicky took care of the hamster during Christmas vacation, but when school started, the hamster vanished. Eventually they found out that she'd let it go in a park on the way to school. When Jack explained to her that it might not survive the cold, Vicky ran to her room and slammed the door maybe ten times. Then she downed a bottle of burgundy during the night and threw up all over the sauna. Later that week, she stole two rings that Elin had inherited from her grandmother and refused to say what she'd done with them. Elin never got the rings back.

Jack was beginning to reach his limit. He started saying that their lives were too complicated to give a child security, especially one who needed as much as this one did. He spent less time at home and stopped engaging with the girl.

Elin realized she was going to lose him.

When the social workers said they wanted to try placing Vicky temporarily back with her real mother, Elin welcomed the news. She felt that both she and Jack needed the break to find their way back to each other. Vicky refused to take the cell phone Elin offered her so they could keep in touch.

The day Vicky left, Elin and Jack had a late dinner at the Operakällaren restaurant, went home and made love, and then slept through the night undisturbed for the first time in months. In the morning Jack said he'd leave if Vicky came back. Elin let him call Vicky's case manager to explain that they couldn't cope with the child and were not able to take her back.

She learned later that Vicky and her mother ran away from their placement at an open care facility in Västerås and were later found hiding in a small playhouse at a playground. The mother started leaving Vicky alone at night, and, after she'd been gone for two days, Vicky walked the 110 kilometers back to Stockholm.

Jack was not home the night Vicky rang their doorbell. Elin had no idea what to do. She pressed her body against the wall by the door, listening to the girl ring the bell and call her name over and over. Finally Vicky started to cry. She opened the mail slot and called, "Please? Can I come back? I want to stay with you. Please, Elin, open the door. I'll be a good girl. Please . . . please . . ."

When Jack and Elin had met with Vicky's case manager after they told her they were dropping out of the program, she'd said, "Do not explain to Vicky why you can't take her in any longer."

"Why not?" Elin had asked.

"Because," the case manager had said, "the child will blame herself. She'll assume it's her fault."

So Elin had stood silently in the hallway and after what seemed like an eternity, she'd heard Vicky's footsteps fade away.

63

Elin is looking in the huge bathroom mirror and watching her eyes sparkle in the indirect light. She's taken two Valium and has had a glass of Alsatian Riesling. Out on her large terrace, Nassim DuBois, the young photographer from French *Vogue*, is setting up. The interview was done last week, when Elin was in Provence for a charity auction. She auctioned off not only her collection of contemporary French art, but also her Jean Nouvel–designed house in Nice. She's donating the proceeds to a guaranteed fund for microloans to women in North Africa.

She moves away from the mirror and picks up the phone to call Jack. Even though Jack's lawyer has told her that any contact regarding Vicky Bennet should go through his office, she wants to tell Jack that the car Vicky stole has been found in the Indal River. She won't care if he seems tired or irritated. She's no longer in love with him, but at times she feels the need to hear his voice. Before he can answer, she changes her mind and ends the call.

She steadies herself, resting her hand against the wall as she leaves the bathroom. She walks through the living room, to the glass doors leading to the terrace.

She steps languidly outside. Nassim whistles.

"You look absolutely wonderful," he says with a smile.

She knows she looks good in her copper-colored dress with its thin shoulder straps, and her necklace of hammered white gold. Her gold earrings—a gold so deep it's almost bronze—cast reflections over her bare skin.

Nassim wants her to stand with her back to the terrace wall and drape herself in a flowing white Ralph Lauren shawl. She lets it billow in a beautiful curve behind her body.

The photographer moves a silver reflecting screen so that her face is filled with light and photographs her from a distance with a telephoto lens. Then he comes closer. He sinks down on his knees. He's wearing tight-fitting jeans. He takes a series of shots with an old-fashioned Polaroid.

She notices the sweat breaking out on his forehead, but he never stops praising her. Still, she knows his concentration is elsewhere: on composition and light.

"You're dangerous, you're sexy," he mumbles.

"You really think so?" she answers with a smile.

He gets to his feet, nods, and then breaks into a wide, self-conscious smile. "Though more sexy than dangerous."

"You're sweet," she says.

Elin is not wearing a bra and she feels her nipples harden in the cool breeze. She's hoping he's noticing and realizes she's tipsy.

Now he's lying down beneath her with an old Hasselblad camera and he's asking her to lean forward and pucker her mouth as if she wants to be kissed. "*Une petite pomme,*" he says.

They smile at each other and Elin feels happy all of a sudden, almost giddy from the flirtation. His thin, tight T-shirt has come untucked and she can see how firm his body is.

She pouts a little and he keeps taking her photograph, keeps mumbling that she's the best, she's just like a top model, then finally he lowers his camera and looks at her.

"I can keep going all night," he says. "But I can see that you're freezing."

Elin nods. "Let's go inside and have a glass of whiskey."

64

The salon feels warm when they get inside; Elin's housekeeper has lit a fire in the tile stove. They sit side by side on the couch with their malt whiskeys and talk about the importance of microloans to women in the third world. The Valium and alcohol still have a spell over Elin. She feels relaxed, becalmed.

Nassim is saying that the journalist from *Vogue* is very happy with the interview. Then he tells Elin that his mother is from Morocco.

"What you've done is incredible," he says with a smile. "If my grandmother had been able to have a microloan, perhaps my mother's life would not have been so hard."

"I do what I can, but . . ."

She falls silent and looks into his serious eyes.

"No one is perfect," he says and slides closer.

"Once I let a little girl down. A girl I never should have abandoned. A girl who . . ."

He touches her comfortingly on the cheek and whispers something in French. She smiles at him, tipsy and tingling. "If you weren't so young, I might fall in love with you," she says in Swedish.

"What did you say?"

"I envy your girlfriend."

She can smell his breath: mint and whiskey. Like herbs, she thinks. She has the sudden urge to kiss him but thinks this will frighten him.

She remembers when Jack stopped sleeping with her. It was after Vicky had left their lives. She realized she no longer excited him. She had thought that it was just stress; they'd had too little time together; they were too tired. So she started to make an effort. She always dressed well, arranged romantic dinners, planned excursions. But he just didn't react to her any longer.

One night he came to her when she was in bed wearing a delicately laced negligee and he told her that he was not in love with her any longer. He'd met another woman. He wanted a divorce.

"Watch out!" Nassim says. "You're spilling your drink."

"Oh God," she whispers as she looks at the drips in her lap.

"Not to worry."

He takes a cloth napkin and kneels in front of her. As he carefully wipes the spill his other hand touches her waist.

"I have to change," she says, and she gets up and tries to stand upright. Her head is spinning.

He supports her and they walk single file through her apartment. She feels weak and leans back to kiss him on the throat.

The bedroom is cool and shadowy. A single lamp beside the bed casts a soft light.

"I have to lie down," she says.

She says nothing more as he lays her on the bed and slowly pulls off her shoes.

"Let me help you," he says softly.

She's acting more intoxicated than she actually is and lies still as if she's not even noticing how he's unbuttoning her dress. She listens to his heavy breathing and wonders if he will dare touch her.

She's lying still in her golden panties and is looking at him as through pulsing fog. Then she shuts her eyes. His fingers are ice-cold as he pulls off her panties.

She opens her eyes slightly to look at him as he gets undressed. His body is thin and tanned, and he has a gray Horus-eye tattoo on his shoulder.

Her heart begins to race as he lies down beside her. She thinks of stopping him, but she's flattered by his desire. She thinks that she shouldn't let him come inside her and instead let him look at her and masturbate as if he were a boy.

She tries to concentrate on what is happening and let herself enjoy the moment. He's breathing quickly as he parts her legs. She's wet and slippery, but her desire is fading. He is now over her and she feels him, warm and hard, against her soft folds. She slowly writhes away and presses her thighs together.

She opens her eyes and meets his puzzled look and then closes her eyes again.

Carefully, as if he does not want to wake her, he opens her legs again. She smiles and lets him look. She feels him over her and then he slides inside.

She moans softly. She wants to respond to his desire, but he's in too much of a hurry. He's thrusting too quickly and too hard. Loneliness catches up to her and what little lust she was feeling dies. She lies still until he's finished and pulls out.

"Sorry, sorry," Nassim whispers as he gathers his things. "I thought you wanted it."

I thought so, too, she thinks, but she's unable to speak. He quickly gets dressed and all she wants is for him to leave. Then she'll get up and wash and spend the rest of the evening praying to God that Vicky is alive.

65

Joona is back at the dam, looking down the high concrete wall where water is gushing from three openings sixty feet beneath him. Below the sluice gates, the concrete wall bends like a massive slide.

Joona's arm is still in a sling and his jacket is hanging over his injured shoulder. He looks back along the river and thinks about the car with the two children inside. It's pouring rain. The car skids into the traffic light in Indal and the windows are knocked out. Vicky's wearing her seat belt but hits her head against the side window. The car is filled immediately with crumbs of glass and the cold rain starts pouring inside.

All is silent.

Then the child begins to scream. Vicky gets shakily out of the car, brushes off the glass, and opens the back door. She unbuckles the boy and looks to see if he is all right. She tries to get him to be quiet and then she drives on.

Perhaps she intends to drive over the bridge until she sees the blue lights of the police car blocking the road on the other side. She swings off the road in panic, brakes hard, but can't stop the car as it drives into the river. Vicky hits her head again, perhaps on the steering wheel, and loses consciousness.

As the car plows through the water, they are probably both already unconscious. The current drags them through the window, softly and quietly, and pulls them along the rocky bottom of the river.

Joona picks up his cell phone to call Carlos Eliasson.

The diver from the rescue service is already standing in his blue wet suit on the dock at the power station. He's checking the fasteners on his regulator.

"Carlos here," Joona hears his boss say.

"Susanne Öst wants to end the preliminary investigation," Joona says. "But I'm not done."

"It's always sad, but the killer is most likely dead, and so, unfortunately, we can't justify the expense of continuing the investigation."

"We haven't found any bodies."

Joona hears Carlos mutter something, then break into a coughing fit. He waits while Carlos takes a drink of water.

"It can take weeks for bodies to appear," Carlos whispers, and clears his throat again.

"But I'm not done," Joona says.

"Now you're being stubborn."

"I have to—"

"This isn't even your case," Carlos interrupts.

Joona is looking at a black log, which is speeding with the current. It hits the edge of the dam with a dull thud.

"Yes, it is," Joona says.

"Joona." Carlos sighs.

"The technical evidence points to Vicky, but there are no witnesses and she hasn't been accused."

"You can't accuse the dead," Carlos says.

Joona thinks about the girl, the lack of motive, the fact that she'd slept in her bed after those violent murders. He thinks about the fact The Needle mentioned: that Elisabet was killed with a hammer but Miranda with a rock.

"Just give me a week, Carlos," Joona says. "I need a few answers before I come back."

Carlos mumbles something.

"I'm sorry, I didn't hear you," Joona says.

"This is not formal," Carlos repeats more loudly. "But as long as the internal investigation is under way, you can do what you want."

"What are my resources?"

"What resources? You're still just an observer and—"

"I've hired a diver."

"A diver?" Carlos says agitatedly. "Do you know how much a diver costs? You can't just—"

"And a dog."

Joona hears the sound of a motor, turns, and watches a small gray car with a rattling engine park beside his. It's a Messerschmitt Kabinenroller from the early sixties, with two wheels in the front and one in back. Joona rings off as the car door flies open and Gunnarsson, a cigarette dangling from his mouth, climbs out.

"I'm the one who decides whether or not to call in a diver!" roars Gunnarsson. He's sprinting toward Joona. "You're not supposed to have anything to do with this case!"

"I'm just observing," Joona says calmly, and heads for the dock.

66

The diver is a man in his fifties. He's starting to put on a bit of weight, but he has wide shoulders and strong upper arms.

"The name's Hasse Boman," he says.

"We can't close the sluice gates as there's a flood risk," Joona says.

"I understand the situation," Hasse says, while he contemplates the unsettled, swirling water.

"There's going to be a strong current," Joona says.

"I know," the diver says, and looks at Joona calmly.

"Can you handle it?" Joona asks.

"I was in mine removal in the KA1 unit . . . Can't be worse than that," Hasse says, and there's a hint of a smile.

"Do you have nitrox in your cylinders?" asks Joona.

"Yes, indeed."

"What the hell is that?" Gunnarsson asks, catching up to them.

"It's air with extra oxygen," Hasse says as he struggles into his vest.

"How long can you be down there?"

"Maybe two hours. Don't worry."

"I'm grateful you could come," Joona says.

The diver shrugs. "My boy is at soccer camp in Denmark. I promised to go with him, but you know how it is. It's just me and the boy, and I need the extra money."

He shakes his head. Then he points at his diving mask and its digital camera. A cable runs from it along the lifeline and into a laptop.

"I always record my dives. You'll see everything I'm seeing. We can even talk while I'm underwater."

Another log thuds into the dam.

"Why are there logs in the water?" asks Joona.

Hasse is putting on his cylinders. "Who knows? Somebody probably dumped timber destroyed by bark beetles."

A woman is heading toward them. Her face is worn and she's wearing blue jeans, rubber boots, and an open down-filled coat. She is leaving the parking lot with a russet-colored German shepherd on a leash.

"And here's a goddamn bloodhound," Gunnarsson says, and shudders.

The dog handler, Sara Bengtsson, unclips the leash and says something in a low voice. The dog immediately sits down. She doesn't look at it as she walks toward them. She knows it will do what she says.

"Good that you could come," Joona says as he shakes her hand.

Sara Bengtsson briefly glances at him as she pulls her hand back. Then she feels for something in one of her pockets.

"I'm in charge here," says Gunnarsson. "And I'm not fond of dogs— just so you know."

"Well, I'm here now," Sara says. She looks back at the dog.

"What's its name?" Joona asks.

"Jackie." Sara smiles.

"We're going to send a diver down in a minute," Joona says. "But it would be helpful if Jackie could mark the spot. Do you think she can?"

"Oh, yes," Sara says, and kicks a stone into the water.

"There's a lot of water and a strong current," Gunnarsson warns.

"Last spring, she found a body at a depth of a hundred and eighty feet," Sara replies, and turns red.

"Well, what the fuck are we waiting for then?" asks Gunnarsson, lighting a cigarette.

Sara Bengtsson ignores him. She looks over the black, glittering water. She stuffs her hands into her pockets before she says, in a soft voice, "Jackie."

The dog leaves her spot immediately and walks up to her. Sara squats down and pats the dog on her neck and behind her ears. She talks encouragingly to the dog and tells her what they are looking for and then they start walking along the edge of the dam.

The dog is trained to recognize the smells of blood and the lungs of the recently dead. The search dogs are trained by rewarding correct identifications, but Sara knows that Jackie gets nervous and needs to be comforted afterward.

They walk past the place where Dante's car seat was found. Sara steers the dog's nose toward the water.

"I don't believe in this crap." Gunnarsson smiles. He throws the butt of his cigarette into the water.

Sara stops and gestures for them to halt as Jackie catches a scent. The dog stretches her nose out over the edge of the dam.

"What did you find?" asks Sara.

The dog sniffs, moves to the side, and then loses the scent and keeps walking.

"A bunch of hocus-pocus," the diver mutters, and adjusts his vest.

Joona watches the dog trainer and her unusual red German shepherd. They are moving slowly along the railing over the open sluice gates where the current is strongest. Hair has loosened from Sara's ponytail and is blowing in her face. The dog stops and whines, leans out, licks her nose, becomes agitated, and walks in a tight circle.

"Is there someone down there?" asks Sara quietly as she looks into the black water.

The dog does not want to stay there. She walks farther, to the electricity box, and sniffs there, then returns to the first spot and whines again.

"What is it?" Joona asks.

"I honestly don't know," the dog handler says. "She hasn't marked a corpse, but she's acting as if she's found something."

The dog barks and the woman squats next to her.

"What is it, Jackie?" she asks tenderly. "What is so strange?"

The dog wags her tail as Sara hugs her and tells her that she's a good girl. Jackie whimpers again and then lies down, scratches behind her ear, and licks her nose.

"What are you doing, you little rascal?" Sara asks with a surprised smile.

67

There's a vibration at the dam. Watertight body bags are folded neatly on top of a plastic tub with attached signal buoys to mark the position of any discoveries.

"I'll start by the power station and take the area in squares," Hasse says.

"No, let's start where the dog reacted," Joona says.

"Are we going to let the ladies tell us what to do now?" Hasse complains.

Deep below the turbulent surface of the water are the openings of the gates, with heavy grates to catch everything brought downstream by the river. The diver checks his air hose, connects the cable from the camera to the laptop, and then puts on his mask. Joona can see himself on the computer screen.

"Wave to the camera," Hasse says, and then he puts in his mouthpiece and slides into the water.

"If the current is too strong, we'll call it off," Joona says.

"Be careful," says Gunnarsson.

"I'm used to diving in heavy current," Hasse says. "But if I don't come up again, tell my boy that I should have gone with him instead."

"Let's have a beer at Hotel Laxen when you're through," Gunnarsson says, and waves.

Hasse Boman disappears beneath the surface, which bubbles, then grows calm again. Gunnarsson smiles and flicks his cigarette into the water. The only thing they can see on the computer screen is the rough surface of the concrete as it slips past the camera. They can hear Hasse's deep breathing in the speaker. On the river, bubbles from his exhalation break the surface.

"How far down are you now?" asks Joona.

"Just thirty feet."

"How hard is the current?"

"It's like someone pulling at my legs."

Joona keeps watching the diver's plunge on the computer screen. The concrete wall slides past. The diver's breathing sounds heavier. Sometimes they catch glimpses of his hands against the wall. His blue gloves shine in the camera's light.

"There's nothing down there," Gunnarsson says, and begins to pace back and forth.

"The dog sensed—"

"But it didn't mark the spot properly." Gunnarsson raises his voice.

"No, but she sensed something," Joona replies stubbornly.

He thinks how the bodies could have traveled with the water, tumbling over the riverbed, getting closer to the midstream current.

"Fifty feet. The current's pretty strong here," the diver says.

Gunnarsson is letting the lifeline out now. It's moving swiftly over the metal railing and disappearing below the surface.

"You're going too fast," Joona says. "Fill your vests."

The diver begins to fill his vests with air from his cylinders. Usually this is done only when it's time to return to the surface, but the diver knows that Joona is right—he has to slow down because of all the flotsam in the water.

"I'm fine," he says after a moment.

"If you can, I'd like it if you can take a look at the nearest grate," Joona says.

Hasse moves slowly and then is caught in the current, which has sped up, as if the sluice gates have been opened wider. Garbage, twigs, and leaves rush past his face and head straight down.

Gunnarsson shifts the lifeline and cable as a log approaches and crashes into the dam.

68

The strong current is pulling Hasse Boman straight down. He's going much too fast again. The water pounds against his ears. He knows he could break both legs if he collides with something. His heart races as he tries to fill his vest more, but the dump valve is giving him trouble. He tries to slow down using his hands. Algae loosens from the concrete walls and disappears with the current. He doesn't tell the police above water that he's getting frightened. The suction is more powerful than he'd believed possible, and everything beyond the camera light is completely black.

"How deep are you now?" asks the inspector from Stockholm.

He doesn't reply because he doesn't have time to look at the depth meter. He has to slow his descent. He's using one hand to work the inflation valve and the other to keep himself upright. An old plastic bag dashes past. He's plunging straight down. He tries to reach the regulator on his back, but he bangs his elbow against the concrete wall. He sways as he's buffeted by the fierce current and feels the adrenaline coursing in his blood. He thinks in panic he must control his descent.

"Eighty-five feet," he finally pants.

"You'll be at the grate soon," the inspector says.

As it's sucked down the concrete wall, the water makes his legs shake uncontrollably.

Hasse is still falling fast and realizes that he's at risk of being speared by sharp branches or broken timber. He knows he'll have to drop some of his weights in order to stop, but he has to keep some so he has a chance of returning to the surface.

The bubbles from his exhalation now head straight down like a string of pearls. The suction increases and a new current of much colder water hits him in the back. It feels as if the entire river is trying to press him against the wall.

He sees a large leaf-covered branch coming at him. The leaves shake as the branch tumbles along the concrete wall. He tries to move away, but the branch is caught in his lifeline and hits him—then it breaks free and disappears down into the darkness.

"What happened?" asks the inspector.

"There's a lot of garbage."

The diver manages to release some lead weights from his vest and is able to break his violent fall. He hangs, shaking, next to the concrete wall. The view in his circle of light is clouded by sand and soil caught in the streaming water.

He stops. His feet have reached the upper edge of the grate, where there's a lip of concrete. Vast amounts of branches, tree trunks, leaves, and garbage have collected in front of the intake grate. The suction is so strong that every movement feels impossible.

"I'm in place now," he says, "but it's hard to see anything. There's a ton of shit down here."

Trying to keep his lifeline free from the branches, he climbs over a vibrating tree trunk. Something is moving slowly behind a misshapen spruce log.

"What's going on?"

"I see something."

69

Bubbles stream in front of the diver's face while he reaches to brush away a tight mass of pine needles clinging to the grate. He's standing on the lip above it, holding on tightly with one hand. Suddenly there's an eye staring straight at him—and teeth, large teeth. In a huge body. Right in front of him, or so it seems. Closeness is an optical illusion of being underwater.

"Moose," he reports, and backs away.

The enormous animal lies directly across the grate, but the throat is stuck between a tree branch and a broken oar.

"That's what the dog reacted to," Gunnarsson says.

"Shall I come up?" Hasse asks.

"Keep looking a little longer," Joona replies.

"Farther down or more to the side?"

"What's that right in front of you?" asks Joona.

"It looks like cloth."

"Can you check it out?"

Hasse can feel the lactic acid in his arms and legs. He looks slowly at the mass of debris that has collected at the grate. He tries to peer beyond the black spruce logs and between the branches. Everything is shaking. He thinks he'll buy a new PlayStation from the earnings from this dive. He'll give it to his son as a surprise when he returns from camp.

"It's just cardboard. From a box."

Hasse tries to move the cardboard box aside but only rips it in half. The loose piece is caught by the current and sucked up to the grate.

"My strength is starting to give out. I'm coming up," he says.

"What is that white thing?" asks Joona.

"Where?"

"In the direction you're looking right now," Joona says. "There was something among the leaves, down at the grate, just a bit farther down."

"Maybe a plastic bag?" suggests the diver.

"I don't think so," says Joona.

"Come on up now," Gunnarsson says. "We've found the moose, that's what the bitch was reacting to."

"A search-and-rescue dog can react to any dead thing, but not like she did," Joona says. "I think she was reacting to more than just the moose."

Hasse Boman climbs down just a bit farther and pulls away leaves and intertwined twigs. His muscles are shaking from the attempt. The strong current keeps pushing him forward. He has to fight it with one arm. His lifeline is vibrating.

"I don't see anything," he says, panting.

"Break it off," says Gunnarsson.

"Shall I break it off?" asks Hasse.

"If you must," says Joona.

"Not everyone is like you," Gunnarsson hisses at Joona.

"What do you want me to do? Right now?" asks the diver.

"Go to the side," Joona says.

A branch hits Hasse Boman on the neck but he keeps searching. He pulls away the reeds and bulrushes covering the lower corner of the grate. New waste keeps accumulating. He digs more quickly and then he sees it: a shiny white shoulder purse.

"Wait! Don't touch it!" Joona says. "Go closer and shine your light on it."

"Can you see it now?"

"Yes. It could be Vicky's. Be careful how you bag it."

70

The river moves inexorably toward the dam, bearing another large log. A branch is sticking up above the surface of the water. Gunnarsson can't shift the lifeline in time and there's a dull thud and some splashing. The digital connection to Hasse is lost.

"We've lost contact," Joona says.

"He has to come up."

"Pull on the line three times."

"He's not answering," Gunnarsson says after pulling.

"Do it again. Use more strength," Joona says.

Gunnarsson pulls three more times on the lifeline, and this time he gets an immediate response.

"He pulled twice," Gunnarsson says.

"That means he's coming up."

"The line is getting slack. He's on the way up." Gunnarsson looks upstream. "There's more timber coming."

"He has to get up quickly," Joona says.

Gunnarsson counts ten huge logs heading swiftly toward the dam. He climbs down the other side of the railing as Joona reels in the lifeline with his good arm.

"I see him." Gunnarsson points at the blue wet suit moving like a flag in the current.

Joona pulls off the sling and grabs the boat hook from the ground as the first log hits the wall two meters away. He manages to keep the second log away. It hits the boat hook and dives beneath the first log. The two logs start rolling together.

Hasse Boman breaks the surface of the water. Gunnarsson leans over and holds out his hand.

"Come up! Come up!"

Hasse looks at him in surprise and grabs at the side of the dam. Joona climbs over the railing with the boat hook and keeps steering the timber away from him.

"Hurry up!" he yells.

A huge log with wet, black bark is approaching, almost hidden beneath the surface.

"Watch out!"

Joona steers the boat hook between the rolling timber and a few seconds later, the black log hits it, breaks the shaft, and changes direction. It misses Hasse's head by mere inches and smashes into the dam, then it tumbles over and bangs Hasse in the back. One of its wet branches pushes him back underwater.

"Try to grab him!" yells Joona.

The log keeps rolling against the dam, wrapping the lifeline around its girth. Hasse is being dragged down. Bubbles break the surface. Hasse manages to pull out his knife and cut the lifeline. He kicks as hard as he can and grabs Gunnarsson's hand.

Another log hits the black one, and just as three more logs loom close, Gunnarsson hauls Hasse out of the water. He lands on his knees and tries to stand, but his legs are shaking. Gunnarsson quickly frees him from his cylinders and Hasse sinks down to the ground. Joona takes the plastic bag from his trembling hands and helps Hasse out of his wet suit. He's bruised and scrapes the length of his back have stained his sweaty T-shirt red. He's in pain and cursing loudly.

"This isn't exactly the smartest thing I've ever done in my life," he says, panting.

"But you found something important," Joona says.

He's looking at the clear plastic bag where the purse is floating in scummy water along with a few yellow blades of grass. Joona holds it up to the sunlight. His fingers press on the plastic until he's touching the purse.

"We're looking for corpses and you're happy with a damned purse." Gunnarsson sighs.

Light through the plastic bag casts a gold shadow on Joona's face. The purse has dark brown stains on it—blood.

"It's bloody," Joona says. "The dog must have smelled it as well as the moose. No wonder she didn't know how to mark it."

Joona turns the heavy bag over, and the purse bobs in the scummy water.

71

Joona is standing by the locked gates to the parking lot behind the police station in Bergsgatan, the industrial area of Sundsvall. The technicians there have the purse and he wants to talk to them, but no one is answering the intercom at the gate. The parking lot is empty and all the station's doors are closed.

Joona gets back in his car and drives to the station at Storgatan. Gunnarsson should be there. In the stairwell, he runs into Sonja Rask. She's in civilian clothes and her hair is still damp from the shower. She's put on a bit of makeup and seems happy.

"Hello," Joona says. "Is Gunnarsson upstairs?"

"He can go to hell," Sonja says. "He feels threatened. He thinks that you're after his job."

"I'm just an observer," Joona says.

Sonja's dark eyes shine. "I heard you dove right into the water and swam to the car."

"I just wanted to look at it," Joona says.

She laughs and pats his arm, but then turns shy and hurries off down the stairs.

Joona keeps going up. In the police station, the radio in the lunch room is on, as usual, and through a glass door, he can see several people sitting around a conference table. Gunnarsson is at one of its ends. A woman sitting at the table catches Joona's eye and shakes her head, but he still opens the door and walks inside.

"What the hell!" Gunnarsson says when he sees Joona.

"I need to look at Vicky Bennet's purse," Joona says tersely.

"We're in a meeting," Gunnarsson says, cutting him off. He looks back at his paperwork.

"Everything is with the technicians at the Bergsgatan station," Rolf says, looking embarrassed.

"There's no one there," Joona says.

"Give it up, for fuck's sake," Gunnarsson growls. "The preliminary investigation has come to an end and as far as I'm concerned, the internal investigators can eat you for breakfast."

Joona nods and leaves the room. He goes back to his car and sits there for a while, then starts driving to the provincial hospital in Sundsvall. Something is still bothering him about the murders at Birgittagården.

Vicky Bennet, he thinks. *The nice girl who isn't always nice. Vicky Bennet, who slashed the faces of a mother and son with a broken bottle. They were seriously injured, but they didn't go to a doctor. They also did not report the incident to the police.*

Before Vicky drowned, she was a suspect for two violent murders.

Everything indicates that she prepared her killings in advance. She waited for nightfall, killed Elisabet with a hammer, returned to the house, unlocked the door to the isolation room, and then killed Miranda.

The Needle says that Miranda was killed by a rock.

Why would Vicky leave the hammer in her room and then go find a stone?

There are times when Joona thinks his old friend must be wrong. It's why he has not yet said anything about his suspicions to anyone. The Needle will have to present his theory in his report.

Vicky went to bed after killing these two women.

Joona saw the blood on her sheets and how it had been smeared by Vicky's arm as she changed positions in her sleep. Holger Jalmert said that this observation was interesting but impossible to prove.

Without witnesses, he would never get an answer to this case.

Joona has read Elisabet Grim's final note in the Birgittagården logbook, but nothing in it indicates the violence that erupted later that night.

The girls did not see a thing.

No one knew Vicky Bennet.

Joona has already decided he needs to talk to Daniel Grim, the therapist. It's worth a try, even though it's difficult to question someone in mourning. Daniel was the person the girls trusted the most. If anyone understands what happened, he's probably the one.

His shoulder is hurting, so Joona pulls out his cell phone slowly. He remembers that Daniel Grim kept himself together in front of the girls when he first got to Birgittagården, but his face had contorted in pain when he found out Elisabet had been killed.

The doctor had called his acute shock "arousal," a consequence of traumatic stress, which might prevent Daniel from remembering much for some time.

"Psychiatric clinic, Rebecka Stenbeck speaking," a woman says after five rings.

"I would like to speak with one of your patients, Daniel Grim."

"One moment."

He can hear the woman typing on a keyboard.

"I'm sorry, but the patient is not allowed to receive phone calls," she says.

"Who made that decision?"

"His doctor."

"Would you connect me to him, please?"

There's a series of clicks and then the phone rings.

"Carl Rimmer here."

"I'm Joona Linna, a detective with the National Police," Joona says. "It's very important that I speak with a patient by the name of Daniel Grim."

"I'm sorry, I can't allow that," Rimmer says immediately.

"We are investigating a double murder and—"

"Nothing will change my decision. The patient needs to recover."

"I understand that Daniel Grim is suffering, but I promise—"

"My decision stands," Carl Rimmer says, but his tone is friendly. "In my opinion, the patient will recover and then the police can talk to him."

"When will that be?"

"I'd guess in a few months."

"I need to talk to him for just a little while, but I need to talk to him now."

"As his doctor, again I must say no." Rimmer is adamant. "He was extremely upset after your colleague questioned him earlier."

72

Flora is hurrying home with a heavy bag of groceries. The sky is dark, but the streetlights haven't come on yet. Her stomach knots as she thinks of how the police rebuffed her. Her face had flushed with shame when the female officer told her that it was a crime to make a false report. Still, she'd called back to tell them she'd seen the murder weapon. Now she keeps going over the conversation again and again in her mind.

"Police," said the same officer who had just given her a warning.

"My name is Flora Hansen. I just called a moment ago," she said, and swallowed hard.

"Yes, about the murders in Sundsvall," the officer said calmly.

"I know where the murder weapon was hidden," she lied.

"Do you realize that I am going to report you, Flora Hansen?"

"I'm psychic. I've seen the bloody knife. It's in the water—dark, glittering water. That's all I saw, but I . . . I can go into a trance and find out more, for a fee. I can point out the exact place."

"Flora," the officer said sternly, "if you persist, you will be under suspicion for a crime and the police will—"

Flora hung up.

Now she's walking past the halal food market. She stops and looks in a garbage can for empty bottles, then she shifts the grocery bag to her left hand and keeps walking to the apartment building. The front lock has been broken and the elevator is stuck in the basement. Flora climbs the stairs to the second floor and unlocks the door to the apartment. She walks into the hall and flicks the light switch.

There's a click, but the light does not go on.

She puts down the grocery bag, locks the door behind her, and slips off her shoes. As she bends over to put them away, the hair on her arms rises.

The apartment suddenly feels extremely cold.

She takes her wallet and the grocery receipt out of her purse as she walks down the hall to the dark living room. She can make out the sofa, the big worn armchair, and the dark pane of the television. There's an odor of electric dust—a short in the wiring.

Without stepping into the living room, she reaches to turn on the lights. Nothing happens when she pushes the button.

"Is anyone home?" she whispers.

The floor shakes and a teacup rattles in its saucer.

There's someone moving through the darkness.

Flora follows. The floor is cold beneath her feet. It feels as if some-one has left the windows open too long on a winter day.

The door to the bathroom is shut. As Flora reaches for the handle, she remembers that Ewa and Hans-Gunnar are not supposed to be home this evening. They are at a pizza parlor, celebrating a friend's birthday. This means no one should be in the bathroom, but still she pushes open the door.

In the gray light of the bathroom mirror, she sees something that makes her stagger backward and gasp for breath.

On the floor of the bathroom, between the tub and the toilet, a girl is lying with her hands in front of her face. There's a huge pool of blood next to her head and tiny red drops have spattered on the bathtub, the floor mat, and the shower curtain.

Flora trips over the vacuum cleaner hose and as her arm swings out, it catches Ewa's plaster relief from Copenhagen. It crashes at the same time Flora does. Her head hits the hall floor.

73

The floor is icy under Flora's back. She lifts her head and stares at the bathroom, her heart pounding.

There's no girl there.

There aren't any drops of blood on the bathtub or the shower curtain. A pair of Hans-Gunnar's jeans is lying on the bathroom floor close to the toilet.

It must have been her imagination.

She rests on the floor as she waits for her heart to stop pounding. She can taste blood in her mouth. She turns her head and looks down the hall. The door to her room is open. She knows she closed her door. She always closes her door. She shudders and goose bumps rise over her entire body. Icy air is being drawn toward her room. Two dust bunnies roll in the draft down the hall and she follows them with her eyes. They stop at her door, between two bare feet.

Flora moans.

The girl who was lying on the bathroom floor is now standing in the doorway to her room. She steps into the hall.

Flora tries to sit up, but her body is frozen with fear. She realizes that she's seeing a spirit—for the first time in her life, she is face-to-face with a real ghost.

The girl's hair is tangled and bloody.

Flora is breathing quickly and her pulse thunders in her ears. The girl is hiding something behind her back as she starts to walk toward Flora. She stops just one step away from Flora's face.

"Do you want to know what I have in my hands?" the girl asks so quietly that the words are almost impossible to hear.

"You don't exist," Flora whispers.

"Do you want me to show you what I have in my hands?"

"No."

"But I don't have anything."

A heavy rock lands with a thud behind the girl. The floor shakes and the pieces of broken plaster jump.

The girl shows her empty hands and smiles.

The rock is silvery-gray and has sharp edges. It looks like it's from an iron-ore mine. The girl steps on it with one foot. It rocks back and forth. She pushes it away.

"Well, go ahead and die!" the girl mumbles to herself. "Hurry up and die already!"

The girl squats down and puts her ashen hands on the rock. She rocks it, trying to get a good grip on it. It slips out of her grasp. She wipes her hands on her dress and tries again. The rock turns over with a thud.

"What are you going to do?" asks Flora.

"Close your eyes and then I'm gone," the girl says, and picks up the sharp rock. She lifts it over Flora's head. Its dark underside looks wet.

The electricity suddenly turns back on. Ceiling lights come on all over the apartment. Flora rolls to the side and sits up. The girl has disappeared. The television starts to blare and the refrigerator resumes humming.

Flora gets up and walks to her room. The door is shut and she opens it. She turns on the ceiling light, opens the wardrobe, and looks under the bed. Then she goes into the kitchen and sits at the table. Her hands are shaking as she dials the phone for the police.

The automatic voice-message system gives her a few choices. She can report a crime, leave a tip, or receive an answer to a general question. The last choice contacts her with an operator.

"Police," says the friendly voice. "What can I do to help you?"

"I would like to talk to someone working on the Birgittagården case," Flora says in a shaky voice.

"What does this concern?"

"I . . . I've seen the murder weapon," Flora whispers.

"I see," the operator says. "I'm going to connect you to our department that takes tips from the general public. Just a moment."

Flora is about to protest, but there's already clicking on the line. Then there's another woman's voice: "How can I help you?"

Flora can't tell if it is the same woman she's talked to before—the one who got angry when Flora told her about the bloody knife.

"I need to talk to someone who is working on the Sundsvall murder case," Flora says.

"Talk to me first," says the voice.

"It was a large rock," Flora says.

"I can't hear you. Please speak louder."

"What happened in Sundsvall. You should be looking for a large rock. Its underside is all bloody and . . ."

Flora falls silent. Sweat runs down her sides.

"How do you know anything about the Birgittagården murders?"

"I've . . . Someone told me."

"Someone told you about the Birgittagården murders?"

"Yes," Flora whispers. Her ears are ringing.

"Keep going," the woman says.

"The murderer used a rock, a large one with sharp edges. That's all I know."

"What is your name?"

"It doesn't matter. I just wanted—"

"I recognize your voice," the policewoman says. "You called earlier about a bloody knife. I've already written up a report on you, Flora Hansen, but I think you should contact a doctor. You need some serious help."

The policewoman hangs up, and Flora looks at the telephone in her hand. She jumps, knocking over the paper-towel roll when the grocery bag in the hallway falls over.

74

Elin Frank got back to her apartment an hour ago after a long committee meeting at the Kingston Corporation to discuss two holding compa-
nies in Great Britain.

She's feeling anxious about having slept with the *Vogue* photographer, but she keeps reminding herself that it was just a small adventure
and she needed one after so long without sex. Still, she finds herself
sweating from embarrassment.

She has changed into her old, faded red sports shorts and an equally
worn ABBA T-shirt, and she's nursing a bottle of Perrier she picked up in
the kitchen. As she gets to her bedroom, she switches on the TV, but
pays little attention to it.

Later this afternoon, she is supposed to have a telephone conference
with the CEO of her subdivision in Chicago while she has a paraffin bath
and a manicure. At eight, she's expected at a charity dinner, where she'll
sit at the head table. The chairman of Volvo has been assigned the chair
beside hers. The crown princess is awarding a prize from the General In-
heritance Fund, and Roxette is providing the evening's entertainment.

From her walk-in closet she can still hear the television, but she's still
not actively listening, and she doesn't yet notice the news is now on. She
opens one of the wardrobes and looks through her clothes. She selects a
metallic-green dress the designer Alexander McQueen made just for
her not long before he died.

". . . Vicky Bennet . . ." She hears the name mentioned on the broad-cast, and she rushes back into the bedroom. On-screen, a detective by the name of Olle Gunnarsson is being interviewed in front of a dreary police station. He's trying to smile patiently, but his eyes are narrowed. He's stroking his mustache as he nods.

"I cannot comment on an ongoing investigation," he says, and clears his throat.

"But you've concluded the underwater search?"

"That is correct."

"Does this mean that you've found the bodies?"

"I can't answer that."

The image changes, and Elin is staring at footage of the salvage of the wrecked car. The crane is lifting it straight up and it breaks the sur-face of the water and starts to sway. Water pours from the car as a voice says that the vehicle that Vicky Bennet stole was found submerged in the Indal River earlier that day and that both the murder suspect, Vicky Bennet, and four-year-old Dante Abrahamsson were feared dead.

"The police are not talking about what they've found, but we've learned that the underwater search has been suspended and the search for survivors called off . . ."

Elin has stopped listening to the news anchor. All she can do is stare at the picture of Vicky they are now showing. The girl looks older and skinnier, but she hasn't changed. Elin feels as if her heart has stopped. She remembers what it felt like to carry the sleeping child.

"No," Elin whispers. "No."

She's staring at the girl's narrow, pale face. Her hair is falling every which way, uncombed and tangled. Just as difficult to care for as always.

She's still a child, and now they're saying she's dead.

Vicky's gaze is defiant, as if she's being forced to look at the camera.

Elin wheels away from the television and steadies herself on the wall, not noticing that she's knocked an oil painting by Erland Cullberg. It falls to the floor.

"No, no, no," she moans. "Not like this. No . . . no . . ."

The last thing she'd heard of Vicky was her crying in the stairwell, and now she is dead.

"I don't want this!" she screams.

She walks over to the china cabinet with the heirloom Seder plate she inherited from her father. She grabs the upper edge of the cabinet and hurls it over with all her strength. Its glass front splinters and shards whirl over the parquet. The beautifully detailed Seder plate breaks into five pieces.

Elin doubles over and drops to the floor as a single thought churns in her mind. *I had a daughter. I had a daughter. I had a daughter.*

She sits up, takes a slice of the Seder plate, and drags its point across her wrist. Blood starts to run out, dripping down onto her knees. Elin makes a second cut, inhaling sharply from the pain. A key rattles in the front-door lock. Someone opens the door and comes in.

75

Joona is browning two thick ox fillets in a cast-iron skillet. He has tied up the meat and seasoned it with roughly ground black and green peppercorns. When the surfaces of the tournedos are glazed, he places them over sliced potatoes in a clay baking dish and salts them, then moves the dish into the oven. As the meat cooks, he makes a sauce of port, currants, veal stock, and truffles. Then he pours two glasses of a red Saint-Émilion.

The earthy aroma of the wine has spread through the kitchen when the doorbell rings.

Disa is there, wearing a red-and-white polka-dot raincoat. Her pupils are large and her face is damp from the rain.

"Joona, I'm going to test you and see if you are as good a detective as they say."

"How can you test that?"

"By asking you if I look normal."

"You're more beautiful than ever."

"That's not it." Disa smiles.

"You've cut your hair and you're wearing that barrette from Paris for the first time in more than a year."

"Anything else?"

Joona runs his eyes over her thin, blushing face, her shining hair, and her slim body.

"Those are new," he says, and points to her high-heeled shoes.

"Marc Jacobs. A little too expensive for me."

"They're nice."

"Anything else?"

"I'm not done yet," he says, and takes her hands in his, turns them over, and inspects her fingernails.

He can't help smiling as he says she's wearing the same lipstick as the time they went to Södra Theater. He gently touches her earrings and meets her eyes and rests his gaze there a moment. Then he moves so that the light from the floor lamp falls on her face.

"It's your eyes," he says. "Your left pupil is not shrinking in the light."

"Good detective," she says. "I've had my eye examined."

"Is there anything wrong?"

"The cornea has developed an astigmatism, but it's not anything I have to worry about."

Disa walks into the kitchen.

Joona says, "The food's almost ready. The meat just needs to rest."

"It smells wonderful," Disa says.

"It's been a long time since we saw each other last," Joona says. "I'm very happy that you've come."

They raise their glasses without saying a word. As always, when Joona looks at her, Disa feels as if she's starting to shimmer. She forces herself to look away from his eyes, then tilts the wine in her glass, sniffs the aroma, and tastes it again.

"Perfect temperature," she says.

Joona starts to arrange the meat and potatoes on a bed of arugula, basil, and thyme. He slowly pours the sauce over the plate as he thinks he should have talked with Disa long before now.

"How have you been?" he asks.

"Without you, you mean?" Disa says. "Pretty darn good."

There's silence at the table and she gently places her hand on his.

"I'm sorry," she says. "But I've been so angry with you. Especially when I'm my bad self."

"Who are you now?"

"My bad self."

Joona takes a sip of wine.

"I've been thinking about the past lately," he starts.

She smiles and raises an eyebrow. "Lately? You're always thinking about the past."

"I am?"

"Yes, you're thinking about it but you never talk about it."

"You're right, I . . ."

He falls silent and his gray eyes seem to shrink. Disa feels a shiver go down her back.

"You asked me here for dinner because we needed to talk," Disa says. "I had decided never to talk to you again. But now . . . Several months have gone by. And when you called—"

"Yes, because I—"

"You're screwing around with me, Joona."

"Disa, you can think of me however you want," Joona says gravely. "But I want you to know that I care . . . I care about you. I think of you all the time."

"I see," she says as she starts to get up without looking at him.

"It's something else. Something horrible, which—"

Joona watches her put on her polka-dot raincoat.

"Goodbye," Disa whispers.

"Disa, I need you." Joona is surprised to hear himself say these words. "You're the one that I want."

She's staring at him now. Her shining black bangs reach her eyelashes.

"What did you say?" she asks after a few seconds.

"You're the one that I want, Disa." He gets up from the table.

"Don't say that."

"I need you. I've needed you all this time," he says. "But I didn't want to put you in harm's way. I didn't want anything horrible to happen to you if we—"

"What could happen to me that is so horrible?"

"You could disappear," he says simply. He is holding her face between his hands.

"You are the one who disappears," she whispers.

"I'm not easily frightened," Joona says. "I'm talking about real events."

Disa goes up on her toes and kisses him on the mouth and stays to feel his warm breath on her face. He searches for her mouth and kisses her again and again until she parts her lips.

As they kiss, Joona unbuttons her raincoat and lets it fall to the floor.

"Disa," he whispers. He strokes her shoulders and slides his hands to her waist. He presses against her and breathes in her silky aroma. He kisses her collarbone and her throat and takes her gold necklace between his teeth. He kisses her chin and her soft, moist mouth.

He searches for her warm skin beneath her thin blouse. The small fasteners snap open. Her nipples are hard. She looks him in the eye then pulls him after her into the bedroom. Her blouse is open and her breasts are gleaming like polished porcelain.

They stop and kiss again. His hands stroke the small of her back, her ass, and then slip beneath the sheer cloth of her panties. Disa slowly draws away and feels warmth pulse in her body. She's already wet. Her cheeks are bright red and her hands tremble as she unbuttons his pants.

76

After breakfast, Disa is propped up in bed, drinking coffee and reading *The Times* on her iPad. Joona is taking a shower.

Yesterday, he decided he would skip going to the Nordic Museum to look at the Sami bridal crown made from braided roots. Sometimes he just had to be near the crown in order to remember his former, entirely different, life. Instead, he is with Disa. He didn't plan what had happened. Perhaps this was because Rosa Bergman's dementia has cut his last remaining tie to Summa and Lumi.

It has been more than twelve years.

He has to understand that he has nothing to be afraid of now.

Still, he knows he should have warned Disa earlier. He should have told her what frightens him so that she could decide for herself. He stands in the bedroom doorway and watches her, unnoticed, for a long time, then slips into the kitchen to call Holger Jalmert.

"I heard that Gunnarsson was being difficult," Holger says, amused. "I've had to promise him not to send you any copies of my reports."

"Are you allowed to talk to me?" asks Joona.

He moves his sandwich and coffee cup from the counter to the table and waves at Disa, who's reading her iPad with a wrinkled brow.

"Probably not," Holger says with a laugh.

"Were you able to look at the purse we found at the dam?" Joona asks.

"Yes, I've finished my examination. At the moment, I'm in my car on my way back to Umeå."

"Were there any notes or papers in the purse?"

"Only a receipt from Pressbyrån."

"A cell phone?"

"No, unfortunately."

"So what do we have?" Joona says as he lets his eyes rest on the gray sky above the rooftops.

Holger takes a deep breath and starts speaking as if he's reading aloud from a list: "There are traces of what is most probably blood on the purse. I cut out a sample and sent it to the National Forensic Laboratory. Some makeup—two different lipsticks and a stump of a kohl stick—a pink plastic barrette, a wallet with a skull on it, some cash, a photograph of Vicky herself, some kind of bike tool, a prescription bottle without its label, which I also sent to the National Lab. A few pills of diazepam. Two pens. And hidden in one of the purse pockets I found a table knife as sharp as a sushi knife."

"Nothing written at all? No names? No addresses?"

"No, that was everything."

Joona hears Disa's footsteps on the wooden floor behind him. He stays where he is. He shivers and a few seconds later he feels her soft lips on the back of his neck and her arms slip around his body.

She releases him and wanders off to take a shower. Joona sits at the kitchen table and dials the number for Solveig Sundström, the nurse responsible for the girls from Birgittagården. Maybe she knows what kind of medications Vicky took.

The phone rings eight times before it's picked up.

"Caroline here, answering an ugly telephone that was left on a chair."

"Is Solveig there?"

"I don't know where she is right now. Can I tell her who's calling?"

Caroline is the older girl. She's a head taller than Tuula. He remembers she had old injection scars on the insides of her elbows, but she seemed to have things together. She appeared intelligent.

"Is everything going all right for you girls?" he asks.

"You're the detective, right?"

"Yes, I am."

"Is it true that Vicky is dead?"

"Unfortunately it seems so," Joona replies.

"It feels strange," Caroline says.

"Do you know what kinds of medications she was prescribed?" Joona asks.

"You mean Vicky?"

"Right."

"I dunno, probably Eutrexa, but it's hard to believe—she was so thin."

"That's an antidepressant, right?"

"Yeah, I used to take it. Now I just take Imovane," Caroline says. "It's fucking nice not to have to take Eutrexa."

"What are its side effects?"

"Different for different people. I put on twenty-two pounds."

"Does it make you tired?" Joona asks. In his mind's eye, he sees the bloody sheets where Vicky slept.

"At first it's the opposite. All I had to do was start sucking on the pill and it took off like gangbusters. It creeps through your entire body and you get angry and yell. I threw my phone against the wall once and another time I ripped down the curtains in my room. After a while, it stops making you angry and does the opposite. It's like you have a warm blanket wrapped around you. You get tired and all you want to do is sleep."

"Do you know if Vicky was taking any other medications?"

"I imagine she was like the rest of us and held on to anything that worked—diazepam, Lyrica, Stesolid, Ketogan."

There's a voice in the background and Joona realizes the nurse has come into the room and seen Caroline talking on the phone.

"I'm going to report you for theft," the woman is saying.

"It rang and I answered," Caroline says. "It's for you, anyway. It's the detective on the line. You're a suspect in the murder of Miranda Eriksdotter."

"Don't be stupid," the nurse says. She takes the phone and clears her throat before saying, "Solveig Sundström."

"I'm Detective Inspector Joona Linna with the National Police and I'm investigating—"

The woman hangs up without a word and Joona doesn't bother to call back since he's already gotten the answer he wanted.

77

A white Opel pulls to a stop underneath the flat roof of the gas station. A woman in a light blue sweater gets out and stands at the pump while searching through her purse.

Ari Määtilainen turns his gaze back to the two thick grilled hot dogs on their bed of mashed potatoes with chili sauce and roasted onions. He glances up at the heavyweight motorcyclist waiting for his food and says mechanically that coffee and soft drinks are available at the opposite counter.

The zippers on the motorcyclist's leather jacket scrape against the glass counter as he leans over to take his food.

"*Danke,*" he says and then heads over to the coffee machine.

Ari turns up the volume on the radio. The woman in the blue sweater has walked away from the pump as it's filling the Opel's tank.

On the radio the news announcer is reporting developments in the recent kidnapping case: "The search for Vicky Bennet and Dante Abrahamsson has been called off. The Västernorrland police are not commenting, but sources have told us that they are feared to have drowned last Saturday. The police are being criticized for sending out a general bulletin. Radio Eko has been trying to reach the chief of the National Police, Carlos Eliasson, for a statement . . ."

"What the hell," Ari whispers.

He looks at the sticky note, which is still next to the cash register. He picks up his cell phone and calls the police again.

"Police, Sonja Rask speaking," a woman says.

"Hi," Ari says. "I saw them, the girl and the little boy."

"May I ask who is calling?"

"Ari Määtilainen. I work at Statoil gas station in Dingersjö. I was just listening to the radio and they said that the kids drowned on Saturday. But they didn't. I saw them here in the early-morning hours Sunday."

"You're talking about Vicky Bennet and Dante Abrahamsson?" asks Sonja skeptically.

"Yes, I saw them here. It was just after midnight, so it was already Sunday. They couldn't have drowned on Saturday and then showed up here on Sunday, right?"

"You're saying you saw Vicky Bennet and Dante Abrahamsson on Sunday?"

"That's right."

"Why didn't you call right away?"

"I *did* call, and I talked to a police officer."

Ari had listened to Radio Gold on Saturday evening. The general bulletin hadn't gone out yet, and the local news was asking the public to keep their eyes open for a girl and a little boy.

At eleven p.m., a long-haul truck parked in the lot behind the diesel pumps. The truck driver napped for three hours.

He saw them in the middle of the night, around two a.m.

Ari was looking at the monitor, which showed everything the security cameras were picking up outside. The picture changed and showed the long-haul truck from another angle. The gas station appeared deserted as the driver started the engine and the truck began to pull away. Then Ari noticed a figure at the back of the building, close to the car wash. He was surprised to see anyone, then realized that there were actually two figures. He stared at the screen. The truck was backing up and turning around. The truck's headlights shone into the window as it turned. Ari left his position behind the counter and ran around the building. The truck was on the exit ramp and the parking lot was empty. The girl and the little boy were gone.

78

Joona parks his car outside the Statoil gas station in Dingersjö, 360 kilometers north of Stockholm. It's a sunny day and the breeze is brisk. Ragged advertising flags are flapping in the wind.

Joona and Disa had been having lunch at Villa Källhagen when Joona received a call from a nervous Sonja Rask, the policewoman.

Now Joona is walking into the shop. A hollow-eyed man with a Statoil cap is placing paperback books in a rack. Joona looks at the menu over the counter and then at the hot dogs rotating on the grill.

"What would you like?" asks the man.

"*Makkarakeitto*," Joona answers in Finnish.

"*Suomalainen makkarakeitto*," Ari Määtilainen says with a smile. "My grandmother used to make sausage soup when I was a boy."

"With rye bread on the side?" asks Joona.

"Yes indeed. But here there's only Swedish food," he says, gesturing to the hot dogs and hamburgers.

"Well, I'm not really here to eat. I'm from the police," Joona says.

"I realized that. I talked to one of your colleagues the night I saw them," Ari says and points at the monitor for the security cameras.

"What did you see that made you call?"

"A girl and a little boy at the back of the building."

"You saw them on the screen?"

"Right."

"Clearly?"

"Well, I'm used to keeping an eye open."

"Did the police come here that night?"

"This guy Gunnarsson stopped by the next morning and didn't think there was much to the video. He told me I could erase it."

"But you didn't."

"What do you think?"

"I imagine you've kept a copy on an external hard drive."

Ari Määtilainen smiles and shows Joona to the minuscule office beside the storage area. A sofa bed is open and some empty cans of Red Bull are lying on the floor. A carton of milk is standing in the frosty window. On a school desk, there's a laptop computer connected to an external hard drive. Ari Määtilainen sits down on a plastic chair and quickly goes through the files.

"I'd heard on the radio that everyone was looking for a girl and a little boy, and this is what I saw in the middle of the night," he says as he opens a file.

Joona leans forward to get a better look. There are four small squares showing the inside and outside of the gas station. A counter in the corner of each square ticks away the time. The gray pictures don't move. Ari is sitting behind the counter. Every once in a while, he turns the page of a newspaper and eats an onion ring.

"This long-haul truck was there for three hours," Ari tells Joona. He points at one of the pictures. "Now it's about to move."

They see a dark shadow in the driver's seat.

"Can you enlarge the picture?" asks Joona.

"Just a moment."

A grove of trees is suddenly lit up by the headlights of the truck. Sensors outside detect motion and banks of lights go on.

Ari points at the second exterior picture and changes it to full screen.

"You can see them here," he whispers.

The long-haul truck is starting to roll forward. Ari points at the back of the gas station with the garbage bins and the recycling boxes. There are many shadows and it's still. Then there's movement next to the black glass of the entrance to the car wash. A small figure appears—a thin being pressed against the wall.

The picture is grainy and flickers. It's hard to make out the face or other details. However, it's obviously a girl. And now there's something else.

"Can you make the picture clearer?" asks Joona.

"Just wait," Ari whispers.

The long-haul truck is turning toward the exit ramp. Light floods the door beside the figures and the glass turns blinding white for a second. Then the entire back of the gas station building is bathed in light.

Joona can see that it definitely is a thin girl standing there with a child. They're looking at the long-haul truck. Then they turn black again.

Ari points at the screen as both figures run along the dark gray wall and disappear from the picture.

"You saw them?" Ari asks.

"Can you show it to me again?"

Ari moves the cursor back to where the two figures are briefly lit up. He plays the video extremely slowly.

It appears that the long-haul truck is barely moving. In jerks, the light goes from the grove of trees, over the back wall of the station, and starts to fill the windows with white light.

The smaller child is looking down and its face is in shadow. The thin girl is barefoot and it looks like she is carrying plastic bags in both hands. The headlights reach them and the girl starts to lift her hand.

Joona sees that she's not carrying plastic bags. Her wrists are wrapped in bandages that have partially come undone and are hanging loosely and swaying in the light. Vicky Bennet and Dante Abrahamsson did not drown in the river.

The digital clock says 2:14 a.m.

Somehow, the two children managed to get out of the car and cross the river. They reached the other shore and traveled seventy-two kilometers farther south.

Hair hangs in tangled strands over the girl's face. Her dark eyes shine and then the two figures move out of the frame.

They're alive, Joona thinks. *They're both still alive.*

79

The head of the National Criminal Investigation Department, Carlos Eliasson, is standing with his back to the door on purpose as Joona walks into his office.

"Sit down," Carlos says with odd expectation in his voice.

"I've just driven here from Sundsvall and—"

"Just a moment," Carlos interrupts.

Joona looks at his back, wondering what's up with Carlos, and then sits down in the leather chair. He lets his eyes wander over the polished desktop, where reflections from the aquarium are shining.

Carlos takes a deep breath and turns around. He looks different. He's unshaven. There's gray-speckled stubble on his upper lip and jaws.

"So, what do you say?"

"You're growing a beard."

"A full beard," Carlos says contentedly. "Well, I think it will thicken up soon. I'm never going to shave again. I've tossed my razor in the trash."

"Nice."

"But I gather you're not here to talk about my beard," Carlos says. "The diver did not find any bodies in the river."

"No," Joona says. He pulls out the print of the security camera picture. "We didn't find the bodies—"

"Here it comes," Carlos mumbles to himself.

"—because there were no bodies in the river."

"And you're sure about that?"

"Vicky Bennet and Dante Abrahamsson are still alive."

"Gunnarsson has already called me about the security film from the gas station and I—"

"Put out a new general bulletin."

"Are you shitting me? You just can't turn a general bulletin on and off like a light switch!"

"Vicky Bennet and Dante Abrahamsson are clearly the children in this picture," Joona says. He points at the printout. "This was taken several hours after the car accident. They are alive and we have to send out another general bulletin!"

Carlos sticks out one of his legs. "Put the Spanish boot on me if you have to," he says, "but there is no way in hell I'm issuing another general bulletin."

"Look at the picture," Joona says.

"The Västernorrland police department went to the gas station today, too," Carlos says. He folds the picture until it is a small, tight square. "They sent a copy of the hard disk to the National Forensic Lab and two of their best people have taken a look and are in agreement. They say it is impossible to definitively identify the people outside the gas station."

"But you know I'm right."

"Okay," Carlos says. "Let's say you're right. You turn out to be right in the end, but I am not going to make a fool of myself and put out another general bulletin for people the police believe are dead."

"I'm not going to give up—"

"Wait a second, just wait a second," Carlos says. He takes a deep breath. "Joona, the internal investigation against you has gone higher up the chain. The head prosecutor has it on his desk."

"But it is—"

"I am your boss. I am taking this report against you extremely seriously, and I want to hear from you that you understand that you are not leading the preliminary investigation in Sundsvall."

"I am not leading the preliminary investigation."

"And what does an observer do if the head prosecutor in Sundsvall chooses to end the investigation?"

"Nothing."

"Then we're agreed." Carlos smiles.

"Not at all," Joona says as he gets up and walks out.

80

Flora lies in her bed and stares at the ceiling. Her heart is thumping. She woke up dreaming that she was in a small room with a girl who did not want to show her face. The girl was hiding behind a wooden ladder. Something was wrong with her. She was wearing only white cotton panties and Flora could see her little breasts. She waited for Flora to come nearer and then she turned away, giggling and hiding her face in her hands.

That evening, Flora had read about the murders of Miranda Eriksdotter and Elisabet Grim in the newspaper. Now she can't stop thinking about the ghost who visited her. It already feels like a dream, although she knows she saw the dead girl in the hallway. She didn't seem to be more than five years old, but in this dream, the girl was the same age as Miranda.

Flora lies quietly and listens. Every creak in the apartment makes her heart beat harder. People who are scared of the dark are not in charge of their own homes. Fear sneaks through and alerts them to the slightest movement. Flora doesn't know where she is supposed to go. It's quarter to eight. She gets up and opens her bedroom door and listens to the sounds of the apartment. No one else is awake yet.

She sneaks to the kitchen to start the coffee for Hans-Gunnar. The rising sun is casting a few rays on the scratched countertop. Flora takes out an unbleached filter and puts it into the basket. When she hears footsteps behind her, she is terrified.

She turns and sees Ewa standing in the doorway to her bedroom. She's only wearing a blue T-shirt and panties. She catches sight of Flora and comes down the hall.

"What's going on?" Ewa asks when she sees Flora's face. "Have you been crying?"

"I . . . I have to know. I think I've seen a ghost," Flora says. "Have you seen her? A little girl here at home?"

"What is wrong with you, Flora?"

Ewa turns to go into the living room, but Flora places a hand on her strong arm to stop her.

"But it's true . . . I'm telling you the truth. Someone had hit her with a rock on the back of her head—"

"You're telling the truth?" Ewa interrupts sharply.

"I was just . . . Perhaps there really are ghosts?"

Ewa grabs one of Flora's ears and drags her around.

"I can't understand why you insist on lying, but you do," Ewa says. "You always have and you always will."

"But I saw—"

"Shut up!" Ewa says and twists Flora's ear.

"Ow!"

"We don't tolerate lying in this household!"

"Let go! Ow!"

Ewa gives Flora's ear one more twist and then releases her grip. Flora stands there a few moments with tears in her eyes and one hand on her burning ear. Then she starts the coffee machine and returns to her room. She shuts the door behind her, turns on the bedside light, and sits on her bed for a good cry.

She's always thought that mediums just pretended that they saw spirits.

"I don't understand anything," she whispers.

What if she's really called out the spirits by doing séances? Maybe it didn't matter whether she believes in them or not. When she called them and built a circle of participants to welcome them, perhaps the door to the other side did open and the ones waiting could just come in.

Because I really saw a ghost.

I saw the dead girl as a child.

Miranda wanted to show me something.

It's not impossible. It must happen sometimes. She's read that the body's energy does not completely disappear on death. Many people believe in ghosts without being considered mentally ill. Flora tries to collect her thoughts and go through what happened the past few days.

The girl came to me in a dream. I know I've dreamed about her, but when I saw her in the hall, I was awake. That was real. I saw her in front of me and she was speaking. She was actually there.

Flora lies down, closes her eyes, and thinks that maybe she passed out when she tripped and hit her head on the floor.

There was a pair of jeans on the floor between the tub and the toilet.

I was afraid, I was startled, and I fell.

She must have been unconscious and dreamed of the girl in the hallway.

That's what happened.

She closes her eyes and smiles to herself. Then she notices a strange smell in her room—the odor of burned hair.

There's something under her pillow. She sits up and shivers then picks up the pillow. The large, sharp rock is lying on her white sheet.

"Why aren't you closing your eyes?" a voice says.

The girl is standing in the dark, behind the lamp on her nightstand, and is looking straight at Flora. She's not breathing. Her hair is sticky and black from dried blood. The light from the lamp interferes with her view, but Flora can see that the girl's thin arms are gray and her brown veins look like a rusty network beneath her dead skin.

"You're not supposed to look at me," the girl says, and turns off the light. It's completely dark and Flora falls off the bed. Light blue spots dance in front of her eyes. The lamp drops to the floor beside her and she can hear the rustle of bedclothes and the sound of naked feet running across the floor, the walls, the ceiling. Flora crawls to the door and pulls herself to her feet. She fumbles with the door handle and stumbles into the hall, her lips clamped to keep from screaming. She walks down the hall, holding the wall so she doesn't fall over. Panting hard, Flora grabs the telephone from the hallway table but drops it on the floor. She crouches down and calls the police.

81

Robert had found Elin on her knees next to the smashed china cabinet.

"Elin, what is going on?"

Without looking at him, she'd climbed to her feet and started walking over the shards of glass en route to her office.

"You're bleeding!"

Elin had glanced impassively at her cut-up left hand, and kept going. He'd offered to call her doctor. "No, I don't want him to come. I don't care."

"Elin," Robert protested, agitated. "You need help."

Elin had studied her wrist again, and admitted that it might be wise to have it bandaged. Then she'd walked into her office, drops of blood marking her path, and she'd shut her door.

Now, she was in front of her computer, searching for the phone number of the National Police. She asked the operator to put her through to the person responsible for the investigation into the murders at Birgittagården.

A man with a high voice answered. "The preliminary investigation is being headed by the prosecutor's office in Sundsvall," he said.

"Is there a police officer I can speak with?"

"The prosecutor's office is working with the Västernorrland police department."

"I was visited by a detective inspector from the National Police. A tall man with gray eyes and—"

"Joona Linna."

"Yes."

The man read a number and Elin scribbled it on the glossy cover of a fashion magazine. She thanked him for his help and ended the call. She dialed the number for the detective, but he did not pick up, and she couldn't figure out a message to leave, so she left none.

Elin was about to call the Sundsvall prosecutor's office when her doctor arrived. The doctor didn't ask her any questions. He had known her since childhood and knew quite well when a conversation was over. Elin sat quietly as he cleaned and wrapped her wound. She looked at her cell phone, which was lying on the August issue of British *Vogue*. Right between Gwyneth Paltrow's breasts was Joona Linna's number.

By the time the doctor had finished and Elin returned to the large salon, the cleaning service had removed all the glass and mopped the floor. The china cabinet had been removed and Robert had spoken to the restorer at the Mediterranean Museum about the broken Seder plate.

82

Elin Frank is not smiling at anyone as she walks down the hall to Joona Linna's office at the police station. Her graphite-gray coat from Burberry is tightly belted and there is a silver silk scarf around her hair. She hides her eyes behind black sunglasses and her wrapped wrist under a long gray cashmere sweater. The wrist throbs. Her heels clack against the scratched floor, and a poster reading IF YOU BELIEVE YOU'RE WORTHLESS AND DESERVE THE BRUISES, COME TALK TO US! flutters in her wake.

A powerfully built woman wearing a bright red angora sweater and a tight black skirt comes out of an office to wait for Elin.

"I'm Anja Larsson," the woman says.

Elin tries to say that she wants to speak to Joona Linna, but her voice won't come out. The large woman smiles at her and offers to show Elin to the detective's office.

"I'm sorry," Elin whispers.

"Not to worry," Anja says. She leads Elin to Joona's door, knocks, and opens it. Anja and Joona exchange a glance, and Joona gently pulls out a chair for Elin.

"I'll bring you some water," says Anja, and closes the door behind her.

The room is silent. Elin tries to calm down enough to be able to speak. She has to wait for a long time. Finally she says, "I know it's too late. I know I wasn't helpful when you came to see me a few days ago. I can just imagine what you think of me."

She can't go on. Tears start streaming down her face from behind her sunglasses. Anja comes in with a glass of water and a bunch of grapes on a tray and leaves again.

Elin collects her thoughts. "I would like to talk about Vicky Bennet now."

"Then I will listen," Joona says in a friendly way.

"She was just six years old when she first came to me and I had her . . . I had her for only nine months."

"I know that."

"What you don't know is that I . . . I let her down. No one should disappoint another human being the way that I disappointed her."

"Sometimes people do that," Joona says.

She takes off her sunglasses and studies the detective sitting across from her: his tousled blond hair, his serious face, and his eyes that mysteriously shift color.

"I can't excuse my own behavior," she says. "But I have an offer for you. I am ready to pay all the costs for finding the bodies . . . so that the investigation can continue and not be shut down."

"Why would you want to do that?"

"Even if things can't be made right, I can . . . I mean . . . What if she's not guilty?"

"There's no evidence pointing that way at the moment."

"No, but I just can't believe that . . ."

Elin's eyes fill until it seems that the whole world is swimming in water.

"Because she was a sweet and good child?"

"She was hardly sweet and good." Elin smiles faintly.

"So I gather."

"Would you be able to continue the investigation if I pay you?"

"We can't take your money."

"I'll find a way to solve the legal issues."

"Maybe so, but that won't change a thing," Joona explains softly. "The prosecutor is ending the investigation."

"What can I do?" asks Elin.

"I am not supposed to say anything, but I will continue the investigation myself because I am absolutely sure that Vicky is still alive."

"But the news on television said—" Elin's hand flies to her mouth.

"I know for a fact that they did not drown in the river," Joona replies.

"Good Lord," whispers Elin.

83

Elin is crying with her face turned away. Joona gives her time. He walks to the window and looks out. A misty rain is falling and the trees are swaying in the afternoon wind.

"Do you have any idea where they could be hiding?" Joona asks after a few minutes have passed.

"Her mother used to sleep in various garages. I did meet Susie once when she was going to try to take care of Vicky one weekend. She'd gotten a place to live in Hallonbergen, but it didn't work out. Vicky was found in the subway tunnel all by herself between the Slussen and Maria-torget stations."

"It could be hard to find her," Joona says.

"I haven't seen Vicky in nine years, but the staff at Birgittagården, they must have talked to her. They have to know something," Elin says.

"I agree," Joona says.

"So what's wrong?"

Joona looks her in the eye. "The only people Vicky talked to were the nurse who was murdered and her husband, who was the therapist. He should know a great deal—or at least something—but mentally he's not well at all and his doctors think that a police interrogation will worsen his condition. We can't do anything."

"But I am not a police officer," Elin says. "I could speak to him."

She keeps looking him in the eye and realizes that this is exactly what he's been hoping she'd say.

Going down in the elevator, Elin feels the heavy exhaustion that comes after prolonged crying. She remembers the detective's voice and his soft Finnish accent. He had unusual eyes, gray and oddly sharp.

His colleague in the red sweater had called the provincial hospital in Sundsvall and found out that Daniel Grim had been moved to the psychiatric ward and that his doctor was still forbidding the police to interview him.

Elin crosses the street and gets into her BMW. She calls the number for the hospital that she's been given and finds out that Daniel Grim is in Ward 52A but that he's not allowed to receive phone calls in his room. However, he can receive visitors daily until six p.m.

She puts the address into her car's GPS, which calculates that it is 407 kilometers from here to Sundsvall. If she starts driving right now, she'll get there at a quarter to seven. She turns around at Polhemsgatan, her tires mounting the sidewalk, and drives down Fleminggatan.

When she reaches the first traffic light, Robert calls her to remind her that she has a meeting with Kinnevik and Sven Warg in thirty minutes at the Waterfront Expo.

"I won't be able to make it."

"Shall I tell them to start without you?"

"Robert, I don't know when I will be back, but it won't be today," Elin says.

When she reaches the E4, she sets the cruise control to precisely twenty-nine kilometers over the speed limit. She doesn't mind paying a fine, but it would be ridiculous to lose her driver's license.

84

Joona feels deep down that Vicky Bennet and the little boy are still alive. He can't give up on them now.

A girl who once slashed two people in the face with a broken bottle has taken a tiny boy from his mother and is hiding somewhere with him. The police have concluded that they are dead. No one is looking for them.

Joona thinks about where he is in the investigation now he's seen Vicky and the boy on the security camera video. He knows that Vicky has taken Eutrexa, and he's checked on the side effects of this medicine with The Needle's wife, who works as a psychiatrist.

There's too much that's still not known, Joona thinks. It is possible that Vicky was suffering from an overdose of Eutrexa. Caroline had told him that the medicine starts to work when a person still has the pill in his or her mouth, inducing restlessness and anger.

Joona closes his eyes and tries to imagine Vicky demanding the keys from Elisabet. She threatens Elisabet with a hammer. Elisabet flees across the yard to the old brewery. Vicky follows and flies into a rage and hits Elisabet again and again. Then she takes the keys from the dead woman, crosses the yard still carrying the hammer, picks up a rock, and opens the door to the isolation room. Miranda is sitting on a chair with a blanket around her. Vicky smashes her head repeatedly with the rock. She carries Miranda's body to her bed and puts her hands over her face. Then her rage dies down.

Vicky must have become confused, Joona thinks. She took the bloody blanket with her and hid it beneath her bed as the drug's calming effect began to work. She probably felt unbelievably tired. All she did after that was kick off the boots into the closet, put the hammer under her pillow, and fall sleep. She woke up a few hours later, realized what she'd done, and became frightened. She fled through the window and headed straight into the forest.

The side effects of the medicine could explain her rage as well as the bloody sheets.

But what did she do with the rock? Had there really been a rock?

Joona feels the tug of doubt—for the second time in his life, he wonders if The Needle could be wrong.

85

At five minutes to six, Elin walks through the door to Ward 52A. She greets a nursing assistant and says that she's here to see Daniel Grim.

"Visiting hours are over," the woman says, and walks away.

"I've driven the whole way from Stockholm," Elin pleads.

The nurse turns and looks at her. "If we make an exception for everyone, we'll be running around twenty-four hours a day," she says.

"Please, just let me—"

"You won't even have time to drink a cup of coffee."

"That doesn't matter," Elin insists.

The nurse looks at Elin doubtfully, but then nods to Elin to follow her. She goes down the hall and knocks on the door of a patient's room to the right.

"Thanks," Elin says, and waits until the nurse leaves before she walks in.

Standing by the window is a man with an ashen face. He hasn't shaved this morning and perhaps not the day before, either. He's wearing jeans and a wrinkled shirt. He looks at her with a slight frown and runs his hand through his thin hair.

"My name is Elin Frank," Elin says softly. "I know I'm disturbing you and I apologize in advance."

"No, it's . . . it's . . ."

He appears to have been crying, crying for many days. In a different context, Elin might have thought he was handsome. He has a friendly face and intelligent eyes.

"I need to talk to you, but I understand if you're not up to it," she says.

"It's all right," he says in a voice that sounds as if it will break at any moment. "The reporters kept coming by the first days, but I couldn't speak . . . I couldn't handle talking to them. There was nothing I could say. I mean, I wanted to help the police, but I couldn't make it work. I couldn't get my thoughts together . . ."

Elin tries to think of a way to bring up the subject of Vicky. She understands that Vicky is a monster as far as he is concerned. She's ruined his life. It won't be easy to make him want to help out.

"Do you mind if I ask you a few things?"

"Honestly, I don't know." Daniel rubs his face.

"Daniel, I'm very sorry about what happened to you."

He whispers a thank-you. Then he looks up and says, "I just said thank you for your sympathy, but I really don't understand what happened. I was worried about Elisabet's heart . . . and . . ."

The light leaves his face, which turns inward and ashen again.

"I truly can't comprehend what happened to you," Elin says quietly.

"I have my own psychologist now," he says. He tries to smile but can't. "I never thought I'd need my own psychologist. He listens to me. He listens and waits while I cry like a baby. I feel . . . You know, he won't let the police talk to me. I would have made the same decision if I were in his place. At the same time, I know myself . . . It wouldn't hurt me to talk. I should tell him I can talk to them . . . not that I know if I'd be of any real help."

"It's probably good to listen to your psychologist," she says.

"Do I sound that confused?" he asks.

"No, but . . ."

"Sometimes I remember something that I think I should tell the police, but I immediately forget what it is. It's strange. I can't keep my thoughts straight. It's as if I am absolutely exhausted."

"I'm sure things will get better again."

He rubs his finger under his nose. Then he looks at her.

"Did you tell me which newspaper you're working for?"

She shakes her head and says, "I'm here because Vicky Bennet lived with me when she was six years old."

86

The room in the psychiatric ward is quiet. Elin can hear steps in the hallway. Daniel is blinking behind his glasses as if he is trying to take in what Elin has just said.

"I heard about her on the news . . . the car and the boy," he whispers.

"I know," she says, keeping her voice low. "But if she is still alive, where would she be hiding?"

"Why do you ask?"

"I don't know. Maybe I want to know the people that she trusted."

He studies her for a second and then says, "You don't believe she's dead, do you?"

"No, I don't," she says quietly.

"You don't believe it because you don't want to believe it," he says. "Do you have any proof that she didn't drown in the river?"

"Please don't be afraid," Elin says. "But we are fairly sure that she and the boy escaped from the car."

"We?"

"A detective inspector and me."

"I don't understand. Why do they say she drowned, if she—"

"Most of the police involved in the case do think that they drowned, and they've stopped looking for her and for the boy."

"But not you?"

"Maybe I'm the only person in the world who cares about Vicky right now just because she's Vicky," Elin says. She can't manage to smile at him and she can't keep her voice gentle any longer.

"And now you want my help to find her?"

"Maybe she will hurt the boy," Elin says. "Maybe she will hurt other people."

"Well, I don't believe that," Daniel says. For the first time, he looks at Elin with an open face. "In the beginning, I said I doubted that she'd killed Miranda. I still can't believe that she would . . ." Daniel mumbles something.

"What did you just say?" Elin asks.

"What?"

"You just whispered something to yourself."

"I don't believe Vicky killed Elisabet."

"You don't?"

"I've worked with troubled girls for many years and I, well, it doesn't fit."

"But—"

"During my time as a therapist, I've met many girls who have dark souls, girls who could kill, who—"

"But not Vicky."

"No, not Vicky."

Elin smiles widely and feels her eyes filling with tears. She struggles to bring her emotions back under control.

"You've got to explain this to the police," she says.

"I already did. They know that, in my opinion, Vicky is not violent. Of course, I could be wrong," Daniel says, rubbing his eyes.

"Can you help me?"

"Did you say Vicky lived with you for six years?"

"No, I said she was six years old when she lived with me," she replies. "What would you like me to do?"

"I have to find her, Daniel. You spoke to her for hours. You must know about her friends, boyfriends, anyone."

"Maybe . . . We talked about group dynamics for the most part and . . . I'm sorry, I'm having difficulty keeping my train of thought."

"Please try."

"I met her at least once a day . . . I don't know for sure, perhaps twenty-five conversations. Vicky, she is . . . The danger with Vicky is that she drifts away in her thoughts. What I would be worrying about is that she might just leave the boy somewhere. In the middle of the road, perhaps."

"Where would she be hiding? Did she have any family? I mean, anyone she particularly liked?"

87

The door to Daniel's room swings open and the assistant nurse enters with his medication for the evening. She stops abruptly when she sees Elin.

"What is this?" she says. "You were only supposed to be here for five minutes."

"I know," Elin says. "But there was something important we had to—"

"It is six thirty," she interrupts.

"I'm sorry," Elin says, and she turns to Daniel. "Where should I start my search?"

"Get out," the nurse orders.

"Please," Elin says, and folds her hands as if in prayer. "I do need to talk to Daniel."

"Are you deaf?" the nurse says. "I told you to get out!"

The nurse swears and leaves the room. Elin touches Daniel's arm.

"Vicky must have talked about places or friends."

"Yes, that's true. I can't think of anything, however. I'm really having trouble—"

"Please try."

"I know I'm completely useless, but . . ." He rubs his forehead hard.

"The other girls, they must know something about Vicky."

"Yes, they should. Caroline maybe."

A man in a white shirt and pants strides into the room. The nurse is right behind him.

"Please follow me," the man says.

"One more minute," Elin pleads.

"Right now," he barks.

"Please," Elin says, her eyes pleading. "It's about my daughter."

"Come with me now," he says, but his tone is milder.

Elin's mouth is trembling as she sinks to her knees in front of them.

"Just a few more minutes," she begs.

"If we have to, we'll drag you out."

"Now that's enough of this," Daniel says, and he helps Elin up from the floor.

The nurse protests. "She is not supposed to be here after six o'clock!"

"Shut up!" Daniel roars. He takes Elin by the arm and leads her from the room. "We'll talk in the foyer or the parking lot."

They walk down the hallway and keep going even as they hear steps behind them.

"I plan to go to Birgittagården to talk to the girls," Elin says.

"They're not there. They've been evacuated."

"Where to?"

He holds the glass door for her and follows her to the landing by the elevator.

"To an old fishing village north of Hudiksvall."

Elin presses the elevator call button. "Will they let me in?"

"If I go there with you, they will," he says.

88

Elin and Daniel drive away from the hospital, neither one of them saying a word. As she pulls onto the E4, she gets out her cell phone and
calls Joona Linna.

"Sorry to bother you," she says, her voice tinged with despair.

"You can call me whenever you want," Joona says. His tone is
friendly.

"I'm in my car with Daniel Grim and he doesn't believe that Vicky
did those horrible things," Elin explains quickly.

"Even though all the technical evidence points to her."

"It can't be true. Daniel says that she's not violent," Elin says.

"She can become violent," Joona says.

"You don't know her!" Elin erupts.

Joona says nothing for a few seconds. Then he says calmly, "Ask
Daniel about Eutrexa. It's a drug."

"Eutrexa?"

Daniel looks at Elin.

"Ask him about side effects," Joona says before hanging up.

Elin drives quickly back along the coast, heading toward the forest.

"What side effects does Eutrexa have?" she asks.

"A person can become extremely aggressive if he or she takes an
overdose," Daniel says matter-of-factly.

"Was Vicky prescribed this drug?"

Daniel nods and Elin says nothing.

"It is a good drug," Daniel tries to explain, but then he falls silent.

Almost all the light from the headlights is swallowed by the trees at the edge of the forest. The shadows overlap until there is nothing but darkness.

"Did you notice that you said Vicky was your daughter?"

"Yes, I know," Elin says. "It just came out."

"She was your daughter for a little while."

"Yes, she was," Elin says, keeping her eyes on the road.

They drive past the vast Armsjön Lake. It gleams like cast iron in the darkness.

Daniel takes a deep breath. "I was trying to think of something Vicky said when she first arrived but now I can't remember it. Oh yes, she said she had some friends from Chile who had a house . . ."

He falls silent and looks out the passenger-side window. There are tears on his cheeks.

"Elisabet and I were hoping to go to Chile and then there was the huge earthquake . . ."

He takes a deep breath, but sits quietly with his hands in his lap.

"You were talking about Vicky," Elin says.

"That's right. Where was I?"

"You said she had friends from Chile."

"Yes."

"They had a house somewhere."

"Did I say that?"

"Yes."

"Damn it," he mumbles. "What is wrong with me? That is . . . Maybe I should have stayed at the hospital. This is kind of crazy."

Elin smiles weakly at him. "I'm glad that you didn't."

89

They leave the highway at Jättendal and head toward the coast on a single-lane road that takes them past old farmhouses and falling-down barns and then back into the dark forest. Where the road ends, there's a cluster of houses in Falun red and before them the opalescent eternity of the sea. The midsummer pole is still standing in the village, its birch leaves and flowers now brown and hanging loose. A large wooden house with a beautiful glass-enclosed veranda faces the water. Once a country store, for several years now it has been owned by the company that manages Brigittagården.

Elin steers the car slowly between the fence posts and parks. As she undoes her seat belt, Daniel warns, "You have to be prepared for these girls. They've had rough lives." He pushes his glasses high on his nose. "They're going to provoke you. They like to test the boundaries."

"I'll be fine," Elin says. "I was a teenager once, too."

"This is something completely different," Daniel says. "It's not always easy, not even for me. They can be really terrible at times."

"So what do you say when they try to provoke you?" asks Elin. She looks him in the eye.

"The best thing is to be as honest and clear as possible."

"I'll keep that in mind." Elin opens the car door.

"Wait, there's one more thing before we go in. They have a security guard there. I think that he should accompany you the entire time."

Elin smiles. "Isn't that a bit excessive?"

"Well, I don't know. Maybe. I mean, you don't have to be afraid, but I think—I know that you shouldn't be alone with two of the girls. Not even for a short time."

"Which ones?"

"Almira and a little girl named Tuula."

"Are they that dangerous?"

He holds up a hand. "I'm just saying I would like the guard to be there if you want to talk to them."

"Okay."

"Don't worry," he says, trying to calm her. "They can also be quite nice, all of them."

The air is cool and carries with it the scent of the sea. Elin pauses after she locks the car.

"One of the girls must know about Vicky's friends," she says.

"Even if one of them does, you can't assume that she'll want to tell you."

A path of black slate leads around the gable and to the front steps. Elin's red heels keep getting caught between the stones. It's late in the evening, but one girl is lying in the hammock next to the lilac tree, smoking. Her pale face and tattooed arms shine in the darkness.

"Hey, Daniel," the girl says, and smiles. She sits up and tosses the cigarette onto the grass.

"Hello, Almira," Daniel says.

"Hello," Elin says, smiling.

Almira stares directly at Elin but does not smile back. Her dark eyebrows meet over her large nose and her cheeks are peppered with acne.

"Vicky beat his wife to death," Almira says. "And when Elisabet was dead, she killed Miranda, too. I don't think she's going to stop until we're all dead."

Almira gets out of the hammock and walks up the stairs and into the house.

90

Elin and Daniel follow Almira into the small kitchen. Lu Chu and Indie are sitting at a pine table in the adjacent dining room, eating ice cream right from the carton while flipping through old comic books.

"Good thing you're here," Indie says when she sees Daniel. "You've got to talk to Tuula. She's sick in the head. I think she needs to go back on her meds."

"Where is Solveig?" asks Daniel.

"She had to go somewhere," Almira says, and takes a spoon from a drawer.

"When did she leave?" asks Daniel with skepticism in his voice.

"Right after dinner," Lu Chu mumbles without looking up from her comic book.

"So there's just the security guard here?"

"Anders. He was only here the first and second nights."

"What are you telling me?" Daniel says. "Are you girls all on your own?"

Almira shrugs and starts to eat the ice cream.

"Tell me," Daniel says.

"Solveig is supposed to come back," Indie says.

"But it's eight in the evening!" Daniel says. He pulls out his cell phone and calls the health company. He is given a complaint number, but no one replies. He leaves an irritated message saying there must always be competent staff on the grounds. They can't cut costs—they have responsibilities.

While Daniel is talking on the phone, Elin watches the girls. Almira is sitting in the lap of a cute girl with East Asian looks, who also has acne all over her face. While she's flipping through an old *Mad* magazine, she keeps kissing Almira on the neck.

"Almira," Elin says. "Do you have any idea where Vicky might be hiding?"

"No idea," Almira says, and sucks on her spoon.

"Vicky is fucking dead," Indie says. "Didn't you hear? She killed herself and that little boy."

"Shit!" Lu Chu exclaims. She points right at Elin. "I recognize you! Aren't you, like, the richest woman in Sweden?"

"Cut it out," Daniel says.

"Fuck! I swear!" Lu Chu says, and drums on the table. Then she yells right at Elin. "Give me some money!"

"Please lower your voice," Daniel says.

"I only said I recognized her. I can say that, right?"

"Yes, you can say what you want," Daniel says.

"We just want to ask if you have any idea where Vicky might be hiding," Elin says.

"She kept to herself," Daniel says. "But you girls had the chance to talk to her. You don't have to be best friends to know something about another person. For example, I know the name of your former boyfriend, Indie."

"We got back together," Indie says with a grin.

"When did that happen?" asks Daniel.

"I called him yesterday. We talked for a long time," she said.

"Wonderful. I'm happy for you," Daniel says with a smile.

"Those last few days, Vicky tended to hang with Miranda," Indie says.

"And with Caroline," adds Daniel.

"Because they had All Day Lifestyle classes together," Indie replies.

"Who is Caroline?" asks Elin.

"She's one of the older girls," Daniel says. "She also was in a class called Life Training with Vicky."

"I don't get how anyone could care about Vicky," Almira says. "She slaughtered Miranda like a pig."

"That's not completely clear," Elin tries to say.

"Not completely clear?" Almira raises her voice. "You should have seen her! She was really fucking dead! There was blood all over the place!"

"Please don't shout," Daniel asks.

"Well, what the fuck are we supposed to say? Are we supposed to pretend that nothing ever happened?" Indie yells. "Are we going to pretend that Miranda is still alive? That Elisabet is still alive? Or what?"

"I only meant—"

"You weren't fucking there!" Almira screams. "Vicky turned Elisabet's head to applesauce with a fucking hammer! You act like she's still alive!"

"Please try to speak one at a time," Daniel says, doing his best to keep his composure.

Indie holds up a hand as if she's in school. "Elisabet was a fucking drug addict! I hate drug addicts and I—"

Almira grins. "Because your mother overdosed."

"I don't give a fuck about Elisabet! She can burn in hell for all I care!" Indie says.

"How can you say something like that?" asks Elin.

"We heard her screaming that night," Lu Chu lies. "She called for help for a long, long time. We just stayed in bed and listened to her scream."

"She screamed and screamed," Almira says, smiling.

Daniel has turned away from them. The girls stop talking. Daniel says nothing and eventually he dries his face with his sleeve.

"You realize that it's a rotten thing to do, to talk like that," he says finally.

"But it's fun," Almira says.

"Do you really think so?"

"I sure do!"

"You, too, Lu Chu?"

Lu Chu shrugs.

"You don't know?"

"No, I don't."

"We've talked about situations like this," he says.

"Okay. I'm sorry. It was a rotten thing to say."

Daniel tries to smile reassuringly at Lu Chu, but it only makes him look unbearably sad.

"Where is Caroline?" asks Elin.

"In her room," Lu Chu answers.

Elin asks, "Can you show us the way?"

91

Lu Chu leads them down the ice-cold hall between the living room and the dining room with its glassed-in veranda facing the water. Beyond the living room, a second hall leads to the bedrooms. Lu Chu points out her room and Tuula's room then stops in front of a door that has a colorful small porcelain bell hanging from the handle.

"Here's where Caroline sleeps," she says.

"Thank you," Elin says.

"It's getting late," Daniel says. "Why don't you brush your teeth and get ready for bed?"

Lu Chu waits for a moment and then heads off to the bathroom. When Daniel knocks on the door, the little porcelain bell rings. A young woman Elin assumes is Caroline opens the door and looks at Daniel in surprise. Then she gives him a careful hug.

"May we come in?" Daniel asks.

"Of course." She holds out her hand to Elin. "I'm Caroline."

Elin greets the girl, and holds her thin hand for a moment. Caroline has a pale, freckled face. She's plucked her sand-colored eyebrows and has carefully applied makeup. Her straight hair is drawn into a thick topknot.

The wallpaper in her room is mottled and the wooden dresser by the window has been stripped. On the wall, there's a picture of an old fisherman wearing a sou'wester, his teeth clamped on a pipe.

"We're here to talk about Vicky," Daniel says.

"I was Vicky's foster mother a few years ago," Elin explains.

"When she was small?" asks Caroline.

Elin nods. Caroline bites her lip and looks out the window.

"You know Vicky a little bit," Elin says.

"I don't think she trusted people," Caroline says, and smiles. "I liked her, though. She was calm and had a sick sense of humor when she got tired."

Elin asks straight-out, "Did she ever talk about people she knew? Friends or boyfriends?"

"We never talk about old shit. It brings us down."

"Good things, then? What did she dream of doing when she got out?"

"We'd talk about working abroad for the Red Cross or Save the Children, but who would ever hire us?" Caroline replies.

"Did you two want to do that together?"

"We were just talking," Caroline says patiently.

"I just thought of something," Daniel says, rubbing his forehead. "I was off duty on Friday, but from what I understand, Miranda was in the isolation room. Do you know why?"

"She hit Tuula," Caroline says in a matter-of-fact way.

"Why did she hit Tuula?" Elin asks.

Caroline shrugs. "Because Tuula deserved it. Tuula steals stuff all the time. She took my earrings the other day. She said they wanted to stay with her."

"What did she take from Miranda?"

"When we were swimming, she took Vicky's purse and she took Miranda's necklace."

"She took Vicky's purse?" Elin asks.

"Yeah, she gave it back, but she took something out of it. I don't know what. Something Vicky's mom gave her."

"Was Vicky angry at Tuula?" Elin asks.

"No."

"Vicky and Caroline never get into fights," Daniel says, and he pats Caroline's thin arm.

"Daniel, we need you," Caroline says. She looks anxious. "You have to take care of us."

"I'll be back soon," he says. "I want to take care of you, but I'm not really in shape for—"

"You will come back, won't you?"

"I will."

Elin glances back as they leave the room. Caroline's face has fallen. She looks as if she's been completely abandoned.

92

Daniel knocks on Tuula's door. No one answers, so they head back to the kitchen.

"Remember what I told you earlier," Daniel says seriously.

As they pass the dining room, its table uncleared from dinner, they see the little red-haired girl. Beyond the large windows of the glass veranda, the harbor is gleaming in the darkness. The faded silver fishing huts stand in a row and are reflected in the water. It's a beautiful view. But the girl has turned her chair away from the windows to face the wall and she's staring right at it.

"Hello, Tuula," Daniel says.

The girl turns her head. Her eyes are pale. Her haunted expression changes into something else, something harder to define.

"I have a fever," she says, and turns back to face the wall.

"Nice view," Daniel says.

"Yeah," she says, but keeps staring at the wall.

"I need to talk to you," Daniel says gently.

"Go ahead."

"I want to see your face as we talk."

"You want me to cut it off?"

"It would be easier if you turned your chair around."

She sighs and gets up, turns her chair, and sits back down. Her face doesn't reveal a thing.

"Last Friday, you took Vicky's purse," Elin says.

"What?" Tuula exclaims. "What did you say? What the fuck did you say to me?"

Daniel tries to minimize the effect of Elin's words. "She was wondering—"

"Shut up!" screams Tuula.

They don't say anything. Tuula presses her lips together while she rips a cuticle from her fingernail.

"You took Vicky's purse," Elin says again.

"You're a fucking liar," Tuula says. She looks at the floor. She's trembling.

Elin leans forward and strokes her cheek. "I don't mean—"

Tuula grabs Elin's hair and yanks, then snatches a fork from the table and pulls back her arm to stab Elin's face. But Daniel seizes her hand and holds on while she screams and kicks.

"Fucking bitch! I'm going to . . ."

Daniel holds Tuula until she quiets down. He takes her onto his lap and she finally starts to relax.

Elin has backed away.

"I know. You only borrowed Vicky's purse," Daniel says.

"She only had crap in there. I should have burned it all."

"So there was nothing in her purse that said it wanted to stay with you?"

"Just the flower button."

"It sounds lovely. May I see it?"

"A tiger is keeping watch over it."

"Oh, my."

"You can nail me to a wall," Tuula whispers.

"Was there anything else that wanted to stay with you?" Daniel says.

"I should have set fire to Vicky when we were in the forest."

Tuula keeps talking to Daniel and Elin leaves the room. The hall is dark and empty. She walks to Tuula's bedroom and listens to make sure that Daniel is still talking to the girl. Then she opens the door.

93

Elin's heart is racing as she enters the small room. There's a narrow bed, a chair, a wooden dresser, and a single window. A table lamp is lying on its side on the floor, lighting the room from below. On one white wall, an embroidered hanging promises "The best thing we have is each other."

Elin can still see Tuula licking her dry lips and shaking right before she tried to stab her face with a fork.

There's an odd, sweet, almost rotten smell in the stale air of the room.

She hopes that Daniel realizes that she's here and will keep Tuula occupied for a while.

The mattress is missing from the narrow bed and beneath the bed slats Elin can see a small red suitcase. Her shadow grazes the slats as she leans over and pulls it out. Inside there's a photo album, some wrinkled clothes, a perfume bottle with Disney princesses on it, and a candy wrapper.

Elin closes the suitcase and pushes it back under the bed. She looks around the room and notices that the dresser has been moved out from the wall. The mattress and bedclothes are on the floor behind it. Tuula has been sleeping there instead of in the bed.

Elin walks over slowly, stopping for a moment when a floorboard creaks. She pulls open each dresser drawer but there are only tangled sheets and small cloth bags of lavender inside. She lifts the sheets, but there's nothing underneath. She hears steps in the hallway. She stands still and tries to breathe without making a sound. She hears the bell ring on Caroline's door. Then silence.

Elin waits a moment, then looks through the bedclothes behind the dresser. She lifts the mattress, and the stench of rotting food makes her rear back. On a newspaper on the floor lies a mound of old food: moldy bread, chicken bones, brown apples, sausage, and fried potatoes.

Tuula mumbles that she's tired. She wiggles out of Daniel's embrace and walks to the window. She starts to lick the glass.

"Have you ever heard Vicky say something?" asks Daniel.

"Like what?"

"That she has a hiding place somewhere or places where—"

"Nope," Tuula says, turning toward him.

"But you like to listen to the bigger girls when they talk," Daniel says.

"So do you," Tuula replies.

"I know," Daniel says. "But right now I'm having trouble remembering things. The doctor calls it 'arousal.'"

"Is it dangerous?"

He shakes his head but he does not try to smile.

"I go to a psychologist and I get drugs for it."

"Don't be sad," she says, and she cocks her head. "It was a good thing that Miranda and Elisabet were killed. There are too many people on the planet anyway."

"I loved Elisabet, I needed her and—"

Tuula slams her head backward into the windowpane and cracks the glass.

"The best thing for me to do right now is to hide behind the dresser in my room," she says.

"Wait a moment."

Elin is on her knees at the end of the bed looking at a trunk. She can tell it's an American chest from the name and address written on the lid in elegant lettering: "Fritz Gustavsson 1861 Harmånger." At the beginning of the twentieth century, more than a quarter of the Swedish population emigrated to America, their belongings packed into these trunks, but perhaps Fritz never got away. Elin tries to lift the lid. She can't get it open and breaks a nail. The trunk is definitely locked.

She hears the sound of glass shattering. Someone screams.

Elin shudders and walks to the window. There are seven small containers on the sill, some tin and others porcelain. She opens the first two. One is empty and the other has a coil of old string.

Through the small window, she can see the dark abyss of the lawn. Beyond it, light from another window falls on the outhouse and the stinging nettles beside it.

She opens another porcelain jar and sees a few old copper coins. A tin jar with a painted harlequin on the side contains a few nails and a dead bumblebee.

She glances outside again as she feels her pulse rise in her temples. Everything is quiet. All she can hear is her own breathing. The shadow of a figure passes over the nettles and Elin drops the jar. Someone could be standing outside and looking right at her. She moves away from the window and is heading for the door when she spots a small sticker on the closet door. It's Tigger from *Winnie-the-Pooh*.

Tuula had said that a tiger keeps watch over the flower button.

Inside the closet, oilskins are hanging from a hook and behind them is an ancient vacuum cleaner. Elin's hands shake as she pulls the vacuum cleaner out. Beneath it, there are flattened tennis shoes and a dirty pillowcase. She grabs a corner of the pillowcase and can feel the weight of what's inside.

She pours out the glittering contents onto the floor: coins, buttons, hair clips, glass marbles, a SIM card for a cell phone, a shiny ballpoint pen, capsules, earrings, and a key ring attached to a little metal fob with a light blue flower. Elin looks at the fob closely. She turns it over and sees the name Dennis engraved on it.

This must be what Vicky's mother gave her.

Elin pockets the key ring and stuffs everything else back in the pillowcase. She puts it back in the closet, lifts the vacuum cleaner back on top, and pulls the oilskins to the front. She hurries over to the bedroom door. She listens for a moment, then opens it and walks out.

Tuula is standing there.

She is waiting in the dark hall a few steps away and she stares at Elin without saying a word.

96

Tuula takes a step toward Elin and holds out a bloody hand. Her face is pale and her eyebrows are invisible. Her hair is hanging in red wisps around her cheeks.

"Go back inside the room," Tuula says.

"I have to talk to Daniel."

"We can go inside together and hide."

"What's happened?"

"Go inside the room," Tuula says, licking her lips.

"Is there something you'd like to show me?"

"Yes."

"What is it?"

"It's a game. Vicky and Miranda played it last week," Tuula says. She raises her hands in front of her face.

"I have to go," Elin says.

"I'll show you how it's done," Tuula whispers.

Elin hears other footsteps in the hallway and catches sight of Daniel carrying a first-aid kit. Lu Chu and Almira are coming from the direction of the kitchen. Tuula runs her fingers through her hair, and they come away coated with fresh blood.

"Tuula, you were supposed to stay in the dining room," Daniel says. He takes her other hand and leads her away. "We have to wash your wound and see if it needs stitches."

Elin stays still and waits until her heart calms down. Reaching into her pocket, she fingers the key ring Vicky got from her mother.

A few minutes later, the door to the kitchen opens again. Tuula walks out, trailing her hand along the wooden paneling. Daniel is beside her, saying something in a serious but calm tone. Tuula nods and then goes inside her room and shuts the door. Elin waits until Daniel turns to her before she asks what happened.

"She's all right. She banged her head on the window a few times until she broke the glass."

"Has Vicky ever mentioned someone named Dennis?" asks Elin. She keeps her voice low as she gives Daniel the key ring.

He looks at it and turns it over in his hand. He whispers the name Dennis to himself.

"Well," he says at last. "I think I've heard the name, but I . . . Elin, I'm embarrassed. I feel totally worthless, because—"

"You're trying—"

"Yes, but I'm not at all sure that Vicky has told me anything that could help the police. She didn't really tell me all that much, and . . ."

He stops talking as they hear the sound of footsteps coming up the steps outside and the front door opening. A massive woman in her fifties enters and she's about to lock the door from the inside when she catches sight of them.

"You're not supposed to be here," she says as she heads toward them.

"My name is Daniel Grim and I'm—"

"The girls cannot receive visitors at this time of night," the woman interrupts him.

"We're just about to leave," Daniel says. "We just need to ask Caroline about—"

"You're not going to ask anyone about anything."

97

Joona is in the police station, riding up the elevator. He's holding a small plastic bag containing the key ring. The fob looks like a large coin, a silver dollar. "Dennis" is engraved on one side and a light blue flower with seven petals is embossed on the other. The coin is linked to a large, empty key ring.

Late last night, Elin called Joona. She was in her car driving Daniel back to the hospital and was planning to stay in a hotel in Sundsvall for the night. She told Joona that Tuula had stolen this key ring from Vicky's purse early on Friday.

"It was important to Vicky. Her mother gave it to her," Elin said. She promised to courier it to him as soon as she'd checked in.

Now Joona is turning the plastic bag over and over in the fluorescent light of the elevator. Then he stuffs it in his pocket and gets off at the fifth floor.

He wonders why Vicky's mother would give her a key ring with the name Dennis on it.

Vicky Bennet's father is unknown. Her mother gave birth outside the health-care system. The child did not enter state registers until she was six. Perhaps the mother knew the name of the father the entire time. Was this a way to let Vicky know?

Anja is at her desk and, before he can ask her if she's learned anything about who Dennis is, she says, "There is no person by the name of

Dennis in Vicky Bennet's life. Not at Birgittagården, not at Ljungbacken, and not with any of the foster families."

"Strange," says Joona.

"I even called Saga Bauer from Säpo," Anja tells him, and smiles. "They have their own records, of course."

"Someone must know who Dennis is," he says as he sits on the edge of her desk.

"Nope," she sighs, and drums her fingers on her desk. Her nails are long and red.

Joona looks out of the window. Clouds are chasing each other in the strong wind.

"I'm stuck," he says. "I can't look at the reports from the National Forensic Laboratory, I can't ask questions, and I have nothing more to go on."

"Perhaps you should recognize that this is not your case," Anja says quietly.

"I can't let it go," he whispers.

Anja smiles, pleased, and her plump cheeks turn red.

"Since you've nothing better to do at the moment, I'd like you to listen to something," she says. "And it's not Finnish tango, for a change."

"I didn't think it was," he says as he pulls up a chair.

"Of course you did," she mutters, typing on her computer. "This is a telephone call I answered earlier today."

"Do you record your calls?"

"As a rule, yes," she replies in a neutral voice.

A woman's thin voice starts speaking.

"I'm sorry that I keep calling," the woman says. Her voice is almost breathless. "I talked to a policewoman in Sundsvall and she said that a detective by the name of Joona Linna might be interested."

"Talk to me," Anja's voice says.

"If you'll listen to me, only listen, there's something important I have to tell you about the murders at Birgittagården."

"The police have a tip line," Anja's voice explains.

"I know," the woman says quickly.

There's a waving Japanese cat on top of Anja's computer. Each time it waves, it clicks.

"I saw the girl. She didn't want to show her face," she says. "There was a large rock. A bloody rock. You have to look for it."

"Are you saying you witnessed the murders?"

They can hear the woman breathing before she answers.

"I don't know why I've seen this," she says. "I'm frightened and I'm very tired, but I am not crazy."

"Are you telling me you saw the murder?"

"Or maybe I'm going crazy," the woman says, as if she didn't hear Anja's question.

The telephone call ends abruptly.

"This woman's name is Flora Hansen. She has a report made against her."

"Why?"

"Brittis at the tip line got tired of her calls. Flora has called in a number of false tips and wanted to be paid for further information."

"Does she call the tip line often?"

"No, she's never called before. It's just the murders at Birgittagården. I thought you should hear this before she calls back. She'll certainly phone you. She keeps calling even though the police have reported her. And now she has my telephone number."

"What do you know about her?"

"Brittis says that Flora has an alibi for the evening of the murder. She held a séance for nine people at Upplandsgatan 40 here in Stockholm," Anja says, amused. "She calls herself a medium. She says she can get answers from the dead if she gets paid for it."

"I'm going to go see her," Joona says, getting up from the chair.

"Joona, people know about this case," Anja says. Her smile is uncertain. "And before too long, someone else will have a tip. If Vicky Bennet is alive, someone will see her sometime."

"Right," he says as he buttons his jacket.

Anja is about to start laughing but catches Joona's gaze and suddenly realizes what he knows.

"It's the rock," she says. "So it's true there was a rock."

"Right," he says. "But only The Needle, Frippe, and I know that the killer used a rock."

98

Joona knows that in rare, difficult cases the police turn to mediums and psychics for help. He remembers the murder of Engla Höglund. The police consulted a medium who described two killers—both descriptions turned out to be completely wrong. The true killer was caught because someone trying out a new camera just happened to take a photograph of the girl and the killer's car.

Joona had read an independent study done in the United States about a medium the police turned to more often than any other. Although the woman had been used in one hundred and fifteen investigations, the study concluded that she'd never contributed any valuable information in any case.

Joona shivers in the chilly afternoon air as he gets out of his car and walks toward a gray apartment building with satellite dishes on every balcony. The door to the entrance has a broken lock and someone has sprayed graffiti in pink all over the entrance hallway. Joona takes the stairs to the second floor and rings the bell at a door with the name Hansen on the mail slot.

A pale woman in gray clothes opens the door. She looks at Joona shyly.

"My name is Joona Linna," he says. He shows his police ID. "You've called the police a number of times."

"I'm sorry," she says, and looks at the ground.

"People are not supposed to call the police unless they have something to say."

"But I called because I saw the dead girl," she says. She looks up into his eyes.

"May I come inside for a minute?" Joona asks.

She nods and leads him through a dark hall with worn-out vinyl flooring to a small, clean kitchen. Flora sits in one of the four chairs and wraps her arms around her body. Joona walks to the window and looks out. The façade of the building across the street is covered in plastic sheeting. The thermometer fastened to the outside window frame rocks slightly in the wind.

"I believe that Miranda is coming to me because I let her in accidentally when I was doing a séance," Flora starts. "But I don't know what she wants."

"When do you hold your séances?"

"Every week. I earn my living by speaking with the dead," she says, and a muscle twitches near her left eye.

"In a manner of speaking, so do I," says Joona quietly.

He sits down across the table from her.

"I've run out of coffee," she says apologetically.

"It doesn't matter," he says. "You said something about a rock when you called."

"I didn't know what to do. Miranda keeps appearing and showing me a bloody stone." She indicates how large it is with her hands.

"So you held a séance," Joona prompts her. "A girl comes and tells you—"

"No, it was later," she interrupts. "It was after the séance, when I got back home."

"And what did this girl say to you?"

Flora looks at him directly, her eyes dark with the memory. "She shows me the rock and tells me to close my eyes."

Joona looks back steadily with his gray fathomless gaze. He has only one thing to say.

"If Miranda comes back, I would like you to ask her where the killer is hiding."

99

Joona takes the plastic bag out of his pocket and dumps the key ring on the table in front of Flora.

"This belongs to the murder suspect," he says.

Flora looks at it without picking it up.

"Dennis?" she asks.

"We don't know who Dennis is, but perhaps . . . perhaps you can feel something from it," Joona says.

"Maybe, but this is my job." She smiles, embarrassed, and hides her smile with her hand.

"Of course," he says. "How much?"

She looks down at the table as she tells him the price for a half-hour sitting. Joona opens his wallet and pays for one hour. Flora thanks him and gets her purse. Then she turns off the ceiling lamp. There's still some light outside, but inside the kitchen it's fairly dark. Flora takes out a tea light and a silk cloth with golden edges. She lights the candle and places it in front of Joona. Then she places the cloth over the key ring.

Joona watches her without presuppositions.

Flora places her left hand beneath the cloth. She sits still and then her body begins to shake. She takes a deep breath. "Dennis, Dennis," she mutters.

She touches the metal tag beneath the black cloth. They can hear voices from the neighbor's television through the walls. Suddenly a car alarm goes off on the street below.

"I'm getting strange pictures. Nothing I can make out yet."

"Keep going," Joona says.

Flora's light, curly hair touches her cheeks. Her skin turns bright red and her eyes dart under her eyelids.

"There's power in this object. There's loneliness and rage. I feel like I'm burning when I touch it," she whispers. She pulls the key ring from beneath the cloth and holds it in her palm. She opens her eyes to stare at it. "Miranda tells me there's a thread of death. They were both in love with Dennis. I can feel jealousy burning in the medallion."

Flora falls silent, then she mumbles that the contact has been broken and pushes the key ring at Joona.

Joona gets up. He was wasting his time coming here. He thought that she might know something real for reasons that she did not want to mention. It's obvious that Flora Hansen is only telling him what she thinks he wants to hear.

"I'm sorry that you feel you have to lie," Joona says. He takes the key ring from the table.

"May I keep the money?" she asks. "I can't manage. I collect bottles and newspapers from the subway and from all the garbage cans . . ."

Joona stuffs the key ring back into his pocket. Flora picks up a piece of paper and follows him into the hallway.

"I really did see a ghost," she says. "I've drawn a picture of her."

She shows Joona a childish drawing of a girl and a heart. She practically holds it in front of his face. Joona pushes her hand away. She drops the paper and it sails to the floor. Joona steps over it, opens the door, and leaves.

100

Joona is still feeling irritated when he parks his car outside Disa's apartment building on Lützengatan near Karlaplan Circle. Vicky Bennet and Dante Abrahamsson are alive and hiding somewhere, and he's lost an hour of valuable time speaking with a disturbed woman who lies for money.

Disa is sitting on her bed with her computer on her lap. She's wearing a white robe and she's pulled her brown hair back into a ponytail.

Joona takes a shower in the hottest water he can stand. Then he lies down beside her. As he leans his face next to her body, he can smell her perfume.

"Have you been to Sundsvall again today?" Disa asks distractedly as he runs his hand down her arm.

"Not today," Joona answers. He remembers Flora's pale, lean face.

"I was there last year on an archaeological dig," Disa tells him. "I dug around the Högum Women's House."

"The Women's House?"

"In Selånger, on the outskirts of Sundsvall."

She looks up from her computer and smiles. "If you have a chance between murders, you should go there," she says.

Joona smiles as he runs his hand over her hip. He follows her thigh to her knee. He doesn't want Disa to stop talking so he asks, "Why do they call it the Women's House?"

"It's an Iron Age grave mound, but it was built over a burned-down house. We don't know what happened there."

"Were there any human bones inside?"

"Yes, the remains of two women," she says as she puts away the computer. "I brushed the dirt away from their combs and jewelry."

Joona rests his head on her knee and asks, "Where did the fire start?"

"We don't know, but there was an arrowhead in the wall."

"So they were attacked from outside?"

"Perhaps the villagers set fire to the house and let it burn," she says. She runs her fingers through his thick, damp hair.

"Tell me more about the graves," Joona says.

"We don't know much," she says, wrapping a strand of his hair around her finger. "The women were inside weaving. Bits of their looms were scattered throughout the site. Isn't it strange that it's the small things, like nails and combs, that survive the ages?"

Joona resolves to visit the Sami bridal crown of braided birch root and then go to Kronoberg Park and its old Jewish cemetery, where his colleague Samuel Mendel lies all alone in his family grave.

101

A soft kiss on his mouth awakens Joona. Disa is already dressed. She's brought him a cup of coffee on a breakfast tray.

"I fell asleep," he said.

"You slept like a rock." She smiles as she heads toward the hall.

Joona hears her close the door after her. Then he gets up and puts on his pants. While he's standing next to the bed, he realizes that he'd visited Flora Hansen because she happened to guess right about the rock. It's called confirmation bias. Unconsciously, all people tend to heed results that confirm their theories rather than those that don't. Flora called the police many times mentioning different murder weapons, but it was only when she mentioned a bloody rock that he paid any attention to her.

Now that Flora is off his list, there are no other clues for him to follow.

Joona walks to the window and opens the thin white drapes. The gray light of dawn still holds some of the previous evening's gloom. Even the splashing he can hear from the fountain at Karlaplan Circle seems melancholy. Pigeons strut around the closed entrance to the shopping center. A few people are already on their way to work.

There was something desperate in Flora Hansen's voice and eyes as she told him how she collected bottles and newspapers in the subway.

Absentmindedly, he puts on his shirt and stares at nothing as he buttons it. He had just made a logical connection, but he lost it immediately.

He tries to go back in his thoughts and remember what it was, but it glides away again.

It was about Vicky, her mother, and the key ring. Was it something he saw?

He puts on his jacket and looks out the window at Karlaplan Circle again. A bus is driving around it. It stops and lets on passengers. Farther down the street, an elderly man with a walker is smiling at a dog sniffing around a garbage can.

A woman in a leather jacket is running toward the subway. She scares a flock of pigeons on the square. They take off and fly in a semicircle before they land again.

The subway.

There's something about the subway.

Joona picks up his cell phone. He thinks he's right about his intuition, but he wants to check some facts first. While he waits for the signal to go through, he walks into the hallway and puts on his shoes.

"Holger here."

"Joona Linna here," Joona says. He opens the front door.

"And a very good morning to you! I have—"

"There's something I have to ask first," Joona interrupts as he locks the door behind him. "You went through the purse we found at the dam, right?"

Joona is starting to run down the stairs.

"I had already taken pictures and listed the contents when the prosecutor told me they were shutting down the investigation."

"I am not allowed to read your report," Joona says.

"There wasn't much to it," Holger says. Joona can hear him shuffle papers. "I mentioned the knife—"

"You mentioned some sort of bicycle tool. Did you find out what it was?"

Joona is rushing down Lützengatan to his car.

"Yes, I did," Holger says. "It took a little time, since I'm from Västernorrland. It wasn't a bike tool at all. It was a key to the driver's cab in a subway car."

"Has this key been on a key ring recently?"

"How the hell should I know!" Holger is quiet for a moment and Joona assumes he's looking at the photograph in his report. "You're right! It's shiny around the eye."

Joona thanks him for his time and runs the last few yards to his car. Elin told him that Tuula steals pretty things from everyone around her: earrings, shiny pens, coins, and lipsticks. Tuula had taken the beautiful key ring with its light blue flower and left the ugly key in Vicky's purse. He taps in Anja's number as he opens the car door.

"Hello, Ghostbusters," Anja says.

"Anja, can you help me? I need to talk to whoever is responsible for Stockholm's subway system." By now Joona is in his car and has started to drive.

"Let me connect with the spirits instead."

"Anja, I'm in a hurry!"

"Well, who got up on the wrong side of the bed this morning?" Anja mutters.

Joona is driving toward the stadium. "Did you know that all the subway cars in Stockholm have their own names as well as numbers?" he asks.

"Of course. I rode in Rebecka this morning and what a fine car she is, too."

"I just figured out that Dennis isn't a person. It's the name of a subway car, and I need to find out where it is right now."

102

All the cars in the subway system have numbers, of course, but for many years the cars have also been given personal names. Joona is fairly certain that the key from Vicky's mother, Susie, fits a mechanical lock that's on all the subway cars, but the name on the fob points at a specific car. Perhaps Susie kept her personal belongings in the driver's cab—perhaps she slept there sometimes. He knows that she sometimes stayed in the subway tunnels or slept on benches in a subway station after it closed. Perhaps she even lived in an abandoned tunnel deep underground.

Somehow she had got hold of a key, Joona thinks as he drives. It couldn't have been easy. It must have been one of her more valuable possessions. Still, she gave it to her daughter. She'd also gotten a key ring with the name Dennis so that the girl would not forget which subway car was the important one.

Maybe she knew Vicky was planning to run away.

Vicky had already run away many times and managed to stay hidden for a long time at least twice. The first time she was only eight years old and she'd been missing for seven months when she was found in the middle of December, severely hypothermic, in a parking garage with her mother. The second time, she was thirteen. Vicky had been gone for eleven months when she was arrested for shoplifting near Globen.

It's easy enough to get into a driver's cab. Any box-end wrench the right size would work.

Even if Vicky is not in the subway car named Dennis, she might have left clues there from her time as a runaway, clues that could lead to her present hiding place.

Joona has almost reached the police station when Anja calls and says she's talked with someone at Stockholm Local Transport.

"There was a subway car named Dennis that was taken out of service some time ago due to serious maintenance issues."

"Where is this car now?"

"He didn't know," she said. "It could be at the depot in Rissne, but more likely it's parked at the service depot in Johanneshov."

"Connect me," Joona says. He turns his car around and the tires thud over the speed bumps. He runs a red light as he turns onto Fleming-gatan.

103

Joona drives toward Johanneshov, south of Stockholm. A man answers his phone call. It sounds as if he's in the middle of eating.

"Subway Traffic Technical Division, Kjelle here."

"Joona Linna from the National Police. Can you confirm that a sub-way car named Dennis is parked with you at Johanneshov?"

"Dennis," the man says, smacking his lips. "Do you have the car number?"

"No, sorry, I don't."

"Hold on, let me check."

Joona can hear the man talking to himself and then the man picks up the phone again.

"There's a Denniz with a *z* at the end—"

"That could be the one."

"Okay."

Joona hears the man swallow his food before he speaks again.

"It's not in the current register. It's a really old car. As far as I can tell from this database, it hasn't been used in traffic for the past few years."

"Where is it now?"

"Probably here, but let me connect you to Dick. He knows every-thing the computer doesn't."

Kjelle's voice disappears and is replaced by the sound of electric buzzing. Then an older man picks up the phone. His voice echoes as if he's in a cathedral or a room made entirely of metal.

"Swinging Dick here," he says.

"I just talked to Kjelle," Joona says. "He thinks that a car named Denniz is parked out by you."

"If Kjelle says it's here, it probably is. But I can go and take a look, especially if it's a vital matter of life and death and the honor of my country."

"It is, actually," Joona replies.

"Are you in a car?"

"Yes."

"Heading here?"

Joona hears Dick climbing down a metal staircase. A large, heavy door creaks. He sounds slightly out of breath when he next speaks.

"I'm down in the tunnel now. Are you still there?"

"Still here."

"It looks like we have Mikaela and Maria. Denniz should be in one of these corners."

Joona can hear Dick's echoing footsteps even as he's driving as fast as he can over the Central Bridge. He thinks about the times Vicky was on the lam. She must have slept somewhere. She must have felt safe and secure somewhere.

"Do you see the car yet?" asks Joona.

"Not yet. We have Ellinor. There's Silvia. Even the lighting down here doesn't work like it should."

Joona can hear footsteps as Dick keeps going down a tunnel beneath the industrial center of Johanneshov.

"Let's see. I haven't been back this far in a long time. Let me turn on my flashlight. It's the deepest in, of course. Here it is. Denniz, totally rusty and looks like—"

"You're sure it's the right car?"

"I can take a picture if you want. What the hell! There's people inside! I can see people."

"Shh," Joona says.

Dick whispers, "There are some people inside the car."

"Keep away from them," Joona says.

"They've put a damned gas cylinder in front of the door!"

There's a rustling sound as Dick moves away swiftly. He's breathing hard.

"It was . . . I saw people in there," he whispers into the phone.

Joona thinks it can't be Vicky because she doesn't have the key and the key ring.

Joona hears sudden high-pitched screaming. It's distant but clear.

"There's a woman screaming in there! She seems out of her mind."

"Get away from there as best you can," Joona says.

He hears more steps and hard breathing. He can still hear the screaming, but it sounds fainter.

"What did you see?" Joona asks.

"A large cylinder for welding was blocking the door."

"What about the people?"

"There was graffiti on the door, but I could tell there was a tall person and a shorter person, and maybe more than that, but I'm not sure."

"How did they get in?"

"We keep the tunnels locked, but if you're determined, you could break in pretty easily."

"Listen to me carefully," Joona says. "I'm a detective inspector and I want you to leave the tunnel now and wait outside for the police to arrive."

104

A black van is being driven at top speed through the gates of the transit depot in Johanneshov. Dry gravel is churned up in a cloud of dust as the van swings around and stops in front of a green metal building.

After he talked to Dick, Joona called the provincial chief of police and told him that this could be a possible hostage situation. A SWAT team was immediately dispatched.

Five police officers climb out of the van, all of them heavily clothed in boots, dark blue overalls, bulletproof vests, helmets, protective glasses, and gloves. They are all armed and keyed up.

Joona walks over to meet the group. Three of them are carrying jade-green automatic rifles with non-magnifying reflector sights from Heckler & Koch. These weapons aren't anything special but they are lightweight and can empty a magazine in less than three seconds. The other two men in the group are carrying sniper rifles.

Joona shakes hands with the SWAT team leader, the doctor in the group, and the other three men, and then explains that the situation could be urgent. "I'd like us to go in at once," he says, "but since I don't know what your run-through has been, let me emphasize that we don't have a positive ID of either Vicky Bennet or Dante Abrahamsson."

While waiting for the SWAT team to arrive, Joona talked with Dick Jansson, who gave him a map of the tunnel on which he drew the locations of the various subway cars.

A young officer, holding a sniper rifle, raises his hand. "Are we assuming that she's armed?" he asks.

"Probably not with any kind of gun," Joona replies.

"So we can expect to meet two unarmed children," the man says, and shakes his head with a grin.

"We don't know what we'll meet. You never know what you'll run into during a situation like this," Joona says.

He shows them a picture of a subway car similar to Denniz.

"Where are we going in?" asks the SWAT team leader.

"The front door is open but blocked with one or two gas cylinders," Joona explains.

"Are you all getting this?" The SWAT team leader turns toward the others.

Joona puts the map over the drawing. He points out the various sidetracks and the location of the subway cars.

"I think we can get this far without being discovered," Joona says, pointing to a curve in the tunnel. "It's hard to say for sure."

The SWAT team leader nods.

"It's not all that far, but I would like a sniper on the roof of the closest car."

"I'll do that," one of the men says.

"And I can go here," says the younger sniper.

They follow Joona to the steel door. One of the men checks his reserve magazine while Joona puts on his bulletproof vest.

"Our primary goal is to get the boy out of the car and our secondary goal is to get the suspect," Joona says as he opens the door. "If you must fire, aim for the girl's legs first and foremost. Otherwise aim for the shoulders or arms."

A long metal staircase leads down to the tunnel where the subway cars wait for repairs. The only sound is the dull tramp of heavy boots.

105

As soon as the team reaches the tunnel, they start to move more slowly and carefully, the sound of their footsteps mere whispers against the metal-clad tunnel walls.

They approach a buckled train that gives off a strange smell, its cars looking like dark ruins from an abandoned civilization. The beams from their flashlights flicker over the rough walls. They're moving single file, quickly and almost soundlessly. The tracks branch out near a manual switch. A red light with a broken shade gives off a weak light, and a work glove lies forgotten in the black gravel. Dim light from induction lamps set at intervals down the tunnel allows them to see the way forward.

Joona signals to the men to turn off their flashlights and they pass through the narrow gap between two cars with broken windows. A box of oil-covered nuts and bolts leans against the wall. Loose cables, outlets, and dusty wires surround it.

They're almost there now, so they move cautiously. Joona points out a car for the first sniper who climbs onto its roof, unfolds a tripod, and begins to adjust his Hensoldt sight. The others mount their weapon lights then approach the next car in the tunnel. Their quick, short breaths are the only indication of the stress they're under, though one of the men keeps compulsively checking the clasp on his helmet. The SWAT team leader exchanges glances with the younger sniper and indicates a line of fire.

Someone slips in the gravel and a loose stone clatters off the rail. A shiny rat jumps toward the wall and disappears.

Joona keeps walking forward at the side of the tunnel, ahead of the others. He sees the car named Denniz on the track closest to the wall. Cables or ropes are hanging from the ceiling of the tunnel. He moves slightly sideways and notices a weak light coming through one of the car's dirty windows. The beam of light moves like a butterfly, making the surrounding shadows grow and shrink.

The SWAT team leader loosens a shock grenade from his belt.

Joona stands still and listens before he resumes walking. He knows he's now in the line of fire and that the sniper's rifle is aimed at his back. He can see the large green gas cylinder lodged in the open door.

When he finally reaches the car, he squats and places his ear against its metal wall. Immediately he can hear someone walking around inside.

The SWAT team leader signals to two men. Like shadows, they run through the darkness. They are big men, but they move soundlessly. All that can be heard is the quiet scrunch of holsters, bulletproof vests, and heavy overalls in motion. Then they're right next to Joona.

Joona has not even drawn his pistol, but sees that the men from the SWAT team already have their fingers on the triggers of their automatic rifles.

It's hard to make out anything through the car's filthy windows, but a small flashlight lying on the floor reveals boxes, empty bottles, and plastic bags. Between two seats, there's a large bundle tied with a rope.

The flashlight beam begins to shake as the whole car vibrates. Somewhere, a subway car is moving on another set of rails.

Thunder rolls along the tunnel.

They can hear weak moaning.

Joona draws his pistol.

A shadow moves deep inside the subway car. It appears to be a large man in jeans and sneakers crawling away.

Joona stuffs the first bullet into the cartridge position and turns toward the SWAT team leader. He points at the man inside the subway car and gestures for the team to move on in.

106

The central door bursts open with a bang and the SWAT team storms the subway car. Windows are broken and shards shower down on the ripped-up seats and the floor. The gas cylinder falls with a thud and rolls through the car, the argon hissing as it escapes. All the inside doors are forced open.

Joona steps over moldy blankets, egg cartons, and old newspapers.

"Lie still!" someone bellows.

They search the car section by section using the light from their weapons. They go between the seats and look through the dirty Plexiglas dividers between sections.

"Don't hit me!" screams a man inside the second section.

"Quiet!"

The SWAT team leader tapes the gas cylinder's vent shut.

Joona rushes toward the driver's cab.

There's no sign of Vicky Bennet or Dante.

The car stinks of sweat and old food. The walls and windows are scratched and covered with scrawls. Someone has recently eaten grilled chicken; the greasy paper is lying on the floor among beer cans and candy wrappers. Newspaper rustles beneath Joona's feet. The light from outside is dappled by the broken windows.

Joona reaches the driver's cab. He's certain the name Dennis on the key ring points to this place, where Vicky's mother used to hide.

The SWAT team has already broken the door open, and Joona steps inside. The cramped space is empty. The walls are covered with graffiti. A syringe without its needle is lying on the instrument panel beside pieces of sooty aluminum foil and empty plastic capsules. On the small shelf beside the pedals, there's a package of painkillers and a tube of toothpaste.

Joona keeps searching and finds a rusty food knife stuck to the foam under the ripped driver's seat. There are more candy wrappers and an empty baby-food jar, which once held plum puree. Through the side window, Joona can see the SWAT team has captured the man in jeans. His face is heavily wrinkled and his eyes are wide with fear. He's coughing blood into his beard. He's yelling. His arms are bound behind his back with plastic handcuffs. He's forced onto his stomach and the muzzle of an automatic rifle is pointed at the back of his head.

Joona keeps searching the cramped cab. His eyes fly over buttons and knobs, the microphone and the stick with its polished handle, and he doesn't know where else to look.

Why did Vicky and her mother have keys to this place? There's nothing here.

He's examining the screws fastening the grille over the ventilation outlet when his glance falls on a word scratched on the wall: *Mamma*.

He takes a step backward and sees right away that everything scrawled on the walls are messages between Vicky and her mother. This must have been a place where they could meet in peace, and whenever they missed each other, they left messages:

Mamma, they abused me, I couldn't stay.

I'm freezing and I need food. Have to go back, but will be here again on Monday.

Don't be sad, Vicky. They put me in detox so I missed you.

Thanks for the candy.

Sweetie!! I'm sleeping here for a while. Uffe's a pig!! If you can leave some money, that'll be great!!

Merry Christmas, Mamma!

You gotta know I can't call you back for a while.

Mamma, are you angry with me for something?

107

Joona leaves the cab and joins the SWAT team. They surround the shaggy man, who's sitting with his back to the wall. He's crying and seems bewildered.

Joona takes off his bulletproof vest, squats down in front of the man, and says, "I'm looking for a girl and a little boy."

"Don't hit me," mumbles the man.

"Nobody is going to hit you. I need to know if you've seen a girl here in this subway car."

"I didn't touch her! I just followed her!"

"Was she alone?"

"I don't know. She locked herself in the cab."

"Did she have a little boy with her?"

"A boy? Yes, maybe . . . maybe—"

"Answer the question!" barks the SWAT team leader.

"You followed her here," Joona says. "What did she do after she got here?"

"She left again," the homeless man answers. His eyes still show his fright.

"Where did she go? Do you know where she went?"

"That way," the man says, using his head to make a helpless gesture toward the opening to the tunnel.

"So she headed toward the opening? Is that what you're trying to say?"

"Maybe not . . . maybe—"

"Answer the question!" snaps the SWAT team leader.

"But I don't really know," the man snivels.

"When was she here?" Joona asks carefully. "Was it today?"

"She left just a minute ago," he says. "She started screaming and then she took off."

Joona begins to run down the sidetrack. Behind him, he can hear the SWAT team leader take over the questioning. His voice brusque and hoarse, he demands to know if the man has done anything to the girl or molested her in any way.

Joona runs along the rusted track to its end, up a set of metal stairs, and into a long hall ribbed with pipes running along the ceiling. At one end, there's a large door, and the damp concrete floor before it shines with the light from outside creeping in. When Joona reaches it, he finds it is broken and is able to push his way through the gap. He's outside, in the middle of a rough stone crossway that spans more than fifteen or so pairs of train tracks. The tracks gather like a ponytail farther up and then curve smoothly to the side.

He can spot the thin figure of a woman farther down the embankment. She has a dog with her. A subway train starts to thunder and passes him, shaking the ground beneath his feet. Joona sees glimpses of her figure as the windows of the train flash by. He keeps running along the embankment through tall weeds and over broken glass, crushed tins, and used condoms. There's electric buzzing and a new train approaches from Skärmarbrink. Joona has almost caught up to the thin figure. He jumps over the tracks in front of the train and grabs her thin arm. He pulls her around to face him. She's surprised and tries to hit him, but he dodges her blow. He loses his grip on her arm, but still has her jacket. She tries to hit him again while she wriggles out of her jacket. She drops her shoulder bag and falls backward onto the gravel.

108

Joona pins the woman down among the thistles and browning cow pars-
ley alongside the tracks. He grabs her hand as she reaches for a stone and
tries to calm her. The dog cringes beyond arm's reach.

"I only want to talk to you."

"Fuck you!" she yells as she tries to wriggle out of his grasp.

She kicks, but he blocks it and keeps her down. Her small breasts
are heaving. She's extremely thin and her face is wrinkled and her lips
badly cracked. She's perhaps forty years old, maybe only in her thirties.
When she can't get free, she starts to whisper soothing phrases to pla-
cate him.

"Calm down, now," Joona says again, and lets her go.

She looks at him shyly as she stands up. She picks her shoulder bag
up from the ground. Her filthy black T-shirt declares "Kafka Didn't
Have Much Fun Either" and her thin arms are mottled with injection
scars. On the inside of her forearm there's a tattoo, which has been cut
to pieces. She runs her hand over her mouth and glances down the
tracks. She shuffles sideways, testing him.

"Don't be afraid. I really have to talk to you."

"I'm busy," she replies quickly.

"Did you see anyone inside the subway car when you were there?"

"I don't know what you're talking about."

"You were staying in a subway car."

She doesn't reply. She shuts her mouth tightly and scratches her throat.

Joona picks up her jacket and turns it right-side out. He hands it to her and she takes it without thanking him.

"I'm looking for a girl who—"

"Fuck you. I haven't done anything."

"I'm not saying you have," Joona says.

"Well, what the fuck do you want from me, then?"

"I'm looking for a girl named Vicky."

"So how does that make it my business?"

Joona pulls out the photo of Vicky that was used for the bulletin.

"No one I know," she says automatically.

"Take another look."

"You wanna give me some money?"

"No."

"Come on, can't you help me out here?"

A subway train passes by them, small sparks flying from its wheels.

"I know that you've been hanging out in the driver's cab," Joona says.

"Susie started it," she says, not wanting to be blamed.

Joona shows her the photograph of Vicky again.

"It's Susie's daughter," Joona explains.

"I didn't know she had kids," the homeless woman says, and rubs her nose.

The buzz of electricity in the lines overhead gets louder.

"How did you know Susie?"

"We kept to ourselves in the garden plots as long as we could. I felt really bad when I ran into her. I had hepatitis and this guy, Vadim, was after me. He used to beat me up and Susie helped me out. She was a tough bitch all right, but I wouldn't have made it through the winter without her, I wouldn't have had a chance, but when Susie died, I took her stuff, because . . ."

The woman mutters something to herself and starts rummaging through her shoulder bag. She takes out a key identical to the one Vicky had in her purse.

"Why did you take it?"

"Anyone would. Anyone. That's the way it is. I took it from her before she died, even," the woman confesses.

"What else was in the subway car?"

She scratches the cracked corner of her mouth and mutters "Fuck this" to herself. She takes a step to the side, farther away from Joona.

Two subway trains are heading closer in the same direction on separate tracks. One is coming from Blåsut and the other from Skärmarbrink station.

"I need to know," Joona says.

"All right, what the fuck," the woman says, rolling her eyes. "There was some stuff to eat and a cell phone."

"Do you still have the cell phone?"

The sound of metal scraping and the thunder of the subway trains keep getting louder.

"You can't prove it's not mine."

The first subway train passes them, shaking the ground beneath their feet. Loose stones jump from the embankment and the weeds twist in the draft. An empty McDonald's cup rolls between the other set of rails.

"Just let me look at it!" Joona yells.

"Yeah, right!" she laughs.

The second train speeds by and their clothes flap in its wake. The dog next to the woman begins to bark. The woman moves backward along the embankment and says something Joona can't hear, then she turns and starts running across the tracks. Joona has no time to react.

The woman doesn't see the third train coming in the opposite direction at top speed. Its thunder is drowned out by the two other trains, but now it is deafening. Yet when its front hits the homeless woman, the impact is silent. She disappears beneath the first car.

The train screams as the brakes are slammed on, and its cars smack one another as they slow to a stop.

Now the only sound is the buzz of insects and the far-off hum of traffic.

The driver is sitting in his seat as if he's turned to stone.

A long trail of blood runs over the rails. There's a dark clump of cloth and flesh under one of the cars. The stench of the brakes starts to spread.

The dog starts to trot back and forth along the tracks with its tail between its legs. It doesn't seem to know where to go or where to stop.

Joona picks up the woman's shoulder bag, which has landed in the ditch.

The dog comes up to him and sticks its nose in the bag as Joona empties out its contents. Candy wrappers flutter away in the wind, followed by a few banknotes. Joona takes the black cell phone and leaves the rest.

He walks over to a concrete piling next to the embankment and sits down.

The westerly wind smells of garbage and city.

He clicks until he reaches the cell phone's voice mail. He calls it and finds out there are two messages.

"Hi, Mamma," says a girl's voice. It can only be Vicky. "Why aren't you picking up your phone? If you're in detox, let me know. I like this new place. Maybe I told you already the last time I called—"

The automatic voice says, "Message: August first, eleven ten p.m."

"Hi, Mamma," Vicky says. Her voice is tense and breathless. "Stuff has happened here and I need to find you. I can't talk long. I've just borrowed this phone. Mamma, I don't know what to do. I don't know where to go."

"Maybe I need to ask Tobias for help?"

The automatic voice says, "Message: Yesterday. Two p.m."

The sun breaks through the clouds all of a sudden. The tops of the subway rails shine in the light.

109

Elin Frank wakes up. She's in a large, strange bed. The green shine of the television clock dimly lights the bedroom of the presidential suite. She can see the decorative curtains hanging in front of the heavy curtains that block the sunlight.

She's been asleep for a long time.

There's a sweet aroma from an arrangement of cut flowers in the living room of the suite. The smell nauseates her. The air conditioner has been spreading an uneven chill, but she is still too weary to get up and turn it off or call the reception desk.

Elin thinks about the girls in the house by the coast. One of them must know something more. There must be one witness to what happened at Birgittagården.

That little girl Tuula was speaking and moving as if she were near the boiling point. Perhaps she saw something that she doesn't dare tell anyone.

Elin has a vivid mental image of the girl grabbing her hair and trying to stab her face with a fork. The memory should make her more frightened than it does.

It's almost impossible for her to understand yesterday's events.

She slides her hand beneath the pillow. The wounds on her wrists ache. She remembers how the girls went on provoking Daniel when they found his weak spot.

Elin twists inside the sheets as she pictures Daniel's face. He has a pleasant mouth and sympathetic eyes. It's ridiculous how she's been faithful to Jack except for that misadventure with the French photographer. She hadn't intended to be faithful. She knows that they're divorced and that he will never come back to her.

After she takes a shower, Elin rubs body lotion into her skin, using the no-name brand provided by the hotel. She rewinds the bandages around her wrist and, for the first time in more years than she can recall, she dresses in the clothes she wore the day before.

During the car ride back, they talked about Vicky's key ring. Daniel did his best to recall Vicky mentioning someone named Dennis. He was frustrated that he couldn't remember anything.

Her stomach has butterflies when she thinks about Daniel Grim. She feels as if she's falling from a great height—and enjoying every minute.

She roots around in her purse and finds an eyeliner pencil and applies it lightly along her eyelids. Her movements are slow and her face shows her conflicting emotions.

It had been very late when they arrived at his house in Sundsvall. A gravel path led through an old garden, and the dark silhouettes of fruit trees waved in the wind before a small red house with a white veranda.

If he'd asked her to come inside, she would have done so. If he'd asked her to sleep with him, she'd have done that, too. But he hadn't asked. He was careful and pleasant, and when she'd thanked him for his help, he'd said that taking this trip had been much better than any amount of therapy. She'd missed him as she watched him walk through the low gate and head toward his house. She'd stayed in her car for a while before she'd driven back to the center of the city and checked into First Hotel.

She can hear her cell phone purr in her purse, which is next to the fruit bowl in the living room. She hurries to answer it. It's Joona Linna.

"Are you still in Sundsvall?" the detective inspector asks.

"I'm just about ready to check out of the hotel," Elin says as a wave of fear rushes through her. "What's happened?"

"Nothing, don't worry," he's quick to say. "I just need some help with one thing if you have the time."

"What's it about?"

"If it's not too much trouble, I want you to ask Daniel Grim about something."

"I can do that," she says in a low voice, a big smile crossing her face.

"Ask him if Vicky has ever mentioned someone named Tobias."

"Dennis and Tobias," she says, thoughtfully.

"Just Tobias. Tobias is the only lead to Vicky we have left."

110

The sun is fairly high in the sky by the time Elin Frank pulls away from the hotel. A few minutes later, she drives along Bruksgatan, past its neat single-family homes, and parks beside a thick hedge. She leaves the car and walks up to the low gate.

Daniel Grim's house is well cared for. Its black gabled roof appears new and the gingerbread trim on the veranda is covered in bright, fresh paint. This was the home Daniel and Elisabet Grim shared until just over a week ago. Elin shivers as she rings the doorbell. She waits for a long time, listening to the wind moving through the leaves of the birch trees.

A motorized lawn mower on one of the lawns nearby shuts off.

Elin rings the bell a second time. She waits a bit more, then decides to walk around the house.

Sparrows take flight from the lawn. A dark blue settee sways gently beside two large lilac bushes. Daniel is lying there, asleep. His face is pale and he's curled up as if he's freezing.

Elin keeps walking toward him and he wakes with a jerk. He sits up and looks at her with a question in his eyes.

"It's too cold to be sleeping outside," Elin says as she sits down on the settee beside him.

"I couldn't go inside the house," he says, and shifts so she has more room.

"The police called me this morning," she says.

"What did they want?"

"Did Vicky ever mention someone named Tobias?"

Daniel wrinkles his forehead and Elin is about to ask his forgiveness for her intrusion when he stops her.

"Wait," he says quickly. "He must be the guy with the loft apartment in Stockholm. Vicky lived with him for a while." His tired face breaks into a large, warm smile. "Wollmar Yxkullsgatan 9."

Elin is surprised. She takes her cell phone out of her purse as Daniel shakes his head.

"How the hell did I remember the address like that?" he asks. "I forget everything these days. I can't even remember my parents' middle names."

Elin gets up from the settee and steps into the sunshine. She calls Joona to tell him what she found out. While she's speaking to him she can hear him start to run, and before she says goodbye, she hears a car door slam.

111

Elin's heart is skipping as she sits back down next to Daniel in the settee. She feels the warmth of his skin next to her leg. He's found an old wine cork between the pillows and is peering at it nearsightedly.

"We took a course in wine and decided to start collecting. Nothing special, but some wines are very nice. I got them as Christmas presents . . . from Bordeaux. Two bottles of Château Haut-Brion, 1970. We were going to drink them when we retired, Elisabet and I. People make tons of plans like this. We even saved some marijuana. It was a joke. We often joked that we'd finally act like kids when we were old, kids who play loud music and sleep in."

"I should head back to Stockholm," Elin says.

"Yes, you should."

They swing for a while and the ropes of the hammock creak against the hooks in the trees.

"You have a nice house," Elin says softly.

She places her hand on his. He turns it over and their fingers intertwine. They sit in silence as they continue to swing. The hammock keeps creaking.

Her glossy hair falls into her face, and she sweeps it away and meets his gaze.

"Daniel," she says.

"Yes," he replies in a whisper.

Elin looks at him. She thinks she's never needed the tenderness of another human being as much as now. Something about his gaze and his wrinkled forehead touches her deeply. She kisses his mouth softly, smiles, and kisses him again. She takes his face between her hands and kisses him deeply.

"Dear Lord," he says.

Elin kisses him again and skims her lips over his beard stubble. She opens her blouse and pulls his hand to her breast. He touches her gently and caresses her nipple.

She kisses him again and slips her hand into his shirt. His stomach trembles at her touch.

Waves of desire go through her body and she feels weak. She wants either to lie in the grass with him or sit astride his hips.

She closes her eyes and pulls him to her. He says something that she doesn't hear. Her blood pulses inside her. She feels his warm hands on her body but then he stops and pulls away.

"Elin, I can't . . ."

"Sorry, I didn't mean . . ." She tries to breathe more calmly.

"I just need some time," he says. There are tears in his eyes. "It's too much for me now, but I don't want to scare you off."

"You're not scaring me off," she says and tries to smile.

Elin gets up and adjusts her clothes as she leaves the garden. She gets into her car.

Her cheeks are flushed and her legs are still trembling as she drives away from Sundsvall. Five minutes later, she has to turn off onto a forest road. Her panties are soaking and her heart hasn't stopped racing. Her blood throbs through every vein. She looks at her face in the rearview mirror. Her eyes are heavy and glistening and her lips are swollen.

She can't remember the last time she felt such sexual power stream through her body. Daniel seems unimpressed by her beauty. Instead, it feels as if he can look right into her heart.

She tries to breathe slowly and waits, but finally she looks around the small forest road. She shifts her dress and lifts her ass so she can pull her panties down over her hips. She touches herself quickly with both hands. Her orgasm comes violently, in quick bursts.

She's panting and sweating with two fingers inside herself. She looks out the windshield at the magical rays of sunlight streaming through the branches of the Scotch pines.

112

Night is falling as Flora heads to the recycling bins behind the grocery store to look for cans and bottles. She can't stop thinking about the murders in Sundsvall. She's started to fantasize about Miranda and her life at Birgittagården.

She imagines Miranda wore suggestive clothing, smoked, and swore. She stops thinking about the girl as she passes the grocery store's loading bay. She looks in the cardboard boxes stacked near the dock. Then she keeps going.

She starts to imagine Miranda as a child playing hide-and-seek with some friends outside of a church. She sees her cover her eyes and start to count to one hundred. A little girl is running among the gravestones and laughing in an exaggerated way, already a bit frightened. Flora's heart is fluttering.

She stops beside the bin for old newspapers and cardboard boxes and puts down her plastic bag of empty bottles and cans. She goes up to the container for clear glass and shines her flashlight into it. The light leaps over both broken and whole bottles. In one corner, Flora spies a bottle that she can get some money for. She reaches in and gropes around, since she can't look in at the same time. Something touches her. It feels like someone is stroking the top of her hand. A second later, she cuts her fingers on a shard of glass. She snatches her arm out and backs away.

She can hear a dog bark far away and then she hears the slow, pro-longed crash of glass inside the large bin.

Flora runs away. Her chest hurts and she can't catch her breath. Her wounded fingers are burning. She looks around. The ghost was hiding among the glass bottles, she thinks.

I see the dead girl as a child. Miranda haunts me because she wants to show me something. She hasn't left me alone since I lured her to this side by my séance.

Flora sucks the blood from her fingertips and relives how the girl tried to catch and hold her hand. She thinks that the girl tried to hiss something. She can hear it now: *Someone was there and witnessed the whole thing. There weren't supposed to be witnesses, but there was one anyway. One witness.*

Flora starts to walk again as quickly as she can. She's looking back over her shoulder and screams when a man bumps into her. He smiles and mumbles an apology as she hurries away.

113

Joona walks briskly through the entrance to the building at Wollmar Yxkullsgatan 9. He runs up the stairs to the top floor and rings the bell beside the only door. His heart starts to calm down as he waits for an answer. The brass plaque screwed to the door bears the engraved name Horáčková. There's a piece of tape above it on which the name Lundhagen has been scrawled. He knocks as hard as he can, but he can't hear a thing inside the apartment. He opens the mail slot and peeks inside. It's dark but he can see the floor is covered with mail and flyers. He rings the doorbell again, waits, and then pulls out his cell phone to call Anja.

"Can you search for Tobias Horáčková?"

"No such person," she replies a moment later.

"Horáčková at Wollmar Yxkullsgatan 9."

"There's a Viktoriya Horáčková at that residence," Anja says. She keeps typing.

"What about a Tobias Lundhagen?"

"Let me just tell you that Viktoriya Horáčková is the daughter of a diplomat from the Czech Republic."

"What about a Tobias Lundhagen?"

"Yes, he lives there. Either he rents it from her or he lives with her."

"Thanks."

"Joona, wait," Anja says hurriedly.

"Yes?"

"Three small details. One: You can't go into a diplomatic apartment without a warrant from the Justice Department—"

"Okay," he says.

"Two: You have a meeting with the Internal Review Board in twenty-five minutes."

"Can't make it."

"Three: At four thirty this afternoon, you have a meeting with Carlos."

Joona is sitting straight-backed in a hard armchair at the office of the Public Prosecutor for Police Cases. The head of the Internal Review Board is reading the report from the first interview with Joona in a monotone. Then he hands it to Joona so he can approve and sign it.

Mikael Båge has a drop of snot hanging from his nostril. He sniffs it into his nose as he takes the report back and hands it to Helene Fiorine, the lead secretary. Then he starts to read the transcript of the testimony given by the witness Göran Stone from Säpo.

Three hours later, Joona is walking the short stretch from Kungsbro Bridge to the police station. He takes the elevator to the eighth floor, walks past Carlos Eliasson's assistant, and knocks on the chief's door. He takes his place at the table where his colleagues Petter Näslund, Benny Rubin, and Magdalena Ronander are already waiting.

"Joona, I am a reasonable person, but this is going too far," Carlos says. He's feeding his paradise fish.

"Bringing in the national SWAT team!" Petter says with a grin.

Magdalena is sitting silently looking at the table.

"Tell them you're sorry," Carlos says.

"Because I wanted to save the life of a little boy?" asks Joona.

"No, because you know you were wrong."

"I'm sorry," Joona says.

Petter giggles. His forehead is sweaty.

"I'm going to have to suspend you from active service," Carlos says, "until the internal investigation is concluded."

"Who is taking over?"

"The preliminary investigation is being shut down—"

"Vicky Bennet is alive," Joona interrupts.

"—probably tomorrow afternoon, once the prosecutor has the chance to formally close it."

"She's alive!"

"Get a grip!" Benny says. "I've also taken a look at that security film—"

Carlos silences Benny with a wave of his hand.

"There's no indication that it was Vicky and the boy on that security film at the gas station."

"She left a message on her mother's cell-phone voice mail two days ago," Joona says.

"Vicky doesn't have a phone and her mother is dead," Magdalena says in a serious tone.

"You're starting to get sloppy, Joona," Petter says in a pitying voice.

Carlos clears his throat and hesitates before he takes a deep breath. "This isn't easy for me," he says slowly.

Petter looks expectantly at Carlos, while Magdalena stares at the table and Benny doodles on a piece of paper.

"I'll go on leave for a month," Joona says.

"That's good," Carlos says. "That will solve—"

"As long as I can enter a specific apartment first."

"An apartment?"

Carlos's face darkens and he sits down behind his desk as if all his strength has just left him.

"It was purchased seventeen years ago by the ambassador from the Czech Republic. He gave it to his twenty-year-old daughter."

"Forget it," says Carlos.

"The daughter hasn't lived there for twelve years."

"Doesn't matter. As long as it's owned by a person with diplomatic immunity, paragraph 21 doesn't apply to it."

Anja Larsson comes into the office without knocking. Her blond hair is arranged in a bun on the top of her head, and she's wearing glittery lip gloss. She walks right up to Carlos, looks at him, and gestures toward his cheek.

"You have a spot of dirt on your face," she says.

"Is it my beard?" Carlos asks weakly.

"What?"

"Maybe I forgot to shave this morning," Carlos says.

"It doesn't look good at all."

"I see," he says as he looks down.

"I need to talk to Joona. Are you done here?"

"No," Carlos says. "We're—"

Anja leans over his desk. The red beads of her necklace jostle in her cleavage. Carlos is about to remind her that he's married when his eyes fasten on the shadow that disappears into her low-cut blouse below the lowest bead.

"Are you about to have a nervous breakdown?" Anja asks.

"Yes, I am," Carlos says weakly.

Their colleagues stare as Joona gets up from his chair and walks out of the office with Anja.

They head toward the elevators and Joona presses the call button.

"So what do you want, Anja?" he asks.

"Oh, here you are, all stressed again," she says, and offers him a piece of candy in a red-and-white-striped wrapper. "I just wanted to tell you that Flora Hansen called back and—"

"I need a decision on a search warrant."

Anja shakes her head. She peels the paper from the candy and pops it into Joona's mouth.

"Flora wants to give you your money back."

"She lied to me."

"She just wants us to listen. She said that there is a witness. She really did sound frightened and she kept repeating that you have to believe her. She doesn't want money. She just wants us to listen to her."

"I must get into the apartment at Wollmar Yxkullsgatan 9."

"Oh, Joona." Anja sighs.

She takes the paper off another piece of candy and holds it to Joona's mouth as she puckers her lips. Joona eats the candy. Anja laughs happily and unwraps a third piece and holds it up. It's too late. Joona is already in the elevator.

There are balloons hanging from a door with a scratched window in the Wollmar Yxkullsgatan building. The high voices of children singing comes from the inner courtyard. Joona opens the door and looks in: It's a small garden with a lawn and an apple tree. In the last light of the evening sun, he can see a table set with colorful paper napkins and cups, as well as streamers and balloons. A pregnant woman is sitting on a white plastic chair. She is made up to look like a cat. She's calling something to the children. Joona is hit with a pang of longing.

One of the girls leaves the group and runs up to him.

"Hi," she says, and pushes past him through the door festooned with balloons.

Her bare feet leave dirty footprints on the foyer's white marble floor. She opens the apartment door and yells that she has to pee. One of the balloons is loosened from the door and falls to meet its pink shadow. Joona sees that the entire foyer is filled with traces of bare feet: back and forth from the entrance, up and down the stairs, past the storage door and the garbage chute.

For the second time, Joona walks up to the loft apartment and rings the bell. He stares at the brass plaque with the name Horáčková and the piece of tape with the name Lundhagen. He is starting to get a headache.

He can still hear the voices of the children coming from the inner courtyard. He presses the doorbell again and is about to take out his break-in tools when a man of about thirty opens the door. His hair is styled so it sticks up. The security chain is not attached, and it clatters against the doorframe. Old mail and advertisements still cover the floor in the narrow entry hall. A tiled staircase painted white leads up into the apartment.

"Are you Tobias?"

"Depends on who's asking," the man replies.

He's wearing a short-sleeved shirt and black jeans. His hair is stiff with gel and his face has a yellow tinge.

"The National Police," Joona says.

"No shit," the man says in English with an amazed smile.

"May I come in?"

"No, I'm just going out, but if—"

"You know Vicky Bennet," Joona says.

"Maybe you should come in for a short while," Tobias says seriously.

Joona is aware of the heaviness of his new pistol in its shoulder holster as he walks up the short staircase and into an attic apartment with a sloped ceiling and rounded windows. A framed poster showing a Goth girl with large breasts and angel wings is hanging on one of the walls.

Tobias sits down on the sofa and tries to zip up a large dirty suitcase on the floor close to his legs, but gives up. He leans back into the sofa.

"So you want to talk about Vicky?" Tobias says, reaching forward to take a handful of candy from a ceramic bowl.

"When did you last hear from her?" Joona asks as he flips through some of the unopened mail on the sideboard.

"Well, that's a good question." Tobias sighs. "I don't know. It must have been a year or so ago. She called from . . . Damn." He has dropped some candy on the floor.

"What were you going to say?"

"She called me from Uddevalla, I think. She talked a lot, but I really don't know what she wanted."

"No calls the past few months?"

"Nope."

Joona opens a small wooden door, which leads to a closet. Four hockey video games are unopened in their packages. There's an old computer on the shelf.

"I've really gotta get going," Tobias says.

"When did she live here?"

Tobias tries to close the suitcase again. One of the windows on the side facing the inner courtyard is slightly open. The children are now singing the birthday song.

"Almost three years ago."

"How long did she stay?"

"She didn't stay here the whole time. About seven months in all," Tobias answers.

"Where did she stay when she wasn't here?"

"Who knows."

"You don't know?"

"I had to get her to leave here a few times. See, you don't get it. She was a kid but she could be really difficult."

"In what way?"

"The usual—drugs, theft, suicide attempts," he says as he scratches his scalp. "I never thought she'd kill anybody, though. I saw it in the tabloids. I mean, it was all over."

Tobias glances at the clock and then meets the detective's eye.

"Why?" asks Joona after a few moments of silence.

"Why what?" Tobias replies.

"Why'd you let her stay here?"

"I had a rough childhood myself," he says, and again tries to close the zipper on the suitcase. Joona can see it is filled with tablet computers in their original packaging.

"Can I help you?" Joona holds the zipper together while Tobias zips it shut.

"Sorry about this stuff," he says, patting the suitcase. "I promise, it's not mine. I'm just watching it for a friend."

"I see," Joona says.

Tobias laughs and a bit of candy flies out of his mouth. He gets up and pulls the suitcase behind him as he goes down the stairs and into the hallway.

"Do you know where Vicky would be hiding?" asks Joona.

"No idea—wherever she finds a spot."

"Who does she trust?"

"No one," he replies. He opens the front door and heads toward the stairwell.

"Does she trust you?"

"I don't think so."

"There's no chance that she'd come here?"

Joona dawdles in the narrow hall a few seconds and opens the key cupboard by the front door.

"No, maybe she'd go to . . . Nah, forget it," Tobias says, his back turned to Joona. He presses the button to call the elevator.

"What were you about to say?" Joona asks.

"I need to get going."

Joona carefully removes the spare set of keys to the apartment from the hook before he leaves. He closes the door behind him and rides the elevator down with Tobias.

115

They leave the building to the happy shrieks of children. The balloons on the apartment door are bumping against each other in the breeze.

They walk out to the sidewalk and into the glare of the setting sun. Tobias stops to look at Joona. He scratches one of his eyebrows and then starts sliding away while peering down the street.

"You were about to tell me where she could be hiding," Joona says.

"I don't even remember his name," Tobias says, shading his eyes with his hand. "He's the stepfather of a girl I used to know, Mickan. I know she used to sleep on a sofa bed at his place, near Mosebacke Square. Don't know why I'm going on and on."

"You know the address?"

Tobias shakes his head and pulls at the heavy suitcase.

"A little white house across from the theater," he says.

Joona watches him disappear around the corner with his stolen goods. He thinks about driving to Mosebacke Square and knocking on doors, but something is holding him to this place. A rising sense of unease chills him. It's evening, and it's been a while since he ate or slept. It's getting more difficult to hold his headache at bay and to keep thinking. Joona starts to walk toward his car but then stops. He's just figured out what didn't fit.

He has to smile to himself.

How could he have missed it? He must be very tired not to realize it until now. Perhaps it was too obvious, like the missing link in a classic detective novel.

Tobias said he'd followed the case in the tabloids, yet he talked to Joona as if Vicky were alive. Journalists throughout the country have been writing and broadcasting since Wednesday that Vicky and Dante drowned in the Indal River. They've been howling about the thought-lessness of the police in aggravating the mother's suffering by categoriz-ing Vicky's file as a missing person report.

Tobias knows that Vicky is alive.

This brings to mind an earlier observation.

Joona is sure he has recently seen something without realizing its significance, so instead of following Tobias, he turns around and returns to Wollmar Yxkullsgatan 9.

He remembers the pink balloon that fell from the door and rolled weightlessly across the marble floor of the foyer. There were a number of footprints made by children. They'd been playing and running back and forth from the inner courtyard.

Joona thinks that Vicky could be barefoot since she'd lost her shoes in the river. He opens the front door and scrutinizes the floor and sees that his mind did catch something correctly.

One pair of the bare footprints leads directly from the front to the basement door but not back again.

116

Joona follows the footprints to the metal door and takes out the keys he stole from Tobias's apartment. He unlocks the door and finds the switch for the ceiling light. The heavy door shuts behind him. It's dark for a moment and then the ceiling lamp flickers on. The walls stream cool air and the putrid odor from the garbage room reaches him from one of the vents. He stands still and listens before he keeps walking down the stairs.

He reaches the bottom and sees an overflowing bike-storage area. He squeezes past bicycles, sleds, and baby strollers and starts down a long hall lined on one side with wire-mesh cages that serve as storage lockers. Insulated pipes run directly below the ceiling.

There's a loud rumble as the elevator motor starts up. The odor of urine permeates the still air.

He hears someone move at the far end of the basement.

Joona remembers the photograph of Vicky, which was used for the general alarm. It's hard to imagine that shy, blushing face contorting with uncontrollable rage. The only way for her to be able to swing that hammer would be with twice her natural strength. He tries to imagine her standing in front of him, swinging the hammer and rubbing blood from her eyes before striking again.

Joona tries to breathe quietly while he uses his left hand to unbutton his jacket and pull out his weapon. He's not yet used to its heft and balance.

In one of the storage cages, there's a brown rocking horse with its nose pressed against the wire. Behind it there are steel-edged skis, poles, and a brass curtain rod.

He shudders as he realizes that Vicky could have hidden among the heap of sleds he's already walked past and could be sneaking up behind him.

There's a rustling sound and Joona turns.

The hall is empty.

The sewage pipes rattle in their place against the ceiling.

As he turns back, the ceiling light goes off automatically. He can see nothing and reaches out with his hand until it touches the wire mesh of a storage locker. Farther away, he sees a small light glow against the plastic case of the circuit breaker. It's a yellow flicker, just enough light for someone to find the button for the ceiling light.

Joona waits for his eyes to adjust to the dark and then starts to walk.

The light disappears. Joona stands still and listens. It takes him a moment to realize that someone has walked in front of the yellow light.

He squats down to make himself a smaller target.

The elevator machinery kicks in. Then the switch is visible again.

Joona moves back and at the same time hears someone shuffling down the hall toward him. Someone is there. Someone is at one of the storage lockers in front of him.

"Vicky," he says into the darkness.

The door is opened to the basement and voices are heard from the top of the stairs. Someone is heading for the bicycle-storage area while the ceiling light flickers.

Joona uses the moment. He takes a few quick strides to the end of the hall and aims his gun at a huddled figure.

The light comes on and stays on. The basement door closes and the voices fade in the distance.

Joona holsters his pistol and kicks the door to the storage locker open. He hurries inside.

The figure inside is much smaller than he'd thought. The bent back heaves with her breathing.

Vicky Bennet is the girl huddling there.

Her mouth has been taped shut and her arms are tied to the wire mesh behind her back.

Joona reaches her and tries to loosen the ropes. Her head is bent and she's breathing hard. Her matted hair is hanging in front of her face.

"Vicky, I'm going to get you free—"

She kicks him hard in the forehead just as he bends forward.

The kick is so hard he stumbles backward. She keeps kicking him in the chest. Her shoulders are going to be dislocated by the force she's using. She kicks again, but this time Joona blocks her kick with his hand. She's screaming underneath the tape and throws her body forward. An entire section of wire mesh gives way. Vicky is pulling with both arms and is trying to reach a sharp steel lathe when Joona knocks her to the cement floor.

He holds her still with one knee and puts handcuffs on her before he unties the ropes and rips off the tape from her mouth.

"I'm going to kill you!" screams Vicky.

"I'm a detective at—"

"So rape me, go ahead, I don't care, I'll find you and kill you and all you—"

"Vicky," Joona repeats in a louder voice, "I'm a detective inspector and I need to know where Dante is!"

117

Vicky Bennet is panting through her half-open mouth and staring at him with her dark eyes. There are patches of dried blood and mud on her face and she seems exhausted.

"If you are a police officer, you have to stop Tobias," she says hoarsely.

"I just talked to him," Joona says. "He was on his way to sell some tablets which he—"

"That son of a bitch!" she says, still panting.

"Vicky, you realize I have to take you to the police station."

"Yeah, whatever, I don't give a fuck."

"First, please, tell me where the boy is."

"Tobias took him. I trusted Tobias," Vicky says, and looks away. Her body starts to shake. "I shouldn't have trusted him again."

"What are you telling me?"

"You're not going to listen," she says as she looks at Joona with tears in her eyes.

"I'm listening."

"Tobias promised to take Dante back to his mother."

"He hasn't done that," Joona says.

"I know. I trusted him. I'm such an idiot . . . I . . ." Her voice breaks and panic glitters in her dark eyes. "Don't you get it? He's going to sell the boy! He's going to sell him!"

"What are you—"

"Don't you get it? You let him go!" she screams.

"But what do you mean by 'sell him'?"

"Tobbe's selling the boy to someone who will sell him again, and you will never be able to find him!"

Now they're both running through the bicycle-storage area and up the steep stairs. Joona is holding one hand around Vicky's thin lower arm while he takes out his cell phone and starts calling the county communications center.

"Send a car to Wollmar Yxkullsgatan 9 to pick up a murder suspect," he says quickly. "I need help to catch a kidnapping suspect . . ."

They head through the entrance and out onto the sidewalk. Joona points out the direction toward his car and says to the duty officer who answered the phone, "The kidnapping suspect is Tobias Lundhagen and . . . wait—" Joona turns to Vicky. "What kind of a car does he have?"

"A big black one. I'd recognize it if I saw it."

"What make?"

"No idea."

"Do you know if it's—"

"What the hell!" Vicky screams. "Sorry."

Joona ends the call and takes both of Vicky's shoulders. "Who is he planning to sell Dante to?"

"I don't know. God, I don't know."

"How do you know that they're planning to sell him? Did he say so?" Joona looks into her frightened eyes.

"I know him. I . . ."

"What is it?"

Vicky's voice is weak as she says, "The slaughterhouse area. That's where we need to go. The slaughterhouse area."

They run to his car. He opens the door to the front passenger seat and she gets in, her handcuffed arms behind her. Joona slams the door and sprints to the driver's side, throws himself in, and hits the gas. Gravel spews from the spinning tires. Vicky falls sideways as Joona turns sharply onto Timmermansgatan.

In one fluid movement, Vicky pulls her handcuffed hands beneath her bottom and feet and rests them in her lap.

"Put on your seat belt," Joona says.

They're doing one hundred kilometers an hour when Joona touches the brakes. The car's tires squeal as it swings into Hornsgatan. A woman is standing in the middle of the street looking at her cell phone.

"Idiot!" Vicky screeches.

Joona passes the woman on the wrong side of the median and almost collides with a bus head-on but manages to swing back into his lane. He drives past Maria Square and speeds up. Near Maria Church, a homeless man is digging through a garbage can and then walks into the street without looking, his sack thrown across his back.

Vicky holds her breath and shrinks down. Joona steers up the curb into the bike lane and down again. An oncoming car honks, but Joona increases his speed after he's passed the long wall across from the church and ignores the traffic lights as he turns right into the Söder Tunnel.

Lights along the walls pulse monotonously into the car as they race through the tunnel. Vicky's dirty face is frozen. Her lips are cracked.

"Why the slaughterhouse area?" asks Joona.

"That's where Tobias sold me."

118

The traffic is light in the Söder Tunnel and Joona is able to drive extremely fast. There's a crackle on Joona's radio as he requests backup from the police as well as an ambulance. He says he's heading for the slaughterhouse area in Johanneshov, but explains he does not yet have a specific address.

Beside him, Vicky gnaws on her nails.

"I'll get back to you," he says as his car thumps over the remains of a truck tire.

The long tunnel ends in a curve between concrete walls, forcing Joona to slow down. The sun has now set and the yellow light from lamps strung overhead across the street flash like a strobe over Vicky's pale face. The car speeds up.

"Drive faster," she says, although she's bracing herself against the glove compartment as if it would protect her in a crash. "I said I'd pay double if he'd get money and a passport for me. He promised he'd return Dante to his mother, and I believed him. Can you believe it? After all he's done to me."

She starts hitting her head with her fists.

"How can anyone be as stupid as me?" she says. "All he wanted was Dante. He whacked me with a pipe and locked me up. I was so stupid. I shouldn't even be alive."

On the other side of Hammarbyleden's water, they pass beneath the viaduct of Nynäsvägen and around the Globen Arena. The arena looks like a dirty white celestial body next to the soccer stadium.

They drive toward a large enclosed area with industrial buildings and parked trailers. Neon signs hang over both lanes of traffic. White letters on a red background tell them they're in the slaughterhouse area. The booms are up, so they drive straight in, tires squealing.

"Where to now?" asks Joona as they pass a gray warehouse.

Vicky is biting her lip as she looks around.

"I don't know."

119

The sky is dark, but neon signs and streetlights illuminate the maze of the industrial area. Almost all work has ended for the day, but on a cross street deep in the maze, a crane is lifting a blue container. The machine is making a grating, scraping noise.

Joona drives past a dirty building with a bent sign advertising steaks and is coming up to some green sheet-metal buildings next to a turn-around. The steel gates are closed.

They drive past a yellow-brick building with a loading dock and rusty containers and turn at the meat center.

They haven't seen a single person.

They pass a less well-lit street. Garbage cans, old trucks, and large blower ducts fill the space. By the parking lot under a billboard that reads HAVE OUR HOT DOGS! there's a van with a pornographic picture painted on the side. There's loud grinding as they drive over a well grid. Joona turns to the left around a crooked railing. A few seagulls fly up from a stack of wooden pallets.

"There! There's his car!" Vicky yells. "It is definitely his! I recognize the building. I bet they're inside!"

A black van with a Confederate flag pasted in its back window is parked in front of a large building as brown as liver. On the other side of the road, four cars are parked in a row along the sidewalk.

Joona drives past the building, turns left, and parks in front of a brick building. Three vertical flag signs are flapping in the wind.

Joona says nothing, but he takes his key and unlocks Vicky's right hand. He fastens the free handcuff to the steering wheel before he leaves the vehicle. Her dark eyes land on him, but she does not protest.

She watches him run back, his figure illuminated by a streetlight. Sand and dust whirl around him. He turns right and disappears.

Between the closed buildings, there's a small alley with loading docks, iron staircases, and containers for slaughterhouse waste. Joona approaches the door Vicky pointed out. He looks back for a moment and takes in the deserted location. Far away, there's a forklift moving around inside a huge building with an open front wall, like an airplane hangar.

He walks up a metal staircase, opens the door, and enters a hall with cracked vinyl flooring. He walks silently past three offices with thin walls. One has a plastic lemon tree inserted into a white pot filled with LECA balls. There are traces of Christmas glitter on its branches. Behind it on the wall there's a framed slaughterhouse license from 1943, issued by the Crisis Committee of Stockholm.

There's a steel door at the end of the hallway and on it is a laminated poster showing the rules and regulations of slaughterhouse hygiene. Someone has scribbled "Rules for Care of Cocks" over the top. Joona pushes the door open a few centimeters to listen. He hears voices in the distance.

He pushes the door farther open so he can look in. He sees a large machine hall for slaughter lines and automated hog splitting. The yellow tiled floor has a slight shine. The stainless-steel counters glisten. A bloodied plastic apron hangs over the edge of a garbage can.

Joona pulls out his gun and his heart leaps when he smells the gun grease.

120

Gun in hand, Joona sneaks inside, bending low behind the large machinery. He can smell the sweet odor from the rinsed floor and the rubber mats. He realizes that he didn't stop to give the county communications center an address. They have probably reached the slaughterhouse area by now, but it might take them some time to find Vicky.

A memory flashes through his mind, a merciless memory of seconds during which lives change and time compresses. Joona is eleven years old and the school principal has come to his classroom, taken him out into the hall, and told him what happened. The principal's cheeks are wet with tears.

Joona's father was a policeman and was on patrol. He'd gone into an apartment and had been shot in the back. His father had been on his own. Against regulations.

Joona has no time to wait for reinforcements.

In front of him, pneumatic knives and casing pullers covered in dirty membranes are hanging from a rack above a stainless-steel roller conveyor. He keeps moving forward. He can hear the voices more clearly.

"No, he has to wake up first." A deep, wheezing male voice.

"Give him a minute."

Joona recognizes Tobias's voice with its innocent, boyish tone.

"What the hell were you thinking?" Another voice, also male.

"I wanted to keep him quiet," Tobias replies.

"He's practically dead," says the wheezing voice. "I won't pay until I know he's all right."

"We can only stay two more minutes," says a third male voice. He is serious.

Joona creeps toward the voices. As he reaches the end of one conveyor, he can see the boy lying on a gray blanket spread on the floor. He's dressed in a stretched-out blue sweater, corduroy pants, and tiny sports shoes. His face has been washed, but he is filthy and unconscious.

A large, heavyset man is standing beside the boy. His beer belly protrudes from a leather vest, and he's sweating so heavily that it's running down his face. He stamps his foot with irritation and tugs at his white beard.

Joona feels a drop hit him. A hose clip is loose and drops of water are falling from it. They run over the tiled floor to the drain.

The large man starts to pace, while constantly looking at his watch. Then he squats beside the boy.

"Let's take a few pictures," comes another voice, a new one.

Joona does not know what to do. Besides Tobias, there are at least four men and he can't tell whether they are armed or not.

He really would like a SWAT team to appear right now.

The large man's face shines as he pulls the shoes from Dante's feet.

The small, striped socks come off with the shoes. The boy's heels hit the blanket.

As the man's huge hands start to unbuckle the boy's pants, Joona can't stand to watch any longer.

He doesn't bother to hide as he heads for the cutting counter with its freshly sharpened knives of various lengths, thicknesses, and blade edges.

He keeps his gun pointed to the floor.

Joona knows he isn't following regulations. He just can't wait any longer. He heads directly for the men.

"What the hell!" yells the heavyset man.

He lets go of the boy but remains squatting.

"You are under arrest for kidnapping," Joona says as he kicks the huge man in the chest.

The man falls backward from the blow. He can't stop his fall and crashes into buckets of trimmings, rolls over the floor grate, and knocks a box of ear protectors down before he lands in the heavy skinning machine.

Joona hears the click of a safety being released and feels a muzzle being pushed against his spine between his shoulder blades. He stands absolutely still as he knows the bullet would go right through his heart if it left the weapon that instant.

A man of about fifty comes up to Joona from the side. He has a blond ponytail and is wearing a brown leather jacket. He moves as softly as a bodyguard and he's pointing a sawed-off shotgun at Joona.

"Shoot him!" someone shouts.

The fat man is on his back, panting heavily. He rolls over and tries to get up but stumbles. He rights himself against the machine and gets to his unsteady feet. Then he disappears from Joona's line of sight.

"We can't stay here," Tobias is whispering.

Joona tries to see what's in the reflections on the gleaming metal of the cutting board and the hanging knives, but it's impossible to make out how many men are behind him.

"Hand over your gun," a calm voice says behind him.

Joona lets Tobias take his pistol. His colleagues must be near by now. He must not take any risks.

121

Vicky Bennet is still in the front seat of Joona Linna's car. She's biting her dry lips and staring at the reddish-brown building. She's holding on to the steering wheel so that her handcuffed wrist won't chafe.

After every time she gets angry or afraid, she has trouble remembering what happened. Her memory bounces around and glances off one detail or another then disappears for good.

Vicky shakes her head and closes her eyes. Then she looks back at the building. She doesn't know how long ago the detective with the pleasant voice went into the building, his coat fluttering behind him in the wind.

Perhaps Dante is already lost for good. He's gone down the black hole, which sucks in children of all ages.

She tries to keep calm, but she's frantic to get out of the car.

She sees a rat scurry along the edge of a damp concrete foundation and run down a drainpipe.

The man who had been driving the forklift has stopped working. He's shutting the high doors to the hangar and locking them. Then he leaves.

Vicky stares at her hand and the shiny metal keeping her prisoner.

Tobias had promised to take Dante to his mother.

Vicky wails. How could she have believed Tobias again? If Dante disappears, it's her own fault.

She twists as far as she can to look out the back window. All the doors to the building are closed and there's no one in sight. The yellow cloth of a ripped awning flaps in the wind.

She pulls against the steering wheel with both hands in an attempt to break it off. It's no use.

"Damn it!"

She's breathing hard as she slams her head against the neck support.

She glimpses a poster advertising fresh meat and Swedish goods. Someone has drawn a pair of eyes and a downturned mouth in the dust.

The detective should have been back by now.

She hears a sudden bang as loud as an explosion. The echo reverberates and then dies away.

She tries to see anything at all and cranes her head in all directions. The area is deserted.

What are they doing?

Her heart beats against her chest. Who knows what can happen in this place?

She breathes harder as she pictures a lonely child, crying from fear in a room with strange men. The image just came to her mind—she doesn't know what it's about.

Vicky feels panic rising and tries to wrench her wrist out of the handcuff. She can't. She pulls harder and the pain makes her catch her breath. The metal glides up the back of her hand but sticks. Vicky is breathing through her nose as she leans back, braces herself with one foot on the steering wheel and the other on the handcuff, and then she pushes her legs with all her strength.

Vicky screams as flesh rips away from the back of her hand and her thumb breaks. Her hand has slipped free from the cuff.

122

The muzzle is removed from Joona's back. He can hear footsteps moving away and he slowly turns around.

A short man in glasses and wearing a gray suit is backing away from him. He holds a black Glock, which he is aiming at Joona. His left hand is hanging at his hip. Joona wonders if the man has hurt it, but then realizes it's a prosthetic.

Tobias is standing behind a dirty counter. He's holding Joona's Smith & Wesson but doesn't seem to know what to do with it.

To Joona's right, the man with the blond ponytail is aiming a sawed-off shotgun at him.

"Roger," the short man with the Glock says, "I want you and Micke to take care of this cop once I've left."

Tobias's eyes are dark with anxiety.

A young man with cropped hair and wearing camouflage pants is walking straight toward Joona, pointing a homemade gun at him. It's a small souped-up submachine gun with ancillary parts. Joona is not wearing a bulletproof vest, but he'd rather take his chances with this gun than with the others. A homemade weapon can have the same firepower as an average automatic weapon, but usually it's been badly built.

A red dot appears on Joona's chest. It's from the laser sight on the gun, the kind the police used a few years ago.

Joona says, "Lie down on the floor and put your hands behind your neck."

The man with cropped hair smiles. The red dot slides to Joona's solar plexus and back up to his collarbone.

"Micke, shoot him," Roger says. He's still aiming at Joona with the sawed-off shotgun.

"We can't have a witness," stammers Tobias. He runs his hand nervously over his mouth.

The man with the prosthetic hand looks at Tobias and says, "Get the boy to my car." Then he leaves the hall.

Tobias doesn't look away from Joona for a second as he walks over to Dante. He grabs his sweater to pull him away over the tiled floor. He is not gentle.

"I'll be after you in a minute!" Joona yells at him.

There's about six yards between Joona and the man called Micke with the homemade gun.

Joona moves slowly toward him.

The young man yells, "Stand still!"

"Micke," Joona says softly, "if you lie down on the floor and put your hands behind your neck, you'll be fine."

"Shoot the cop!" yells the man named Roger.

"You do it!" Micke says.

"What? What did you just say?" Roger says, and lowers his rifle.

123

Micke is breathing hard. The laser dot jumps around Joona's chest. It disappears and reappears.

"I can tell that you're scared," Joona says. He comes closer.

"Shut your mouth and keep it shut!" Micke says, backing away.

"You're shaking."

"Shoot him! What the hell are you waiting for?" yells Roger.

"Put down the weapon," Joona says.

"Shoot him!"

"He's too afraid," Joona says.

"I'm not afraid! I'll do it!" Roger raises the rifle.

"I don't believe you," Joona says. He can see a Thor's hammer on a chain around Roger's neck.

"You want me to prove it? You want me to shoot you?" Roger is screaming as he edges closer.

Roger puts his finger on the trigger and aims it at Joona.

"I'll shoot off your head!" he hisses.

Joona looks at the floor and waits until the man is close enough. Then he whips his arm around and catches the barrel of the rifle, pulls it toward himself, and jerks it around. Its butt bashes Roger's cheek. His head jerks to the side and he stumbles into the line of fire of the submachine gun. Joona is now behind him and aims the rifle between Roger's legs. He fires. The sound is deafening and the weapon jumps. The cluster of bullets passes between Roger's legs and slams right through Micke's left ankle. His foot is torn off and rolls beneath the cutting table.

Blood pours from the stump of Micke's leg and he reflexively fires the submachine gun. Six bullets slam into Roger's chest and shoulders. Micke falls while still screaming and the rest of the shots go wild toward the ceiling, ricocheting among the pipes and the overhead cranes.

Roger falls to his knees and leans forward. His ponytail hangs over his cheek. He is holding himself up with his arms, but a steady stream of blood flows from his chest and drains through the grate for pigs' blood.

The short man with the prosthesis and the Glock is running toward them. Joona leaps behind one of the machines, one for inflating pigs' carcasses to make slicing easier. He can hear the man follow him and kick away a rattling cart. The man's breathing is ragged.

Joona moves backward and opens the rifle. It has just one bullet.

Micke is still screaming and calling for help.

Ten more steps back and Joona spots a yellowed plastic strip curtain over an opening. He realizes that behind it is a refrigerated room. He can glimpse slaughtered pigs hanging there tightly side by side. He thinks that on the other side of the room there must be a door to the loading dock facing the road.

124

The door to the reddish-brown building is propped open by a rolled-up newspaper. A white metal sign above it says LARSSON'S BOUTIQUE MEATS.

Vicky walks up to the black metal door, stumbling over the shoe grate, and goes inside. Blood drips from the wound on her hand onto the newspaper. She has to find Dante. That's all she can think about. It's her only plan.

She heads through the employee dressing room, past wooden benches lined up in front of bent red metal lockers. A poster of the soccer player Zlatan Ibrahimović is taped to one of the walls. In the niche by the windows, a few plastic coffee mugs are standing on a brochure from the Food Workers Union.

Vicky hears screaming on the other side of the wall. A man is calling for help.

She looks around the dressing room. She opens a cupboard and pulls out a few sand-colored plastic boxes. She opens the next cupboard and keeps going. She sees the garbage can and looks inside. Among the tobacco papers and candy wrappers, she spots an empty glass bottle.

The man is still screaming for help, but his voice is weaker.

"What the hell," Vicky mutters, and she picks up the empty bottle. She holds it tightly in her good hand and rushes out the door at the far end of the room into a cool storage room with pallets and packing machines.

She runs as silently as she can toward a large garage door. As she passes a pallet of plastic-wrapped cardboard boxes, she sees movement from the corner of her eye and stops.

A shadow is moving behind a bright yellow forklift.

She sneaks forward to the forklift. She touches the vehicle and slowly moves around it and catches sight of a man leaning over a bundle on a blanket.

"I don't feel good," comes the voice of a small child.

"Can you stand up?" the man asks.

Vicky takes one step toward them. The man turns around. It's Tobias.

"Hey, Vicky, what are you doing here?" Tobias smiles in surprise.

She comes closer, wondering what is going on.

"Dante? Is that you?" she asks.

The boy lifts his head from the blanket and peers at her as if he can't make her out in the darkness.

"Vicky, can you help me out here? Can you take him to the van?" asks Tobias. "I'll be right there."

"But I am—"

"Just do what I say and everything will be fine," he says.

"All right," she replies tonelessly.

"Hurry up. Just get the kid to the van."

The boy's face is gray and he lies his head back down on the blanket and closes his eyes.

"You're going to have to carry him." Tobias sighs.

"Okay," Vicky says as she walks up to Tobias and breaks the bottle on his head.

He looks surprised at first. He sways and lands on one knee. He touches his hairline and feels glass splinters and blood.

"What the fuck are you . . ."

She hits him as hard as she can with the rest of the bottle. It lands on the side of his neck and she twists it. His warm blood starts to run over her fingers. Her rage is so strong she feels drunk with it. Her anger burns like overheated insanity.

"You never should have touched this boy!" she screams.

She takes aim at his eyes. His hands are grabbing at air but he gets hold of her jacket and pulls her toward him. Then he hits her in the face with his fist. She falls back and it's as if the light has gone out.

As she falls, she remembers the man who paid Tobias for her.

Remembers waking up with pain in her vagina. Remembers the doctor saying that her ovaries were damaged.

She lands on her back but she's tucked in her head to keep it from hitting the ground. She blinks and her sight is restored. She gets up unsteadily, but she keeps her balance. She feels blood running from her mouth.

Tobias has found a board with nails in it. He's trying to get to his feet as he reaches for it.

Vicky's left hand is throbbing from her broken thumb. She clutches the remnant of the broken bottle with her right hand and slams it into his outstretched hand. Her own blood sprays into her eyes. She hits wildly. She stabs his chest and his forehead and finally the remnant of the bottle breaks apart, slashing her hand. Still she keeps hitting him until he falls to the ground and doesn't move.

125

Vicky can't run any longer with Dante in her arms. She feels as if she's going to vomit. She's losing feeling in both her arms and she's afraid she's going to drop him. She stops so she can shift his position, but falls to her knees instead. Vicky sighs as she carefully lays the boy on the ground. He has gone back to sleep. His face is colorless and Vicky can hardly hear him breathe.

They have to either hide or get out of here.

She pulls herself together and drags him by his sweater to a garbage container, hoping they can squeeze behind it. Dante moans and she pats him and watches him open his eyes for a moment before closing them again.

Ten yards away is a glass door next to a large garage entrance, but Vicky can't carry the boy any farther. Her legs are trembling from exertion. All she wants to do is lie down next to him and go to sleep. She knows she can't. She's in pain and her hands are bloody and her arms are numb.

She can see an empty street through the glass door.

She sinks to a sitting position, breathing hard. She tries to collect her thoughts as she looks at her hands and at the boy. She pushes hair out of Dante's face and leans toward him.

"Wake up now," she says.

He blinks and looks at her blood-covered face. He seems frightened.

"I'm all right," she says. "It doesn't hurt. Have you ever had a bloody nose?"

He nods.

"I can't carry you any longer, Dante," she says, fighting the urge to cry. "You have to walk the last bit."

"I just want to sleep," Dante says as he yawns.

"It's all over now. You are going to go home."

"What?"

"You are going home to your mother," she says, and smiles. It lights up her exhausted face. "All you have to do is walk."

He nods and sits up. He runs a hand through his hair.

Somewhere within the large storage area there's a loud bang as something falls. It sounds like steel pipes are starting to roll.

"Try and stand up now," Vicky says.

They both get up and start toward the glass door. Each step is unbearably hard. Vicky realizes that she might not make it. Then she sees the revolving blue light of a police car. More cars pull up beside it. Vicky thinks that they're saved.

"Hello?" It's a man's harsh voice. "Hello?"

The man's voice echoes between the walls and the ceiling. Vicky is dizzy and has to stop. Dante keeps going.

Vicky leans against the cold metal of the container.

"Go straight out the door," she says. Her voice is weak.

Dante looks back and it seems as if he is going to turn around.

"No, no. Go straight out," she pleads. "I'll be right there."

She sees three uniformed police officers running in the wrong direction. They're heading to a building on the other side of the street. Dante keeps going toward the door. He pulls down the handle and pulls. Nothing happens.

"Hello?" the man's voice is closer.

Vicky bites her lip and spits bloody saliva on the floor, then starts to walk again.

"Won't open," Dante says as he pulls hard on the door.

Her legs are shaking but somehow she manages the last few steps. Her hand burns with pain as she pulls on the door handle as hard as she can. The door does not budge. She pushes it, but it is locked. She tries banging on the glass, but there's not much sound. She can see four police cars outside. Their blue lights flash over the façades and windows of the surrounding buildings. She waves to get their attention, but no one sees her.

Heavy footfalls are approaching swiftly behind them. Vicky turns and sees a heavyset man heading right for them. He is smiling.

126

Beneath the ceiling is an electric conveyor hung with tightly packed pig carcasses. The chill of the refrigerated room dampens the sweet smell of the meat.

Joona runs bent over beside the bodies of the animals deeper into the room, looking for something to use as a weapon. He can hear dull screams from the machine room, followed by a few quick thuds. He tries to spot his pursuer through the plastic slats that cover the opening. An indistinct figure is moving between the cutting counters. He appears as wide as four people and then as thin as a stick.

He is running Joona's way and he is carrying a pistol in his right hand.

Joona backs up and bends over. He looks underneath the pig carcasses and sees a white bucket against the wall. Next to it are a pipe and a few dirty rags. He could use the pipe.

He inches toward the bucket but stops when the short man moves aside the heavy plastic slats with his prosthetic hand.

Joona stands still and glimpses his pursuer in the narrow reflections on the chrome edge of the doorway.

He watches the man enter, holding his pistol with his arm straight out. His eyes search the room.

Without making a sound, Joona takes a few more steps toward the wall. He's hidden behind a pig and can no longer see his pursuer, but he can still hear him walking and breathing.

Fifty feet farther on is an exit, which probably leads toward the loading dock. Joona could run down the aisle between the hanging carcasses, but right before he reaches the entrance, his pursuer would have a clean line of fire for a few seconds.

A few seconds too many, Joona thinks.

He can still hear quick footsteps and then a thud. One of the pigs starts to swing and the connection to the conveyor gibbet creaks.

Joona reaches the wall and sinks down next to the cooling unit. His pursuer's shadow appears not more than thirty feet away.

Time is beginning to run out. The man with the prosthetic hand will find him soon.

Joona slides to the side and picks up the pipe. It's made of plastic. It's absolutely useless as a weapon. He's starting to move away when he notices that there are tools in the white bucket. Three screwdrivers, a pair of pliers, and a knife with a powerful short blade.

Joona draws the knife from the bucket slowly. Metal scrapes against metal. The blade slides against the jaws of the pliers.

He figures out where his pursuer is from the sound of his footsteps and realizes he has to move now.

A shot is fired and the bullet slams into a carcass eighteen inches from Joona's head. The one-handed man is running at him. Joona rolls away under the row of meat.

127

The cop has no weapon. He must be afraid, the man thinks as he pushes his hair out of his face with his prosthetic hand.

He stops so he can aim his gun. He tries to peer through the row of slaughtered pigs.

He has to be afraid, he repeats to himself. He's hiding right now, but he is going to make a run for the door facing the street.

He's panting and the air is dry and cold in his lungs. He coughs weakly and turns completely around. He looks at his pistol and then raises his eyes. He has to blink hard. Perhaps there was just something there by the cooling unit. He starts to run alongside the row of pigs.

He has to end this. All he has to do is catch up to the cop and shoot him point-blank: first through the trunk and then a shot through the temple.

He stops. The space along the concrete wall is empty. There are a few dirty rags and a white bucket on the floor—nothing else.

He spins on his heel and begins to walk back to where he'd come from.

All he can hear is his own breathing.

He pushes a pig with his left hand. It's heavier than he thought. He has to really heave it to get it to swing, and it hurts him where the stump of his arm presses against the prosthesis.

The gibbet's fastener squeaks.

The pig swings to the right and he gets a glimpse into the next row.

He can't go anywhere, the man thinks. *He's in a tiny cage.* All he has to do is keep a line of fire open toward the exit in case the cop tries to get out, while also monitoring the plastic-sheeted opening.

His shoulder is getting tired and he lowers his pistol slightly. He knows he's risking valuable seconds, but the weapon will start to shake if his arm gets too tired.

He sneaks forward and thinks he sees a human back. He aims and fires. The recoil bumps against him and the spray from the fuse burns his knuckles. Adrenaline pumps through his body and chills his face. It was only a pig hanging crookedly.

This is going to hell, he thinks. He has to shoot the cop. He can't let him get away, not now. *But where the hell is he? Where has he gone?*

The ceiling creaks and he looks up at steel girders and overhead cranes. He can't see anything. He backs up and stumbles. He grabs a pig for balance and feels the moisture of the cold meat through his shirt. The rind glitters with small drops of condensation. He feels nauseated. Something is not right. Anxiety is starting to overwhelm him. He can't stay here much longer.

The man keeps retreating. He sees a quick shadow against the wall and raises his weapon.

All of a sudden, there's an electric buzz from the ceiling and all the pigs start swaying. It's hard to make out where one carcass starts and the next leaves off. Then the conveyor system roars to life. The heavy carcasses start to revolve. They are moving along the conveyor and pulling an ice-cold breeze through the room.

The man turns around and blinks. He tries to look in all directions at once and thinks that the job isn't worth this.

It was supposed to be simple: buy a Swedish boy the police believed was dead. He'd get a good price for him without going much farther than Holland or Germany. It's not worth all this trouble.

The pigs stop suddenly and swing in place. A red lamp glows on the wall. The cop has hit the emergency button. The room falls silent and the man feels uneasy.

What the fuck am I doing here? he asks himself.

He bends down to look beneath the carcasses and then takes two steps forward.

The exit to the street is still closed.

He turns around to check the exit with the plastic slats. The cop is standing right in front of him.

A shiver goes up his back.

128

Joona can see the short man starting to take aim at him. He tracks the
man's arm motion as he steps toward him and knocks his pistol upward
as he grabs his wrist. He slams the man's hand over his head against a
pig carcass and drives the knife through the palm. The blade plunges
deep between two ribs. The man screams.

· Joona lets go of the knife and moves away.

The short man fumbles his lifeless prosthetic fingers over the knife
handle, then gives up. He's caught. He can't move or the pain will in-
crease. Blood runs from his palm and down his shirtsleeve.

Joona picks up the pistol and leaves the refrigerated room without
looking at the man.

The air in the large machine hall feels warm. He races along one of
the walls in the direction Tobias disappeared with Dante. He stops at a
green metal door and checks the pistol. There is at least one bullet in
the chamber. There could be more in the magazine. He opens the door
and steps into a warehouse area. Goods are stacked on pallets and there
are forklifts standing still.

He can hear a rustling, moaning sound.

Joona determines the direction and runs over to a large garbage container. Blue light is dancing through a window and over the floor. He
raises the pistol and creeps around the container. The fat man in the
leather vest is on his knees with his back to Joona. He's breathing heavily

as he bangs Vicky's head on the floor. Dante is lying a few feet away, curled into a ball and crying as if he's been completely abandoned.

Joona reaches the fat man before he can get up. He grabs him around his throat with his arm and pulls him up and away from Vicky. He cracks him on the collarbone with his pistol, heaves him backward, and then lets go of the man's throat and kicks him in the chest so hard that he flies through the glass door. The fat man lands on his back among the splinters of glass and the blue lights revolve over him.

Three uniformed policemen run up with drawn weapons. They aim at the man on the ground, who is trying to sit up.

One of the policemen looks up. "Joona Linna?"

The policemen stare at the tall detective standing in the broken door. Glass is still falling from the frame.

"I'm just an observer," Joona says.

He throws the Glock on the ground and heads back to Vicky. He kneels on the ground. She is on her back and her breathing is irregular. Her arm is at an odd angle. Dante has stopped crying and looks at Joona in surprise. Joona rolls Vicky onto her side into the recovery position then squats beside her. He strokes her cheek and whispers that everything is all right now. An even stream of blood starts flowing from her nose. She does not open her eyes or respond to his words, but her feet are twitching.

129

The man who flew through the glass door tried to sit up, but two police-men grabbed him and forced him onto his stomach before they hand-cuffed him.

The first paramedics to arrive put an oral airway into Vicky's throat and immobilized her head before they lifted her onto a stretcher.

Joona told the operations leader what had happened while two po-lice units entered the building, one on each side.

In the refrigeration room, they found a silent, pale man with one hand impaled to a pig carcass by a knife. The police officer who found him called the paramedics and needed the assistance of a fellow officer to wrestle the knife out of the meat. The blade grated against the ribs and came out with a sucking sound. The injured man pulled his hand to his stomach using his other, prosthetic hand but then twirled to the ground.

The man who had been hit in the chest by the homemade automatic rifle was dead. The young man who had pulled the trigger when Joona shot him was still alive. He'd saved himself from bleeding to death by cinching his belt just below his knee as a tourniquet. When the police patrol unit approached with raised guns, he pointed to his foot, which had been shot off. It was lying beneath the cutting counter.

The last man they found was Tobias Lundgren. He'd hidden among the garbage in the warehouse room. His face was cut to bits and was bleeding profusely, but none of his wounds were life-threatening. He tried to crawl deeper into the mound of garbage. When the police pulled him out, he was shaking from fear.

Carlos Eliasson has already been informed of what took place in the slaughterhouse area when Joona calls him from the ambulance.

"One dead, two seriously wounded, and three slightly injured," Carlos reads out loud.

"But the children are alive. They survived."

"Joona." Carlos sighs.

"Everyone decided they'd drowned, but I—"

"Yes, you were right. Absolutely," Carlos interrupts. "But you are still the subject of an internal investigation and you had other orders."

"So I was supposed to just let it be?"

"Yes, that's what you were supposed to do."

"But you know I couldn't do that."

The sirens abruptly stop wailing as the ambulance turns into the entrance of the Söder Hospital emergency receiving area.

"The prosecutor and her people are going to be the ones to question the witness. You are now on sick leave and cut off from everything."

Joona takes this to mean that the internal investigation is not going his way, and it crosses his mind that he may even be charged with dereliction of duty. Nevertheless, the only emotion he feels is relief. Vicky Bennet has been found and the little boy ripped from the jaws of wolves.

Joona climbs out of the ambulance unassisted, but he heeds the paramedics' request to lie down on a stretcher. They lift the rails and roll him away.

Instead of waiting in line for an X-ray after he's been examined and his wounds dressed, he heads out to find the doctor in charge of Vicky's care.

A nurse points to where a short woman is studying the automatic coffee machine.

Joona explains that he has to know whether Vicky can be questioned today.

The short woman listens to him without looking up. She presses the button for mocha and waits for her cup to be filled. Then she says that she's done a CT scan of Vicky's brain in order to determine whether there has been intracranial bleeding. Vicky has received a severe concussion, but luckily there has been no cerebral hemorrhage.

"We must keep her here for observation, but there's nothing to indicate she can't be questioned tomorrow morning if it's important," the doctor says. She walks away with her coffee cup in her hand.

The prosecutor Susanne Öst is on her way from Sundsvall to Stockholm. Tomorrow morning at eight o'clock sharp, she intends to start her initial interrogation of Vicky Bennet, the fifteen-year-old girl who has just been arrested and charged with two murders and one count of kidnapping.

130

Vicky is sitting up in bed, the curtains drawn around her, when Joona Linna shows his ID to the young policeman guarding the door and walks in. Her head is bandaged; her face is covered in bruises and grazes; her broken thumb is in a cast. Susanne Öst is also there. With her is a younger woman. Joona does not greet them but pulls up a chair beside the girl.

"How are you feeling?" he asks.

She gives him a muddled look and asks, "Is Dante with his mother now?"

"He's here at the hospital and his mother is sitting next to him."

"Was he hurt?"

"No, he's fine."

Vicky nods and then stares into space.

"And you? How are you feeling?" Joona asks again.

She looks at him but is not able to answer before the prosecutor clears her throat.

"I would like Joona Linna to leave this room right now," Susanne says.

"Now you've done it," Joona says, and doesn't look away from Vicky.

"You are not part of this initial investigation." Susanne raises her voice.

"They're going to ask you a ton of questions," Joona says to Vicky.

"I want you to stay here," she says in a quiet voice.

"Honestly, I can't," Joona says.

Vicky whispers something to herself and then she looks at the prosecutor.

"I'm not saying anything unless Joona stays."

Susanne says, "He can stay if he keeps quiet."

Joona is watching Vicky and thinking about how to get through to her.

Two murders are a heavy burden to bear. Most girls her age would have already broken down and confessed, but Vicky is calm and expressionless. She won't let anyone inside her mind. She creates quick alliances, he thinks, but hides her true motives to keep as much control as she can over her situation.

"Vicky Bennet," the prosecutor starts with a smile, "my name is Susanne and I'm going to be asking you questions, but before we begin, I have to let you know that we are recording everything so that we can listen to it later. This means I don't have to write much down, which is nice . . . I'm lazy that way."

Vicky is not looking at her and doesn't react. Susanne waits a moment and keeps wearing her smile. Then she rattles off the time, date, and the names of the people in the room.

"We usually do this before we get started," she explains.

"Do you understand who we are?" asks the second woman. "My name is Signe Ridelman and I've been appointed as your lawyer."

"Signe is here to help you," the prosecutor says.

"Do you know what a lawyer is?" asks Signe.

Vicky gives a slight nod.

"I need an answer," Signe says patiently.

"I understand," Vicky says, and then she smiles broadly.

"What's so funny?" asks the prosecutor.

"All of this," Vicky says. Then she lifts her arm and pulls out the narrow tube from the inside of her forearm and watches her blood trickle down.

131

The room is silent except for a scraping noise from outside. A bird has landed on the windowsill. The fluorescent light hums overhead. A nurse has been summoned and Vicky's IV is fastened once more to the catheter in her arm. The nurse pulled open the curtain around the bed before leaving the room, the better to keep an eye on this patient.

Susanne Öst drags a chair back to the side of the bed.

"I will be asking you about some things that you've done," she says. "I want you to tell us the truth."

"And nothing but the truth," Vicky says, looking down.

"Eleven days ago you left your bedroom at Birgittagården in the middle of the night. Do you remember this?"

"I haven't been counting the days," Vicky says. There's no emotion in her voice.

"But you remember leaving Birgittagården in the middle of the night?"

"Yes."

"Why did you leave?" Susanne Öst asks.

Vicky pulls at a loose thread on the bandage around her hand.

"Had you ever done it before?"

"Done what?"

"Left Birgittagården in the middle of the night?"

"No," says Vicky. She sounds bored.

"Why did you do it this time?"

When the prosecutor doesn't get an answer, she smiles and asks in a milder tone, "Why were you awake in the middle of the night?"

"Don't remember."

"And so let's move back a few hours. Do you remember what was going on then? Everyone went to bed and you were awake. What did you do?"

"Nothing."

"You didn't do anything until you left Birgittagården in the middle of the night. Don't you think that's strange?"

"No."

Vicky is staring out the window. The sun is playing hide-and-seek in the clouds crossing the skies.

"I want you to tell me why you left Birgittagården," Susanne says. Her tone turns serious. "I won't stop asking until you tell me what happened. Do you understand?"

"I don't know what you want me to say," Vicky replies quietly.

"I know it's difficult but I want you to tell me anyway."

The girl looks up at the ceiling and her mouth moves as if she's searching for words. Then she says in amazement, "I killed . . ."

She stops and pulls at the IV tube.

"Keep going." Susanne is tense.

Vicky shakes her head and moistens her lips.

"You might as well tell me," Susanne said. "You just said you killed—"

"Right . . . There was an irritating fly in the room and I killed it and I—"

"What the hell? Excuse me, I'm sorry, but isn't it strange that you remember killing a fly but not why you left Birgittagården in the middle of the night?"

132

Susanne Öst and Signe Ridelman have requested a break and have left the room for a moment. The gray morning light is reflected in the IV pole and the chrome bed railings. Vicky Bennet is sitting up in bed and cursing to herself.

"Isn't that the truth," Joona says. He has taken Susanne's place on the chair beside the bed.

"All I can think about is Dante," she says.

"Dante is going to be just fine."

Vicky is going to say something else, but the two women return. Joona gets up and walks over to the window.

"So," Susanne says, full of energy. "You have admitted that you left Birgittagården in the middle of the night and went straight into the forest. This is not something that people do for no reason. You did have a reason to run away, didn't you?"

Vicky looks away, runs her tongue over her lips, and says nothing.

"Answer me," says the prosecutor.

"Yes."

"Why did you go on the run?"

The girl shrugs.

"You did something that's hard to talk about, right?"

Vicky rubs her face.

"I have to ask you these questions," Susanne says. "You think I'm being difficult, but I know that you'll feel much better after you confess."

"Will I?"

"You will."

Vicky shrugs her shoulders and meets the prosecutor's eyes.

"So what do you want me to confess?"

"Just tell me what you did that night."

"I killed a fly."

The prosecutor leaves the room abruptly without saying another word.

133

It's eight fifteen in the morning as Saga Bauer opens the door to the appeals room at the offices for the Public Prosecutor for Police Cases. Mikael Båge, who's responsible for internal investigations, rises from his armchair.

Saga is still damp from her shower and her long blond hair with its colorful bands winds over her narrow shoulders and down her back. She has a bandage on the bridge of her nose, but she's still beautiful in a way that makes an observer feel unhappily in love.

Saga has run six kilometers this morning and, as usual, she's wearing a hoodie from Narva Boxing Club, faded jeans, and sneakers.

"Are you Saga Bauer?" Mikael asks with an unusually large smile.

"That's right," Saga replies.

He wipes his hand on his jacket before he takes Saga's.

"I'm sorry. Don't mind me . . . It's just . . . If only I were twenty years younger! You must have heard this before."

Mikael Båge is blushing as he sits back down and loosens his tie. He can't take his eyes off Saga.

The door opens and Sven Wiklund comes in. He greets them both and then stands in front of Saga at a loss for what to say. Finally he just nods then places a carafe of water and three glasses on the small table before he sits down.

"Saga Bauer is an inspector with Säpo," Mikael Båge begins. Then he smiles that uncontrolled smile.

"I have to say this before I can continue. You look like one of those princesses in a John Bauer painting." He waits a beat and then pours himself a glass of water.

"You have been called here as a witness," Mikael continues, now in his role of internal investigator. He taps a folder. "You were present at the action in question."

"What would you like to know?" Saga asks.

"The petition against Joona Linna . . . He is suspected of warning—"

"Göran Stone is my colleague, but he is a complete idiot," she says. "He's nothing but a climber."

"You don't have to get angry," Mikael Båge says.

Saga Bauer remembers very well the time she and Joona had entered the secret headquarters of the Brigade, a far-left group. Daniel Marklund, the Brigade's expert on hacking and eavesdropping, had given them the information they'd needed to save the life of Penelope Fernandez.

"So you don't believe that the operation was unsuccessful?"

"Of course it was. I was the one who warned the Brigade."

"The petition says—"

"Joona is the best officer in the country!"

"It's always good to be loyal, but we are going to prosecute—"

"Then go to hell!"

Saga gets up and knocks Mikael Båge's folder out of his hands, setting his papers flying. As she leaves, she stomps on them, then slams the door behind her so hard the window shade snaps up.

Saga Bauer may indeed look like a fairy-tale princess, but she feels like what she is: a detective with the security police. She is one of the best sharpshooters in the corps, and she's a boxer at the highest level of the sport.

134

Saga is still swearing as she storms outside onto Kungsbro Bridge. She has to force herself to walk more slowly while she tries to calm down. Her cell phone in the pocket of her hoodie rings. She pulls it out and looks at the display. It's her boss at Säpo.

"We have an inquiry from the National Police," says Verner, his deep voice rumbling in her ear. "I've checked on Jimmy and Jan Petersson, but they can't do it, and I'm not sure Göran Stone is up to it."

"What's it about?"

"The interrogation of a minor, a girl. She's psychologically unstable, and the head of the preliminary investigation needs someone trained in questioning techniques and who also has some experience—"

"So that's why you went to Jimmy first," Saga says, not hiding her irritation. "But why Jan Petersson? Why would you ask him before you'd ask me? And why in the world would you ever think that Göran Stone . . ."

Saga forces herself to shut up.

"You want a fight?" asks Verner with a sigh.

"Who the hell went to Pullach and did the German National Defense training and—"

"Please—"

"I'm not finished! You know I was there when Muhammed al-Abdaly was interrogated."

"But you weren't the head of the investigation."

"No, but I was the one who made him spill. Whatever."

She ends the call. She thinks she'll resign tomorrow.

The cell phone rings again.

"Okay, Saga, we'll put you on it."

"Just shut up!" she yells, and turns off the phone.

Carlos spills fish food on his jacket when Anja flings his office door open. He starts to scrape the flakes into his palm but then his desk phone rings.

"Can you please put it on speaker?" he asks Anja.

"It's Verner," Anja says as she presses the button.

"What a surprise," Carlos says cheerfully as he brushes his hands over the aquarium.

"It's Verner here again. Sorry it took me a while to get back to you."

"Not to worry."

"Well, I've looked high and low but all my best guys are already on loan to Alex Allan at the Joint Intelligence Committee," says the head of Säpo. He clears his throat. "We have one woman, though. You might have met her. Saga Bauer. She might be able to sit in."

Anja leans toward the telephone and barks, "So, sit in and look pretty, is that what you mean?"

"Hello? Who's that?" asks Verner.

"Shut up!" Anja hisses. "I know Saga Bauer and I can tell you that Säpo doesn't deserve such a hardworking, diligent—"

"Anja," Carlos says, wiping his hands on his trousers and placing himself between her and the phone on his desk.

"Sit down!" Anja roars.

Carlos sits down at the same time as Verner's voice says, "I am sitting down."

"You call Saga right up and beg her pardon," Anja says to the speaker.

135

The policeman on duty blushes as he looks at Saga Bauer's ID. He opens the door to room 703 for her and tells her that the patient will be back soon.

Saga walks inside and finds two women in an almost empty room. The bed is gone but the IV is still there, along with two chairs.

"Excuse me?" asks the woman in a gray dress suit.

"Yes?" asks Saga.

"Are you one of Vicky's friends?"

Before Saga is able to answer, Joona Linna walks in.

"Joona," she says in surprise. She smiles and shakes his hand. "I thought they'd cut you off from everything."

"I am cut off," he says.

"How wonderful for you," she says.

"The internal investigation folks are doing a great job," he says, smiling so broadly that dimples appear in his cheeks.

Susanne Öst looks more closely at Saga.

"Säpo?" she asks. "I thought . . . I mean . . . Excuse me for—"

"Where's Vicky Bennet?" Saga asks Joona.

"The doctor is doing a new CT scan," Joona says, and walks over to the window. He looks out.

"This morning I decided to take Vicky Bennet into custody," the prosecutor says. "It would be nice if we had a confession before I do so."

"You're going to prosecute her?" asks Saga.

"You weren't there," Susanne says. "I was. I saw the bodies. And it does mean that she will go to jail. She's fifteen years old and is beyond juvenile closed care."

Saga smiles although she's skeptical. "But to send her to prison—"

"Don't get me wrong," the prosecutor says. "But I was expecting a more experienced interrogator."

"I understand," Saga says.

"Still, you should have a try. You really should."

"Thanks," Saga says.

"I've already spent half a day here and I can tell you, this is not your average interrogation," Susanne Öst says, taking a deep breath.

"How so?"

"Vicky Bennet is not afraid. She seems to enjoy the power struggle."

"And you?" Saga asks. "Do you enjoy the power struggle?"

"I don't have time for her games and not for yours, either. Tomorrow I will be in court to request an arrest order."

"I listened to the recording of this morning's questioning. I don't believe that Vicky is playing a game with you," Saga says.

"I am absolutely sure that she is," the prosecutor says.

"Still, murder can be traumatizing for the murderer. Her mind may have created islands of floating memories with no clear borders."

"Is that what they teach you at Säpo these days?"

"The interrogator must begin by assuming that everyone wants to confess and to be understood," Saga says, ignoring Susanne's provocation.

"Is that all?"

"Any confession is connected to feelings of power. The person who is confessing has power over the truth." Saga keeps her tone friendly. "That's why threats don't work. But using a friendly attitude and respect—"

"Don't forget that this girl is suspected of two brutal killings."

They hear the sound of the bed being wheeled up to the door of room 703.

136

Two nursing assistants steer the bed through the door. Vicky's face has swollen considerably since the morning. Her cheeks and forehead are covered in scabbed wounds. Her arms have been freshly bandaged and her thumb is in a cast. The assistants park the bed in place and move the drip bag to the freestanding IV pole. Vicky is lying on her back, staring at the ceiling. She doesn't listen to the two women pushing the bed, who are trying to carry on a conversation with her. She looks grim.

The side bars of her bed are up, but all the belts used to tie her down have been loosened.

As they leave, Saga notices that there are now two officers posted outside the door.

Saga waits until the girl looks her way before she goes up to her side and sits down.

"My name is Saga Bauer, and I'm here to help you remember the past few days."

"Are you a social worker or what?"

"I'm a detective."

"From the police?"

"From Säpo," Saga replies.

"You are the prettiest person I've ever seen in real life."

"What a nice thing to say!"

"I've cut open pretty faces," Vicky says, and smiles.

"I know," Saga says calmly.

She takes out her cell phone and presses Record. She quickly mentions the date, time, place, and the names of everyone in the room. Then she looks at Vicky quietly for a while.

"You've been through some awful stuff," she says.

"I saw a newspaper," Vicky says. She swallows, continues. "My face and Dante's. They wrote some terrible things about me."

"Did you recognize yourself in their articles?"

"No."

"Tell me what happened instead. Use your own words."

"I ran and ran and I froze . . . was freezing."

Vicky looks at Saga wondering what to say next. She's trying to remember what she's already said. Has she told them the truth? Has she lied? She doesn't know.

"I know nothing about why you ran away, but if you would like to tell me, I'm listening," Saga says.

"I don't want to," Vicky says.

"Okay. Then let's start with the day before," Saga continues. "I know that you had classes in the morning, but after that."

Vicky closes her eyes. "The usual. Boring stuff. Routines."

"Don't you normally have activities in the afternoon?"

"Elisabet took everyone down to the lake. Lu Chu and Almira went swimming all naked. You're not supposed to swim naked, it's against the rules, but they do whatever they want." Vicky suddenly smiles. "Elisabet got angry with them and then everyone took off all their clothes."

"You, too?"

"No, not me. Not Miranda and not Tuula."

"What did you do?"

"I paddled a little bit and watched the others play around."

"What did Elisabet do?"

"She got all naked, too, and went swimming." Vicky is still smiling.

"What did Tuula and Miranda do?"

"They sat and threw pinecones at each other."

"While Elisabet was swimming with the other girls?"

"She swam like all the old ladies do."

"And you? What did you do?"

"I was bored so I went back."

"How did you feel that evening?"

"Fine."

"Were you really feeling fine? Why did you cut yourself, then? You cut yourself on your arms and stomach, right?"

137

Saga is watching Vicky's response to that last question. Her face is darkening and her expression hardening. The edges of her mouth turn down.

Saga explains, "There's a note in the log about you cutting your arms."

"Yes, but it wasn't a big deal. We were watching TV and I was feeling a little bit sorry for myself, so I cut myself. I went to Elisabet and she patched me up. I like it when she takes care of me. She is calm and she knows I need a lot of bandages around my wrists . . . because it always turns my stomach later when I think about my veins being open."

"Why were you feeling sorry for yourself?"

"It was my turn to talk to Elisabet, but she said she didn't have time."

"What did you want to talk to her about?"

"I don't know. Nothing big. It was just my turn to have private time with her, but I couldn't because Miranda and Tuula had a fight."

"That doesn't sound fair," Saga says.

"So I was feeling sorry for myself. So I cut myself and then Elisabet patched me up."

"You had your time with Elisabet after all, it seems."

"Yeah." Vicky smiles.

"Are you Elisabet's favorite?"

"No."

"Who is?"

All of a sudden, Vicky lashes her good hand at Saga's face, but Saga rolls her head away in time. The rest of her body doesn't move. Vicky doesn't know how she missed and why Saga is now gently stroking her cheek.

"Are you tired?" asks Saga.

Vicky looks at her and reaches to stop Saga from taking her hand away. Then she turns her back to her.

"You usually take thirty milligrams of Eutrexa before you go to sleep," Saga says after a moment has passed.

"That's right." The girl sounds irritated.

"What time?"

"Ten."

"Were you able to sleep then?"

"No."

"You couldn't sleep all night, I understand."

"I don't want to talk anymore," Vicky says, and she closes her eyes.

"That's enough for today," the lawyer says.

"We have twenty more minutes," Susanne protests.

"My client needs to rest," Signe Ridelman says as she walks up to Vicky's bed. "You're tired, aren't you? Do you want something to eat?"

While Signe talks to her client softly, Susanne listens to her voice mail. She looks out the window, her face expressionless.

Saga is just about to turn off the recorder on her cell phone when she catches sight of Joona and stops.

He is looking at her with eyes the color of ice. Then he abruptly leaves the room. Saga asks Signe to wait a moment and then follows him. He walks past the officers on guard and waits for her at the door to the stairwell.

"Have I missed something?" she asks.

"Vicky slept that night. In her own bed. The clothes she was wearing were covered in blood," Joona says quietly.

"What are you telling me?"

"It's not in the report."

"But you noticed it at the crime scene?"

"Yes."

"So she fell asleep after the murders?"

"I don't have access to the lab reports, but one thought I've had is that she may have overdosed on her medicine, since she was not feeling well. You'd think the medicine would help, but it doesn't—you just get more and more restless, and finally you become enraged. I don't know for sure, but it could be that she was angry at Miranda for robbing her of her private time with Elisabet, or maybe she was angry with Elisabet because she let Miranda do so, or perhaps it is something else entirely."

"You think that it's possible she murdered Elisabet, took the keys, went into the isolation room, killed Miranda—and then went to sleep?"

"Yes. The evidence in the isolation room shows two sides to the killer: uncontrolled violence and then tenderness."

Joona is trying to read Saga's eyes, but they give nothing away.

"Once Miranda is dead, her rage dissipates," he says. "She lifts her body onto the bed and she places her hands over her face. After that, she returns to her own room as the medicine is starting to take effect—it's strong—and she feels overwhelmingly tired."

138

When Saga returns to Vicky's room, the prosecutor says that the remaining fifteen minutes they have are too few to get anything of value. Saga nods as if she agrees and walks over to the end of the bed. Signe looks at her in surprise. Saga waits with her hands on the rails until Vicky turns her battered face toward her.

"I thought you'd been awake the entire night," Saga begins, very slowly. "However, Joona says that you slept in your bed before you ran away from Birgittagården."

Vicky shakes her head and Signe tries to get between them.

"Any questioning is over for today and—"

Vicky whispers something and scratches next to one of the cuts on her cheek. Saga wants to get the girl to tell her something more, not much, just a few honest words about her flight through the forest and why she kidnapped the boy. She knows that the more the interrogator gets the suspect to say about the events leading up to the crime, the more probable it is that the suspect will tell them everything.

"Joona is never wrong," Saga says, with a smile.

"It was dark and I was in bed while everyone was screaming and slamming doors." Vicky's voice is barely above a whisper.

"So you're lying in bed and everyone is screaming," Saga says. "What are you thinking? What do you do next?"

"I'm scared and I'm lying under the blanket and trying not to move,"

Vicky says, not looking at anyone. "It's totally dark. I'm soaking. I think I pissed on myself, or maybe my period was starting. Buster is barking and Nina is screaming about Miranda. I turn on the light and see that I'm covered in blood."

Saga decides not to ask about the blood or the murders. She does not want to force a confession but to allow Vicky's story to unfold as it will.

"Were you also screaming?" asks Saga.

"I don't think so. I doubt it. I wasn't able to think," Vicky says. "I just wanted to get away . . . get out of there. I usually go to sleep in my clothes. I always sleep in my clothes. So I put on my shoes and grabbed my purse. I got out the window and ran into the forest. I'm scared and I walk as fast as I can. I walk for ages and it gets light and I just keep going. Then I see a car—it's almost new—just left out there in the middle of nowhere with the keys in the ignition. Even the door is open. I know how to drive because I drove a lot last summer, so I just get into the car and start to drive. I want to go to Stockholm and get some money so I can go see my friend in Chile. Then there's a bang and the car turns around. Bang! Just like that. And I wake up, my ear is bleeding, and I look up and see I've driven right into a fucking traffic light and I don't know how I did that. All the windows are gone and it's raining right into the car. The engine's still running and I'm alive so I keep driving. Then I hear someone crying and I turn around and I see a little boy in a car seat—a little boy. It's totally crazy. I don't know where he came from. I yell at him to shut up. The rain's just pouring down. I can hardly see but right when I turn to go over the bridge I see blue lights on the other side of the river. I reckon it's the cops and I get a little panicked and I turn the wheel and we drive off the road. It goes fast, we go right down the side and into the water and I hit my face on the steering wheel. The water is over the hood and we're just sliding into the river like crazy. We're sinking, but I know enough to take deep breaths from the air right under the roof and I go back to the boy and get the car seat unbuckled, and hold him up so he can breathe but the seat's too heavy with him still in it, so I get the seat belt off him but the car seat floats up too so I grab it and push it out the window and I hold on to it and I hold on to the boy and we go up. I'm pulling the car seat toward the shore. The other side of the river. But the river is too strong and I have to let go of the car seat and I swim as best I can. And we get to the shore. My shoes and purse are gone, but the boy is all right and in a bit we start to walk."

Vicky stops for a moment and takes a deep breath.

Saga notices the prosecutor shift slightly but her eyes are fixed on Vicky.

"I ask Dante his name and tell him that we're going to find his mother," Vicky says, and her voice has started to shake. "I hold his hand and we walk and walk and we sing a song he learned in preschool—an old man who wore out his shoes—and we go down a big road with posts along the sides, and a car stops and we get in the backseat. This guy asks us if we want to go to his house and get some new clothes and some food . . ." Vicky falters and blinks hard, then carries on in a whisper.

"We might have gone with him except he said we'd get some money too, and when he stopped to fill up his tank we snuck out and kept walking. I don't know how far we walked but there was a rest area by a lake. And there was a truck from IKEA parked there and we found a heap of sausage sandwiches in plastic bags and a thermos on one of the picnic tables, but before we can swipe the food, this man comes up to us and asks if we're hungry. He says he's from Poland and we can ride with him all the way to Uppsala. I borrow his phone and call my mom, and I keep thinking if he touches the boy I'll kill him, but he lets us just sit there and we fall asleep. He doesn't want anything from us. He just lets us off and we take the train the last bit in to Stockholm and we hide among the suitcases. I don't have the key to the subway car, and I don't know anyone, it's been too long. I lived with a couple at Midsommarkransen for a while but I didn't remember their names but I remembered Tobias, of course I remembered Tobias, and also he lives on Wollmar Yxkulls-gatan, and you take the subway to Mariatorget and I'm such a fucking idiot I really don't deserve to live."

She falls silent and turns her face away.

139

Saga is still standing at the end of the bed and looking at Vicky, who is lying on her side, motionless. Only her index finger moves along the rail of the bed.

"I'm thinking about what you told me about the man in the car," Saga says. "The man who wanted you to come home with him. I think your feeling that he was dangerous was absolutely correct."

Vicky slowly sits up and looks into Saga's cornflower-blue eyes.

"Do you think you could help me trace him down once all this is over?" asks Saga.

Vicky nods and swallows hard. Then she wraps her arms tightly around her knees. It's difficult for Saga to see how this thin, delicate girl could have broken the skulls of two human beings.

"Before we go any further, let me just tell you that people always feel better when they tell the truth," Saga says.

Saga feels the tingling calm she gets when she enters a boxing ring. She knows that she is close to a truthful confession. She can feel the change in the room: it's in the tone of voice, the warmth, the level of moisture in the eyes. Saga pretends to write something in her notebook and waits for a few moments before she looks at Vicky as if the girl has already confessed to the killings.

"So you were sleeping in bloody sheets," Saga begins, softly.

"I killed Miranda, didn't I?" Vicky whispers.

"Tell me about it."

Vicky's mouth trembles and her face darkens into a blush.

"There are times I get really, really mad," she whispers as she covers her face.

"Were you angry at Miranda?"

"I was."

"What did you do?"

"I don't want to talk about it."

Signe walks over to Vicky and says, "You know that you don't have to say a word, don't you?"

"I don't have to tell you anything," Vicky says to Saga.

"The interrogation is over," Susanne Öst says.

"Thanks," whispers Vicky.

"She needs time to remember what happened," says Saga.

"We have a confession," says Susanne.

"I don't know if I—"

"You just confessed to killing Miranda Eriksdotter," Susanne says in a louder voice.

"Don't yell at me!"

"You hit her, didn't you? You hit her in the head."

"I don't want to say anything else."

"This interrogation is over," Signe says sharply.

"How did you hit Miranda?" Susanne asks.

"It doesn't matter." Vicky's voice breaks and she starts to cry.

"Your fingerprints were on a bloody hammer, which—"

"I can't talk about it! What the hell do you want from me?"

"You don't have to say anything," Saga says. "You have the right to remain silent."

"Why did you get angry at Miranda?" Susanne asks. "So angry that you—"

"I'm making a note of this," the lawyer says.

"How did you get into Miranda's room?"

"I unlocked the door," Vicky says, and tries to get out of bed. "I really can't talk about this anymore."

"How did you get the keys?"

"I don't know, I—"

"Elisabet had them, am I right?"

"I borrowed them," Vicky says as she stands up.

"Did she want to give them to you?"

"I smashed her skull in! That's what you want to hear, isn't it?" Vicky screams. She throws her food tray at the prosecutor and orange juice and yogurt with cornflakes spatter the wall.

"Go to hell!" she screams at Signe, who is so startled she falls backward into one of the chairs.

Before Saga and Joona can reach her, Vicky rips out her IV and seizes the pole. She hits Susanne as hard as she can. The bag flies off and bursts against the wall.

140

Afterward, Joona remembers how he and Saga leaped between Vicky and the two women. They tried to calm her. IV liquid ran down the wall. Vicky was panting and looking at them with wild eyes. She'd hurt herself and blood dribbled from one of her eyebrows. The policemen on guard outside and the two nursing assistants rushed in and forced Vicky to the ground. Four people in all. Vicky fought, screaming and kicking to get free. She managed to kick over the patient cart.

Vicky was forced onto her stomach and injected with a tranquilizer. She screamed hoarsely for a while longer and then went quiet.

A few minutes later, they were able to lift her into bed. She started crying and tried to speak, but her speech was slurred. The nursing assistants tied her hands and feet to the bed rails and then her legs and, finally, they fastened a large star-shaped belt over her chest. Vicky's blood had stained the sheets as well as their white clothes. There was liquid and food all over the floor.

Half an hour later, Vicky lay completely still, her eyes shut. Her face was gray and closed off, and the cracks in her lips had widened. Her eyebrow had been stitched and a new IV was in place. The two police officers were back in position outside the door and a cleaning woman had just finished mopping the floor.

Joona knows that the prosecutor, Susanne Öst, is suspicious of him and that he is not supposed to get involved, but he doesn't like what is going on. Susanne has decided that there will be no more interrogations before the hearing. It would have been better to wait until all questioning had been concluded and all test results had been returned from the lab before starting the legal process, but Susanne intends to take the girl into custody tomorrow.

He's certain that if Saga Bauer had been given just a bit more time, Vicky would have told her everything. Now they had a confession that could be considered forced.

As long as the technical evidence holds up, it won't matter anyway, Joona thinks as he leaves the room once the girl is fast asleep.

He walks along the hallway, only subconsciously aware of the strong odor of disinfectant escaping from an open door.

There's something bothering him about this case. If he ignores the rock, the course of events is fairly clear. It would hold up but it's not fixed. It's like a pulsing shadow world—it's still changeable.

He wants to look through all the evidence: the autopsy report, the technical reports, and the lab reports. But he's not allowed access.

Why were Miranda's hands over her eyes?

He remembers how the bloodied room looked, but he needs to read the reports from the crime scene to go deeper into the course of events.

Susanne is standing at the elevator, holding the door for him. They nod. The prosecutor seems untroubled.

"Everybody hates me because I was too tough," she says as they get into the elevator. She presses the button. "Still, a confession is hard to ignore, even if the defense wants to protest it."

"How does the technical evidence look?" asks Joona.

"It's pretty good. I'm going with the highest level of suspicion."

The elevator stops at the ground floor.

"Will I see the reports?" Joona asks.

Susanne Öst looks surprised. She hesitates a moment before she says, "It's not really necessary."

"Good," Joona says, and starts to walk away.

"Do you think there's a hole in my case?" the prosecutor asks. She trots to keep up with his pace.

"No," Joona says brusquely.

"I have the reports right here," she says, and stops to open her brief-case.

Joona keeps walking to the exit. He can hear her behind him, shuf-fling through her papers, then she runs to catch up to him. He's already reached his car when she gets to him.

"It would be fantastic if you could look at these today," she says breathlessly. She's holding out a thick folder. "It's the preliminary results from the National Forensic Lab as well as the cause of death from the autopsy reports."

Joona looks her in the eye, nods, and throws the folder onto the pas-senger seat before he gets in his car.

141

Joona sits down by himself in the inner room of Il Caffé and places Susanne Öst's folder on the table. He's convinced she's made a big mistake in provoking a confession that morning.

He doesn't believe that Vicky meant to take Dante. He thinks she was telling the truth about not noticing him in the backseat when she stole the car. And he can't dispute that she saved him from drowning. Yet for some reason she killed Miranda and Elisabet.

Why?

Joona opens the folder hoping that the answer lies in one of these reports.

Why does Vicky get so enraged? It's not just the Eutrexa. She hadn't taken it before she came to Birgittagården.

Joona quickly flips through the pages. He knows that crime scenes and other places where there's evidence reflect more than the actions of the suspect. There are traces of the motive in the pattern of blood spatter, in where overturned furniture lies, in the footprints, and in the positions of the bodies. Nathan Pollock would probably say that the careful reading of the crime scene is more important than evidence collection. The victim plays a role in the killer's inner drama and the scene of the crime is the stage, complete with stage directions and props. There are multiple clues, including coincidence, but there's always that bit which is part of the inner drama and can be connected to the motive.

For the first time, Joona has the reports from the crime scene investigation. He starts to study the documents, which detail the evidence collection and the analysis of the crime scene.

The police have done a good job and were more careful than Joona would have expected.

A waiter in a knit wool cap comes by with a large mug of coffee on a tray, but Joona is concentrating so hard that he doesn't notice. A young woman with a ring through her lower lip, sitting in the booth next to his, says with a smile that she saw Joona order the coffee.

Although the results from the National Forensic Laboratory are not part of this report, Joona realizes that the results themselves are clear: the fingerprints are Vicky's. The highest level of certainty, grade 4+, has been noted.

There is nothing in the crime scene analysis to contradict anything he observed when he was there. However, many of his observations are not there. For instance, there's nothing about how the blood that had coagulated on Vicky's bed must have soaked into the sheets for at least an hour. The report also does not state how the blood spatter changed angle after the first three blows.

Joona reaches for his coffee and takes a sip. He studies the photographs again. He flips through them slowly until he's gone through the entire stack. Then he pulls out two pictures from Vicky's room, two from the isolation room where Miranda Eriksdotter was found, and two from the brewery room where Elisabet Grim was found. He moves his coffee cup to one side and places the six photographs on the table. He stands up so that he can look at all six at once. He's looking for a pattern.

After a while, Joona turns over all the photographs except one. He studies this photograph carefully. He remembers how this scene looked when he was in the room. He puts himself into the emotions and aromas of the murder. In the photograph, Miranda is lying on the bed. She's wearing cotton panties and her hands are over her face. The flash of the camera makes her panties and the sheets blaze white. The blood from her crushed head is a dark, formless shape on the pillow.

Joona sees something he didn't expect.

He takes a step backward, hastily putting his mug on the floor by his feet.

The girl with the silver ring through her lower lip watches him and smiles to herself.

Joona leans over the photograph of Miranda but he's thinking of his visit to Flora Hansen. He'd been irritated about wasting his time talking to her. As he was leaving, she'd followed him into the hallway, trying to show him the drawing she'd done of Miranda, but he'd pushed her hand away and it had fallen to the floor. Still, he'd caught a glimpse of it as he stepped over it on his way out the door.

Now, as he's looking at Miranda's arranged body, he's remembering the drawing. It looked like it had been done in two stages. Flora had first drawn a stick figure and then filled in the limbs. The girl in the drawing had shaky contours in certain areas, but other parts of her body were still as thin as thread. Her head was disproportionately large. Her straight mouth could barely be seen, since her unfinished skeletal hands were over her face. The drawing was similar to what had been described in the newspapers.

What the newspapers hadn't revealed was that Miranda had been hit in the head and that the blood had run into the pillow. No photographs from the crime scene had been released. The press had speculated about what the hands over her face meant, but no one outside the police and the justice system had known about the injury to the head. Strict confidence had been kept and will be kept until the moment the court process begins.

"You figured it out, didn't you?" the girl in the next booth says.

Joona meets the girl's glittering eyes and nods before he looks back at the photograph on the table.

What he realized while looking at Miranda's body in the photograph was that Flora had drawn a dark heart next to the girl's head right where the blood had been in reality. The same size, the same place.

It's as if she'd seen Miranda lying on her bed.

It could just be a coincidence, but if he remembers Flora's drawing clearly, the similarity is striking.

142

The bells in Gustav Vasa Church are tolling when Joona meets Flora outside Carlén Antiques on Upplandsgatan. She looks terrible. She's tired and washed out. A fading bruise is visible on her right cheek. Her eyes are heavy. On a narrow door next to the store, there's a small sign declaring that a séance will be held there that evening.

"Do you have the drawing with you?" Joona asks.

"Yes," she says as she unlocks the door.

They walk down the stairs to the basement. Flora turns on the ceiling lamps and goes into the room on the right, which has a small window near the ceiling facing the street.

"I'm sorry I lied to you," Flora says as she rummages in her purse. "I didn't really feel anything with that key ring, but I—"

"May I just see the drawing?"

"I did see Miranda," she says as she gives him the sheet of paper. "I don't believe in ghosts and yet . . . there she was."

Joona unfolds the paper and looks at the childish drawing. A girl is lying on her back, holding her hands over her face and her hair is undone. There's no furniture or bed. He'd remembered correctly. Next to the girl's head is a heart, shaded in, right where Miranda's blood had run from her head and had soaked into the pillow.

"Why did you draw a heart next to her?"

Flora looks down at the ground and blushes.

"I don't know. I don't even remember that I did it . . . I was scared and shaking all over."

"Have you seen the ghost since?"

She nods and her blush deepens.

Joona is trying to understand how this fits. Could Flora have guessed her way to the truth? Could she have guessed the rock as well? If she had, she somehow knew she'd guessed right. Because if the rock was right, it would be logical for her to assume that it had been used to hit Miranda in the head and that there'd be blood on the bed.

But she drew a heart, not blood, he thinks. *That wouldn't be right if she were trying to deceive.*

It doesn't fit.

She must have seen something.

She somehow saw Miranda in the bed, but she didn't see her clearly, or she saw her for a brief moment, and then she drew what she remembered without thinking too much about it.

He has a vivid mental image of the photograph of Miranda with the bloodstain next to her head.

She sat down and drew what she'd seen. She remembered a body lying down with hands over her face and that there was something dark beside her head. A dark shape.

When she drew the picture, she interpreted the shape as a heart. She didn't think about any connection or even logic.

Joona knows that Flora was far away from Birgittagården when the murders took place. He knows she has no connection to any of the people involved or to what has happened.

He looks at the drawing again and is struck by another thought.

Perhaps Flora learned about the crime from someone who was actually there. Perhaps a witness to the crime described it to her and told her what to draw.

A child witness who saw the shape of a heart.

Perhaps all this talk about a ghost is Flora's way of protecting the witness.

"I would like you to contact the ghost," Joona says.

"No, I can't—"

"How does it usually work?"

"I'm sorry, but I can't do it here."

"You must ask the ghost if she saw what happened."

"I don't want to," Flora says. "I can't take much more of this."

"I can pay you," Joona offers.

"I don't want to be paid. I just want you to listen to what I've seen."

"I'll listen," Joona says.

"I'm beginning to think that I'm really going crazy," she says.

She looks at him while wiping tears from her cheeks. Then she stares into space and swallows hard.

"I'll try," she says. "But I don't really believe—"

"Go ahead and make an attempt."

"You'll have to wait there," she says, and points to the pantry. "Miranda only comes when I'm completely alone."

"I understand," Joona says. He gets up and leaves the room.

143

Flora is sitting absolutely still, watching as the detective closes the door behind him. A chair creaks as he sits down in the pantry, and then there's silence. She doesn't hear anything, not even the sound of a dog barking or a car driving past and nothing more from the room where the inspector is sitting.

Now she can feel how exhausted she is.

Flora does not know what to do. Should she light a candle or burn incense? She closes her eyes for a moment. Then she looks at the drawing.

She remembers how her hand shook as she drew what she'd seen and how she had trouble concentrating. She glances around the room to see if the ghost has come back and looks at her picture again. She's not good at drawing, but she can see that the girl is lying on the floor. She sees the small crosses and realizes she was trying to draw the fringe on the bathroom rug.

Her hand had been shaking, so one of the girl's legs was as thin as a bare bone. The fingers are just lines. She can see part of the straight mouth behind them.

She hears the chair in the pantry squeak.

Flora blinks and stares at the drawing. It seems as if the fingers have spread. Flora can see one of the eyes.

The girl is looking at her.

Flora jumps when there's a rattling in the pipes overhead. She looks around the room. The sofa is black with shadows and the table is hidden in a dark corner.

She looks back at the drawing. The eye is gone. A crease in the paper runs over the face.

Flora's hands are shaking as she tries to smooth the drawing. The girl's thin fingers are hiding her face and she can only see part of the mouth on the grid paper.

The floor creaks behind her and Flora whirls around.

No one is there.

She looks back at the drawing and tears come to her eyes. The heart next to the girl's head is becoming blurry. She looks at the tangled hair and then again at the fingers in front of the face. Flora jerks her hands back from the drawing when she sees that the mouth is open. She can tell it's screaming.

Flora stumbles to her feet as she stares at the screaming mouth and is just about to call for the detective when she really does see the girl.

She's climbed into the cupboard and is trying to shut the door behind her, but it won't close while she's inside. It swings open. The girl is standing still and her hands are in front of her face. Then her fingers glide open and she looks at Flora with one eye.

Flora stares at the girl.

She's saying something but Flora can't make out the words.

Flora walks closer and says, "I can't hear what you're saying."

"I'm pregnant," the girl says. She takes her hands away from her face. She touches the back of her head in surprise, brings her hand back, and stares at the blood. She sways. Blood has started to flow from her head down her back and onto the cupboard floor.

She opens her mouth, but before she can say anything, her head shakes and her thin legs give way.

Joona hears something crash in the room next door. He rushes in and sees Flora lying on the floor in front of a cupboard that has fallen over. She sits up and looks at him in confusion.

"I saw her. She's pregnant."

Joona helps Flora to her feet.

"Did you ask what happened?"

Flora shakes her head and looks at the cupboard.

"Nobody is allowed to see anything," she whispers.

"What are you trying to say?"

"Miranda said she was pregnant." Flora is crying now and starts to walk away.

She dries her tears, looks back at the fallen cupboard, and abruptly leaves the room.

Joona takes Flora's coat from the chair and follows her. She's already halfway up the stairs to the street.

144

Flora is sitting on the steps in front of Carlén Antiques. She's buttoning her coat. Color is coming back to her face, but she says nothing. Joona has his cell phone to his ear and has just called Nils Åhlén, the head of forensic medicine at Karolinska Hospital.

"Wait a sec," Joona hears The Needle say. "I've just gotten a smartphone."

There's static in Joona's ear.

"Yes? What can I do for you, Joona?"

"I have a short question," Joona says.

"By the way, Frippe's in love," The Needle says in his nasal voice.

"How nice," Joona says.

"I'm afraid that he'll be miserable if things don't work out," The Needle continues. "You know what I'm saying?"

"Yes, but—"

"So what was your question?"

"Was Miranda Eriksdotter pregnant?"

"Absolutely not."

"You remember, the girl who—"

"I remember everyone," The Needle says.

"You do? You never told me that."

"You never asked."

Flora has gotten to her feet and is smiling anxiously.

"Are you absolutely sure?"

"Absolutely," The Needle says. "She couldn't even get pregnant."

"She couldn't?"

"She had large cysts on her ovaries."

"All right. Now I know. Thanks. Oh, and say hi to Frippe."

"Will do."

Joona ends the conversation and looks at Flora. Flora's smile starts to fade.

"Why do you do things like this?" Joona asks in a serious tone. "You told me the murdered girl was pregnant, but she couldn't even get pregnant."

Flora gestures back to the door to the basement. "I remember that she—"

"But it isn't true," Joona says. "She wasn't pregnant."

"I meant to say," Flora whispers. "I meant to say she thought she was pregnant. She wasn't pregnant, but she thought she was. She believed it."

"*Jumala*," Joona swears in Finnish. He starts to walk along Upplandsgatan toward his car.

145

The food is just a touch too expensive. Daniel is embarrassed as he looks through the wine list. He asks Elin if she wants to choose, but she shakes her head with a smile. He clears his throat weakly and asks the waiter about the house wine, but before he gets an answer, he changes his mind and asks the waiter to recommend a red wine. The young man looks through the wine list and offers three wines in three different price categories. Daniel chooses the cheapest, saying that the South African pinot noir would be perfect.

The waiter thanks him and takes the menus and the wine list. There's a family eating at another table.

"You didn't have to invite me for dinner," says Elin.

"I wanted to," he says, smiling.

"It was very nice of you," she says. She sips some water.

A waitress comes and changes their silverware and wineglasses, but Elin continues to speak as if she's not there.

"Vicky's lawyer has resigned from the case," she says in a low voice. "But my family lawyer, Johannes Grünewald, has agreed to take it on."

"It will all work out," Daniel says in a calming manner.

"There won't be any more interrogations because she's confessed," Elin says. She clears her throat carefully. "I can also see how Vicky's background fits. Foster homes, institutions, running away, violence—everything points to her. Still, I don't believe she's guilty."

"I know," Daniel says.

Elin lowers her face as her tears start to run. Daniel gets up and gives her a hug.

"Sorry I keep talking about Vicky," she says, shaking her head. "It's just that you've said that you don't believe she did it. I mean, otherwise I wouldn't have . . . But it seems as if you and I are the only ones who believe she's innocent."

"Elin," he says, "I don't believe anything at all. It's just that the Vicky I knew was not capable of this."

"May I ask you a question? Tuula seems to have seen Vicky and Miranda together," Elin says.

"That night?"

"No, earlier . . ." Elin falls silent and Daniel holds her shoulders and tries to catch her eyes.

"What is it?"

"Vicky and Miranda played some game, where they held their hands over their face," Elin says. "I don't want to tell the police because that would add to their evidence."

"But Elin—"

"Perhaps it doesn't mean anything," Elin says quickly. "I'm going to ask Vicky when I have a chance. She should be able to explain what they were doing."

"What if she can't?"

He falls silent as the waiter returns with the bottle of wine. Elin dries her tears and Daniel returns to his seat. He places his napkin on his knee and then tastes the wine. His hand shakes.

"Good," he says, a little too quickly.

They are silent while the wine is poured. They thank the waiter and look carefully at each other when they're left alone.

"I want to foster Vicky again," Elin says in a serious tone.

"Are you sure?"

"Do you think I'm not up to it?" She smiles.

"It's not that, Elin," he says. "Vicky is suicidal. She's gotten better but she still has a great deal of self-destructive behavior."

"Does she cut herself?"

"She cuts herself and she overdoses. In my opinion, she'll need twenty-four-hour care."

"So you wouldn't recommend me?"

"She needs professional help," Daniel says. "I mean, I don't think she got enough care at Birgittagården, actually. We didn't have the money for it, but—"

"What does she need?"

"People to care for her around the clock."

"And therapy?"

"I only had one hour a week with each student, sometimes two. It was much too little if you—"

Elin's cell phone rings and she excuses herself as she looks at the display. It's Johannes Grünewald, so she answers right away.

"What's going on?" she asks.

"I've looked into the matter and the prosecutor has decided that the girl will be arraigned without further interrogation," the lawyer replies. "I'm going to talk to the court about the time for arraignment, but we'll need a few more hours."

"Will Vicky accept help from us?"

"I talked to her and she's hired me as her lawyer."

"Did you mention me?"

"Yes, I did."

"Did she say anything?"

"Well, she said . . . They've medicated her and—"

"What did she say about me?"

"Nothing at all."

Daniel can see a wave of pain pass over Elin's beautiful face.

"Meet me at the hospital," she says. "It's just as well to talk to her directly before we go much further."

"Good."

"How soon can you get there?"

"Twenty minutes at the earliest, it should—"

"Good, I'll see you there," she says, and ends the call. She looks at Daniel, who has a questioning look.

"Okay then," she says. "Vicky has taken Johannes on as her lawyer. I have to go now."

"Now? But we haven't eaten yet!"

"I know . . . I'm sorry." She gets up. "Maybe we can meet for dessert later on."

"Of course," he says with a weak smile.

"Would you like to come with me to Söder Hospital?"

"I don't think I'm up to it," he replies.

"I don't mean that you should see her," she says swiftly. "I was thinking of myself. I would feel calmer if I knew you were waiting outside."

"Elin, it's just . . . I haven't come so far that I can think about Vicky . . . I need more time. Elisabet is dead and even if Vicky didn't do it—"

"I understand," Elin says. "It wouldn't be good for you to see her."

"Or maybe it would," he says. "Maybe it would help me start to remember. I just have no idea how I would react."

146

Vicky turns her face away when Saga enters the room. White straps around her ankles and wrists and a belt across her chest tie the girl to the bed.

"Take away the straps," Saga says.

"I can't do that," the nurse says.

"It's a good thing that they're scared of me," Vicky says.

"Have you been kept like this all night?" asks Saga as she sits down on the chair beside the bed.

"Yeah."

Vicky is lying with her face turned away.

"I'm going to meet your new lawyer," Saga says. "There's going to be an arraignment later today and he needs the transcript of the interrogation."

"I just get so angry sometimes."

"The interrogation is over, Vicky."

"Can't I talk?" She turns her head to look at Saga.

"It would be best if you asked your lawyer for his advice first before you—"

"But if I want to," she says.

"You can talk, but it won't be recorded," Saga says calmly.

"It's like a strong wind," Vicky tells her. "Everything just . . . It thunders in my ears and I go along so I don't fall over."

Saga looks at the girl's bitten fingernails and then repeats in a calm, almost indifferent voice, "Like a strong wind."

"I can't explain. It's like one time . . . They hurt Simon really bad. He was a little boy. We were in the same foster home," Vicky says. Her mouth is trembling. "The big boy in the family, he was their real son, he was mean to Simon. He'd torture him. Everybody knew. I even talked to the social worker about it, but nobody cared."

"What happened?"

"I came into the kitchen. The big boy had forced Simon's hands into a pot of boiling water and the mom was there and she wasn't doing anything. She looked totally afraid. I was seeing all of it and I got really strange and suddenly I found myself hitting them and cutting them up with a piece of glass."

Vicky pulls at the straps. Her body is tense, but she calms down when there's a knock at the door.

A gray-haired man wearing a dark blue suit enters the room.

"I'm Johannes Grünewald," he says as he shakes hands with Saga.

"Here's the latest transcript," Saga says, and hands him a folder.

"Thanks," Johannes says. "I don't have to read it right away. I managed to get the arraignment moved to tomorrow morning."

"I don't want to wait," says Vicky.

"I understand, but I still have some work to do on your case," he says, smiling. "And there's someone I want you to meet before we start going through all sorts of questions."

Vicky looks up and her eyes grow wide as she sees the woman who heads straight for her without stopping to greet the police officers. Elin Frank's eyes are shimmering and nervous. Her lips tremble as she realizes the girl is strapped to the bed.

"Hello," Elin says.

Vicky looks away as Elin gently unfastens the straps.

"May I sit down?" she asks. Her voice is thick with emotion.

Vicky's gaze becomes hard and she does not say anything.

"Do you remember me?" asks Elin.

Elin's throat hurts from the words she can't force out and the sobs she can barely control.

A church bell starts ringing somewhere in the city.

Vicky touches Elin's wrist and then withdraws her finger.

"We have the same bandages." Elin smiles. "You and me."

Vicky turns her face away.

"I don't know whether you remember me," Elin says. "You stayed with me when you were a little girl. I was just a temporary foster mother, but I've never stopped thinking about you."

She takes a deep breath. Then her voice breaks: "I know I betrayed you, Vicky. I wasn't up to taking care of you."

Elin is studying the girl in the bed: her messy hair, her worried forehead, the dark rings around her eyes, the wounds on her face.

"I know that to you I'm nothing. Just another person in a long line of people who've let you down." Elin has to stop speaking and swallow hard before she can continue.

"The prosecutor wants you in jail, but I don't think that jail is the right place for you. It's not good for anyone to be locked up."

Vicky shakes her head. The gesture is barely noticeable, but Elin sees it and her voice is intense as she says, "It's really important that you listen to what Johannes and I have to tell you."

147

There's an arraignment room on the ground floor of the National Police building. It's a simple conference room with chairs, a desk, and a table of lacquered fir. About twenty journalists have already collected in the glass-enclosed foyer and TV vans are parked on Polhemsgatan.

The hard rain of the previous night has streaked the triple-paned windows of the arraignment room, and wet leaves are stuck to the white window frames. A uniformed policeman is standing by the wall next to the door, and the judge, an older man with bushy eyebrows, sits behind the desk.

Susanne Öst appears pale and tense, and Vicki looks small and exhausted. She sits between Elin Frank and her lawyer, bent over as if her stomach hurts.

"Where's Joona?" she whispers.

"We don't know if he can come," Johannes says.

Susanne stands up. "If it please, Your Honor, I would like to request that Vicky Bennet be jailed on suspicion of the murders of Elisabet Grim and Miranda Eriksdotter, as well as on suspicion of kidnapping Dante Abrahamsson."

The judge writes something down and Susanne hands him a Cerlox-bound collection of documents before she begins to relate the conclusions reached during the preliminary investigation.

"All the technical evidence points to Vicky Bennet and no one but Vicky Bennet."

Susanne pauses for a moment before she begins to go through the reports from the crime scene investigation. Barely restraining her eagerness, she puts special emphasis on the biological evidence and the fingerprints.

"The boots found in Vicky Bennet's closet have been matched to footprints from both crime scenes. Blood from both victims have been found in her room and on her clothing. Vicky Bennet's bloody handprint was found on the windowsill."

"Why do they have to talk about all of this?" Vicky whispers.

"I don't know," Elin replies.

"If Your Honor would look at the appendices to the National Forensic Laboratory's expert opinion." Susanne waits for the judge to find the right document. "On page 9 the murder weapon can be seen. Vicky Bennet's fingerprints have been lifted from the handle. See pages 113 and 114 for photos of them. The comparative analysis has concluded that Vicky Bennet has used the murder weapon."

The judge looks through the material. Then Susanne begins to relate the conclusions from the expanded forensic autopsy report: "Miranda Eriksdotter died from blunt trauma to the head. This is beyond a doubt. She had compression fractures on her temporal bone and—"

"Susanne," the judge says in a friendly manner, "we are only discussing whether the suspect should be kept in jail until trial or not. We're not at the main trial."

"I know." The prosecutor nods. "However, considering the young age of the suspect, I thought it would be important to demonstrate the reasons why she should be in jail."

"As long as you don't take up too much time," the judge says.

"Thank you," Susanne says. She then describes all the injuries on both victims, including Elisabet Grim's serious defensive wounds, and how long the victims had been dead before they were discovered, based on the lividity.

"Where is Joona?" Vicky asks again.

Johannes places a hand on Vicky's arm and whispers that if Joona hasn't appeared by the break, he'll give him a call.

When they return to the room after the break to resume the hearing, Joona still hasn't shown up. Johannes shakes his head at Vicky's questioning face. Vicky is pale and again sits bent over and silent.

Susanne reports the results of the crime scene investigation by the Västernorrland police department: how Vicky pursued Elisabet Grim to the brewery house and how she took her life so that she could get her hands on the keys to the isolation room.

Vicky has lowered her face and tears are running down her cheeks.

The prosecutor describes the second murder, the flight through the forest, the theft of the automobile, the impulse kidnapping, and finally the suspect's capture in Stockholm. She then details the girl's violence during the interrogation and the need for her to be strapped to the bed.

For kidnapping, the sentence can vary anywhere from four years to life. For murder, the sentence is a minimum of ten years.

Susanne Öst concludes by saying that although Vicky Bennet is extremely violent and dangerous, she is not a monster. In order to be ahead of the defense team, she takes pains to point out the suspect's positive attributes. She has presented her side competently and ends her speech by quoting the interrogation synopsis.

"During the third interrogation, the suspect confessed to both murders. I quote: 'I killed Miranda' and later, in response to whether Elisabet Grim wanted to lend her the keys, the suspect replied, 'I smashed her skull in.'"

The judge, who is looking tired, turns to Vicky Bennet and Johannes Grünewald and asks them formally if they have any objections to the case presented by the prosecutor. Vicky stares at the judge with a frightened expression. She shakes her head. Johannes, however, holds back a smile as he says he would like to go through the confession again to make sure that the court has not missed anything.

"I knew when I saw you that this wouldn't be easy," the judge says calmly.

In his objections, Johannes does not raise any of the technical evidence or even question Vicky's guilt. He lists Vicky's positive qualities, which the prosecutor had just mentioned, and emphasizes the young age of the suspect.

Then Johannes says, "Even if Vicky Bennet and her previous lawyer signed the interrogation, the prosecutor should not have done so."

"The prosecutor shouldn't have?" The judge looks surprised.

Johannes goes up to him and points out Vicky's response in the transcript. The prosecutor has highlighted the words "I killed Miranda" in yellow.

"Could you read her entire answer?" Johannes asks.

"'I killed Miranda,'" the judge reads.

"Not just the highlighted words, please."

"'I killed Miranda, didn't I?'"

"Would you consider that a confession?" asks Johannes.

"No," the judge says.

Susanne Öst stands up. "But her next response," she says. "Her next confession—"

"Quiet," says the judge.

"Would Your Honor be so kind as to ask the prosecutor to read it aloud?" Johannes suggests.

The judge nods. Susanne's voice trembles as she says, " 'I smashed her skull in. That's what you want to hear, isn't it?' "

"This sounds like a confession," the judge says, turning to Johannes.

"Please look carefully at the entire transcript, Your Honor," Johannes says. He points.

" 'This interrogation is concluded,' " the judge reads.

"Who says that the interrogation is concluded?"

The judge runs his hand down the page and looks at the prosecutor.

"I did," she says quietly.

"And this means?" the judge asks.

"That the interrogation was concluded," Susanne says. "But I just wanted—"

"You should be ashamed." The judge stops her sharply.

"To use this confession in an arrest consideration is against Swedish law, Article 40 of the United Nations Convention on the Rights of the Child, and the Council of Europe agreement," Johannes says.

150

Susanne Öst sits down with a thump. She pours water into her glass and spills some on the table. She wipes the drops up with her sleeve and drinks. Her hand is shaking. When she hears Johannes call Daniel Grim as a witness, she understands how completely her hand has been undermined. She'll have to lower the level of suspicion required if Vicky is going to be sent to jail at all.

Elin tries to look at Vicky's face, but the girl is keeping her head down.

Using his warmest voice, Johannes introduces Daniel Grim, mentioning how long he has worked at Birgittagården and all the institutions where he's worked previously. Vicky looks up for the first time. She tries to meet Daniel's eyes, but he's staring straight ahead, his lips pursed.

"Daniel," Johannes begins, "please tell us how well you know Vicky Bennet."

"Know," Daniel repeats, thinking. "No, I . . ." He stops speaking.

Vicky scratches one of the scabs on her wrist.

"Is there any psychologist or counselor who knows her better than you do?"

"No, there isn't," Daniel whispers.

"Not one?"

"No, well, it's hard to judge. I don't believe she had much therapy, if any, before she came to Birgittagården. So it's my understanding she was in therapy longer with me than with anyone else."

"You had one hour of cognitive behavioral therapy with Vicky every week until she ran away, is that correct?" Johannes asks.

"Yes. I also took part in her All Day Lifestyle training."

"That's training to prepare patients for a normal life back in society," Johannes explains to the judge.

"It's a big step," Daniel tells the judge.

Johannes contemplates Daniel for a while and his tone is serious when he says, "Now I have to ask you a difficult question."

"All right."

"There is a great deal of technical evidence that points to Vicky Bennet being involved in the murder of your wife."

Daniel nods so slightly it can barely be seen. The room fills with tension.

Elin is trying to read Daniel's expression, but he isn't looking at her. Vicky seems on the point of tears.

Johannes, however, stays calm and doesn't let Daniel escape his gaze.

"You were Vicky Bennet's therapist," he says. "Do you believe that she is capable of murdering your wife?"

Daniel Grim lifts his chin. His lips are pale. His hand trembles as he wipes his eyes, nudging his glasses off-kilter.

"I have not discussed the case with any of my colleagues. I haven't been able to. But in my professional opinion, well, no, I don't believe that Vicky Bennet is capable of this."

"How did you reach that opinion?"

"Vicky was responsive to therapy and medication," Daniel says. "But most important, in my profession, you meet people who are . . . that is, she did not have any violent fantasies and she was not violent in the manner that such people are."

"Thank you," Johannes says quietly.

151

After lunch, Johannes is the last person to get back to the arraignment room. He's holding his cell phone to his ear. The judge waits until the room is silent and then summarizes the results of the morning. Then he says, "The prosecutor has reduced the level of suspicion to the next-lowest level. She still requests that the accused be held in custody as a suspect for the crime of kidnapping."

"Yes, indeed," Susanne Öst says. "You cannot ignore the fact that Vicky Bennet kidnapped Dante Abrahamsson and held him captive for more than a week."

"There's just one thing," Johannes says.

"What now?" asks the judge.

Johannes walks to the door and opens it. Joona Linna enters, followed by a woman and a little boy. They stop as soon as they cross the threshold.

"I would like to introduce Joona Linna," Johannes says.

"I know who he is," the judge replies. He leans forward with increased interest.

Joona turns to the little boy hiding behind his mother's legs. "Here are the old guys I was telling you about."

"They don't look like trolls," the boy whispers, and starts to smile.

"You don't think so? Look closely at that one over there." He points to the judge.

The boy shakes his head and grins.

"Everybody, say hi to Dante and his mom, Pia Abrahamsson," Joona says.

Everyone in the room says hi. When Dante sees Vicky, he waves. Vicky waves back and her smile is heartbreaking. Susanne closes her eyes and tries to breathe slowly.

"You're waving at Vicky, but wasn't she mean to you?" Joona says.

"Mean?"

"Someone told me she was really mean," Joona says.

"She gave me piggyback rides and all her Hubba Bubba."

"But you wanted to go back to your mom."

"I couldn't," the boy says.

"Why not?"

The boy shrugs.

"Tell them what you told me," Pia says to her son.

"What about?"

"That she called."

"Oh yeah, she called."

"Can you tell Joona all about it?" Pia nods encouragingly.

"Vicky called on the phone but they wouldn't let her come back."

"Where did she call from?" asks Joona.

"From the truck."

"Did someone let her borrow a phone in the truck?"

"Don't know." Dante shrugs.

"What did she say on the phone?"

"She wanted to go back."

Dante's mother lifts him up and snuggles him and whispers to him until he wriggles free.

"Can you explain this?" the judge asks Joona.

"Vicky borrowed a cell phone from a truck driver who worked for IKEA. His name is Radek Skorża," Johannes Grünewald explains. "Joona Linna has traced the call. The call was placed to Birgittagården. It was automatically rerouted to the central office of Orre, the company that manages the home. Vicky spoke to a woman named Eva Morander. Vicky asked for help and repeated that she wanted to return. Eva Morander remembers the conversation. She told Vicky that the central office doesn't handle specific cases."

"Do you remember this conversation, Vicky?" the judge asks.

"Yes," says Vicky. Her voice is naked. "I just wanted to go back. I wanted them to take Dante back to his mother. But she said I couldn't go back."

Joona walks over and stands next to Johannes.

"I know that it's strange for a detective inspector to be on the side of the defense," he says. "But in my opinion, Vicky Bennet told the truth during Saga Bauer's questioning. I do not believe we have a kidnapping case here, just a terrible coincidence. So I talked to Dante and his mother and asked them to come, and that's why I'm here, too."

Joona's sharp gaze lands on the girl's face: no makeup, bruises, and scabs.

"But murder is something else, Vicky," he says sternly. "You may think you can keep silent, but I will not rest until I find out the truth."

152

The hearing concludes twenty minutes later after Susanne retracts her request for the suspect to be kept in custody on the kidnapping charge. Elin is sitting with her back straight and her face is expressionless as the prosecutor speaks. Vicky stares at the table and shakes her head slightly.

The judge leans back in his chair and declares that Vicky Bennet is free on her own recognizance in the matter of the murders of Elisabet Grim and Miranda Eriksdotter until the case is brought to trial.

Vicky Bennet would have been returned to Orre, the company that runs Birgittagården and other group youth homes, but the Swedish Organization for Institutionalized Care has confirmed Elin Frank as Vicky's temporary foster mother.

As the judge turns to Vicky and tells her that she is free to go, Elin breaks into a large smile. She can't help herself. Afterward, though, Johannes takes her aside and warns her: "Even though Vicky is not in custody, she is still a suspect in two murders and—"

"I know that."

"If the prosecutor presses charges, we might be able to win in court. That wouldn't mean she's innocent," Johannes says. "She could still be guilty."

"I know she's innocent," Elin says, aware of how naïve she must sound.

"It is my job to warn you," Johannes says.

"Even if Vicky were involved . . . Well, she's much too young to go to jail," Elin tries to explain. "Johannes, I can give her the best care in the entire world. I have already hired people to help me, and I've asked Daniel to stay with us, since Vicky feels secure around him."

"That's good of you," Johannes says softly.

"We'll consider all the options and find out what is best for her. That's all I really care about," Elin says, taking Johannes's hands. "Maybe Daniel can continue her therapy for a while. Maybe we will entrust someone else with that. But I will not let her down again. I won't do that."

153

While Johannes Grünewald meets with the journalists in the National Police Bureau press room, Elin and Vicky leave Stockholm in Elin's Jeep. They have already passed between Haga Park, where Crown Princess Victoria lives in her castle, and the enormous cemetery where the socialist August Palm lies buried.

The aroma of Italian leather fills the roomy interior. Elin's left hand on the steering wheel is bathed in the amber light from the instrument panel, and the autumnal sound of Bach's first cello suite pours from the speakers.

Elin looks at Vicky's calm face and smiles to herself.

In order to escape media attention, Elin is taking Vicky to her mountain cabin, where they will stay until the trial starts. The cabin is a 4,500-square-foot house in the foothills of Tegefjäll outside Duved.

There, Vicky will have around-the-clock care. Elin's local maid, Bella, is already at the cabin, and Daniel set out just ahead of them in his own car. A nurse will arrive tomorrow.

Vicky showered and washed her hair at the hospital, and her hair now smells of cheap shampoo. Elin bought her jeans, shirts, underwear, socks, and sports shoes, as well as a Windbreaker, and Vicky picked out the pair of black Armani jeans and a baggy gray sweater from Gant. The rest of the clothes are still in their bags in the backseat.

"What are you thinking about?" Elin asks.

Vicky doesn't answer. She's staring at the road. Elin turns down the music a little.

"You'll be found innocent," Elin says. "I'm absolutely sure of it."

They've now passed through the suburbs and there are fields and patches of forest on either side of the highway.

Elin offers Vicky some chocolate, but she shakes her head.

She looks much better today. Her face has more color and the bandages are gone. Only the cast on her thumb is still there.

"I'm so glad that Daniel is able to join us," Elin says.

"He's good," Vicky says.

Elin caught a glimpse of his golden Audi Kombi near Norrtull, but she's fallen behind him since.

"Is he better than the other therapists you've met before?" asks Elin.

"Yeah."

Elin lowers the volume a bit more.

"Do you want him to continue to work with you?"

"If I have to."

"It would be a good idea for you to continue therapy for a while," Elin says.

"In that case, then Daniel."

The farther north they drive, the more autumn makes itself known. Mile by mile, there's less green and more yellow and red. The fallen leaves form glowing lakes around the base of the tree trunks. They whirl over the highway.

Elin and Vicky do not speak for a while, then, out of the blue, Vicky says, "I need my stuff."

"What stuff?"

"My things. The stuff I left behind."

"Your belongings have been moved to the house where the other girls are living now," Elin says. "At least, the things the police didn't take with them. I can see that someone picks them up for you."

She glances at the girl and thinks that her things are important to her.

"Or would you like to get them now?"

Vicky nods.

"All right, if that's what you want. I'll call Daniel," Elin says. "After all, it's on the way."

154

The sun is setting behind the evergreens when Elin turns off the highway at Jättendal and parks behind Daniel's car. Daniel is waiting for them,
a pink cooler by his side. He waves and they get out of the car and stretch
their legs. Daniel unpacks the cooler, and they each have a cheese sandwich and a bottle of Trocadero while leaning against the car and gazing
over the train tracks to the fields beyond.

"I called my substitute at the house up there," Daniel tells Vicky.
"She doesn't think it's a good idea for you to come inside because of the
other girls."

"What harm would it do?" asks Elin.

"I don't want to see them anyway," Vicky says. "I just want my
stuff."

They get back into their cars. A winding road leads them past lakes
and Falun-red cottages and barns, through the forest, and to the coast.

They park outside the house where the girls from Birgittagården are
staying. On the other side of the road, a World War II naval mine is
standing beside an old gas pump. Seagulls are perched on the telephone
poles.

Vicky unfastens her seat belt but stays in the car. She watches Elin
and Daniel head straight toward the house and disappear behind the lilac bushes.

Just ahead, where the road forks, there's an old midsummer pole and the harbor lies beyond. Vicky looks out over the calm surface of the water, then she takes the new cell phone Elin has given her out of its box and peels the plastic from the screen.

The girls are standing by the window when Daniel and Elin walk up the steps to the large veranda. Daniel's substitute, Solveig Sundström, is already standing outside the front door. It is clear that she's not happy to see them. She tells them that they are not welcome to stay for dinner.

"Could we come in and say hi at least?" asks Daniel.

"Preferably not," Solveig replies. "It would be better if you tell me what you need and I go to look for it."

"There are quite a few things—" Elin begins to say.

"I can't promise I'll find them all."

"Just ask Caroline, then," Daniel says. "She usually has things under control."

While Daniel asks how the girls are doing and what they are up to, Elin is looking at their faces in the window. They're pushing one another and she can hear their voices through the glass although she can't make out what they are saying. Indie and Nina are standing next to each other, and Lu Chu pushes herself to the front of the pack and waves. Elin waves back. The only girl that Elin can't see is little red-haired Tuula.

Vicky is putting a SIM card into her cell phone. She looks up. A shiver goes down her back. She thinks she's seen someone moving outside the car. Maybe it's just the wind tossing the leaves of the lilac bushes.

It's twilight now.

Vicky looks back at Daniel's car, at the midsummer pole, the fence, and the lawn in front of the dark red house.

A light is shining on the mast of a boat moored far out on the pier. Its reflection quivers on the black water. Frames used for cleaning fishing nets, abandoned long ago, stand in the meadow near the harbor like soccer nets lined up in a row. Hundreds of iron hooks are still fastened to them.

Vicky catches sight of a red balloon rolling along the lawn in front of the house where the girls live.

She gets out of the car and walks slowly toward the house. She stops and listens. The light from the windows is falling on the birch tree's yellow leaves.

She can hear mumbling and wonders if someone is out there in the darkness. She leaves the gravel path. The balloon rolls past a volleyball net and finally stops when it gets tangled in a hedge.

"Vicky?" a voice whispers.

Vicky whirls around but sees no one. All her senses are heightened.

The settee creaks and starts to swing. The old weathervane turns in the wind.

"Vicky!" A sharp voice close beside her.

Vicky turns to the right and stares into the darkness. It takes her a few moments before she sees Tuula's narrow face peeking out from among the lilac bushes. She's holding a baseball bat. It is so heavy that the tip of the barrel is resting on the ground. Tuula wets her lips and stares at Vicky with bloodshot eyes.

Elin leans against the veranda railing and looks to see if Vicky is still in the car. It's too dark to make her out. Daniel is talking to Solveig. Elin listens to him explain that Almira needs to continue her therapy and that she reacts badly to high doses of antidepressants. He asks again if he can come in, but Solveig says that the girls are now her responsibility. However, she lets Caroline come out on the veranda. Caroline hugs Daniel and greets Elin.

"I've packed all of Vicky's things," she says.

"Is Tuula inside?" Elin asks. Her voice is tense.

"Yeah, I think so," Caroline says, surprised. "Would you like me to get her?"

"Yes, please get her," Elin replies. She tries to look calm.

Caroline goes back inside and calls for Tuula. Solveig looks at Daniel and Elin with mistrust.

"If you're hungry, you can have some apples. I'll tell one of the girls to get some," she says.

Elin doesn't reply. She walks down the steps into the garden. Behind her, she can still hear Caroline calling for Tuula.

It is so dark now that the ocean is invisible. The settee squeaks as it swings.

Elin is trying to be quiet, but her high heels clatter on the paving stones as she hurries around the corner of the path. The lilac bushes are rustling. It sounds like a rabbit running away. The branches move and Elin almost runs into Vicky.

"Good God!" Elin exclaims.

They look at each other. Vicky's face is pale in the weak light. Elin feels her pulse beat in her temples.

"Let's go to the car," she says, leading Vicky away from the house.

Elin glances over her shoulder and sees Caroline running up to them. She's holding a big plastic bag.

"I couldn't find Tuula," she says.

"Thanks for your trouble," Elin replies.

Vicky takes the bag and looks inside.

"Most of your stuff is there," Caroline says. "But Lu Chu and Almira used your earrings to bet with when they were playing poker."

As Vicky and Elin drive away, Caroline stands and watches them go. Her face is deeply sad.

155

Elin can see Daniel's headlights in her rearview mirror the entire time she's driving on the E14. There's almost no traffic, just a few freight trucks, but it still takes them three hours to reach the ski resort area. Even in the darkness, they can see the lifts and support poles for Åre's immense cable car on the mountainside. Six kilometers before Duved, they turn onto a narrow gravel road that zigzags up Tegefjäll. Leaves and dust swirl in the beams of the headlights.

Soon they pass through the open gates and wind up the driveway to Elin's cabin. It is a large, modernist house of poured concrete, all right angles and straight lines. Its huge rectangular windows are hidden behind aluminum shutters.

They park the cars in a garage with room for five vehicles. A tiny blue Mazda is already there. Daniel helps Elin carry the luggage into the living room. Some lights are already on and Elin walks to a switch and presses it. The aluminum shutters creak as their panels separate. Light from the security lamp outside slips in through hundreds of small holes and, with a great deal more creaking, the metal shutters begin to roll up.

After a while, it's quiet again. The mountainous landscape looms outside the enormous windows. The security light has switched off and there are small glimmers of light from houses in the distance.

"Wow," Vicky says as she looks out.

"Do you remember my ex-husband, Jack?" Elin asks Vicky. "He built this mountain hideaway. Well, he didn't build it himself, he had other people build it. He just told them he wanted a bunker with a view."

An older woman wearing a green apron comes down the stairs from the upper floor.

"Hello, Bella," Elin says. "I'm sorry we were so late." She hugs the woman.

"Better late than never," Bella smiles, and explains that she's made up the beds in all the rooms.

"Thanks," Elin says.

"I didn't know whether or not you would do any grocery shopping on the way up, so I just bought a little bit of everything. There'll be enough for a few days."

Bella starts a fire in the huge fireplace. Afterward, Elin follows her to the garage and says good night. When she returns, she finds Daniel in the kitchen, making supper. Vicky is sitting on the sofa, crying. Elin hurries over and kneels in front of the girl.

"Vicky, what's wrong? Why are you crying?"

The girl gets up and locks herself in the guest bathroom, off the living room. Elin rushes back to the kitchen.

"Vicky has locked herself in the bathroom!"

"Would you like me to talk to her?"

"Hurry!"

Daniel follows Elin to the bathroom door. He knocks and tells Vicky to open the door.

"No locked doors," he says. "You remember the rules, don't you?"

A few seconds later, Vicky comes out of the bathroom. Her eyes are damp. She heads back to the sofa. Daniel exchanges a look with Elin and then sits down next to the girl.

"Do you remember how you were sad when you came to Birgittagården?" he says after a while.

"I know. I should have been happy," she replies without looking at him.

"Coming to a place is always the first step toward leaving it," he says.

Vicky swallows hard and tears spring back into her eyes. She lowers her voice so that Elin can't hear what she says.

"I'm a murderer."

"Don't say that unless you are absolutely sure that it's true," Daniel says calmly. "I can tell by your voice that you don't believe it is."

156

Flora pours steaming hot water into the bucket and, although she hates the smell of the rubber gloves, she puts them on. The scent of lemon cleanser spreads through the small apartment. Cool air pours in the open windows. The sun is shining and birds are singing.

When the detective left her standing on the sidewalk, she had stayed right there. She should have started preparing for the séance, but she didn't dare go downstairs by herself. Instead, she waited for the first participants to arrive. Dina and Asker Sibelius came at their usual early time, fifteen minutes before the séance. Flora pretended that she'd arrived late. They came downstairs with her and helped her set up the chairs. By five after seven, nineteen participants had arrived.

The séance lasted much longer than usual. Flora gave each of them her time and pretended to see friendly old ghosts, happy children, and forgiving parents.

She had been able to figure out why Dina and Asker kept coming.

Their grown son was left in a coma after a car accident, and they had reluctantly agreed with the doctor to turn off life support and to donate his organs.

"What if he can't get to God?" Dina had whispered.

This evening, Flora talked to their son and was able to reassure them that he was in the light. He was happy that they'd donated his heart, lungs, corneas, and kidneys, which were now living on.

After the séance, Dina kissed Flora's hands. She was weeping and kept saying that she was now the happiest woman on earth.

Now Flora is scrubbing the floor of the apartment. Ewa is at a sewing circle with a few friends. Hans-Gunnar is in the living room, watching a soccer match against Italy. He has the volume turned up high.

Flora rinses the mop and squeezes out the water while she stretches her aching back. Then she gets back to work.

She knows that Ewa is going to open the envelope and pay the bills on Monday.

"Pass, Zlatan, pass for God's sake!" yells Hans-Gunnar from the living room.

Flora's shoulders have started to ache by the time she carries the bucket to Ewa's bedroom. She closes the door behind her and places the bucket in the way. She takes the key hidden behind the wedding photograph and unlocks the desk.

A crash makes Flora jump.

It was just the mop falling over.

Flora listens for a moment before she lifts the heavy desk lid. She tries to pull open the tiny drawer inside, but her hands are trembling. The drawer is stuck. She pokes among the pencils and erasers and finds a letter opener. She carefully inserts it into the spring above the drawer and gives it a gentle tug. The drawer slides open an inch.

She can hear a scraping sound close-by, but sees it's just a pigeon on the windowsill.

Flora gets her fingers into the drawer and manages to pull it all the way open, but the postcard from Copenhagen gets bent. She takes out the envelope for the bills and replaces the exact amount she took.

She puts everything back in its proper place. She tries to straighten the postcard, pushes the drawer back in, and makes sure the pencils, pens, and letter opener are arranged as she found them. She closes the lid and locks it.

She goes over to the nightstand and has just lifted the wedding picture when the door to Ewa's room crashes open. The bucket tips over and the water spills out.

"You goddamn thief!" Hans-Gunnar yells as he storms inside. He's not wearing a shirt.

She turns toward him. His eyes are wide open and he's punching wildly. The first blow hits her shoulder and she doesn't feel it. Then he grabs her hair and beats her with his other fist. The third blow lands under her chin. The next on her cheek. She falls and feels her hair rip out. The wedding picture falls to the floor and the glass breaks into pieces. She lies on her side in the spilled water. She can hardly breathe from the pain in her eye.

Flora feels nauseated and rolls onto her stomach. She tries to keep herself from vomiting. Spots appear before her eyes. She tries to focus and sees that the photograph has fallen from the frame and is leaning against the nightstand. On the back someone has written: Ewa and Hans-Gunnar, Delsbo Church.

Flora remembers what the ghost has whispered to her. This wasn't the last time, right before the séance, but earlier, here at home. She doesn't remember exactly. Miranda had whispered about a church bell tower. The girl was holding the wedding photo and pointing at the bell tower in the background as she whispered: *She's hiding there. She saw everything and she's hiding in the tower.*

Hans-Gunnar is standing over her, breathing heavily, when Ewa comes in, still wearing her coat.

"What is going on here?" she demands in a frightened voice.

"She's been stealing! I knew it!"

He spits on Flora, picks up the bronze key, and goes to the desk.

157

Joona is sitting in his office with a complete set of the documents presented at the arraignment hearing spread before him. He thinks there's enough evidence here for a conviction.

The telephone rings, and Joona would not have picked it up if he'd looked at the display.

"I know you think I'm a liar," Flora says breathlessly. "But please don't hang up! You have to listen to me. I'm begging you. I'll do anything if you just listen—"

"Calm down and tell me about it."

"There's a witness to the murders," she says. "A real witness. Not a ghost. I'm telling you there's a real witness who is hiding—"

Her voice is thin from hysteria and he tries to calm her down.

"That's good," he says. "However, the preliminary investigation shows—"

"You have to go there!" she interrupts him.

Joona doesn't know why he's even listening to this person. But she seems so desperate that he doesn't hang up.

"Where is the witness, exactly?" he asks.

"In a bell tower. The black bell tower at Delsbo Church."

"Who told you—"

"Please, that's where she is! She's afraid and she's hiding."

"Flora, the prosecutors are supposed to—"

"No one is listening to me!"

Joona hears a man's voice in the background yelling at Flora to leave the telephone alone. Then there's a rustling sound.

"Time for your little chat to end!" the man says, and then the phone call is over.

Joona sighs as he puts his cell phone down. He can't understand why Flora keeps on lying.

Once Vicky was arrested, the preliminary investigation came to an end and Joona had finally been sent all the paperwork. But now the case was out of the hands of the police. It was the prosecutor's job to prepare the evidence for the trial.

I missed something in this case, Joona thinks. He feels oddly desolate.

Something is troubling him about the rock. He doesn't know what.

The Needle mentions in his report that a rock was used as a murder weapon, but no one has followed this up since it doesn't fit with the other evidence.

Joona decides he's not going to leave this case alone. Out of sheer stubbornness he flips through the National Laboratory test results. Then he reads the autopsy report. Joona had left before The Needle and Frippe cut open the body and did the internal autopsy, so their findings are news to him.

He stops at the description of Elisabet Grim's defensive wounds. He rereads the description of the wounds on her hands. Then he reads on.

The light from the window slowly moves over Joona's bulletin board. It has the notification of the internal investigation and the latest postcard from Disa pinned to it. The postcard shows a chimpanzee wearing lipstick and heart-shaped glasses.

There is nothing unusual in Miranda's stomach contents. The tissue was shiny and smooth. Same thing for the lungs and the heart. Tissue shiny and smooth.

84. Heart is normal configuration and weighs 198 grams. Pericardium shiny and smooth. Ventricles and atria normal. No plaque in the aorta. In the walls of the coronary artery no plaque layer. Heart muscles are gray-red and structure normal.

Joona holds a finger in the autopsy report and flips to the National Forensic Laboratory test results. Miranda's blood was type A. It had traces of venlafaxine, an ingredient in many antidepressants. Otherwise normal.

104. Ureters appear normal.
105. In bladder 100 ml. light yellow, clear urine. Mucosa pale.

Joona flips back to the test results and finds the urine test. There are traces of the sleeping substance nitrazepam and the hCG level is unusually high.

Joona gets up quickly and grabs his phone to call The Needle.

"I'm looking at the test results from the National Forensic Lab and I notice that Miranda has a high hCG level in her urine," he says.

"Of course," The Needle replies. "The cysts on her ovaries were—"

"Wait a minute," Joona says. "Isn't a high hCG level a sign of pregnancy as well?"

"That's right, but as I said—"

"But if Miranda did an over-the-counter pregnancy test, she might think she was pregnant."

"Yes," The Needle says. "She would have had a positive reading."

"So Miranda could well have believed she was pregnant."

Joona dashes out of his office and calls Flora while he rushes along the hall. He hears Anja calling him, but he ignores her and runs down the stairs. No one is answering the phone. He keeps repeating to himself that Flora had changed her story.

"I meant to say she thought she was pregnant," Flora had said. "She wasn't pregnant, but she thought she was."

Joona dials her number again. The phone keeps ringing as he races through the lobby. He's already out the revolving door when a man answers. He's breathing heavily.

"Hans-Gunnar Hansen."

"My name is Joona Linna and I'm from the National Police."

"You found my car?"

"I need to talk to Flora."

"What the hell!" the man yells. "I wouldn't have asked if you'd found my car if Flora was here! She's the one who stole it! You policemen can't do your fucking job—"

Joona ends the call and sprints to his black Volvo.

158

Elin sleeps in the room next to Vicky's, keeping the doors to both rooms open. She wakes several times in the night to the slightest noise. Each time, she listens and then gets up and looks into Vicky's room. When morning comes, she stands for a while at the door, watching the girl sleep, before she goes downstairs to the kitchen.

Daniel is standing at the stove, making creamy scrambled eggs. The kitchen smells like coffee and freshly baked bread. The view from the open windows is almost frightening in its immensity: mountaintops and pools of water with mirror surfaces; valleys covered in trees shimmering red and yellow.

"It's almost impossible to look outside," Daniel says. "It's like it hurts my heart."

They embrace and he kisses her on the top of her head. She stands still, breathing in his scent and feeling a little dizzy with unexpected happiness.

A timer beeps on the countertop. Daniel loosens himself from their embrace to get the bread out of the oven.

They sit down at the large dining table, and as they eat breakfast, they touch each other's hands. They drink coffee and look out the window, and the beauty of the view takes away their words.

Finally Elin says in a low voice, "I'm so worried about Vicky."

"It will all work out just fine."

She puts down her coffee cup.

"Promise?"

"All I have to do is get her to talk about what happened," he says. "I'm afraid that her feelings of guilt are making her more and more self-destructive. We really need to keep our eye on her."

"The nurse from Åre is coming in an hour. I'll drive down and pick her up at the bus station," Elin says. "Should I ask Vicky to come with me? What do you think?"

"I don't know," he says. "It might be better for her to stay here."

"That's right. We've just gotten here," Elin agrees. "Still, I can't help worrying. Promise me you'll keep her in sight the whole time."

"She knows she can't even lock the bathroom door," Daniel says.

At that moment, Elin glimpses Vicky through the window. She is on the lawn, kicking through the colorful leaves. Her long hair is still tangled down her back. She looks cold. Elin takes her sweater from the back of her chair and goes outside to hand it to Vicky.

"Thanks," the girl whispers.

"I will never ever let you down again," Elin says.

Without saying another word, she takes Vicky's hand and squeezes it. A moment later, Vicky returns the gesture. Elin's heart is so filled with joy that she can't speak.

159

The sky is getting dark as Joona leaves the E4 and turns onto Route 84 toward Delsbo. His guess is that Flora has taken the car to drive to Delsbo Church.

He can still hear her agitated voice telling him about a witness hiding in the bell tower there.

Joona can't figure her out. It's as if she's mixing lies and truth without being aware of it herself. Even so, he can't let go of the feeling that she knows more about the murders at Birgittagården than anyone else.

This story about a witness could be another one of her lies, but on the off chance it's true he can't ignore it.

Low-hanging clouds make the fields appear gray and the evergreens blue. Falling leaves dance over the road. It's difficult to keep up his speed, as the road is winding and filled with potholes.

A few kilometers farther on, he turns onto a wide boulevard lined with trees, which leads to Delsbo Church. Beyond the trees is wide-open farmland. In the distance, a lone harvester is driving through a field, its blades whirling over the ground like scythes. Birds rise and sink in the swirling air.

He's almost at the church when he sees a car crashed into one of the trees. The hood is smashed, a fender is lying in the grass, and one of the windows has shattered. The engine is still running and the driver's door is wide open. The rear lights stain the grass in the ditch red.

Joona slows down, but when he sees the car is empty, he keeps driving. Flora must have gotten out and run toward the tower.

Joona parks and races over the raked gravel to the pitch-covered bell tower, which is standing on a hill not far from the church. He can see the church bell hanging beneath the onion dome behind a railing. Beyond the bell tower, there's a rushing river, its waters black and foamy. The sky is dark and it looks like it will start raining at any moment.

The door to the tower is slightly ajar.

Joona walks the last few feet. He can smell the pitch.

The wide ground-floor section is paneled in dark wood. There's a steep wooden staircase leading to a platform below the bell.

Joona calls out, "Flora?"

160

Flora appears at the top of the stairs. She looks very sad and there are dark rings around her eyes. Her face is bruised.

"There's no one here," she says. She bites her lip.

"Are you sure?"

She starts to cry and her voice breaks. "I'm sorry. I was so sure."

She climbs down the stairs all the while apologizing, but without looking at him. She starts to walk back toward the ruined car.

Joona follows her. "How did you find your way here?" he asks. "Why did you think that the witness would be hiding here?"

"My foster parents' wedding photo. The bell tower was in the background."

"What does this have to do with Miranda?"

"The ghost said . . ." Flora falls silent.

"What is it?" asks Joona.

He thinks back to the drawing she made of Miranda with her hands in front of her face and the dark blood beside her head in the shape of a heart. She drew the picture not to deceive anyone but because she'd actually seen something and no longer remembers the circumstances.

When she was standing outside Carlén Antiques, Flora talked about the ghost as a memory. She tried to say that she remembered what the ghost had said.

A ray of sunlight streams out between the heavy rain clouds.

As a memory, he repeats. He looks at Flora's pale face.

Yellow leaves are falling from the trees. All of a sudden, the pieces fall into place. Joona realizes how things fit. He feels as if he's just pulled open the curtains and light is flooding in. He knows he has the key to the case. Flora is the witness hiding in the bell tower.

"You are her," he whispers. He shudders at his own words.

She is the witness, but it wasn't Miranda she saw being killed.

Someone else was killed in the same manner.

A different girl, but the same killer.

His instinct is so clear that it is followed by a sharp migraine. It feels as if a bullet is going right through his brain. He tries to find something to hold on to as he hears Flora's voice through a great darkness. Then as suddenly as it arrived the pain disappears.

"You saw everything," he says out loud.

"You're bleeding," Flora says.

He has a nosebleed. He finds a tissue in his pocket.

"Flora," he says, "you were the witness hiding in the bell tower."

"I haven't seen anything," she protests.

Joona holds the tissue to his nose. "You've just forgotten it."

"But I wasn't there. You know that. I have never been to Birgittagården."

"It was something else you saw."

"No," Flora says, shaking her head.

"How old is the ghost?" asks Joona.

"Miranda is about fifteen whenever I'm dreaming, but when she's real, when it looks like she's right in the room with me, she's a little girl."

"How old?"

"About five."

"How old are you now, Flora?"

Flora is fearful as she looks into his gray eyes.

"Forty," she says in a low voice.

Joona has realized that Flora has been describing a murder that she witnessed as a child, but that she thought she was describing Miranda's murder. He knows he's right. He takes out his cell phone and calls Anja. Flora had seen what she'd been through only now, decades later. This is why her memories are so strong and confusing.

"Anja?" he asks when she picks up the phone. "Are you in front of your computer?"

"Are you in a better place?" she says, amused.

"Can you see if anything happened in Delsbo about thirty-five years ago?"

"Anything special?"

"A five-year-old girl would be involved."

As Anja taps away on her computer, Joona watches Flora walk toward the church. She runs her hand over the façade. Then she goes inside. He follows her to keep her in sight. A hedgehog waddles away between a few gravestones.

Beyond the tree-lined boulevard, he can see the harvester in the field and the clouds of dust that rise behind it.

"Yes," Anja says. "There was an unusual death thirty-five years ago. A five-year-old girl was found dead by Delsbo Church. Nothing more. The police wrote it off as an accident."

Joona watches Flora turn around and look at him with a question in her eyes.

"What was the name of the policeman in charge of the investigation?"

"Torkel Ekholm."

"Can you find an address for him?"

161

Twenty minutes later, Joona parks his car on a narrow gravel road. He opens an iron gate, and he and Flora walk through a shady yard up to a wooden house painted red with white trim. The roof is made of asbestos cement tiles. The autumn greenery is filled with buzzing insects. The thunderstorm is still building overhead.

Joona rings the doorbell. Its chime is deafening.

They hear a shuffling sound, and then an elderly man opens the door. He's wearing a vest, suspenders, and slippers.

"Are you Torkel Ekholm?" asks Joona.

The man is leaning on a walker. He's looking at them with old, watery eyes. There's a hearing aid behind his large, wrinkled right ear.

"Who wants to know?" he asks. They can hardly hear him.

"Joona Linna. I'm a detective inspector with the National Police."

The old man peers at Joona's ID and smiles slightly.

"Ah, the National Police," he says softly. He gestures for Joona and Flora to come inside. "Let's have a cup of coffee."

They sit down at the kitchen table as Torkel goes to the stove after apologizing to Flora for having no cookies to offer her. He talks quietly and appears to be quite hard of hearing.

A clock is ticking loudly and over the kitchen bench there's a moose-hunting rifle, a well-oiled Remington. An embroidery piece with bent corners is hanging crookedly nearby. It reads "Happiness in the home comes from contentment."

Torkel Ekholm scratches his chin and looks at Joona.

Once the water is boiling, he takes out three cups and a tin of instant coffee.

"When you live alone, you keep things simple," he says, and shrugs as he hands Flora a teaspoon.

"I'm here to ask you about an extremely old case," Joona says. "Thirty-five years ago, a five-year-old girl was found dead at Delsbo Church."

"That's right," the man says without meeting Joona's gaze.

"Was it an accident?" Joona asks.

"Yes," the man says.

"I don't think it was an accident," Joona says.

"I'm relieved to hear that," the old man says. His mouth trembles and he pushes the sugar bowl toward Joona.

"Do you remember the case?" asks Joona.

The spoon clinks against the coffee cup as the old man pours in the coffee powder and stirs. He looks back up at Joona.

"There are certain cases that I wish I could forget."

He gets up and shuffles over to a dark dresser and unlocks the top drawer. He explains that he's kept his notes from that case all these years.

"I knew that someday, someone would want these from me," he says so softly they can hardly hear him.

162

Torkel nods toward the papers on the table in front of them.

"The dead girl was named Ylva. She was the daughter of a farm fore-man working on the Rånne estate. When I arrived on the scene, they'd already moved her onto a sheet. They told me she'd fallen from the bell tower . . ."

The old policeman leans back against his chair and the wood creaks. A heavy fly buzzes against the windowpane.

"They said there was blood on the railing under the roof. They pointed and I looked, and I noticed that something wasn't right."

"Why did you end the preliminary investigation?"

"There were no witnesses. I had nothing. I questioned everyone but got nowhere. I was told not to disturb the folks at the Rånnes' manor any-more. They gave the girl's father leave from work and . . . it was . . . I have a picture that Janne took. He worked for *Arbetarbladet* and we used him as a crime scene photographer."

The old policeman shows them a black-and-white photograph. A lit-tle girl is lying on a sheet on the lawn. Her hair is spread out. At the side of her head, there's a pool of blood looking just like the one on Mi-randa's bed. The same place.

The bloodstain looks like a heart.

The little girl's face is soft and her cheeks are round. Her mouth is closed, which makes her appear as if she's asleep.

Flora stares at the picture with her hand on her hair and her face loses all color.

"I didn't see anything," she moans, and then she begins to weep.

Joona moves the photograph away. He tries to calm Flora, and after a few moments she gets up and takes the photograph from Torkel. She dries her tears and stares at it, bracing herself against the sink. She doesn't notice when she knocks an empty beer bottle into the soapy water.

"We were playing a game called shut-your-eyes," she says at last.

"So you were covering your eyes?"

"Yes, we were supposed to cover our eyes with our hands."

"But you looked, didn't you?" Joona asks. "You saw who hit the little girl with the rock."

"No, I had my hands over my eyes."

"Who hit her?"

"What did you see?" asks Torkel.

"Little Ylva. She was happy . . . She covered her eyes with her hands, then he hit her."

"Who hit her?" Joona asks.

"My brother."

"You don't have a brother," Joona says.

Torkel shakes so much his coffee cup rattles in its saucer.

"So it was the boy," he mutters. "Could it have been the boy?"

"Which boy?" asks Joona.

Flora's face is completely white. Tears run freely down her face. The old policeman gets up from his chair with difficulty and rips a paper towel from the roll on the counter. Flora is shaking her head, but Joona sees that her mouth is moving slightly.

"What did you see?" asks Joona. "Flora?"

Torkel reaches her and hands her the towel. He says carefully, "Are you little Flora? The silent little sister?"

163

The memory comes to Flora as she's standing in the old policeman's kitchen with her hand on the sink. She feels her legs start to buckle as she remembers what she'd seen.

The sun was shining. They were playing on the lawn by the church. She was holding her hands in front of her face. The light was shining right through her spread fingers. The other two children had golden halos around them.

"Oh God!" she moans. "Oh God!"

She remembers seeing her brother hit the little girl with a rock.

The memory is so strong it feels as if the children are there with her in the kitchen.

She hears the thud and sees Ylva's head jerk.

Flora remembers seeing the girl falling down on the grass. Her mouth opened and closed. Her eyes shook and she mumbled something. He hit her again.

He was hitting as hard as he could, yelling that they should keep their eyes shut. Ylva stopped moving. He placed her hands over her face.

"But I didn't—"

"Are you Flora?" the old policeman asks again.

She's still looking between her fingers when her brother gets up. He's still holding the rock. He tells Flora she should close her eyes. She has to close her eyes to play the game. He is coming closer to her from the side. He lifts the blood-covered rock. She jumps backward as his blow came. The rock cut her chin and hit her shoulder, and she fell to her knees. She picked herself up and ran as fast as she could.

"Are you little Flora who lived at the Rånne mansion?"

"I don't remember much at all," she answers.

"Who is her brother?" asks Joona.

"The forestry magnate Rånne, we called them fine folk," Torkel said. "They were like nobility. They adopted two children. It was even in the newspapers. Their good deed. A noble deed and a caring deed. After the accident, the girl was sent away. They kept the boy."

"Daniel," Flora says. "His name is Daniel."

Joona's chair scrapes the floor as he gets up from the table. He leaves the house without saying a word. He runs through the garden with the cell phone to his ear and leaves a message as he gets into his car.

"Anja, you have to help me, it's urgent. See if Daniel Grim has any connection to a family named Rånne in Delsbo."

Joona has just turned on the car's radio to alert police at the national communications center when Anja calls him back.

"Yes, those are his parents."

"Find out everything you can about him," Joona says.

"What's this about?"

"Girls," Joona replies.

He ends the call and before he radios the police, he calls Elin Frank.

164

Elin is driving carefully down the steep gravel road toward Åre to pick up Vicky's nurse from the bus station. Her window is rolled down and fresh, cool air has flooded the Jeep. The mountains here are close together like giant Viking burial mounds, rounded and overgrown.

She remembers Vicky taking her hand and squeezing it. Everything is going to be better from now on.

The narrow road is passing beneath a cliff when she hears her cell phone buzz in her purse. She drives slowly until she finds a place to stop. She has a bad feeling as she takes out the phone. It's still ringing in her hand and she can see it's Joona Linna calling. She doesn't want to hear what he has to say, but she answers anyway.

"Hello?"

"Where's Vicky?"

"She's here with me," she says. "I have a house in Duved which—"

"I mean, can you see her right now?"

"No, I—"

"Get Vicky at once, get in your car, and drive to Stockholm right now. Just you and Vicky. Don't stop to bring anything with you—"

"I'm already in the car!" Elin shrieks. She feels alarmed. "Vicky is with Daniel at the house."

"That's not good," Joona says in a tone that fills Elin with dread.

"What's happened?"

"Listen to me. Daniel was the one who killed Miranda and Elisabet."

"That can't be true," she whispers. "He's keeping an eye on Vicky while I pick up the nurse from the bus station."

"Then she may no longer be alive, and you are in danger," Joona says. "Get away from there right now. That is my advice as a police officer."

Elin stares at the sky. In the last few minutes, low clouds have gathered. They push over the mountaintops, threatening rain.

"I can't leave her," Elin hears herself say.

"The police are on the way, but it could take a while."

"I'm turning around right now."

"I understand," Joona says. "Be very careful. Daniel Grim is an extremely dangerous man and you'll be on your own until the police get there."

Elin's mind is blank. She turns the Jeep around and speeds up the steep road, the gravel clattering against the underside of the vehicle.

165

Vicky is sitting on the white leather armchair, downloading apps onto
her cell phone. Daniel comes into her room and sits down on the bed.
He's quiet for a moment as he looks out at the gray, ancient top of Mount
Åreskuta and the dark clouds gathering around it.

"Did it feel wrong yesterday?" Daniel says. "I mean, just sitting and
waiting in the car when we got your stuff."

"No. I knew nobody wanted to see me," she says, still busy with her
phone.

"When I went inside the house, I saw Almira and Lu Chu playing
the shut-your-eyes game," Daniel says. "Miranda taught you that game,
didn't she?"

"Yeah," Vicky says.

"Do you know where Miranda learned it?" Daniel asks.

Vicky nods as she reaches for the cell-phone charger.

"I use the game in therapy sometimes," Daniel says. "It's a game to
practice trust."

"Miranda popped some chocolate in my mouth," Vicky says. She
smiles. "Once, she drew a heart on my stomach."

Vicky stops talking. She's remembering her meeting with Tuula.
Tuula had told her things when she met her by the lilac bushes.

"Have you told anyone about the game?" Daniel asks.

"No," she says.

"I was just wondering."

Vicky looks back down at her phone. She thinks about Tuula, standing in the darkness with a baseball bat in her hand. She was saying that the murderer only kills whores. Only whores need to be afraid. Typical Tuula, trying to scare her with her crazy stories. Vicky had tried to smile, but Tuula said that she'd found a pregnancy test in Miranda's purse when she took her necklace. Yesterday, the only thing Vicky had thought about that was Miranda must have been sleeping with some guy she'd met through the All Day Living program.

Now she realizes that it has to be Daniel.

Vicky had the feeling that something was wrong when Miranda was trying to explain the game. It struck her that Miranda was only pretending that the game was fun. She was giggling and giving her chocolate, but the real reason she was doing it seemed to be to find out what Vicky knew about the game.

She remembers how unconcerned Miranda tried to look when she asked if Daniel had ever come into her room and played with her.

"Miranda didn't say anything," Vicky says. "She didn't tell me anything about what you guys did in therapy."

Vicky blushes as she realizes how everything fits together. Daniel had killed Miranda and Elisabet. The killings had nothing to do with Miranda being a whore. Daniel killed Miranda because she was pregnant.

Perhaps Miranda had told Elisabet everything.

Vicky tries to breathe calmly. She doesn't know what she is supposed to say. She pulls at the frayed edge of her cast.

"It was—"

Daniel leans forward and takes her cell phone out of her hand.

"The therapy . . . It was about trusting one another," Vicky says. She feels sure that Daniel has seen through her, that he's aware she knows he killed Miranda and Elisabet with the hammer and tried to pin the murders on her.

"Yes, it's an important step in therapy," Daniel says. He's watching her closely.

"I know," she whispers.

"We can play the game now. You and me. Just for fun," he says.

Vicky nods and realizes with panic that he's already decided to kill her. He helped her avoid jail so that he could find out what she knew. He wanted to be absolutely sure that he was safe.

"Shut your eyes," he says with a smile.

"Right now?"

"It's a fun game."

"But I—"

"Just do it," he orders.

She shuts her eyes and puts her hands in front of her face. Her heart is pounding. He's doing something. It feels as if he's pulling the sheet off her bed beneath her.

"I have to pee," she says.

"You'll have a chance soon," he says.

She sits with her hands over her face and flinches when she hears the scrape of the chair being moved. But she keeps her hands over her face.

166

Elin is driving recklessly fast up the steep hill. Last spring the runoff corrugated the road, and the key ring is rattling violently in the spare-change cup by the gearshift. Tree branches slap the sides of her Jeep and the gravel beats against its underside. She brakes during a steep curve and almost skids. The tires slide over the gravel, but she shifts into neutral, comes around, and hits the gas again.

Elin is driving too quickly when she reaches the turnoff to her house. She slows down just a little, but she swings wide and scrapes the side of the Jeep against one of the gateposts, knocking off a side mirror. She hits the gas and it seems like she's about to launch into the air as she reaches the top. The case of mineral water in the back falls over with a crash.

She brakes hard at the house and leaps from the car, leaving the engine running. She runs straight inside. The metal shutters are closed. It's dark and she stumbles over boots in the hall as she hurries into the large living room.

"Vicky!" she yells.

Elin turns on the lights and runs up the stairs. She slips and bangs her knee, jumps back up, and rushes toward Vicky's room. She pushes down the handle. It's locked. Elin bangs on the door and can hear the hysteria in her voice as she screams, "Open up!"

She can't hear anything inside. She looks through the keyhole. A chair has been overturned and shadows are jerking across the walls.

"Vicky?"

She moves back and then kicks the door. There's a thud, but nothing happens. She kicks again. Then she runs to the room next door, but there's no key in the lock. She runs to the next room, and there's a key to that bedroom still in the keyhole. She grabs it and runs back, knocking over a glass sculpture, which thuds to the floor. Her hands are shaking, but she manages to get the key into the lock and throw the door open.

"Oh God!" she whispers.

Vicky is hanging from the whitewashed beam by a bed sheet made into a noose. Her mouth is open and her face has lost color, but she's kicking her feet. She's still alive. She's holding on to the noose, trying to relieve the pressure on her throat.

Elin doesn't stop to think. She runs to Vicky and lifts her as high as she can.

"Try to get loose!" she exclaims, crying, as she holds her up by her thin legs.

The girl fights with the cloth. Her body is cramping and she has to get oxygen. She's panicking and tearing at the cloth to get the noose off.

Elin hears Vicky draw in a lungful of air. She coughs and takes another deep breath. She starts to pant and her body goes tense.

"I can't get it off." Vicky coughs.

Elin stands on her toes and struggles to lift Vicky higher.

"Try to climb!"

"I can't!"

The noose tightens again and Vicky can't get enough air. She's jerking in panic-induced convulsions. Elin's arms are shaking from the effort of holding her.

She won't give up.

She tries to reach the fallen chair with her foot so she can climb on it. She can't reach it. Vicky is covered in sweat and her body spasms. Elin tries to change her grip, but it's too hard. Still, she lowers one of her hands just a bit so she can lift higher. Vicky uses the last of her strength to fight the noose and manages to slip it over her chin and then off her head. Coughing, she falls to the floor in a tangled heap with Elin.

Vicky's neck has a red bruise and she's taking quick, shallow breaths, but she is breathing. She's alive. Elin kisses her cheek and wipes her damp hair from her face. She whispers to Vicky to keep quiet.

"It was Daniel."

"I know," Elin says. "The police are on the way. Stay here. I'm going to lock the door, and you must keep completely quiet."

167

Elin locks the door with Vicky inside. She's shaking and her arms and legs are numb from the effort she's just made. Her cell phone rings and she sees that she's gotten a text message from Vicky's cell phone.

Sorry. I can't tell more lies. Don't be sad. Hugs, V

Elin feels nauseated and her heart is hammering. Her thoughts are tumbling too quickly in her head. It takes her a moment to understand what's going on. Daniel must have just sent her this message from Vicky's cell phone. She heads downstairs to the large living room. The metal shutters are still closed throughout the house.

She catches sight of someone: Daniel. He's at the head of the basement stairs and must have just come up from the garage. She knows that she'll have to keep him occupied until the police arrive.

"She went through with it," Elin says. "Vicky locked the door. I couldn't get it open in time. I don't understand."

"What are you saying?" Daniel says slowly, looking at her with shining eyes.

"She's dead. I've got to call someone about this."

"That's right," he says.

"Daniel, I don't get it."

"You don't?"

"No, I'm—"

"After killing you, Vicky went to her room and hanged herself."

"What?"

"You shouldn't have come back so soon," Daniel says.

Elin catches a glimpse of the ax Daniel is holding behind his back. She makes a run for the front door, but he's right behind her. She twists to the right and pulls a chair over behind her. He trips over the chair so now she has a slight head start. She runs through the kitchen and into the hall. He's right behind her. There is nowhere to hide. She runs into Jack's old bedroom and locks the door behind her. She hits the button to open the metal shutters.

I'm not going to get out, she thinks. *It takes too long for the shutters to open.*

The motor whirs and then there's the creaking sound as the aluminum panels start to part. Light starts to stream through the tiny holes.

Elin screams when the first ax blow hits the door. The blade goes through the wood by the lock, is turned to the side and drawn back out.

The shutters slowly rattle upward. She can see a few inches of window when the ax falls a second time.

She can't wait in Jack's bedroom. She stumbles into the bathroom as she hears Daniel break open the door. She can hear the wood splinter and the door being pushed aside.

She catches a glimpse of herself in the large mirror as she runs through the bathroom past the tub, the shower, the sauna, out the other door, and into Jack's office. It's so dark, she runs into Jack's pedestal desk. Folders and files crash to the floor. She opens a desk drawer, dumps out pens and pencils, and gropes through them. She grabs the letter opener.

She can tell by the silence that the shutters have finished opening in the bedroom. She hears something fall into the large bathtub. Daniel is still coming after her. Elin kicks off her shoes and sneaks out the door to the hall, closing it silently behind her.

She thinks perhaps she could follow Daniel and get in the bedroom through the broken door and try to open the window.

She takes a few steps and then changes her mind and runs down the hall.

"Elin!" Daniel calls behind her.

The door to the large guest room is locked. She turns the key, but the lock sticks. She looks back and sees Daniel striding down the hall. She pulls at the door handle but it won't budge. A shadow crosses the door and she leaps to the side.

The ax misses her head. The blade clangs into the concrete wall behind her and changes direction so fast that Daniel loses his grip on it. The ax slams to the floor.

168

The lock clicks and Elin shoves the door open with her shoulder. She stumbles into the room. Daniel is right behind her and tries to grab her. She whirls around and stabs him with the letter opener. It goes into his chest, but not very far. He catches her hair and pulls her to the side and then pushes her onto the floor. She tumbles into the TV stand and a lamp crashes to the floor.

Daniel pushes his glasses up his nose and walks back to where the ax has fallen. Elin crawls beneath the large bed.

Elin is hoping that Vicky is all right. She's beginning to hope she'll have enough time until the police arrive.

She can see Daniel's feet and lower legs. She wriggles to the center under the bed and curls up. She can hear him walk around the bed and then crawl on top of it. The slats beneath the mattress creak. Elin doesn't move.

He reaches in and grabs her foot. She screams, but now he's on his knees next to the bed and hauling her out. She tries to grab a slat to hold on to, but she can't. He's holding her foot with one hand and raising the ax with the other. She kicks him in the face as hard as she can with her free foot. He loses his grip on her ankle and his glasses fall off. He tips over backward and hits the bookshelf. He holds his hand over one eye and stares at her with the other.

She gets to her feet and rushes toward the door. From the corner of her eye, she can see him pick up his glasses. She runs past Jack's bedroom and into the kitchen. Daniel's footsteps are behind her.

All kinds of thoughts are scrambled in her mind. The police should be here at any moment. Joona said they were on the way.

Elin grabs a frying pan as she darts through the kitchen. She runs across the living room and opens the door to the garage. She throws the frying pan down the stairs to the basement and hears it clang as she rushes up the stairs to the upper floors.

Daniel has reached the basement stairs, but he hasn't been fooled. He's heard her running up the stairs. She's almost out of ideas. She races past the floor where Vicky is hiding and then deliberately slows down to lure Daniel toward her and away from the girl. She's now in the big open room on the top floor. It is almost completely dark.

Elin knows she must hold on until the police arrive. She has to keep Daniel following her and ignoring Vicky's room.

She hears his footsteps on the stairs and knows that he is coming after her.

She runs to the tile stove in the corner and grabs the poker from the rack of implements, then crosses to the middle of the room and smashes the ceiling lamp with one blow. The large dish of frosted glass crashes to the floor and slivers fly everywhere. Then the room is silent.

There is only the sound of heavy steps on the stairs.

Elin hides in the darkness next to a bookcase beside the door.

Daniel is panting when he reaches the top. He's not in a hurry. He knows there's only one staircase down from the top floor of the house.

Elin tries to stifle the sound of her breathing.

Daniel stands in the doorway holding the ax. He stares into the room and then hits the light switch.

There's a click, but nothing happens. The room stays dark.

169

Elin hides in the darkness with a poker in both hands. She is shaking with the adrenaline coursing through her, but she feels remarkably strong.

Daniel slowly steps into the room. Elin can't see him, but she hears the glass crackling beneath his shoes.

Then there's a loud buzz and the metal shutters start to open. Light begins to seep into the room. Daniel is standing right inside the doorway and he is waiting until he can see where Elin is. Bit by bit, light pours into the room.

There is nowhere to hide.

He spots her. He stares at her and she backs away, aiming the poker at him.

Daniel has the ax in his right hand. He glances at it and then approaches her.

She hits at him, but misses. He moves away. She's panting from the strain as she aims at him again. Her foot burns. She's stepped on a shard of glass. She keeps staring at Daniel.

The ax sways in his hand.

She hits, he dodges the blow.

His eyes are boring into hers.

He slashes the ax down with all his strength. But he hasn't aimed it at her. Instead, the blade hits the poker. The clang of metal against metal. The poker is knocked out of her hand and thuds to the floor.

She can't defend herself. She just keeps stepping backward. She realizes with a kind of astonishment that things aren't going well for her. Fear floods her body but clears her mind. She feels uninvolved, as if she's merely observing what is happening.

Daniel keeps approaching.

She looks him in the eyes and he looks back. He seems calm, as if none of this has touched his emotions.

Finally she has her back to the large window. Behind her, it is three and a half stories to a stone patio.

Her feet are bleeding and red footprints mark her path over the blond wood floor.

She can't do anything more. She thinks that she should try to negotiate, promise him anything, just get him to talk.

Daniel is breathing heavily and watches her for a while. Then he swiftly crosses the last few feet while lifting the ax. He strikes as hard as he can. Instinctively, Elin jerks her head to the side. The ax smashes into the window. She feels the thick glass vibrate behind her back and crack. Daniel lifts the ax again but before he can land a blow, Elin leans back. She's throwing all her weight at the broken window and she can feel it give way. Her stomach churns. Then she's falling through the air with glass showering down all around her. Elin Frank closes her eyes and does not feel the ground when she hits it.

Daniel steadies himself on the windowsill and looks down. Splinters of glass are still falling from the window as Elin lies on her back down below, a steady stream of blood flowing from her head onto the stones of the patio.

Daniel begins to breathe more calmly. His shirt is stuck to his back from sweat.

He has a spectacular view from this uppermost window. He can see Tyskhuvud close-by but Åreskutan is lost in the clouds. On the road from Åre, the bright blue lights of emergency vehicles are heading this way. The road to Tegefors, however, is completely empty.

170

Joona had put the puzzle together the moment Flora said her brother's name. Daniel Grim was the boy who had been adopted by the Rånne couple in Delsbo. He was the same Daniel whom Flora saw kill a little girl at Delsbo Church thirty-five years ago.

Now Joona understood why Elisabet had wounds on the backs of her hands, not her palms. She hadn't been trying to defend herself, she'd been holding them over her face. Daniel wasn't leaving any witnesses. No one could see what he had done.

Once he'd phoned Elin and warned her of the danger she was in, Joona radioed the national communications center asking them to send a helicopter, an ambulance, and police cars to Elin's house near Duved. He was told that the helicopters were already in use in Kiruna, so it would take at least half an hour for the police to get to the house by road.

Joona couldn't get there himself—it was more than 150 kilometers from Delsbo to Duved.

He was starting the car engine when Carlos Eliasson called, wanting to know why Joona thought Daniel Grim was the murderer.

"Thirty-five years ago he killed another girl in the same way as the girl at Birgittagården," Joona said as he started driving down the gravel road.

"Anja showed me the photo from the accident at Delsbo Church." Carlos sighed.

"It wasn't an accident," Joona said.

"What makes you believe they are connected?"

"Both victims had their hands over their faces when they were killed," Joona said.

"I know Miranda did, but this victim is lying on a sheet and her hands are at her sides."

"The body was moved before the police arrived," Joona said.

"How do you know?"

"I just do."

"Is this your usual stubbornness or did that psychic woman tell you about it?"

"She is an eyewitness to the Delsbo murder."

"That's well past the statute of limitations," Carlos said with a slight laugh, and then he continued in a more serious tone. "We have a prosecutor who is leading the investigation for the case against Vicky Bennet. You are still under internal investigation."

Now Joona is turning east onto Highway 84 toward Sundsvall. He contacts the Västernorrland police and requests a patrol car and a technician to Daniel Grim's home. Over the radio, he can hear the Jämtland police estimate the time of arrival at ten minutes.

171

The first patrol car stops right outside Elin Frank's house on the side of Tegefjäll. One of the police officers runs over to the Jeep and turns off the engine. The other one pulls out his gun on his way to the front door. A second patrol car is turning into the driveway, followed by an ambulance. The light from a second ambulance behind it is flashing on the gravel road.

There is no noise coming from the house. The windows are shuttered.

Everything is frighteningly quiet.

Now both officers from the first patrol car are entering the house with their guns drawn. A third officer stays in place, while a fourth starts to walk around the house. He walks up a wide white concrete staircase.

The house appears abandoned. It is as dark as a locked treasure chest.

The fourth police officer walks onto the terrace and past a cluster of outdoor furniture. He sees blood, glass splinters, and two human beings.

He stops.

A girl with a pale face and dry, cracked lips looks up at him. Through her messy hair, her eyes look almost black. She's on her knees beside a woman who appears lifeless. A pool of blood has surrounded them both. The girl is holding the woman's hand in hers. She's moving her mouth, but the police officer can't hear what she's saying until he comes closer.

"She's still warm," Vicky is whispering. "She's still warm."

The officer lowers his weapon and picks up his radio to call the paramedics.

Vicky can't stop weeping. She keeps a tight hold on Elin's hand.

The paramedics roll two stretchers to the wounded people. They determine immediately that the woman is still alive. She has a skull fracture and possible damage to her spine. They secure her breathing, then brace her head and neck and lift her onto a backboard before lifting it carefully onto the stretcher. The girl does not once let go of the woman's hand.

The girl is also seriously wounded. She's bleeding from kneeling on the glass. Her neck is swollen and badly bruised, and her neck vertebrae might be injured. She refuses to lie down on a stretcher. She won't leave the woman's side.

The paramedics are in a hurry now, so they don't argue with the girl. They let her sit beside Elin Frank and hold her hand while they drive to Östersund, where they'll both be examined. An ambulance helicopter can take Elin on to Karolinska Hospital in Stockholm.

172

Joona is bumping over rusty train tracks when the coordinator for the operation at Duved answers the phone. His voice is jumpy and he's speaking to Joona at the same time that someone else in the operation bus is talking.

"Things are a bit jumbled right now—but we're on the scene," he says, coughing.

"I have to know if—"

"Damn it, no! Before Trångsviken and Strömsund!" the coordinator shouts.

"Are they alive?" Joona asks.

"Sorry, I'm trying to get some roadblocks set up."

"I'll wait," Joona says. He starts to pass a long-haul truck.

He hears the coordinator put down the phone and talk to the operational leader, confirming the positions of the roadblocks and telling Alarm Communication Central to use patrol cars to block the roads.

"I'm back," he says, when he picks up his phone again.

"Are they alive?" Joona asks again.

"The girl is fine. She's not in danger. The woman is in critical condition. They're going to do emergency surgery in Östersund and then fly her by helicopter to Karolinska in Stockholm."

"What about Daniel Grim?"

"There were no other people in the house. We're putting up the roadblocks right now. Still, if he knows the side roads . . . We don't have the resources to cover everything."

"What about helicopters?"

"We're talking to a hunt club in Kiruna to see if we can borrow theirs, but it will take some time," the coordinator answers in a voice harsh from strain.

Joona is now on the outskirts of Sundsvall. He can't imagine what Elin has been through, but she obviously was able to reach the house in time to save the girl.

Elin is seriously injured, but Vicky is still alive.

Daniel Grim might get caught in one of the roadblocks, especially if he doesn't think that the police are after him. If he gets through the roadblocks, the earliest he can reach his house is in two hours. The police will have to set a trap for him.

We have to finish the technical search for evidence before he gets there, Joona thinks.

He stops on Bruksgatan behind a patrol car. The front door to Daniel Grim's house is wide open and two uniformed officers are waiting for him in the hall.

"The house is empty," one of them says. "Nothing unusual."

"Is the technician on the way?"

"He'll be here in ten minutes."

"Let me look around," Joona says.

Joona walks through the house without knowing what he's looking for. He opens closets, pulls open drawers, looks inside a wine cellar, goes to the kitchen, looks through the cupboards, the refrigerator, the freezer. He runs up to the second floor and pulls off the tiger-striped bed covering, turns over the mattress, opens the closet, throws Elisabet's clothes to the side and knocks on the wall. He kicks away old shoes and pulls out a box of Christmas decorations. Then he goes into the bathroom and looks in the medicine cabinet. Shaving cream, medicine bottles, makeup. Then he runs down to the basement and looks over the tools hanging on the wall. He tries the door to the furnace room, looks under the lawn mower, and lifts the lid to the floor drain. He looks behind bags of potting soil.

Joona closes his eyes and thinks. First, the trapdoor in the ceiling, which leads to the attic. That was in the bedroom. Second, the locked door to the furnace room. Finally, the wine cellar. He thinks that it should be much larger considering where it is.

He opens the door to the wine cellar again. It's situated beneath the stairway and has a sign on it: ALLWAR OCH SKÄMT.

About a hundred bottles are stacked on their sides in small boxes on a tall wooden shelving unit. The shelving appears to be freestanding, and when he checks he sees that there is at least a twelve-inch gap between the back of the wine storage unit and the wall. He pulls at the shelving, but it doesn't budge. He moves a few bottles from both ends and finds a bolt far down on the left. He carefully lets the unit swing open on its hinge.

The space behind it is empty, except for a shoe box on the floor. A heart has been painted on the lid.

Joona gets out his cell phone to take a picture of the shoe box and then he puts on latex gloves.

173

The first thing Joona sees when he lifts the lid of the shoe box is a photograph of a girl with reddish-blond hair. It's not Miranda. This girl appears to be twelve years old.

She is holding her hands in front of her face.

It seems to be just a game—she's smiling and her glittering eyes show through her spread fingers.

Joona lifts out the photograph and finds a dried rose and another photograph. This one shows a girl curled up on a brown sofa and eating some chips. She's looking at the photographer with curiosity.

Next there's a paper bookmark in the shape of an angel. Joona turns it over and sees someone has written "Linda S" in gold ink.

There's a lock of light brown hair, a hair band with a rosette, and a cheap plastic ring sitting on a pile of photographs held together by a rubber band.

Joona flips through the photographs. None of them is pornographic, but they are all of young girls. They all resemble Miranda in some way, but most of the girls are much younger. In some of the pictures, they're covering their faces with their hands or they have their eyes shut.

There's a very little girl in a pink tutu and pink leg warmers. She's standing with her hands over her face.

Joona turns over the photograph and reads "Dearest Sandy." A mass of hearts has been drawn around the words in red and blue ink.

A girl with short hair is grimacing at the camera. Someone has drawn a heart and written the name "Euterpe" next to her.

At the bottom of the box, there is a polished amethyst, a few dried petals from what looks like a tulip, some old candy, and a piece of paper on which a child has written: Daniel + Emilia.

Joona picks up his cell phone, holds it in his hand for a while, looks at the box of photographs again, and finally calls Anja.

"I don't have anything," Anja tells him. "I don't even know what I'm supposed to be looking for."

"Deaths," Joona says. He's looking at a photograph of a girl with her hands in front of her face.

"Well, sorry, but Daniel Grim has worked at seven different institutions for troubled girls throughout Västernorrland, Gävleborg, and Jämtland. He has no record and he has never been a suspect in any crime. There are no internal investigations against him. There's not even a reprimand."

"I understand," Joona says.

"Are you sure you have the right person? I've been comparing, and during the time he was at each institution, there was a lower than average death rate."

Joona is still looking at the photographs and all the flowers and hearts. It would seem sweet if it had been a young boy who'd hidden the box.

"Anything unusual or unexpected?"

"At least two hundred and fifty girls passed through those institutions while he was working there."

Joona takes a deep breath.

"I have seven first names," he says. "The most unusual name is Euterpe. Was one of the girls Euterpe?"

"Euterpe Papadias," Anja says after searching the database for the name. "She committed suicide while in emergency care in Norrköping. Daniel Grim wasn't at that institution."

"Are you sure?"

"She arrived at Fyrbylund emergency care with a history of bipolar depression, self-injury, and two serious suicide attempts."

"Was she moved there from Birgittagården?" Joona asks.

"Yes, she was moved in June 2009. On July second, that is, two weeks later, she was found in the shower with her wrists slit."

"But Daniel wasn't working there."

"No," Anja replies.

"Were any of the girls named Sandy?"

"Yes, two. One of them is dead. She overdosed on pills at a home in Uppsala."

"I found the name Linda S on a bookmark."

"Linda Svensson. Reported missing seven years ago after she returned to a comprehensive school in Sollcftcå."

"So they all die somewhere else," Joona says.

"Oh my dear Lord."

"Is there a girl named Emilia?"

"Yes, Emilia Larsson left Birgittagården. There's supposed to be a photo of her body in her file. Wait one sec . . . Yes, here it is. Good Lord. Her arms are cut open from the wrist to the elbow. He must have cut them himself and prevented her from calling for help. He probably just watched as she bled to death."

Joona leaves the house and sits in his car, shaken by what Anja has told him. Sorrow for those girls blows through him like an icy wind. He looks through the windshield without seeing the glory of the trees around him and takes a deep breath. The police will hunt down Daniel Grim until he is found. He's sure of that. He starts the car.

As soon as he's on the E4, he calls the coordinator in Duved, who tells him that the operational leader no longer expects that they'll catch Daniel Grim at any of the roadblocks.

Joona can't stop thinking about the shoe box with the photographs of the girls Daniel chose. All the hearts, flowers, and small notes show that his love for them was clearly childish. The whole collection was pink and lighthearted—a candy coating over a vile reality.

The girls had all been locked up in institutions and youth homes. They may even have been tied down or heavily medicated when he forced himself on them.

He was the only person they could talk to. No one else listened to them. No one would miss them. He'd chosen girls who were self-destructive and had a history of suicide attempts. Their relatives may have given up on them long ago. Miranda was an exception. She was killed while still at the home where he was working. Had he killed her because she'd told him she was pregnant?

The box is evidence of the connections between Daniel Grim and all these girls. It's enough for the police to arrest him for a number of murders. They can look into these other deaths and give these girls some justice at last.

174

Torkel Ekholm's late wife's embroidery still adorns the well-worn kitchen tablecloth, but her crocheted curtains have turned yellow with age and Torkel's trousers are worn at the knees.

The old policeman has taken his pills from his dose box and then shuffled to the kitchen bench, using his walker.

On the kitchen table in front of Flora are all the notes concerning the accident, the newspaper clippings, and the tiny death announcement.

The old man has told Flora everything he knows about the lumber baron Rånne and his wife: the family manor house, their forests and fields, their childlessness, and their adoption of Flora and her older brother, Daniel. He's told her about the field foreman's daughter, Ylva, who was found dead beneath the bell tower and how the people of Delsbo kept quiet about it afterward.

"I was so little," Flora says. "I didn't realize they were actual memories. I thought the children were fantasies."

She remembers how she thought she was starting to go crazy after she'd heard about the murders at Birgittagården. She's been thinking about what happened there all the time, especially the girl with her hands over her face. She's dreamed about her and has seen her everywhere.

"You were there," Torkel says.

"I tried to tell people about what Daniel had done, but everyone just got angry with me. When I told him what had happened at the bell tower, my father took me into a big office and told me that all liars will burn up in a lake of fire."

"So I have my witness at last," the old man says quietly.

Flora remembers that as a child she'd been terrified about burning up. Just the thought of her hair and clothes catching fire tormented her. She believed she would turn as black as coal if she ever talked about what Daniel had done.

"What happened to the little girl?" Torkel asks.

"I knew Daniel liked Ylva. He was always holding her hand. He gave her raspberries . . ."

She sees the golden-tinged memories in her mind. They shimmer as if they are about to catch fire.

"We were playing that game where you cover your eyes and the other person does something to you. When Ylva covered her eyes, he kissed her on the mouth. She opened her eyes and laughed and said that he'd just given her a baby. I laughed too, but Daniel . . . he said that we weren't supposed to look. His voice sounded strange. I peeked through my fingers as I always did. Ylva looked happy as she covered her face again. I saw Daniel pick up a rock and hit her and hit her . . ."

Torkel sighs and then lies down on the large kitchen bench.

"I see Daniel sometimes. He often comes back to visit the Rånnes."

The old policeman is soon asleep.

Flora quietly stands up and takes the moose rifle down off the wall. She checks that it's loaded, then leaves Torkel Ekholm's house.

175

Flora is walking up the narrow tree-lined driveway to the Rånnes' manor house. She's carrying the heavy moose rifle in both arms. Blackbirds observe her from their perches in the yellowing trees.

She feels as if Ylva is walking beside her. She is remembering playing here with her and Daniel.

Flora thought it had all been a dream: the fine house they'd come to, her own bedroom with its floral wallpaper. Images she'd buried and forgotten keep swelling up from the depths of her memory.

The old cobbled courtyard hasn't changed a bit. A few shiny cars are standing at the entrance to the garage. She walks up the wide, shallow steps to the house, opens the door, and goes inside. She remembers this hall, with its dark paneling and huge oil paintings.

She feels odd being inside a familiar place while carrying a loaded weapon.

Massive chandeliers light her way as she walks silently across dark Persian rugs.

She hears voices coming from the dining room, but no one has seen her yet.

She walks through the four salons one by one until she can see into the dining room. There are fresh-cut flowers in the vases standing in the window niches. Her former family is seated at the table, eating and conversing. None of them is looking in her direction.

She shifts the moose rifle so that it is resting in the crook of her arm, holds it under the barrel, and puts her finger on the trigger.

She sees a movement from the corner of her eye and whirls around with her weapon raised. It's just her own reflection in a mirror that goes from floor to ceiling. She's aiming at herself. Her face is gray and her expression wild.

Still aiming the moose rifle, she walks into the dining room.

The table is decorated with tokens of the harvest: small sheaves of wheat, bunches of grapes, and clusters of plums and apples.

Flora remembers it is the day of thanksgiving.

The woman who was once her mother looks thin, fragile. She's eating slowly with trembling hands. A napkin is spread over her lap.

A man is sitting between her parents. He's just a bit older than she is. She does not recognize him, but she knows who he is.

Flora stops and the floor creaks beneath her feet.

Her father sees her first.

When the old man looks at her, he lowers his knife and fork and straightens his back. He says nothing. He just stares at her.

Her mother follows her father's gaze and blinks several times as she sees the middle-aged woman with the rifle.

"Flora?" the old woman says, dropping her knife. "Flora, is that you?"

Flora stands in front of their well-set table. She can't speak. She swallows and gives her mother a quick glance. Then she turns to her father.

"Why are you carrying a gun into this house?" he asks.

"You made me out to be a liar," she says, finding her voice.

Her father smiles shortly, but without joy. The wrinkles on his face show him to be a bitter and lonely man.

He says tiredly, "The liars are cast into the lake of fire."

She nods and has a moment of doubt before she asks her question.

"You knew that Daniel killed Ylva, didn't you?"

Her father dries his mouth on a white linen napkin.

"We had to send you away because of all your terrible lies," he says. "And here you are, coming back and telling those lies again."

"I was not lying."

"You told me you were, Flora. You confessed that you'd made it all up," he says.

"I was just five years old. You were telling me that my hair would catch on fire and that I would burn right up if I didn't say that I was lying. You were yelling at me that my face would melt and my blood would boil. And so I said I'd lied and then you sent me away."

176

Flora peers at her brother, who is sitting in front of the window, his face in shadow. She can't tell if he is looking at her or not.

"Time for you to leave," her father says, and he picks up his knife and fork.

"Not without Daniel," she says. She points at him with the rifle.

"It wasn't his fault," her mother says weakly. "I was the one who—"

"Daniel is a good son," her father interrupts.

"I'm not saying he isn't," her mother says. "But he . . . You don't remember. We were watching television—theater—the night before it happened. We were watching Strindberg's *Miss Julie* and she's pining after the servant so badly, and I said . . . I said it would be better for her—"

"What kind of stupidity is this?"

"I keep thinking about it. Every day," the old woman continues. "It was my fault. I said that it would be better for the girl to die than to be with child."

"Stop this nonsense!"

"And just when I said this, I saw that little Daniel had come up behind me. He was staring at me . . ." She is trying to explain with tears in her eyes. "I was only talking about Strindberg's play."

She brings her napkin up. Her hands are shaking.

"After what happened to Ylva . . . a whole week after the accident. It was evening. I was praying with Daniel when he told me that Ylva was with child. He was just six years old. He didn't understand a thing."

Flora is looking at her brother. He pushes his glasses up his nose and stares at his mother. It is impossible to tell what he is thinking.

"You are coming with me and telling the truth to the police," Flora says to Daniel. She aims right at his chest.

"What would be the good of that?" asks her mother. "It was an accident."

"We were playing," Flora says without looking at her. "But it was not an accident."

"He was just a child!" roars her father.

"Yes, but now he's killed other people. Two people at Birgittagården. One was a girl who was just fourteen and she had her hands over her face just like—"

"Stop your lying!" her father shouts. He hits the table with his fist.

"You are the ones who are lying," Flora whispers.

Daniel gets up. His expression starts to shift. Perhaps it is cruelty, perhaps it is disgust or fear. Flora can't tell. Perhaps his feelings are mixed.

A knife has two sides but only one edge.

His mother is pleading with him and holding on to his arm. He takes her hands and says something Flora can't hear. But it sounds as if he's swearing.

"We're going now," Flora says to Daniel.

Her father and mother stare at her. They have nothing to say.

She leaves the dining room with her brother.

177

Flora keeps the rifle pointed at Daniel's back as they leave the manor house and walk down the wide stone staircase, over the courtyard, and onto the gravel road. They walk past an annex to the manor house and down a slope past some sheds. The weight of the rifle is making her arms ache, but she doesn't notice.

"Keep moving," Flora mutters, when Daniel slows down.

They are walking on the gravel road, heading toward the field.

She is starting to remember even more fragments of her two years on this estate, but also a single vivid memory from before then, of standing at the door to the orphanage with Daniel.

There must have been a time before that when she was with her real mother.

"Are you going to shoot me?" Daniel asks.

"I could," she says. "But I'm taking you to the police."

Sunshine breaks through the heavy rain clouds and blinds her for a moment. She wants to wipe her damp hands, but she doesn't dare risk taking them off the rifle.

They keep walking along the gravel road, which makes a wide semi-circle past the enormous, empty barn. They pass by stinging nettles and milkweed and sacks of LECA balls stacked on pallets beside the wall. A crow caws in the distance.

It is a long way around to reach the field.

The sun is hidden behind the barn until they reach its other side.

"Flora," Daniel mumbles to himself in amazement.

Flora's arms are beginning to shake from the weight of the rifle.

On the other side of the large field is the road to Delsbo. It looks like a pencil streak between the yellow pastures.

Flora pushes Daniel between the shoulder blades with the barrel of the rifle. They walk across the dried mud in front of the barn.

Flora quickly wipes her hand on her pants and returns her finger to the trigger.

Daniel stops and waits to feel the pressure of the gun before he starts moving again. They walk past a concrete foundation with rings of rusted iron. Weeds are growing along its broken edge.

Daniel has started to limp and is walking more slowly.

"Keep going," Flora says.

Daniel lets his hand run along the weeds. A butterfly takes off and glides into the air.

"I think we can stop here," he says, slowing down again. "This is the old slaughtering spot, when we used to have cattle. Do you remember the slaughterhouse and how they killed the animals?"

"I'm going to shoot if you don't get moving," Flora says, adjusting her finger on the trigger.

Daniel catches a marguerite daisy and pulls it from its stalk. He turns as if he wants to give it to Flora.

She steps back and thinks she has to shoot now. She has no time. Daniel has grabbed the barrel and pulled the rifle toward himself.

Flora is so surprised that she can't dodge him. He slams the rifle butt into her chest. She falls on her back. She gasps for breath, coughs, and scrambles back up.

Now they're standing and staring at each other. Daniel is looking at her. His eyes are dreamy.

"You shouldn't have peeked," he says.

She doesn't know what to say to him. She realizes that she might die on this spot.

Daniel raises the rifle and meets her eyes. He places the muzzle directly on her right leg and pulls the trigger.

The bullet goes straight through Flora's muscle. She doesn't feel any pain, just a kind of cramp.

The recoil makes Daniel step back. He watches Flora drop to the ground, her leg no longer holding her weight.

She tries to break her fall, but her hip and chin hit the ground hard. She lies there a moment. She can smell hay and gunpowder. Small insects are crawling over the weeds beside her.

"Time to cover your face," he says as he takes aim.

Flora is lying on her side and blood is bubbling from her leg. She turns her head to look at the barn. Things go black before her eyes for a moment. She wants to throw up. The fields and the red barn are whirling around as if she's riding a carousel.

She's having trouble breathing. She coughs so she can take a deep breath.

Daniel is standing above her, the sun behind him. He pushes her shoulder with the rifle so she rolls onto her back. She's starting to feel pain in her leg and lets out a moan. He is saying something she can't understand.

She tries to lift her head and her gaze slides over the ground, the weeds, and the concrete foundation with its rings of iron.

Daniel aims the rifle at her forehead and then moves the muzzle along her nose to her mouth.

She can feel the warm metal on her lips and chin. She is breathing too quickly. Blood pulses from her leg. She looks up into the sky and then down to the barn. She blinks and tries to make out what she's seeing. A man is running inside the large barn, behind the sparse boards, right through the rays of light.

She wants to call out, but she has no voice.

The rifle's mouth is wandering toward her eye. She shuts it and feels the pressure against her eyeball and does not hear the shot.

178

It has taken Joona forty minutes to drive from Sundsvall to Hudiksvall. Now he has just turned west onto Highway 84 to Delsbo. All this time, he couldn't let go of the thought of the photographs and mementos in Daniel Grim's shoe box, so completely innocent at first glance. Perhaps the initial phase was always the same for him. A crush, with kisses, gazing, and words filled with longing.

Once the girls moved on, Daniel showed his twisted mind. He went to visit them in secret and then he killed them to ensure their silence. Their deaths surprised no one. Those who took pills were killed with overdoses; those who cut themselves had their wrists slashed.

The owners of the youth homes are profit-driven and probably didn't want the deaths made public. They certainly wouldn't have wanted the Ministry of Health to start any kind of investigation.

No one has ever connected those deaths to Daniel Grim.

But something went wrong with Miranda. It didn't fit his pattern. Perhaps he panicked when Miranda told him she was pregnant. Perhaps she threatened to reveal his secret.

She shouldn't have done that, because Daniel doesn't like witnesses.

Joona is still feeling deeply troubled when he calls Torkel Ekholm to tell him that he'll be there in ten minutes. He wonders if Flora is ready to go home.

"Oh my, I fell asleep," the old policeman says. "Give me a moment."

Joona hears Torkel put the phone down and shuffle across the floor. He's already over the bridge at Badhusholmen when the old man picks the phone back up.

"Flora's gone," he says. "She's taken my rifle."

"Do you know where she might have gone?"

There's a moment of silence on the other end. Joona pictures the little house, its kitchen table and embroideries.

"I think she went to the Rånnes' manor house," Torkel says.

Joona takes a sharp right onto Highway 743 instead of continuing to Torkel's house. He hits the gas pedal. He radios the national communications center and requests backup and an ambulance to the Rånnes' manor house. He's reaching 110 kilometers an hour when he has to brake to swing between the gates and onto the lane leading to the manor house.

From a distance, the house looks like a great white ice sculpture. It seems darker the closer he gets. Joona stops in front and leaps from the car. He's headed up the steps into the house when he catches sight of two figures walking around a wall and disappearing behind a huge red barn.

Joona understands what he's glimpsed: Flora holding a rifle to Daniel's back. Joona starts to run along the gravel road past the annex and down the slope on the western side of the shed. Flora is walking too close to Daniel, he thinks. Her brother could take the rifle away from her with no trouble at all. He knows she's not ready to shoot him, that she doesn't want to shoot him. She just wants the truth to come out.

Joona leaps over the remains of an old fence and slides down the slope. His hand rips through the weeds, but he keeps his balance.

He thinks they are somewhere behind the barn. Its black doors are wide open and shafts of sunlight are falling between its wide boards.

He runs past a rusty gasoline tank and is right at the huge barn when he hears the shot. The sound resonates among the buildings then dies away over the fields.

It's too far to get around the barn and the wall. There's not enough time. Perhaps it's already too late.

179

Joona pulls out his pistol as he runs into the empty barn. Sunbeams thrust in all directions through the gaps between the boards, making a cage of light. Joona races over the dry gravel floor of the barn. He stops when he catches sight of both figures on the other side.

Flora is lying on the ground and Daniel is standing over her with a rifle aimed point-blank at her face.

Joona stands and aims with his arm straight out. The distance is much too far. Through a gap, Joona watches Daniel put his head to the side and press the rifle against Flora's eye.

It all happens fast.

The pistol's front sight shakes before Joona's gaze. He aims at Daniel's stomach, follows Daniel's movements, and pulls the trigger. There's a loud crack and the recoil runs up Joona's arm. The flash burns over his hand.

The bullet goes straight between the gap in the boards. Dust motes whirl in the light.

Joona doesn't stop to see if he's hit his mark. He keeps running through the barn. The sunbeams flash over him. He kicks open a narrow back door and runs out into the waist-high weeds. Daniel has dropped the rifle into the grass. Joona hopes he did not have time to pull the trigger again.

Daniel is walking out into the field, clutching his stomach, blood running between his fingers. He can hear Joona behind him and he turns, swaying, and gestures to Flora, who is lying on her back in the grass and breathing hard.

Joona keeps heading for Daniel with his pistol aimed at his chest.

Daniel sinks to the ground and groans as he looks up. Sunlight reflects from his glasses.

Without saying a word, Joona kicks the rifle away from him. He grabs one of his arms, drags him over to one of the iron rings on the concrete foundation, and handcuffs him to it.

Flora has not fainted, but she looks at Joona with a stiff, unnatural gaze. She's bleeding heavily from her leg. Her face is gray and she's breathing fast. So fast that Joona can tell she is about to go into shock.

"Thirsty," she whispers.

One leg of her pants is soaked with blood and new blood keeps bubbling out. There's no time to make a tourniquet. He grabs her leg with both hands and presses his thumb into the wound right against the artery. The flow of warm blood diminishes immediately. He presses even harder as he looks at Flora's face. Her eyes have shut and he can feel her pulse racing.

"The ambulance will be here soon, Flora," he tells her. "It's going to be all right."

Behind his back, Joona hears Daniel try to say something.

He turns toward Daniel and sees an elderly man wearing a black coat over a black suit walking toward Daniel. The man's strict face is colorless and his eyes are sorrowful. He looks over at Joona.

"Let me just embrace my son once more," the old man says. His voice is gruff.

Joona can't let go of Flora's leg. He must not move or Flora might die.

The man walks slowly past him as if in a spell. Joona can smell gasoline.

The old man has soaked his coat in gasoline. He's drenched himself in gasoline and he's holding a matchbox.

"Don't do it!" Joona yells.

Daniel stares at his father and tries to crawl away. He yanks at the handcuff holding him back.

The old man stops and gazes down at Daniel. He says nothing, but his fingers are trembling as he opens the matchbox and pulls out a match. He closes the box and runs the match along the side.

"She's lying! She's lying!" Daniel howls.

There's a puff of air as his father's coat catches on fire. A band of light blue fire embraces him. The heat reaches Joona's face.

The burning old man sways, then he kneels beside his son and embraces him with fire. The grass around them begins to burn. Daniel fights, but the old man holds on tightly. Daniel stops struggling as the flames burn around them both. It sounds like a flag whipping in the wind as the fire swirls upward. A tower of black smoke rises, and pieces of soot, glowing, rise to heaven.

180

When the fire behind the large barn has been put out, only two black-
ened bodies are left, entwined in a pile of ashes.

The ambulance drives away with Flora.

Just as it is leaving, the old woman walks out. The lady of the
manor stands completely still as if she froze the moment the wall of pain
hit her.

Joona starts to drive back to Stockholm. He is listening to the Radio
Book Club, but he's thinking about the weapons Daniel used at Birgittagården.

The hammer and the rock had confused him.

Now it's clear. Elisabet was not killed because the killer needed her
keys. Daniel had his own key to the isolation room. Elisabet must have
seen him, and he must have known she had. He followed her and killed
her solely because she had witnessed him murder Miranda.

Rain, hard as glass, spatters the windshield. A ray of the setting sun
pierces the clouds and steam rises from the asphalt.

Daniel probably went in to Miranda after he thought Elisabet had
taken her sleeping pills and gone to bed. Miranda did as he asked because she did not have a choice.

She took off her clothes and sat with the blanket around her to keep
her warm.

Something went wrong that night.

Perhaps Miranda told him she was pregnant. Perhaps he found the pregnancy test in her room. Perhaps he felt suffocated. Perhaps he panicked. Joona may never know. But he does know that something made Daniel decide that he had to get rid of a problem, that Miranda was a problem.

Joona can picture him putting on the boots that always stood in the hallway, going outside, and searching the garden for a sharp rock. Then he returns, tells her to shut her eyes and place her hands over her face, and hits her again and again.

She was not supposed to see him. She was supposed to have her hands over her face, just as Ylva had all those years ago.

Nathan Pollock had interpreted the covered face as a sign that the killer wanted to make the girl into an object before he killed her. The reality, Joona thinks, was that Daniel was in love with Miranda and he wanted her to put her hands over her eyes so that she wouldn't be frightened.

He'd had plenty of time to prepare the deaths of the other girls, but not Miranda's. He beat her to death without thinking of what would happen next.

At some point in the middle of this—as he hit her with the rock, lifted her onto the bed, and covered her face again—Elisabet burst in on him. Perhaps the sound of his car woke her.

Perhaps he'd already gotten rid of the rock. Perhaps he'd thrown it far into the forest.

Daniel hunted Elisabet down, grabbing a hammer from somewhere, following her into the brewery, and ordering her to cover her face before he hit her.

When Elisabet was dead, he decided to place the blame on the new girl, Vicky Bennet. He knew that she took strong sleeping pills, which meant she'd slept through the events of that evening.

Daniel had to hurry. Any minute someone could wake up. He took Elisabet's key to the isolation room from her ring of keys, returned to the main building, put the key in the isolation room lock, scooped up Miranda's blood, went to Vicky's room, placed the hammer under her pillow, and smeared the blood on her sleeping body. Then he left the grounds.

He'd probably used garbage bags or some newspapers to protect his car while he drove back to his house. He probably burned them along with his clothes in the cast-iron stove.

Afterward, he had to stay nearby to see if anyone was figuring out what had happened. He played the role of helpful director as well as victim.

Joona is nearing Stockholm. The Radio Book Club is almost over. They'd been discussing *Gösta Berling's Saga* by Selma Lagerlöf.

Joona turns off the radio and puzzles through the rest of the case.

When Vicky was arrested and Daniel heard that Miranda had told her about the face-covering game, he realized he was vulnerable. His secret would be revealed if Vicky had the chance to tell her story to a competent psychologist, and one would have been assigned to her in jail. That's why Daniel did everything he could to make sure that Vicky was released—so he could arrange her suicide.

For most of his career, Daniel had worked with troubled girls who had neither parents who cared nor any sense of security. Whether he was acting on a conscious or unconscious level, he sought out those jobs and kept falling in love with little girls who reminded him of his first crush. Daniel used the girls and once they moved away, he made sure that they would never tell anyone about what he'd done.

Joona slows down for a red light and shudders. He thinks of the hours Daniel spent with these girls as their psychotherapist, twisting their minds; of all the reports he wrote detailing their insecurities, their hatred of themselves. He has met a number of killers in his work as a police officer, but Daniel's careful preparations for these girls' deaths—preparations he started long before he killed them, and probably shortly after he fell for them—makes him almost the worst killer Joona has ever dealt with. Only one other murderer was worse.

181

There is a light fog in the air as Joona parks his car and walks across Karlaplan to Disa's apartment.

"Joona?" Disa says as she opens the door. "I almost thought that you weren't coming. I have the TV on and they're talking about what happened at Delsbo."

Joona nods.

"So, you caught the killer," Disa says with a slight smile.

"Or however you want to put it," Joona says, thinking of the father's fiery embrace.

"What happened to that poor woman who was always calling you? They said she'd been shot."

"Flora Hansen," Joona says.

He bumps his head on the light in the hallway. Light flashes back and forth over the walls. Joona is barely aware of it. He's thinking now about the young girls whose photographs were in Daniel Grim's shoe box.

"You're tired," Disa says, pulling him by the hand.

"Flora was shot in the leg by her brother and . . ."

She doesn't notice that he's stopped in the middle of a sentence. He's tried to clean up at a gas station on the way back, but his clothes are still covered in Flora's blood.

"Go take a bath. I'll pick up some food at the corner shop," Disa says.

"Thanks." Joona smiles.

In the living room, the news is showing a photo of Elin. They stop to look at it. A young journalist is reporting that Elin Frank has undergone an operation during the night and that her doctors are very optimistic. The picture switches to footage of Elin's assistant, Robert Bianchi. He looks exhausted, but he smiles tentatively and tears leak from his eyes as he tells the reporters that Elin is going to live.

"What happened?" Disa asks.

"She fought this killer all on her own. She saved the girl's life, the one—"

"My God," Disa whispers.

"Yes, well, Elin Frank, she's . . . she's actually quite exceptional," Joona says as he rubs Disa's narrow shoulders.

182

Joona is sitting at Disa's kitchen table wrapped in a bathrobe. They're eating chicken vindaloo and lamb tikka masala.

"Good . . ."

"Mamma's Homemade Finnish recipes, and I won't reveal what they are!" Disa is laughing.

She tears a naan in half and hands one piece to Joona. He's looking at her with smiling eyes. He drains his wineglass, and then picks up his story about the case.

He's started at the beginning and told Disa about Flora and Daniel, the siblings who were placed in an orphanage at a young age.

"Were they really siblings?" she asks as she refills their wineglasses.

"Yes, and it was a big deal when the rich couple, the Rånnes, adopted them."

"I can see that."

They were small children who played with the foreman's daughter on the grounds of the estate, in the fields, and around the churchyard and its bell tower. Daniel had a crush on Ylva, who was still a little girl herself. Joona tells her what Flora, wide-eyed, had said about Daniel kissing Ylva when they were playing the close-your-eyes game.

"The little girl laughed and said she was now with child," Joona says. "Daniel was six years old and he panicked for some reason."

"So what did he do?" whispers Disa.

"He ordered both girls to close their eyes and then he picked up a heavy rock and hit Ylva so hard in the head that she died."

Disa stops eating and listens intently as Joona describes how Flora fled and told her father what happened.

"But her father loved Daniel and defended him," Joona says. "He demanded that Flora take back her accusation. He threatened her by telling her that all liars end up in a lake of fire."

"So she took it all back?"

"She said she lied, and because she'd lied so terribly, they banished her from their home forever."

"So Flora took back what she'd said. She lied about lying," Disa says thoughtfully.

"Yes," Joona says, and he reaches across the table for her hand.

He is thinking about Flora and how, even as a little girl, she managed to bury her memories of what happened at Delsbo so deeply she also soon forgot all about her earlier life, her adoptive parents, her own brother.

He realizes Flora had little choice but to create a whole life based on lies. She lied for others to make them happy. Her memories began to return only after she heard about the girl with her hands over her face who'd been murdered at Birgittagården. It cracked open the vault of her memories, and the past started to catch up to her.

"How could she forget such things?" Disa asks, gesturing to Joona to help himself to more.

"I called Britt-Marie on the way here," Joona says.

"The Needle's wife?"

"Exactly. She told me how they have a number of theories concerning repressed memories after traumatic events. It's a form of PTSD. Apparently the huge amounts of adrenaline and stress hormones released at the time of the trauma affect long-term memory. Seriously traumatic events are stored deep within the brain and are hidden. They are not dealt with on an emotional level. However, the right stimulus can trigger the memory to surface in physical responses and pictures. Flora was first just shaken up by what she'd heard on the radio and didn't know why. She thought she might earn some money by leaving a tip with the police. But when the real memories began to appear, she thought they were ghosts."

"Perhaps they were ghosts," Disa says.

"Well, perhaps. In any case, she started to tell the truth and she became the witness who solved the case."

Joona stands up and blows out the candles on the table. Disa joins him and snuggles beneath his robe. They stand holding each other for a long time. He breathes in her scent and feels the pulse of her heart.

"I'm so afraid something could happen to you. This is why our relationship has been so rocky. I get afraid and I withdraw," he says.

"What could ever happen to me?" she asks, smiling.

"You can disappear off the face of the earth."

"Joona, I'm not going to disappear."

"I once had a friend named Samuel Mendel," he says, and then he falls silent.

183

Joona leaves the police station and as he's done many times before walks up the steep path and over to the ancient Jewish burial ground. With practiced hands, he loosens the bar inside the gate, opens it, and walks inside.

There's a relatively new family grave among the older stones: Samuel Mendel; his wife, Rebecka; and sons, Joshua and Reuben.

Joona places a small pebble on the top of the gravestone and stands there with his eyes closed for a moment. He inhales the smell of damp earth and listens to the breeze soughing in the treetops.

Samuel Mendel was a direct descendant of Koppel Mendel, who opposed Aaron Isaac, the founder of Sweden's Jewish community, and bought this land for use as a cemetery in 1787. Although the cemetery has not been actively used since 1857, the descendants of Koppel Mendel are still buried there.

Detective Inspector Samuel Mendel and Joona were partners at the National Police, and they became very good friends.

Samuel Mendel was forty-six years old when he died. Joona knows that he is alone in his grave, although the gravestone says something else.

Joona and Samuel's first case together was also their last.

One hour later, Joona is back in the appeals office of the Public Prosecutor for Police Cases. Mikael Båge, the head of the internal investigation, is there, along with Helene Fiorine, the department secretary, and the prosecutor, Sven Wiklund.

"I will now be deciding whether to start prosecuting your case," Wiklund says. He runs his hands over a pile of paperwork and adds, "In these documents, there is nothing favorable."

His chair creaks as he leans back and meets Joona's eyes. The only sound in the room is the scratch of Helene Fiorine's pen and her shallow breathing. The yellow light from outside plays over the polished furniture and the glass doors protecting the many leather-bound volumes of law, police regulations, and the writings and binding judgments of the Swedish Supreme Court.

"As I see this," Wiklund continues drily, "the only way you can avoid prosecution is by giving me a really good explanation."

"I bet Joona has an ace up his sleeve," whispers Mikael Båge.

The contrail of an airplane dissipates in the light sky. The chairs creak. Helene Fiorine swallows and puts down her pen.

"Just tell us what happened," she says. "Perhaps you had a very good reason for warning them of Säpo's intended action."

"Yes, I did," Joona says.

"We know that you're a good police officer." Mikael Båge smiles, embarrassed.

"I, on the other hand, must go by the letter of the law," Wiklund says. "My job is to break people to pieces when they break the rules. Don't make me break you here and now."

It's as close to a plea as Helene Fiorine has ever heard her boss make.

"Your entire future is up in the air, Joona," Mikael whispers.

"You understand that the decision was entirely my own," Joona says. "I do have an answer for you, which perhaps . . ."

Joona's cell phone rings. He gives it an automatic glance, and his eyes darken.

"Please excuse me," he says. "I must take this call."

The three others look at him as Joona listens to the voice on the other end.

"Yes . . . yes, I know," he says. "I'll get there as soon as I can."

Joona ends the call and looks at Wiklund as if he's forgotten why he's here.

"I have to go," he says, and leaves the room without saying another word.

184

One hour and twenty minutes later, the scheduled flight from Stockholm lands at Sveg Airport in Härjedalen. Joona takes a taxi to Blåvingen, the assisted-living home where Maja Stefansson lives. He's been here before, when he traced Rosa Bergman, the woman who had followed him from Adolf Fredrik Church and asked him why he was pretending his daughter was dead.

Rosa Bergman had changed her name to Maja Stefansson. She'd used her middle name and her maiden name instead of the name she'd had most of her adult life.

Joona gets out of the taxi and heads straight to Maja's ward. The nurse he'd met the last time he was here waves from behind the reception desk. The light from the window makes her hair shine like copper.

"That was fast," she says cheerfully. "I was thinking of you and we have your card here behind the desk so I called—"

"Can I speak with her?" Joona says.

The woman is surprised by his serious tone. She runs her hands over her light blue skirt.

"We have a new doctor. She's young. I think she comes from Algeria. Anyway, she changed Maja's medicine and, well, I've heard people tell me about cases like this, but I haven't seen it before . . . Maja woke up this morning and told us quite clearly that she needed to talk to you."

"Where is she?"

The nurse leads Joona to a narrow room with closed curtains, and then she leaves him alone with the elderly woman. Over a tiny desk, there's a photograph of a young woman sitting next to her son. The mother is holding the boy's shoulders protectively.

A few pieces of her furniture have been moved here. A dark desk, a vanity, and two golden pedestals. Rosa Bergman is sitting on a daybed, dressed neatly in a blouse and skirt, with a knitted afghan around her shoulders. Her face is swollen and covered in wrinkles, but Joona can see that she's fully aware and calm.

"My name is Joona Linna," he says. "You have something to tell me."

The woman nods and gets up with difficulty. She opens a drawer in her nightstand and takes out a Gideon Bible. She holds the book by its covers over the bed. A small piece of folded paper falls out.

"Joona Linna," she says as she picks up the piece of paper. "So you are Joona Linna."

He says nothing, but feels the burning intensity of a migraine coming on. It's like a glowing needle pressed through his temples.

"How can you pretend your daughter is dead?" Rosa Bergman says. She glances at the photograph on the wall. "If my boy was still alive . . . If you knew what it was like to see your child die . . . Nothing would ever make me abandon him."

"I did not abandon my family," Joona says. "I saved their lives."

"When Summa came to me, she said nothing about you, but she was broken," Rosa continues. "Your daughter had it much worse. She stopped talking and didn't start again for two years."

Joona feels a shiver go down his spine.

"How did you contact them?" he asks. "You were not supposed to be in contact with them."

"I could not let them disappear completely," she said. "I felt extremely sorry for them."

Joona knows that Summa would not have mentioned his name unless something had gone terribly wrong. There was not supposed to be a single thread connecting them—not one. That was the only chance they had of surviving.

He has to lean on the desk. He swallows hard and looks at the old woman.

"How are they doing?" he asks.

"It's very serious, Joona Linna," Rosa says. "I used to go see Lumi once a year. But these days . . . somehow I've gotten very forgetful and confused."

"What's happened?"

"Your wife has cancer," Rosa says. "She was going to have surgery, but might not survive. She wanted you to know that Lumi was going to be handed to the authorities if she—"

"When did you hear this?" Joona's jaw is clenched. His lips have turned white. "When did she call you?"

"I'm afraid it might be too late," Rosa whispers. "I've been so forgetful lately."

She hands him the wrinkled sheet of paper. It has an address on it. She lowers her head and stares at her arthritic hands.

185

There are only two destinations from Sveg Airport. Joona chooses to fly back to Arlanda Airport and then change planes to Helsinki. He feels as if he's in the middle of a dream. He's looking out the window at the veils of clouds over the Baltic Sea. A flight attendant offers to serve him something, but he can't make himself answer.

His memories are drowning him in their deep ocean.

Twelve years ago, Joona cut off the finger of the Devil himself.

Nineteen different people had disappeared—from their cars, their bicycles, their mopeds. At first it seemed like a coincidence. When none of the disappeared showed up anywhere, the case was given highest priority.

Joona was the one who insisted that they had a serial killer on their hands.

Working with Samuel Mendel, Joona was able to trace the whereabouts of their prime suspect, a man named Jurek Walter, and catch him in the middle of committing a crime. They found him in Lill-Jans Forest, forcing a fifty-year-old woman into a coffin. The coffin was a few feet underground, and he'd been keeping her there for two years. They were able to rescue her.

When the woman was examined at the hospital, the enormity of what she'd undergone was revealed. Her muscles had atrophied and bedsores had deformed her. Her hands and feet were frostbitten. She was not only psychologically traumatized but had also suffered brain damage.

The way Joona sees it, the Devil resides in the worst cruelty of humankind. It is impossible to kill the Devil, but twelve years ago, he and Samuel Mendel cut off one of his fingers when they caught the serial killer Jurek Walter.

Later, Joona was at the Swedish Supreme Court in Wrangelska Palace on the island of Riddarholm in Stockholm. The case had gone through the system. Now Jurek Walter was being sentenced to a life in a closed insane asylum with special requirements for parole. He was moved to a high security institution twenty-one kilometers north of Stockholm.

Joona will never forget Jurek Walter's wrinkled face as he turned to face Joona.

"Both of Samuel Mendel's sons are going to disappear," Jurek said in a tired voice as his defense lawyer collected his paperwork. "Samuel's wife, Rebecka, will also disappear, but . . . No, listen to me, Joona Linna. The police will never find them, and once they call off the search, Samuel will keep looking. When he realizes that they will never be found and he will never see them again, he will kill himself."

Joona got up to leave.

"And as for your little daughter—" Jurek Walter continued.

"Watch out," Joona said, though there was no rage in his voice.

"Lumi will disappear, then Summa, and when you realize you will never see them again, it will be your turn to commit suicide. You will hang yourself."

One Friday afternoon, a few months later, Samuel's wife drove from their apartment in Liljeholmen to their summer house on Dalarö Island. Their sons, Joshua and Reuben, were with her in the car. When Samuel arrived at their summer house a few hours later, no one was there. The car was found abandoned on a nearby logging road. Samuel never saw his family again.

One chilly morning in the beginning of March, he went down to the beach where his boys used to play. The police had ended the search for them eight months earlier. He'd now given up himself. He took his service pistol from its holster and shot himself in the head.

Joona watches the shadow of the plane move over the waters of the Baltic Sea and thinks back to the day his life shattered. There was no sound in his car. The world seemed to be bathed in an odd light. The sun shone red behind veils of clouds. It had rained and the rays of the setting sun made the puddles shimmer as if they were burning underground.

186

Joona and Summa had planned the road trip together. They took it in stages: first up to Umeå, past Storuman, over the mountains to Mo i Rana in Norway, and then back down the west coast. They were now driving to a hotel in the middle of the Dalälven area and they'd promised Lumi they'd visit a zoo the next day.

Summa changed the channel on the radio to some dreamy piano music. The notes wove in and out like a tapestry. Joona reached back to check that Lumi was fastened properly in her car seat. He wanted to make sure her arms weren't caught at an odd angle.

"Pappa," Lumi said sleepily.

Joona felt her small fingers on his hand. She held on tightly, but released her grip when he pulled his hand back.

They drove past the exit to Älvkarleby.

"Lumi's going to love the zoo," Summa said quietly. "The chimpanzees and the rhinos."

"I already have my own monkey!" exclaimed Lumi.

"What?"

"I'm her monkey," Joona said.

"That suits you."

"Lumi takes good care of me. She's a nice vet."

Summa's sandy brown hair was hanging in her face, partially covering her deep, dark eyes, but Joona could see the dimples appear in her cheeks.

"Why would you need a vet? Is there something wrong with you?"

"I need glasses."

"Is that what she said?" Summa laughed. She was flipping through a magazine and didn't notice that he'd missed the turnoff and was now heading in the wrong direction entirely. They were already north of the Dalälven.

Lumi had fallen asleep with her doll resting against her cheek.

"Are you sure that we don't have to book a table?" Summa asked. "I want to sit outside on the veranda this evening so we have that great view of the river below us."

Joona took the exit toward Mora, and that's when Summa realized that something was wrong.

"Joona, we missed the exit to Älvkarleby, didn't we? Aren't we staying in Älvkarleby? That's what we were planning, weren't we?"

"Yes, that's what we planned."

"What are you doing?"

He didn't reply, but kept staring at the road. The afternoon sun made the puddles shimmer. A long-distance truck ahead of them swung into the middle lane without signaling.

"We said that we'd—"

Summa stopped and took a deep breath. Then her voice changed and fear was in it.

"Joona? Have you lied to me? Tell me you didn't lie to me."

"I had to," he whispered.

Summa stared at him. He knew how upset she was. She struggled to keep her voice low so that Lumi would not wake up.

"You can't be serious," she said. "You can't do this. You told me we weren't in danger any longer. You said it was all over and I believed you! I believed you'd changed your mind, I believed that—" Her voice broke and she turned away and looked out the window.

"I lied," Joona confessed.

"You are not supposed to lie to me. You must never lie to me."

"You're right. I'm sorry."

"We can leave the country, the three of us together. It'll all work out. You'll see."

"You have to understand, Summa. You must understand. If I thought it was at all possible . . . if I had any other choice—"

"Stop this nonsense right now," she says. "This threat can't be real. It can't be. You're seeing a connection that doesn't exist. Samuel Mendel and his family have nothing to do with ours. Do you hear me? We're not under any real threat."

"I've tried to tell you how serious this is, but you won't listen."

"I don't want to listen. Why would I want to?"

"Summa, I have to . . . I've arranged everything. There's a woman named Rosa Bergman waiting for you in Malmberget. She'll give you new identity cards. You will be fine."

His hands have started to shake.

"You really are serious," Summa whispers.

"I'm more serious than I've ever been," he says. "We are going to Mora, and you and Lumi will take the train to Gällivare."

He could tell that Summa was working hard to keep her emotions in check.

"If you leave us at the station, you've lost us for good. Do you realize this? There's no way back." She stared at him with defiant and sorrowful eyes.

"Tell Lumi that I had to go work abroad," he continued, keeping his voice low. Summa had started to weep.

"Joona," she said. "No, don't do this."

He kept staring straight ahead. He swallowed hard and kept his eyes on the road.

"And in a few years," he went on, "tell her that I'm dead. You must never ever contact me again. Never try to see me. Do you understand?"

Summa was now crying out loud.

"I don't want to! I don't want to!"

"Neither do I."

"You shouldn't do this to us!"

"Mamma?" Lumi had woken up and sounded frightened. Summa quickly dried the tears from her cheeks.

"Don't worry," Joona says to his daughter. "Mamma is sad because we're not going to the hotel by the river."

"Tell her," Summa said.

"Tell me what?" asked Lumi.

"You and Mamma will be taking the train," Joona said.

"What about you?"

"I have to work," he replies.

"You told me we were going to play monkey and vet."

"He doesn't want to play," Summa said harshly.

They were near the outskirts of Mora. They passed scattered houses and a few industrial buildings. Then they passed shopping malls and car repair shops. The dense forest fell back, and the fences to keep the wild-life off the highway disappeared.

187

Joona slowed down as they drove up to the train station. He parked and opened the trunk and lifted out the huge suitcase on wheels.

"Did you remove your things last night?" Summa asked.

"I did."

"Did you put other stuff inside?"

He nodded and looked away toward the station: four parallel lines of tracks, embankments of rust-colored gravel, weeds, and dark crossties.

"Your daughter needs you in her life."

"I have no choice." He looked inside his car's rear window to where Lumi was pushing her big, soft doll into her backpack.

"You have many choices," Summa continued. "Instead of fighting, you're giving up. You have no idea if this threat is real. I just don't understand all this."

"I can't find Lollo!" Lumi complained.

"The train leaves in twenty minutes," Joona said.

"I don't want to live without you," Summa said, and took his hand. "I want things to go on as they were."

"I know."

"If you do this to us, you will be all alone."

He didn't answer. Lumi climbed out of the car and dropped her backpack on the ground. A red barrette was hanging loosely in her hair.

"Are you ready to live the rest of your life alone?"

"I am," he said.

Joona could not look at her. He gazed across the tracks. Between the trees on the other side of the tracks, the northern bay of Lake Siljan was glittering.

"Say goodbye to Pappa, now," Summa said. She pushed her daughter toward her father.

Lumi stood still and didn't look up.

"Hurry up," Summa says.

Lumi looks up and says, "Bye-bye, Monkey."

"Properly. Say goodbye properly." Summa showed her irritation.

"I don't want to," Lumi said.

She clung to her mother's leg.

"Do it anyway," Summa said.

Joona squatted down before his tiny daughter.

"Can I have a hug?"

She shakes her head.

"Well, here comes the monkey with his long, long arms!" he joked.

Joona lifted her up. He felt her little body resist—she knew something was seriously wrong. She wriggled to get down, but Joona held her close, just for a while, just to inhale the scent of her neck.

"You silly!" she shouted.

"Lumi," Joona whispered against her cheek. "Never forget that I love you more than anything else."

"Time to go," Summa said.

Joona set his daughter down. He wanted to pet her on the cheek but couldn't bring himself to do so. He felt as if he was shattering into pieces. Summa was staring at him in fear. Her neck was stiff. She grabbed Lumi's hand and pulled her away.

They waited for the train in silence. There was nothing more to say.

Downy dandelion seeds blew over the tracks.

There was a burned smell from the brakes as the train rolled away from the platform. He stood and stared at his daughter's pale face through the train window. Her little hand was waving slowly. Summa was a black shadow sitting rigidly next to her. She did not look at him. Before the train reached the bend toward the harbor, Joona turned and walked back to his car.

188

Joona drove the 145 kilometers to Ludvika without thinking. His head was roaring but empty—frighteningly so.

He drove without thinking and finally arrived.

His headlights lit up massive metal structures. He turned into the industrial area and drove down to the empty harbor near the power station. A large gray car was already parked between two huge piles of sawdust. Joona pulled up next to it. He was remarkably calm; so calm that he knew he was in some form of shock.

He got out of his car and looked around. The Needle was waiting for him, standing next to a door. He was wearing white overalls and his face looked worn and serious.

"So? They've left?" he asked in the sharp tone he used whenever something bothered him.

"They're gone," Joona said.

The Needle nodded a few times. The white frames of his glasses shone coldly in the weak light.

"You didn't give me a choice in this matter," The Needle said glumly.

"True enough," Joona said. "You had no choice."

"We're both going to get fired if this comes out."

"Then we'll be fired."

"Two at the same time. I moved as fast as I could when they arrived."

"Good."

"Two of them," The Needle repeated, almost to himself.

Joona thought back to just a few days ago, when he woke up next to his wife and daughter. His cell phone was ringing in his jacket in the hall.

Someone had sent a text message. The minute he saw it was from The Needle, he knew what it was about.

They had agreed. Once The Needle found two bodies that were approximately right, Joona would leave town with Summa and Lumi on the pretext of going on the vacation they'd been talking about for such a long time.

Joona had waited to hear from The Needle for more than three weeks. Time was running out. He was keeping watch over his family as best he could, but he recognized that this was not going to work in the long run. Jurek Walter was a man who could wait.

Joona knew right away that The Needle's message meant he was about to lose his family. He could ensure that Summa and Lumi would be protected, but only if he never saw them again.

The Needle opened the hatchback of his gray car.

On two stretchers, covered in a cloth, were two body bags, one large and one small.

"A woman and a girl. They died in a car crash three days ago," The Needle explained. He began to pull out the larger body.

"I've worked on them a little. There's not a trace left that could identify them. Not a single identifying mark."

He groaned as he removed the body from his car. The undercarriage of the stretcher fell into place. The small wheels clattered as they hit the gravel.

Without saying a word, The Needle zipped open the body bag.

Joona clenched his jaw and forced himself to look.

A young woman lay there. Her eyes were closed and her face was calm. Her chest was crushed. Her arms appeared to have been broken in many places and her pelvis had been wrenched awry.

"The car drove off a bridge," The Needle said. "The reason she has so many injuries is that she'd unbuckled herself. Perhaps she was picking up the pacifier for the little one. I've seen it before."

He reached for the second stretcher and pulled it out of the car.

Joona contemplated the woman. He could see no fear or pain in her face. Nothing in her expression revealed the injuries done to her body.

The Needle unzipped the small bag. When Joona saw the little girl inside, tears filled his eyes.

The Needle mumbled something to himself and then zipped the body bags up again.

"Well, then," he said. "No one will ever find Catharina and Mimmi. No one will ever identify their bodies."

His emotions overwhelmed him for a moment, and then he continued, almost angry.

"The little girl's father has been going from hospital to hospital looking for them. He's even called my department. I had to talk to him."

The Needle's mouth twisted.

"They're going to be buried as Summa and Lumi. I've already arranged false dental records for them."

He gave Joona one last questioning look.

Joona said nothing.

Then they put the bodies in Joona's car.

189

It felt strange to be driving with a dead woman and child as passengers. The roads were dark. Roadkill hedgehogs were lying beside ditches. A badger stood on the narrow shoulder, hypnotized by Joona's headlights.

When he arrived at the hill he'd chosen weeks earlier, he dislodged the airbag fuse. Then he placed the woman in the driver's seat and loosely strapped the little girl into Lumi's child seat. The only sounds were his breathing, the rustle of cloth against cloth, and the thud of lifeless arms and legs.

He leaned into the car and released the emergency brake. He gave the car a shove from behind and it started to roll down the hill. He walked beside it and reached in to give the wheel a tug in the right direction. The car picked up speed and he ran to keep up. The car hurtled away from him, then it left the road and crashed into a massive Scotch pine. The woman's body smashed into the steering wheel. The little girl's body jerked violently in the car seat.

Joona took a gasoline can out of the trunk and began to splash it inside the car. He poured gasoline over the little girl's legs and the woman's heavily damaged body.

It was getting hard for him to breathe. He had to stop.

He leaned over, holding his knees, and tried to calm himself down. His heart was breaking.

Joona couldn't bear it. He pulled the little girl's body from the car and walked with it back and forth, cradling it and singing lullabies and whispering in her ear and crying. Then he placed her on her mother's lap in the front seat.

He closed the car door in silence. He poured the rest of the gasoline over the car. Then he threw a lit match through the open window into the backseat. Flames leaped up and raced through the car.

He stared at the woman's unnaturally calm face while her hair caught fire.

The fire was voracious. To Joona it looked as if a blue-tinged angel of death was claiming its own. The flames began to roar and they seemed to contain the sound of weeping.

Joona suddenly snapped awake. He wanted to get the bodies out. He burned his hands on the car door, but he was able to get it open. The fire in the car burned higher once the door let in more oxygen. He tried to grab the woman's jacket, which was already on fire. Her slim legs were already smoking and licked by flames.

Pappa, Pappa, help me, Pappa!

Joona knew that it couldn't be real. He knew they were already dead. He still couldn't bear it. He reached into the fire again and grabbed the girl's hand.

Then the gas tank exploded. Joona heard the bang just as his eardrums burst. He fell backward and felt the blow as his head hit the ground. His hands were empty. Blood trickled from his ears.

His heart was screaming and burning.

Before he lost consciousness, he watched the blazing pine needles come swirling down.

190

Joona is staring out the window and doesn't hear the announcement that the plane has started its descent into Helsinki International Airport.

Twelve years ago, he'd cut off the finger of the Devil himself, and his punishment had been loneliness. It was a high price, yet he felt that it was still too mild. The Devil was waiting to take more from him. The Devil was waiting for him to imagine that everything was forgotten or forgiven.

Joona bends over in his seat and waits, trying to slow his breathing. The man sitting next to him looks at him nervously.

It's not the migraine, it's that other thing, the immense darkness behind everything.

He had stopped the serial killer Jurek Walter. That can't be written off or forgotten.

He had no choice, but the price was too high, much too high. It hadn't been worth it.

His skin is covered with goose bumps. He pulls at his hair with one hand. He presses his feet against the floor with all his strength.

He is going to see Summa and Lumi. He is going to do the most unforgivable thing. Only as long as Jurek Walter believes they are dead are they safe.

Perhaps he's already leading the serial killer to his family.

Joona has left his cell phone in Stockholm. He's using a forged passport and is paying for everything in cash. When he gets out of the taxi, he walks two blocks to the door of the apartment.

He waits for a moment and then goes to a café down the street. He pays ten euros to borrow a phone and calls Saga Bauer.

"I need help," he says in a voice thick with emotion.

"Don't you know everyone is looking for you? Things have gone completely haywire here."

"I need help with one thing."

"Yes," she says without hesitation.

"When you've given me the information I need, erase the search history," Joona says.

"All right."

Joona swallows hard and looks at the slip of paper Rosa Bergman gave him. Then he asks Saga to search the Finnish health records for a woman named Laura Sandin who lives at Liisankatu 16 in Helsinki.

"Let me call you back in a minute," she says.

"No, I'll hang on while you search," he says.

Those minutes are the longest of his entire life. He stares at the glittering dust on the countertop. He looks at the espresso machine and the marks on the floor where chairs have been pushed in.

"Joona?" Saga says at last.

"I'm here," Joona whispers.

"Laura Sandin was diagnosed with liver cancer two years ago."

"Go on," Joona says.

"Well, she had surgery last year, a partial hepatectomy. And she . . . well . . ." Saga Bauer is whispering something to herself.

"What is it?" Joona asks.

Saga clears her throat and says, "She just had surgery again last week."

"Is she still alive?"

"Apparently so. She's still in the hospital."

191

As Joona walks down the hospital corridor, it seems as if everything is sinking. His steps are heavy and the distant murmur of voices and televisions seems to get slower and slower.

He opens the door to Summa's room and walks in.

A thin woman is in the bed, her back to the door.

A light cotton curtain is drawn across the window. Her thin arms lie on top of the covers. Her hair is sweaty and dull.

He doesn't know if she's sleeping or not. He must see her face. He walks up to her. The room is completely silent.

The woman who had been Summa Linna in another life is extremely tired. Her daughter sat up with her most of the night. Now Lumi is sleeping next door in the room reserved for relatives.

Summa can see the weak light of dawn filtering through the curtain. She's thinking that human beings are helplessly alone. She has a few good memories, which she tries to bring to mind when she feels most alone and frightened. When they put her under for the operation, she'd remembered the light, light summer nights of her childhood; the first hours after her daughter was born and her baby fingers wrapped around her own; the wedding that summer day when she wore the bridal crown her mother had woven from birch root.

Summa swallows, fully aware of the life in her body. She is breathing and her heart is beating. She is so afraid of leaving Lumi all on her own.

The stitches from her operation burn as she turns over. She closes her eyes, but then opens them again. Joona Linna is standing over her.

She blinks a few times. Her message has reached him.

He sits beside her on the bed and she reaches up to touch his face. She runs her hand through his thick blond hair.

"If I die, you must take care of Lumi," she says.

"I promise."

"You must see her before you leave again," Summa says. "You must see her."

He strokes her face and whispers she's the most beautiful woman ever. She smiles at him. Then he leaves the room and Summa no longer feels so afraid.

The room for relatives is simply furnished. There's a TV suspended from the ceiling and a pine table scarred with cigarette burns alongside a saggy corduroy sofa.

A fifteen-year-old girl is lying on the sofa, fast asleep. Her eyes are swollen from too much crying. One of her cheeks is creased from the pattern of the cushion. She wakes with a start. Someone has put a blanket over her. Her shoes have been taken off. They are lined up on the floor by the sofa.

Someone has been here. In her dream, she'd felt someone sit next to her and hold her hand.

192

Between Stockholm and Uppsala, on the old highway, is the old Löwenströmska Hospital. Gustaf Adolf Löwenström had it built at the beginning of the nineteenth century in penance for his family's guilt. His brother had assassinated King Gustav III at a masquerade for the Royal Opera.

Anders Rönn is thirty-three years old and has just received his license to practice medicine. He's slender and has a handsome, sensitive face. He has just been hired to work at Löwenströmska and today is his first day on the job.

The low sunlight of autumn is playing between the leaves of the trees as he enters the building.

Behind the hospital's modern main building there's a structure that, from above, looks like two joined crosses. It's the psychiatric unit, which includes a secure division for criminals sentenced to psychiatric care.

A bronze sculpture of a boy playing the flute stands near the building on the forested hillside. There's a bird sitting on the boy's shoulder and another on his wide-brimmed hat. On one side of the pathway that leads to the building a park stretches out toward Fysingen Lake. On the other side, there's a fifteen-foot-high barbed-wire fence. Inside it, there's a shadow-filled dirt yard with cigarette butts around its single park bench.

No visitors under the age of fourteen are allowed. Taking photographs or recordings is forbidden.

Anders Rönn walks up the concrete path, underneath a canopy of flaking tin, and enters the building. He walks quietly across the bone-colored vinyl flooring, scuffed and stained with wheel marks. When he gets to the elevator, he sees that he's already on the third floor of the building. The rest of it is underground, including the closed psychiatric ward, number 30.

The elevator doesn't go all the way down. Two floors down, behind a steel gate, there's a spiral staircase to the bunkerlike isolation unit. The unit has room for a maximum of three patients. For the past twelve years, there's only been one: Jurek Walter.

Anders has been told that Jurek Walter is sentenced to psychiatric care with special parole requirements, and that when he arrived, he was so aggressive that he was physically restrained and tranquilized.

Nine years ago, he'd been diagnosed: schizophrenia (unspecified) with chaotic thinking. Acute psychotic condition with bizarre, extremely violent features.

So far, that was the entire diagnosis.

"I'm going to let you in now," says a woman with round cheeks and calm eyes.

"Thanks."

"Do you know the patient, Jurek Walter?" she asks, but she doesn't wait for an answer.

193

Anders hangs his keys in the cupboard before the woman opens the first door in the gate. He walks inside and waits as the door is shut behind him. Then he goes to the second door. The woman is listening for a signal, and when she hears it, she opens the second door. Anders turns and waves before he heads down the corridor to the staff lunch room.

A powerful man of about fifty is waiting for him there. His shoulders are slumped and he's smoking beneath the ventilator grille in the pantry. He nips off the end and throws it into the drain. He stuffs the half cigarette back into the pack, which he puts in the pocket of his lab coat.

"Hi, Roland Brolin, chief physician," he says, introducing himself.

"Anders Rönn."

"Why did you end up here, out of all the possible jobs out there?" the chief physician asks.

"I have young children and wanted to work near home," Anders Rönn replies.

"Well, you picked a hell of a day to start." Roland Brolin smiles.

He leads the way down the soundproof corridor to the security door, where he takes out his card and swipes it through a lock. He waits for the click from the steel door and then pushes it open with a deep sigh. He lets go of it before Anders has fully cleared it. The door hits him in the shoulder.

"Is there anything I need to know about the patient?" asks Anders, blinking away the pain.

Brolin waves his hand and rattles off a list: "He must never be alone with any employee. He is never to leave the premises under any circumstances. He may never meet another patient. He may never receive guests. He may never go to the recreation yard. Not even—"

"Never?" Anders repeats, doubtfully. "It's against regulations to keep a patient—"

"So it is," Roland says.

The atmosphere chills between them. Finally Anders asks, "What has he done?"

"Only nice things," Roland says.

"Such as?"

They pass through a second security door. A woman with pierced cheeks waves at them.

"Come back alive!" she says.

"Don't worry," Roland says. "Jurek Walter is a quiet older man. He doesn't fight or even raise his voice. He keeps to himself and we never enter his room. However, today we'll have to go in, because the night shift observed him hiding a knife underneath his mattress."

"How the hell would he have gotten a knife?"

Roland's forehead is now sweaty. He wipes his hand over his face and dries it on his coat.

"Jurek Walter can be extremely manipulative and . . . well, we'll be doing an internal investigation. But who knows?"

194

The chief physician pulls his card through a third security lock and taps in a code. There's a beep and the door opens.

"So why would he want a knife?" asks Anders as he hurries through the door. "If he wanted to kill himself, he'd already have done so by now, right?"

"Maybe he likes knives," Roland replies.

"Do you think he plans to escape?"

"He hasn't tried it once during all these years."

They have reached another locked gate.

"Wait a minute," Roland says. He holds out a small box with yellow earplugs.

"You just said he doesn't scream."

Roland looks extremely tired as if he hasn't slept in weeks. He looks at his new colleague for a while and sighs heavily before he starts to explain.

"Jurek Walter will talk to you, very calmly, very pleasantly," he says. His tone is serious. "Later this evening, when you're driving home, you'll find yourself driving into the lane of oncoming traffic and crash into a truck, or you'll go past a hardware store and buy an ax before you pick up your children from day care."

"Are you trying to scare me?" asks Anders with a smile.

"Not really, but I want you to be careful," Roland says. "I've had to enter his room once before, sometime last year, because he had a pair of scissors in there."

"He's an old man, right?"

"Don't worry. We're going to make it through this all right."

Roland's voice dies away and his expression is vague and hard to read. Then he says, "Before you walk through these doors, make sure you look as bored as possible. Your days are boring, boring, boring. You act like you're doing nothing that you haven't done a thousand times before."

"I'll try."

Roland's face is tense. His gaze is hard and nervous.

"We're going to act as if we're giving him his usual dose of Risperdal."

"But?"

"But instead we're giving him an overdose of Eutrexa," the chief physician says.

"Intentionally give an overdose?"

"I did it the last time, so, yes, all right. At first he was extremely aggressive. It lasted a short time. Then the muscle relaxant worked. First the face and tongue—he wasn't able to speak properly. Then he fell on the floor and lay on his side. He was breathing. Then there were a number of cramps, like epilepsy. It took a while. After that, he was tired and dazed, almost out of it, unable to move. When that happens this time, we'll run in and grab the knife."

"Why not just use a barbiturate?"

"That would be better," Roland nods. "But it's best to keep to the kinds of drugs he's already getting."

They walk through the final grid gate into the ward devoted to Jurek Walter. Ahead is a metal door painted white, with a small bulletproof glass window, a boom, and a slot.

Roland Brolin gestures to Anders to wait. He is moving cautiously.

Perhaps he is afraid of being surprised.

He keeps his distance from the glass and moves sideways. Then his face relaxes and he waves to Anders to join him. They stand in front of the window and look into a large room without windows.

195

A man in blue jeans and a denim shirt is sitting on a plastic chair. He's leaning forward, his elbows on his knees. Then his blue eyes look up at the door and Roland Brolin takes a step back.

Jurek Walter is clean-shaven and his gray hair has been combed with a straight part. His face is unnaturally white and deeply furrowed with wrinkles. It's a net of pain.

Roland walks back to the grid gate and unlocks a cupboard. He takes out three small glass vials with wide necks and aluminum caps. He adds two milliliters of water to each bottle, turns them upside down, and then swirls them carefully so that the powder dissolves in the liquid. Then he draws the liquid into a needle.

They walk up to the bulletproof glass on the door. Jurek Walter is now sitting on his bed. Roland puts his earplugs into his ears and then opens the slot in the door.

"Jurek Walter," he says in a relaxed voice. "It's time . . ."

Anders watches the man get up from the bed and walk to the door while unbuttoning his shirt.

"Stop and take off your shirt," Roland says, although the man is already doing so.

Jurek Walter walks slowly toward them.

Roland shuts the slot and fastens it with movements that are just a bit too fast, too nervous. Jurek stops and slips out of his shirt. He has three round scars on his chest. His skin hangs limply from his arms.

Roland opens the slot again and Jurek walks the last few steps.

"Hold out your arm," Roland says. A slight hiccup betrays his fear.

Jurek puts his arm through the slot but does not look at Roland at all. He's staring intently at Anders.

Roland jabs the needle into an upper-arm muscle and injects the liquid quickly. Jurek's hand jerks in surprise, but he does not withdraw his arm until he has received permission.

Roland shuts the slot and locks it as swiftly as he can. Jurek Walter stumbles back toward his bed. He sits down. His movements are jerky. Roland drops the needle and they watch it roll across the concrete floor.

When they look back through the glass, it's misty. Jurek Walter has breathed on it. He's written a single word backward in the haze: JOONA.

"What's that say?" asks Anders, his voice weak.

"He's written 'Joona.' "

"Joona? What the hell does that mean?"

Before the haze dissipates, they look in. Jurek Walter is sitting on his bed as if he'd never moved.

a note about the author

Lars Kepler is the pseudonym for a literary couple who live and write in Sweden. Their novels, including *The Fire Witness*, *The Nightmare*, and *The Hypnotist*, have been number-one bestsellers in more than a dozen countries, including France, Spain, Germany, Italy, Holland, and Denmark.